Tara Pammi can't remember a moment when she wasn't lost in a book—especially a romance, which was much more exciting than a mathematics textbook at school. Years later, Tara's wild imagination and love for the written word revealed what she really wanted to do. Now she pairs alpha males who think they know everything with strong women who knock that theory *and* them off their feet!

Jackie Ashenden writes dark, emotional stories, with alpha heroes who've just got the world to their liking only to have it blown wide apart by their kick-ass heroines. She lives in Auckland, New Zealand, with her husband, the inimitable Dr Jax, two kids and two rats. When she's not torturing alpha males and their gutsy heroines she can be found drinking chocolate martinis, reading anything she can lay her hands on, wasting time on social media or being forced to go mountain biking with her husband. To keep up to date with Jackie's new releases and other news sign up to her newsletter at jackieashenden.com.

Discover more at millsandboon.co.uk.

THE SURPRISE BOLLYWOOD BABY

TARA PAMMI

THE WORLD'S MOST NOTORIOUS GREEK

JACKIE ASHENDEN

MILLS & BOON

First Published in Great Britain 2021
by Mills & Boon, an imprint of HarperCollins*Publishers*
1 London Bridge Street, London, SE1 9GF

The Surprise Bollywood Baby © 2021 Tara Pammi

The World's Most Notorious Greek © 2021 Jackie Ashenden

ISBN: 978-0-263-28235-1

THE SURPRISE BOLLYWOOD BABY

TARA PAMMI

To all the readers
who have picked up a book of mine—thank you!
This journey wouldn't be possible without you.

CHAPTER ONE

After a decade-long affair, Bollywood Queen Zara Khan is dumped by Vikram Raawal for a younger model!

"Nobody Naina" steals boss Zara Khan's man right from under her nose!

Vikram Raawal's massive biopic set to sink even before release!

ZARA KHAN LOOKED at the headlines on three different websites in dawning horror and put away her cell phone. She stole a quick glance at her assistant, Naina, also her longtime best friend Vikram Raawal's fiancée. Her signature curls framing her small face, Naina sat at the back table with Vikram's sister, Anya. Even from this distance, Zara could see the strain on Naina's face.

Had Naina already seen these? Was that the reason for how subdued she'd been for the past week—this ridiculous suggestion that somehow she'd stolen Vikram away from Zara? That she'd destroyed Zara's chance at happiness?

Where and how did the media come up with these disgusting lies?

This was the last thing the happy couple needed, just a week before their wedding—Zara's rabid fan base to send ill wishes their way. After standing by Zara through thick and thin, after a lifetime spent righting the mighty ship of his family's rocky finances and reputation and that of the Raawal House of Cinema, Vikram deserved to have his and Naina's happiness unmarred by all this drama and dirt.

Even though she had already made a public statement about how happy she was for Vikram and Naina, it hadn't made a speck of difference to her legion of fans.

And it wasn't limited to silly rumors, either, that she wished all of them could simply weather until something more salacious hit the news cycle.

This gossip about Vikram's supposed breakup with Zara and his simultaneous engagement to Naina was becoming the defining narrative around the upcoming biopic telling the story of how Vikram's grandfather, Vijay Raawal, had been inspired to create his production house. Every interview Vikram had tried to give about the project had been hijacked by the media to ask him about his relationship struggles.

Frustration filled her muscles and Zara struggled to keep her expression smiling and graceful as the program for the launch of the lifestyle website *SuperWomen*, which Zara was one of the prime investors for, continued on stage.

If she hadn't promised the group of smart young women who had created the website that she would throw her weight and name behind the launch, and if she hadn't already spent the considerable goodwill she had in the industry to wrangle powerful men into attending it, Zara would have walked out of the event. The last thing she wanted to do right now was to be her graceful self on stage while every man and woman watching wondered if she was secretly nursing a broken heart.

Damn it, no one was going to reduce her to the role of victim. She hadn't done that even when she had just cause to. She certainly wasn't going to begin now.

It was time to take action. The last thing Vikram needed this close to his wedding to Naina was this much bad publicity.

With the biopic in full production already and slated to be finished within the next few weeks, this much bad sentiment toward Vikram had real consequences, especially as he'd sunk everything he had into the project. It was time to give the media a new distraction. Time to give her fan base something even more delicious and exciting to speculate about than Vikram and Naina's engagement. Time to bring the focus back to the biopic, where it belonged.

A niggle of a plan began to hatch at the back of Zara's mind the moment she saw Virat Raawal walk in from the foyer, all casual grace and swaggering masculinity. Heads turned toward him and whispers abounded as they always did whenever he appeared.

While Vikram was traditionally handsome and had established himself as the uncrowned king of the acting industry through various carefully designed blockbusters, his brother, Virat, stood at the top of the directing hierarchy in a way no one could even compete with. Known for his brilliant storytelling across a number of internationally acclaimed movies, Virat was a true rebel in every way that mattered. Actors and actresses vied with each other to star in his movies, while writers created stories for him to bring to life on the silver screen.

With a patrician nose and rugged features, *beautiful* or *handsome* were words too…simple to describe the brilliant director. *Untamed* was the only word that came to Zara's mind every time she saw him. A man who wouldn't be caught by the simple constraints of a relationship or the boundaries by which everyone else lived.

A shiver of awareness gripped Zara—as familiar to her when he was anywhere in the vicinity as her own reflection. His tall, lean frame rounded the banquet hall, radiating an intensity that belied the cocky smile on his lips.

Zara always had the feeling he was laughing at the world, instead of with it. With pure contempt. As if they were all insignificant pawns in a game only he knew how to play.

While every man here—most of them pioneers in their industry—was dressed to the nines in three-piece suits, Virat of course flouted the dress code in a fitted white shirt and black trousers that molded to his six-foot-two-inch frame. His pristine shirt, three buttons undone, formed a deliciously contrasting V against his dark skin.

Ten years ago, at just twenty years old, he'd been full of an innate confidence and wicked charm that Zara hadn't been able to resist. Now he wore his power as comfortably and as effortlessly as his custom-made shirts.

The shadow of a beard and a cigar hanging from the edge of his full mouth completed the picture of the disreputable genius, as the world called him. With him looking like that, the recent news of his dangerous affair with a powerful cabinet minister's young wife was all too easy to believe.

Apparently, the man lived his life the way he made his movies—skating the edge of propriety, pushing the boundaries of society, with a hefty dose of mockery and contempt. No one had missed the showdown the minister had tried to force on Virat not a week ago. No one in the industry could be oblivious to the rumors that the minister was using every ounce of his reach to hurt Virat where it would do the most damage.

Zara sent a silent thanks to the universe that at least he hadn't shown up at this launch with the minister's young wife in tow. She had wondered if he would even show up at all.

But now that he was here, she didn't have a moment to lose to execute her plan. If she thought about it too much, if she pondered on what she was putting into motion with the man who hated her very guts, the one man who'd always be her weakness, then she would talk herself out of it.

She would run far away.

Instead Zara stood up from her seat and dragged in a few deep breaths under the guise of straightening her white silk shirt and emerald green skirt. Her knees wobbled as she made her way toward the group of men that were laughing uproariously at whatever brilliant piece of wit Virat had bestowed on them.

Once, Zara hadn't been his equal. She had walked out of his life because she hadn't trusted herself to be good enough for him.

Now, at least when measured by the world's superficial and arbitrary definition of success, Zara Khan—sometimes dubbed Bollywood Queen for her continued and sustained success at the age of thirty-five in an industry that swapped veteran actresses for the latest young thing like they were yesterday's leftovers, was more than good enough to take on Virat Raawal.

If it meant giving Naina and Vikram a better start to their life together, if it meant saving all their asses with regards to the biopic, Zara would do anything. Even if it meant tangling with the reckless playboy who hated her very guts, who would take every opportunity to use what she was giving him to torment her for God only knew what sins.

She was up to something.

Zara Khan, actress extraordinaire and astute business-woman, should be firmly embedded in his distant past but kept shimmering like an enticing beacon in his present. No, strike that. She was more like a niggling thorn lodged in his skin.

And damn it all to hell, but Virat Raawal felt every inch of him practically vibrating with an anticipation and excitement he hadn't tasted in a long time. He ran a hand through his hair, cursing his tunnel focus on his current project for the last eighteen months.

From the moment he had stepped into the banquet hall and found her watching him with undisguised attention, Virat had known something was afoot. Tracking his every move from that wide-eyed gaze. Making his skin prickle with awareness.

She couldn't have been more obvious if she'd thrown herself at him—all grace and curves and self-confidence oozing out of every inch of flawless skin she revealed.

No wonder his long-denied libido was now wagging its tail like an excited puppy at the sight of a much-coveted fancy treat.

Because that was what Zara was to him. A delicious treat that made him act like a man barely out of his teens, riding the roller coaster of horniness and emotional turbulence all over again.

Even after all these years. Even after he'd reminded himself countless times that she'd made her choice a long time ago. That she'd left no doubt as to whom she preferred, between the famous Vikram Raawal—the uncrowned king of Bollywood who'd slogged night and day for years, to save his family and the prestigious Raawal House of Cinema from dire straits—or him, Virat Raawal, the man whose questionable paternity was always a fan-favorite topic of conversation on the weekly chai-and-chat shows.

In the decade since she'd used him to climb up the ladder of success, Virat had built up a reputation both within the industry and with the critics—a reputation that his grandfather and cinema visionary Vijay Raawal had garnered more than half a century ago. A reputation and a body of work that had every artist in the industry salivating to work with him.

Even though they'd regularly butted heads on the direction of the family's production house, Virat had always had Vikram's support. The brothers' bond had been borne out of their parents' incapability to provide them with a modicum of emotional and mental stability in their lives. So Virat had actively worked on not letting the bitterness of Zara's choice or her long-standing relationship with his brother rot the bond between himself and Vikram. And he'd succeeded for the most part.

While he'd never understood their relationship, he'd left it alone. And now, with his brother about to marry the lovely Naina and the resulting nasty rumors about Vikram breaking Zara's heart, Virat had been thinking a lot more about their purported, decade-long relationship.

Tucking his hands into his trouser pockets, he absently nodded at some comment on his left when the subtle hint of Zara's scent hit his nostrils. Virat stiffened, as if bracing himself against an oncoming attack. He didn't have to turn and look at her to know that she had sidled up to him, closer than a woman he hardly ever talked to in ten years should have done.

Her bare arm rubbed up against his, the warmth of her curvaceous body a teasing caress. Virat scowled and was about to ask her what the hell she was up to when the roaming strobe light focused on them both and a cheer went up around the hall.

An announcement flashed on the huge screen propped at the top corner next to the stage just as a short, bespectacled woman announced his and Zara's names together as the primary investors in the web mag, calling out giveaways including and not limited to scholarships for female junior college students, a featured monthly charity drive for innovative small businesses from around the country's rural villages, and an opportunity for the chosen SuperWoman of the month to meet Zara and Virat. As their schedules allowed, of course.

"Shall we, darling?" Zara said then, loosely linking her arm through his, in that husky voice of hers that he could recognize in his sleep.

He turned his head to look at her then, beyond stunned. And Virat knew that everyone in the hall was watching them, with the same wide-eyed fascination that Zara was faking as she looked at him.

As if he was the answer to all her dreams and wishes. Their gazes met and the world around them seemed to stand still. With her silky hair in a soft cut framing her sharp-angled face, Zara was the consummate actress. Her eyes shone with some inner resolve he couldn't read and the smile she offered him was wide and not in the least bit awkward. The lush lower lip painted a soft pink taunted him.

With her palm pressed to his chest, she winked at him and pouted. His blood pressure went up another notch, shock and desire twining into an inseparable rope. "I know you don't like PDAs, sweetie, but you promised to do this with me, remember?" Her thigh bumped against his when she leaned closer and it was a miracle that he didn't jump away like a scalded cat. Or more like an outraged heroine fending off the caricature villain in one of his brother's latest box-office hits.

He noted the flare of awareness in her eyes before she pulled back. Reaching for her waist, Virat twirled her out of earshot of the rest of the group, keeping his own expression mildly amused. She came as easily as if she were floating on air, her face barely betraying her shock. He pushed her against the far wall, and the circle of light followed them.

"Now what the hell are you playing at, *shahzadi*?" he whispered, while she clasped her hands at the nape of his neck. The slide of her soft fingers there sent tension and desire rolling through him in fast waves.

Her breath was a silky caress against his jaw as she whispered, "It's all for a good cause, Virat. Play along, won't you?"

"Play along as what? Your latest boy toy?"

She laughed and shrugged. "Something like that, yes."

The warm, husky sound wrapped around his heart like a tight fist, rushing in vivid memories he'd buried deep for ten long years. There had always been something sensuous and magical about Zara's ability to laugh. Both at the world and at herself. Her sheer verve for life.

Was he the only one to be so besieged by those memories? Still so haunted? Was she so completely unaffected?

Their legs tangled all the way now, but she didn't back down. The slight tremble she tried to hide gave him a sudden stab of savage satisfaction. "I would love to, Zara. Even though playing games is your forte, not mine." He tucked a strand of silky hair that had fallen forward back behind her ear and she hissed in a breath. Yes, two could play these games apparently. But whatever it was, this time, he would win. Not come second to his older brother. "But I like the rules to be clear and upfront before I play with any woman, *shahzadi*. I have standards that have to be met. Even with repeat participants like yourself who want another round on the roller coaster."

"That's an awful thing to say about me. And yourself," she said, planting those long nails on his arm, her lovely smile out in full force.

"But accurate, yes?"

She sighed and nodded. "You're mistaking my intent here."

"Am I? Do you want me to pretend that we're innocents who don't know how the game is played?"

She glared at him, a glittering intensity to her brown eyes. But the damned woman didn't back down. Of course, she didn't. Despite everything she had done to get to where she was now, Virat couldn't help but admire her sheer tenacity in forging the glittering career she'd always wanted, and for sustaining it for so long.

In four-inch heels, she made up the difference between their heights. When she leaned closer still, her luscious, pink mouth reached his ear. Virat had to fight down a shiver. Gilded by long eyelashes, her eyes held his with a stubborn resolve. "Fine, then. Believe me when I say that this is a much-needed distraction. One small farce to be played out so that..."

Those expressive eyes flicked to someone in the back. Virat followed her gaze and found his on Naina, his soon-to-be sister-in-law, who was trying to downplay her curiosity at Zara's sudden public display. And with him, of all men.

But what he didn't miss was the sudden surge of curious whispers that already filled the hall, like the drone of bees.

"So that what?" he prompted, having already noted the dark circles under Naina's eyes when he'd met her earlier in the day. Caught up as he'd been in his own work, he still hadn't been oblivious to all the nightmarish, nasty rumors swirling around his brother and his fiancée. With Zara at the center of it all, being portrayed as the poor rejected ex-lover.

Zara noted his impatience. "So that other genuinely deserving people like Naina and Vikram can be given a respite from all the drama. So that you can save your own backside from the powerful minister's reach. So that we can both stop Vikram's biopic from sinking before it even gets released."

For a few seconds there, he'd wondered if Zara had started all the rumors to make herself look better in the world's press. But Virat couldn't discount the genuine quality of her friendship with his brother or the generosity with which she had taken Naina under her wing.

He had no idea what she saw in his eyes but she sighed and said, "Oh, for God's sake, Virat, don't look at me like that. You can't be surprised that I know of the troubles you're having thanks to your affair with the minister's young wife. Or that the biopic has been mired in one trouble after another ever since production began."

"I'm not surprised that you have your finger on the pulse of it all, as usual," he countered, as hundreds of eyes stared at the spectacle unfolding right in front of them. As much as he hated it, he couldn't discount the genius of her idea. Of how close he was to wrapping up everything he needed for the documentary series he was secretly filming, and how much he didn't need the extra scrutiny from the powerful and corrupt cabinet minister he was about to expose. "Or that you have contacts in high places and know how to use them."

She blinked and he had a feeling he'd hurt her with that last comment. But he'd learned his lesson the hard way to never trust Zara. To never believe the bright, intelligent eyes, or the flashes of vulnerability that had once fascinated him. Even now apparently. "So what is your concern, then?" she asked, a bite to her tone.

"For myself, of course," he added, his blood buzzing on a new high already. There was nothing more addictive than going toe to toe with this woman. Mere words bandied with her had more effect on his libido than rolling around naked with any other woman he'd known. He traced the line of her jaw, wrestling with his own hunger. "I don't know that I'm up to playing the role of your willing slave again, *shahzadi*. I don't know that I'm strong enough to survive it."

She gasped and swatted him. And he had a feeling that at least a hundred cameras were recording them right now. Of course, that was why she'd made her move at this launch party. Where she was already playing the central role. "It's not like I mean to swallow you and spit you out. You're not some innocent prey caught in the claws of some hungry female predator."

He raised a brow, a smile tugging at his lips. "Those are your words, Zara. Not mine."

"So?"

"So what?"

"So will you play along and pretend we're together?"

"For now, yes. Not that you have left me much of a choice."

He flicked his finger at the tip of her nose, refusing to give weight to the flash of hurt in her face. "Let's finish what you started. Then you and I will walk out of here and have a long talk."

"Long talk about what?" Uncertainty filled her voice for the first time this evening.

"You sound scared, Zara."

"Of course I'm not scared of you. I ambushed you tonight, didn't I?"

"Ah...of course. The cryptic message I got about a source if I came here tonight was from you."

She shrugged. "You left me no choice. I had Naina call your assistant three times in the last week since I returned from my shoot. You were incommunicado."

"I was busy."

"With the minister's young wife, of course."

"Beginning to feel jealous of younger women like the papers are hinting at, are you?"

"Of course I'm not. You should know that everything they're writing about this strangely perverted love triangle between Naina, Vikram and me is...utter rubbish at best. Disgusting drivel at worst. Also remember that while I can shove it under the rug and rise above it, your soon-to-be sister-in-law can't. This has cast such an awful pall over Naina. I'd hate for it to cause more problems at the wedding or for their life together to begin on such a sour note."

The worry in her tone forestalled his instinctive response. "We will talk about terms and conditions for this new game, then. So that we can ensure both of us get what we desperately want out of this new...adventure."

"I want nothing from you," she retorted defensively and then blushed. Protesting much?

"One evening in my company and you might be ready to revise that declaration, Zara. In fact, if I remember right, there was one particularly delightful evening ten years ago when we were supposed to sneak into one of Vikram's launch parties so that he would notice you and instead we—"

Her palm landed on his mouth and their gazes held. An electric current arced between them, every bit as powerful and intense as it had been ten years ago. "If you think I've forgotten even one second of the things we did, then you have me all wrong, Virat. But this...this is about something more than you and me.

"Something that's bigger than our petty differences and ego wars."

"Petty differences, *shahzadi*? We will see about that."

Virat wrapped his fingers around her wrist and gently pulled her away from the wall. Her skin was so utterly soft against his calloused hands. "Lead the way," he said, finally breaking eye contact and releasing a long breath.

She nodded and they turned toward the stage as one.

He didn't remove his arm from around her waist and she didn't put any distance between their brushing bodies. They walked down the red carpet to the dais, their strides in rhythm as if they'd done this a thousand times before. As if they shared an intimacy that the world knew nothing about.

As if they knew each other inside out, better than anyone else.

A long time ago, he'd foolishly assumed that they did. With one move, Zara had proved to him that he didn't know her at all. That she wasn't the woman he'd thought her. And yet, this evening, something new had already begun. Something that was beyond both of them. Something that his entire body was primed for.

Zara and he had circled each other for ten years in the same industry, never coming too close. Never working on a project together, until with the biopic now. Never engaging with each other. There had been nothing to say or do while rumors of her continued entanglement with his brother abounded.

Now this, a fake romance, and the next few weeks of being together on the set of the biopic filming the final scenes meant the past was surely going to repeat itself.

He hadn't missed the flicker of interest she'd fought to hide from her eyes. He didn't lie to himself over his own interest in her. But this time, he reassured himself as they climbed the steps to the stage amid roaring applause, the ending of their relationship would be different. This time, he would make sure he was the one that walked away.

CHAPTER TWO

THE EVENING TURNED out to be a fantastic success—in terms of getting the man with a notorious reputation for not playing by the rules to cooperate with her and agree to behave as Zara's man of the hour.

As the evening came to an end, Zara signaled to Naina that she was free to leave. The last thing she wanted was to appease the curiosity shining in Naina's eyes when she and Virat still had to discuss "terms and conditions," as he'd put it. When the media was out in full force, hungry for the details of what they had teased out tonight.

Now it was time for their own personal showdown, to find out what the devil would demand as his due. Zara braced herself for it. She wasn't naive enough to think Virat's compliance as her boy toy for the near future would come without a very high price...

Her clutch in hand, Zara walked through the coffee lounge hidden behind a colorful, paneled wall on the hotel's ground floor. The pub was a well-kept secret, especially when one wanted to hide from the media.

Dark marble floor, handcrafted accents and clusters of low lighting gave the bar a retro, fun atmosphere. Virat sat at one of the high barstools around a table in a dimly lit corner. His discarded jacket was draped on the other barstool, his shirt still casually unbuttoned, a glass of

Old Monk rum in a tumbler by his hand. His hair, piled high in a stylish haircut to accentuate those blade-like cheekbones, was mussed up.

As always, he had a tablet in front of him that he studied with that laser focus of his. Even in the quiet atmosphere of the bar, his restless energy dominated the space.

"Are you going to stand there and watch me all night, *shahzadi*?" came his deep voice in a husky murmur, his head still bent over the screen in front of him.

The endearment hit Zara low in the belly, and then moved up through her body, lodging painfully in her chest. Once upon a time, she'd loved it when he'd teased her like that. And if she was honest, there was a part of her that still liked it. A bit too much.

Except there wasn't that sweet indulgence in his voice anymore, and she wasn't a naive, gauche girl with stars in her eyes.

"Come closer. I won't bite. Unless you want me to."

Zara remained still, letting the longing pass through her. She'd had enough practice, having watched him afar for more than a decade. Having watched him go through woman after woman. He'd earned the reputation of being a brilliant director and an utter womanizer, both justly deserved.

"That endearment didn't make sense ten years ago," she said, covering the distance between them. "Given my lowly background, I've always been the farthest thing from a princess."

He still didn't look up when she arrived at the table, and the casual arrogance in the gesture stole her breath. "I'm used to thinking of you as a princess in training, *shahzadi*. Bad habits, as you know, are hard to shake."

"Was I a bad habit, then?" she fired back, before she could curb the self-indulgence. At least she sounded challenging, full of that verve she portrayed on-screen. At least she hadn't betrayed how much his opinion of her still mattered.

"Oh, the worst kind, *shahzadi*," he said, finally looking up. Cool brown eyes held hers, full of mockery and something more. Only a second's attention on her, then he flipped over another page on the device with his finger. "If one isn't careful, one could slide headlong back in…again and again."

Whether he meant to let her feel the heat in his words or not didn't matter. Zara felt memories sliding into the present, claiming her senses, lodging inside her muscles. God, he'd been such an incredible lover. And it shouldn't surprise her that within minutes of standing this close to him for the first time in a decade, her good sense wanted to fly away.

She waited for her heart to resume its normal pace. Tried to tell her swooping belly that the man was an incurable flirt. She bent her head and clicked the tiny button on his tablet closed. The screen turned black. "Ah… so you were telling the truth when you said you had to protect yourself from me? You're afraid of what I might do to you."

A smile curving his mouth, Virat leaned back into the seat. He rubbed a hand over his jaw, considering her. With one long leg, he pushed out a barstool for her to perch on. If Zara thought he might sputter at her innuendo, she'd have been wrong. This was not the Virat she'd known ten years ago—so full of raw emotions and intensity that it had been like looking at the sun. A man eager to prove himself to the world. Determined to leave the dirty rumors of his paternity behind.

This was a man who'd built and tasted success beyond

his own wildest dreams. A man who lived his life by his own damned rules and no one else's.

"Is that why you picked me for this role, Zara? Because you think you can play me however you want?"

Zara snorted. "No, I picked you because this farcical affair will help you, too. And because I believe that, despite your differences, you do care about your brother."

A cold reserve entered his eyes. "So this is all about Bhai, then?"

Zara frowned. "It's not just Vikram that needs my help right now."

"I don't need you to save me, *shahzadi.*"

"From the world? No. From yourself, yes," Zara retorted. "You were kind to me when I was at the worst point in my life. Let's just say I'm finally returning the favor. Maybe even taking the burden of talking some good sense into you off Vikram's shoulders."

"I forget how good you are at calculating your pros and cons. How risk averse you are. No wonder you and Bhai got along so well for so many years."

Zara stared at the clear contempt in his statement. That Virat and Vikram had always had differences in their vision for Raawal House of Cinema was publicly known. But to say *she* was calculating was…unfair. She wasn't calculating so much as she was risk averse. In both her career and in her personal life.

Especially when it came to men. Because she'd learned the hard way to be calculating. To deal with her head and not her heart.

Did Virat really believe the myriad rumors about her and Vikram's on-off relationship that was purported to have lasted throughout an entire decade? Did he think she'd simply traded one brother for the other when the fancy took her?

The very thought made her sick and angry. No, to think Virat was still affected in any way by the past was nothing but self-indulgence.

Virat Raawal attracted women like honey attracted bees. Maybe because he was such a generous lover. Maybe because he didn't play ego games like other men. Maybe because when he put his mind to it, he could be the kindest, funniest man a woman would ever meet.

He enjoyed the women who came to him and everything they offered. He gave them everything but his heart.

In the last ten years, he'd been through countless women, and she was a fool if she believed he'd been hung up on her even for a few days.

She shook her head, refusing to let the past cloud the present. "The point is, this situation you've created with your crazy antics with that minister's wife is bigger than both of us. Vikram's spent over fifteen years building up Raawal House of Cinema again, and he's finally found some measure of happiness with Naina. He's poured his heart and soul into this biopic, put everything he owns on the line. You're out of control, and if someone doesn't stop you, you'll bring everything down."

Virat's mouth tightened. "If I've become such a big liability because of my recent actions, then Bhai will simply fire me and find a new director. Like you, he's not sentimental."

"I don't think Vikram will fire you. Not when the production's more than half done. Not when this project already has your brilliant stamp all over it. This biopic is not any average project that you two have butted heads over. This is about your grandfather. This is Raawal House's magnum opus. This is a legacy that you and he will leave for generations to come…"

Zara softened her voice, knowing how long and how deep that old wound festered within him.

Virat Raawal's paternity had been fuel for speculation in countless magazine articles for over two decades. It was the alleged reason for his parents' scandalous second split, the reason for the huge chasm between his father and him, and it had been a painfully humiliating thorn in Virat's side from a young age.

Because his mother—the famous Bollywood star of yesteryear Vandana Raawal—had had a secret lover after her first split with her husband. Then had come their publicized reunion and mere months later, Virat had been born.

For most of his life, Virat had had to contend with exposés and articles and trashy interviews speculating about his paternity. With his father's cold rejection of him.

"Are you okay with being thrown out of that legacy, Virat?" Zara asked softly. "Have you decided that you don't want to be a Raawal after all?"

He ran his hand through his hair and groaned. "Enough with the regurgitation of the same sentimental rubbish, *shahzadi*. Mama's already put me through that speech, using the grand Raawal name to corral me." He looked up, his eyes shining with unholy mirth. "Of course, what you're offering as an incentive to behave is…clever."

"I'm not offering you anything," Zara blurted out, like a green girl afraid of the slick charm in his words.

The rascal grinned, having successfully baited her.

"So you trust me to behave as you want, then?"

Zara refused to let him play mind games with her. Even though her pulse raced with his every word, smile and touch. "What's there to not trust? You need to distract the minister's attention away from you. Vikram and Naina need to begin their wedded life not enveloped in dirty rumors. The biopic needs some good publicity after being continually stalled by people baying for Vikram's blood. All of these reasons, I believe, should appeal to your good sense."

"What if I still harbor hatred for you over how you threw me over a decade ago when greener pastures called? What if I take this chance to tumble you into love, and ruin you once and for all? What if—"

"I didn't throw you over for any…" she faltered, the resolute conviction in his gaze stealing away her words. For a few seconds, Zara had no idea what to even say. What was he talking about? She wanted to demand he explain what he meant by that. But he wouldn't. She knew that from the wicked look in his eyes. It was abundantly clear that he would enjoy seeing her squirm if she asked him. "It seems we see the past differently," she said carefully, unable to curb those words. She didn't give him a chance to say more. "Do I wonder why you're constantly getting involved with unsuitable women? Yes. But do I worry that you've become a man who would find pleasure in a woman's pain, in my pain? Never.

"As we get older, we become better prepared to deal with the world, we start wearing masks, we hide our fears, but at the core, we remain who we've always been. Isn't that the gist of your national award–winning movie?"

"A woman with all the answers," Virat said, finding comfort in her innate trust in him, despite everything. Maybe the fact that the entire world—including his mother—thought him a dangerous seducer of innocents had begun to grate. He was a rebel at heart but not how the world imagined it.

He was a decade older, wiser, and more cynical. The whole world thought him brilliant. And he was the first to admit he had a unique point of view. But that knowledge had come at a high price.

The more he saw of the world, the less he wanted to be vulnerable in front of it. It was only through the medium of film that he could share parts of himself. Truly, it was a lesson he'd been taught even as a nine-year-old boy, when his father had shown up for both Vikram and their younger sister, Anya, at the annual school day, but not for Virat. And at sixteen, when his father had called him his mother's not so little dirty secret.

When he'd met Zara, he'd thought he'd met a kindred soul. A woman who was also looking for a place to belong. But Zara had proved to him that he wasn't enough for what she wanted, only confirming what he'd always known about himself. He wasn't good enough to be a Raawal.

And yet when Virat had stopped trying to please others, he'd found his own power. In his art and in his career. And in his personal life.

"No one really appreciates what it takes to be a well-informed woman," she said with a long-suffering sigh.

He smiled. He shouldn't be surprised that it was easy to talk to her. They had always had an inexplicable connection. An undeniable chemistry. A strange sort of magic happened whenever they came together.

After her screen test for the biopic—Virat wasn't going to hire anyone without one—Bhai had seen the kind of performance Zara was capable of giving in Virat's hands. He'd had to needle her, push her, draw her out to give her best to the role. Consummate professional that she was, she'd taken every criticism and suggestion he'd made with a grace he'd rarely seen on a film set.

And in the end, when Zara had tried that scene again, she'd been vibrating with energy and nuance. She'd been magnificent. Ever the businessman, his brother was counting on that alchemy to show up on the screen. With Virat at the helm and Bhai and Zara on screen, Virat had no doubt the movie would be extraordinary.

His own magnum opus. His legacy.

He couldn't give up on the docuseries he'd started secretly filming that would expose the dirty underbelly of a lot of powerful men, but he didn't want to miss the chance to add his name to the Raawal legacy.

Zara had hit the nail on its head. That she'd so clearly known what would motivate him to behave was like a thorn stuck under his skin. He didn't want to be aware of how perceptive she could be when it came to him. He didn't want her in his life at all. But since he was responsible for the rumors surrounding him and the minister's wife, who was actually helping him to bring down her abusive husband, not sleeping with Virat like everyone believed, and because he did care about his brother and Naina, he would behave.

Because this served him, as well. And because, as he was discovering, there was a lot of fun to be had in tripping Zara's confidence. In poking at the Queen's untouchable poise. Already there was that slight buzz in his blood from just parrying words with her.

"If you're signing up to be my keeper," he said, meeting her eyes again, "the woman who will transform me from being a marriage-wrecking womanizer to someone totally respectable, you should know I'm not as malleable as I used to be."

Color seeped into her cheeks but she held his gaze boldly. "You, malleable? Virat, you are the most intense man I have ever met. Even at twenty, there was this…

energy about you. This vitality. This thirst to prove yourself to the world.

"Maybe your memories are skewed. Maybe you've even convinced yourself that I took advantage of a younger man. But I remember otherwise."

"Do you? Remember, that is?" Curiosity overcame his resentment.

"I do. Regularly," she said vehemently and then blushed. Her lashes fluttered down, her silky hair cooperatively falling onto her face. Her honesty added to that hum under his skin.

He held her gaze. "A fake romance where I end up dumping you in a few weeks' time is only going to make me even more the villain. It's bad enough your entire fandom thinks Bhai traded you in for a younger model. I can just imagine the headlines if they thought I was playing with you, too—'Raawal Brothers bounce Zara Khan between them' or some such rot." He let his words sink in. "If this is to have the immediate positive impact we want it to have, we should announce our engagement."

"Absolutely not!" Her stubborn mouth drew into a line, her eyes flashing fire. "An engagement is a step too far, Virat. I… Maybe you have no plans for your future other than playing games with other men's wives, but I…"

"You what, Zara? You're still waiting for your prince? Still waiting for your happily-ever-after?"

She flinched and looked away, and Virat felt a moment's tenderness for her. Which was entirely misguided. He was still bitter about what she'd done ten years ago, but now he'd had years of experience working in the film industry, he did at least understand how valuable networking was if you wanted to get anywhere.

But nevertheless, he wasn't ever going to buy into

those flashes of vulnerability he glimpsed in her eyes sometimes. Not again.

"Think of it, Zara. If you truly want to pull the negative attention away from Bhai and Naina's wedding next week, if you want to create some good PR for the biopic, then logically our engagement provides you with better value. Like Bhai's super-sentimental sagas where you get action, drama and the romance of a lifetime all wrapped up in one," he said, mimicking the reviews of Vikram's last blockbuster.

A smile peeked from the edges of her mouth and she sighed. "Fine. You always could get me with your logic."

He shrugged. "It makes sense. The minister and his powerful cronies will be distracted by my beautiful fiancée, who's taming me away from their young wives. Once the biopic releases, we can slowly untangle from each other, pretending we both made a mistake."

"I'm sure they're all going to pray that I have the power to make you stay with me. Really, Virat, of all the things I expected from you, this wasn't—"

He leaned forward on the table and Zara felt the force of his attention like a laser beam. "And what is that, *shahzadi*? What were your expectations of me? I've been waiting for a long time to hear them."

The intensity of his softly spoken words played on Zara's skin. Maybe he wasn't a completely different man. Maybe he'd just learned to mask all that emotional turmoil better. "Playing games with powerful men's innocent twenty-year-old wives…that was the last thing I expected of you."

Fury flared in his eyes but he banked it with an ease he hadn't possessed before. "Of all the shortcomings I attributed to you, *shahzadi*, hypocrisy wasn't one of them."

"I'm not moralizing to you, Virat. I'm just—"

"You and I both know innocence is not a measure of age, Zara. You had no problem having wild sex with me when I was barely twenty."

"That's different. I'm only five years older than you and you were never simply an innocent, and…" Zara said, flushing at the blunt way he put it. "I…you…we meant something to each other."

"Did we?" Again, two soft words but with a wealth of emotion brimming beneath them. "Have you revised our entire history together into some romantic fairy tale, Zara?"

His question contained a strange mixture of contempt and pity. Again, Zara had the feeling she was walking through a minefield. Blindfolded. "It did mean something to me. It meant a great deal," she replied, refusing to look away. As if she'd done something wrong. "And I'm not going to sit here and let you twist and manipulate our past into something lurid and dirty. This will never work if you make me out to be some vampy villainess that…"

Whatever his earlier comments, he surprised her into silence by taking her hand in his, the pads of his thumbs more abrasive than the rough grain of the solid oak of the table, from years of playing stringed instruments. The man could strum women with the same ease. "You're right. The past is done with."

Zara fought the urge to pull away, and raised her brows in question.

The very devil danced in his eyes, sending a shiver down her spine.

"So we're agreed, then?" he asked now, all politeness and easy smile. "We'll announce our engagement, maybe tomorrow at the awards show. And then arrive at Bhai's wedding together next week."

Zara nodded, a strange cocktail of apprehension and excitement swirling through her belly.

"Should we practice, then, *shahzadi*?"

"Practice what?" she whispered.

"A little intimacy. If you'd like, I can script it for us."

"And how would that go?" Zara whispered, some devil in her goading her on. For the life of her, she didn't want to back down now. And she had a feeling that was what the rogue wanted.

In one smooth movement, he was standing before her. His sharp features in shadow, only that plump curve of his lower lip illuminated, his intensity tugged at Zara. Then he bent from his great height and his fingers were mere whispers away from her mouth. "A little touching. Followed by some light petting. And then maybe, if we both can stand it, one kiss?"

CHAPTER THREE

ZARA DIDN'T JUMP about like a scalded cat through sheer willpower. So the devil meant to torture her for the next few months. For what reason, she had no idea. She traced the veins on the back of his hand lightly. "You change moods like Mumbai's monsoon, Virat. One second, you're ripping into me and the next, touching me as if you can't stop."

"There's a man with his cell phone camera trained on us behind the bar." His voice was a husky whisper over the rim of her ear. "Look at me as if you can't get enough of me, *shahzadi.*"

Zara's belly swooped on a wave of disappointment. But if he thought she was going to act like the scared mouse she'd been ten years ago, he was in for a shock. And if her memory served her right, Virat had been such a cynical soul even back then that he'd adored anything that could shock him.

Zara leaned forward on her barstool, pressed her hand to his chest and looked up. With his jacket discarded, the fabric of his shirt was no barrier to the thud of his heart or the warmth of his body under her palm. "Should this give him the perfect clip of us, do you think?" she whispered, all wide eyes and angelic compliance.

The dark laughter in his light brown eyes made her

want to shout in delight. Long fingers grazed her bare shoulder, and then he was leaning down. "I should apologize for any doubts I had about you seeing this through, Zara. In this moment, I might be forgiven for thinking you truly want me."

There was no way Zara could miss the bite of scorn in those words. Especially since he was right. She did want him. And that want, that vulnerability made her angry. Not ashamed. She'd never again be ashamed of her desires or her dreams again—Virat himself had taught her that. But she was angry that it took no more than an hour in his company for the floodgates of her desire to open up. For him especially. All this frantic need under her skin was to please him. To see true desire for her reflected in his eyes.

Something rose up inside her at the calm humor in his gaze, some wickedly desperate need to knock him off balance. To make him acknowledge that her presence in his life was not some willingly tolerated headache.

"So am I allowed to take complete advantage of this moment, Virat? Am I allowed to show them why my heart's not broken over Vikram's impending wedding?" she threw back.

"Do your worst, *shahzadi*," he retorted, all laughter gone. His fingers tightened over her skin just a fraction. "Or is it your best that I should demand?"

That was all the nudge Zara needed. She pushed off from the stool and landed in front of him. With the high table digging into her back, she was neatly wedged right up against him. And in front of her was the challenge simmering away in his eyes.

It was all there—the laughing dare in his raised brows as he surveyed her from his slight height advantage, the stubborn tilt of his mouth, the casual, laid-back attitude in his tall frame. That she could not move him. That she could have no effect on him. Not anymore. That this agreement between them couldn't be anything but a mutually beneficial drama being played out just to distract an avid audience.

That there wasn't even a hint of anything real between them. Not anymore.

It was an eminently sensible attitude Zara should be embracing, too, and yet something in her rebelled against it.

In four-inch heels, she found her mouth was perfectly placed just below his. Holding his eyes, she clasped his jaw, tilted her head and pressed her mouth to his. This close, she could see the shadows cast by the sweep of his lashes, the sharp highs and hollows of his cheekbones, the small scar at the edge of his mouth.

He tasted of rum and cigars and something so inherently male and irresistible that her knees wobbled beneath her. With a soft groan that she couldn't let out or swallow, Zara increased the pressure of her mouth, needing more contact, more friction, more everything.

She'd forgotten how soft his lips were. How his ever-present stubble created a delicious contrast against the sensitive skin of her jaw. How solidly built he was. How good he tasted. How much she'd adored having him to herself like this.

The gorgeous rebel Virat Raawal that every girl in the country was gaga over. The man who refused to follow in his legendary brother and father's footsteps and take up acting but chose to remain a mystery behind the camera instead.

A sudden furor swelled in her breast, an urgency taking root in her veins as Zara thought of all the ways she had had him and then lost him. This chaste press of her lips she allowed herself wasn't enough. It brought back all the longing she'd suppressed for this man. All the pain of walking away from him. All the ache of a decade as she'd watched him rise up through the industry and chase woman after woman while he didn't even acknowledge her existence. While he looked through her, past her at award ceremonies and charity events, as if he hadn't known her more intimately than any other man in the world.

God, she had wanted this kiss for ten years, she'd wanted it from the moment she had walked away from him, and she was so tired of waiting. Tired of being careful with her feelings. Tired of locking herself up in a cage she had built for herself. She kissed him more urgently then, as if she had to get all of this need and longing out of her. And into him.

But not even his breathing changed.

His nostrils flared but he stood there like a motionless giant, his hands dangling at his sides. Unmoved and mocking. As if she was nothing but one more woman in his impressive lineup. As if she couldn't make a dent in that damned self-possession of his. And Zara had enough.

Her hands crawled over his shoulders to the nape of his neck and demanded he bend. When he didn't, she pressed her face to his throat and let her tongue play with his pulse hammering away there.

She dragged her teeth softly against the hollow of his throat. Trailing soft kisses up and down the line of his jaw, she breathed him in. She licked the small scar on the side of his lip. Scraping her nails into his scalp, she pulled him closer until her breasts touched his chest. And then when Zara went for his mouth again, she knew she'd finally smashed through that steely control of his. He wasn't happy to be a silent spectator anymore. A faint energy vibrated underneath his stillness now, giving her a jolt of her own power.

His fingers sank into her hair, his other hand sweeping around her waist to pull her closer. Zara thrilled at the intimate contact with his hard body. Every muscle in her was singing, every nerve vibrating with need.

"I know what you should call me instead of princess," she murmured, holding his gaze, knowing she was setting the tone for the rest of their arrangement, however long it played out. Knowing that while it was okay to want Virat again like this, with an all-consuming need, she could never let him see how much it scared her, how much power he could still have over her given half the chance. She could never let him realize how much she still cared about his opinion. About him.

She'd worked hard and made enough sacrifices to be where she was today. If there was one thing she'd learned from surviving this industry for a decade, it was that she had to own her success, her choices. She couldn't show vulnerability, regrets, doubts to anyone.

Not to this man, of all people, who knew exactly where and how she had gotten started.

"What?" he said, after a slow blink. A soft word. Desire was a glimmering truth in his eyes and she realized he'd needed a moment to understand what she'd said.

She smiled. She didn't care why she was kissing him now. Or why he was kissing her back. She just wanted. More of him and more of his kisses. "Queen. After all, I built my own kingdom."

His laughter reverberated through her own body, leaving echoes. "Now that I won't disagree with, Zara." He pushed at a strand of her hair, his thumb drawing a barely there line on her jaw. Her skin, her entire being shimmered with anticipation and want. Because through all this, Zara knew he hadn't fully unleashed his own desire. He'd let her get to him, yes, but not tipped over. Not yet. "So should I test if I can make the Queen quake and tremble in my arms? Should I see if there's anything left of that sweet woman I knew a long time ago?"

"That woman was so afraid, Virat. Of everyone and her own dreams. This is me now—full of thorns and ice. A woman who sees a problem and wrangles the notorious playboy of Bollywood into behaving."

His smile wasn't mocking anymore. Those perceptive eyes studied her with a hunger she wanted to revel in. "And you can take everything I want to give? Because I have the most disreputable urge to mess you up, *shahzadi*."

"Do your worst, Virat," Zara said, her heart thudding so loudly that she couldn't hear anything else.

And then his mouth came for hers. He stole her breath and the ground under her feet with the soft, almost gentle press of his lips. This was no possession, as she'd expected. No rough passion that she so wanted. This kiss was charged with curiosity, exploration, almost as if he was willing himself to find something had changed. To find her changed. This kiss was nothing but pure tasting.

The rough bristle of his beard scraped sensuously against her lips and Zara gasped into his mouth. With her body pressed against his from chest to thigh, he was a fortress of heat and desire, touching small sparks in every limb and muscle.

Zara would have shouted her victory if he so much as allowed her another breath. Her heart raced deafeningly in her ears as his kiss turned from gentle exploration to pure possession at her unguarded response.

He kissed and nipped and licked her lips in a frenzy of hunger that would have turned her into a molten puddle if he wasn't holding her up. The table dug into her back but the ache of it contrasted sweetly against the hum of pleasure he evoked. His hands roved restlessly over her body, never landing in one spot, making her mindless with desire.

She pulled at his hair, and he bit her lower lip. When she moaned, he soothed her hurt with a swipe of his tongue. He tasted the warm cavern of her mouth as if he had to quench his thirst again and again.

Restless need slithered under Zara's skin, the rasp of her bra an imposition against her taut nipples. But his hands on her waist controlled her movement, never letting their lower bodies touch. She didn't know how long they kissed like that. She didn't care if it lasted an eternity or just a moment. She lost herself in his hunger. She celebrated herself in his need.

And then, slowly he called a halt to it.

He clasped her jaw in a gentle hold, their foreheads touching, and his harsh exhales coated her sensitive lips. And into the soft silence came his curse—filthy and full of an emotion Zara couldn't name. It snapped her out of the miasma of desire clouding her rationality. His anger at himself was a slap against her senses.

She stepped sideways, tottered on her heels, and he immediately shot out a hand to steady her. She raised a confused gaze to his, her body still made of pleasure currents. After ten years of drought, his touch, his kiss, his body was a haven she didn't want to give up so abruptly. "Virat?"

"Congratulations, *shahzadi*. That was a smashing engagement kiss, don't you think? If I had known you'd morph into such a wonderful actress, I'd have hired you ages ago for one of my projects."

Zara poked him in the chest, anger washing over her.

"I wasn't acting. And neither were you." She also had no idea why she wasn't simply taking the out he was giving her. Laughing away the kiss. "I won't let any man shame me for my desires or my dreams. And do you know who taught me how freeing it could be to truly embrace one-self? You.

"Maybe you need a reminder, Virat. Maybe you do need saving from yourself."

She didn't wait to hear his answer. Holding her head high, Zara walked away from him, wondering what the hell she had started tonight.

Zara leaned against the giant statue of an elephant covered in shimmering mosaic tiles and watched the laughing gaggle of young women surrounding the beautiful bride and grinning groom in the center of the courtyard of the palatial hotel where Vikram and Naina's three-day wedding was underway.

The architecture of the centuries-old palace restored into a luxury hotel had been one delight after the other since she and Virat had arrived together two days ago.

As expected, the world had exploded with the news of their engagement and that kiss had gone viral in a matter of hours. Both she and Virat had been besieged by the press at the awards show—where he'd triumphantly declared that the Queen had accepted his proposal of marriage—and afterward at the post-awards party. Social media had lit up with gossip about them, just as they'd wanted.

When they returned to the biopic's shoot in a few days, they already had more than one interview lined up—to talk about themselves and the movie, to present a united front with Vikram, her and Virat in front of the world.

Of course, the one thing neither had foreseen was

the effect it would have on Naina and Vikram. Zara and Virat had barely arrived at the venue when they'd both been cornered by the bridal couple, demanding to know what the hell was going on.

While she'd stood there flustered, Virat had smoothly taken over the entire conversation. His corded arm around her shoulders, the rogue had pulled her in and whispered, "What can I say, Bhai? She can't stay away from me."

Vikram had stared at them intently before Naina had pulled him away. Whatever magic she'd weaved on her bridegroom—and perceptive Naina had always known Virat and Zara had shared history—Vikram had looked slightly mollified. Still, he'd added, "Don't hurt her, Virat."

At which, her fake fiancé had thrown his head back, laughed uproariously and then muttered, "Have you given Zara the same warning, Bhai? Maybe I'm the one that needs protecting from her."

Zara had been happy to get away from all the perceptive looks flying around. Not that the lonely, foolish part of her had minded being caught up between two men who had always meant so much to her. Not that she and Vikram had ever been together, however.

It was only when she and Virat had fallen apart that her career had taken off and she'd built a platonic friendship with Vikram.

If their mother, Vandana Raawal, had anything to say about the entire matter—and Zara was sure the older woman did—Zara wasn't going to give her half the chance to come at her again. The last thing she wanted to remember was how the older woman had confronted Zara a decade ago. How she'd used all of Zara's insecurities against her to make her leave Virat.

When you threw me away for greener pastures...

That bitter comment of Virat's still bothered her as Zara picked up the hem of her heavy, custom-designed dark green velvet *lehenga*—one of Anya Raawal's superb creations—and walked into the evening's festivities.

Tonight the expansive courtyard glittered with a thousand tiny lights dotted along white-stoned pathways. Small blue pools sparkled with colorful flowers and *diyas*—lit lanterns—floating across the water. Divans with plush velvet pillows had been scattered around while uniformed staff passed out lassi, cocktails and chai.

And in the center of it all sat Naina, dressed in an off-white *kanchivaram* silk sari with a heavy pearl necklace and matching *jhumkas*, her unruly curly hair pulled back into a bun with a jasmine *gajra* wound around it. The young bride was dressed the simplest of them all and yet there was a radiance about Naina that shone bright, as if she was the sun in the sky making every other star dim in comparison.

A bittersweet pang made Zara's chest feel tight as she caught a look between Naina and Vikram, sitting on opposite divans, surrounded by prettily dressed sisters and cousins teasing them as part of another fun ritual. There was nothing but pure adoration, nothing but the deepest form of love in that look.

Once upon a time, Virat had looked at her with that open affection and she had basked in it. Had come out of the shell she'd built around herself during her disastrous marriage.

She laughed when music broke out over cleverly hidden speakers and Vikram dragged his shy fiancée into a slow beat. Zara joined in the group surrounding them, even as her heart felt heavy in her chest. Today, of all days, it was hard to pretend that the past didn't still have its talons sunk into her, hadn't made her build a cage around her heart.

Hard to act as if she was only the successful, bold-as-brass actress and businesswoman the world knew her to be and nothing more. Hard to lie to herself that sometimes she wasn't achingly lonely. Like now, being surrounded by so much love and happiness.

Heat prickled across her skin, and she looked up. Like a magnet seeking its true north, she found him—the man who had always been able to look straight into her heart.

Virat was standing on the open terrace right in front of her. Fading sunlight gilded the strong planes of his face with a glowing outline. In the off-white Nehru-collar kurta, he looked like a king surveying his kingdom. His gaze devoured her—from the gold dupatta falling off her shoulders to the sleeveless velvet blouse with its low, square cut, to her kohl-lined eyes and her ruby-red lips.

A current arced between them, even across the distance and the beat of the music and the laughter surrounding her. The memory of their kiss awakening the hunger and heat that had flared so easily between them. It had been so real that she'd seen the staggering shock of it in his eyes.

Long into the night, after she'd returned to her flat, she'd run her fingers over her lips again and again. As if she could catch and bottle the essence of him. As if she could find the imprint of his hunger and his hardness on herself.

That kiss had been like stepping back into the past. Like finding the pieces of the soul she'd scattered behind her somewhere on the climb to stardom, in her fight to prove to herself that her marriage hadn't completely broken her.

That she'd survived the trauma intact.

Ten years ago, she'd desperately wanted everything Virat had given her, but she'd been tentative, wary, passive, still reeling from the events surrounding the end of her marriage. Now Zara knew her own needs, could demand what she wanted. For a few indulgent seconds, Zara couldn't help but lull herself into thinking he knew exactly what she was thinking. That he could see how much she'd needed that kiss. How much she needed him right now. Even after everything that had happened.

Would he give it to her if she asked?

She didn't know what he saw in her eyes, but a mocking smile curved his lips and he dipped his head in a blazing challenge. Zara looked away, her pulse hammering through her body.

A group of laughing, excited young women surrounded her, alleviating some of the tightness in her chest. She took the dark shades one of them offered and they all struck up a fun pose for the photographer.

And when one of the young women looked up at Virat and then back down at her and whispered, "How does it feel to have hooked the notoriously single playboy whose girlfriends don't last more than a month at most?" Zara faked a laugh and said, "All I know is that man can rock my world with one simple kiss."

Pretending to be hot for Virat Raawal was the easy part. Not falling into the fantasy she weaved every time he so much as looked at her…not so much.

CHAPTER FOUR

VIRAT WALKED ONTO the terrace as dusk streaked orange in the sky. He felt restless at too much partying and posing. He wanted to be back at work. And what bothered him the most was how easily he'd lost control of himself in Zara's kiss.

How much he still wanted her.

Was that such a bad thing, he asked himself with the same honesty that he did everything else. Would it be so wrong to indulge himself? And her? Judging by their kiss, they both clearly had a hell of a lot of heat still brewing between them.

She wanted him. And unlike ten years ago, this Zara clearly had no qualms asserting herself. Demanding that he give her more. Indicating what she wanted from a lover.

She thought she was saving him, he had no doubt. And at least until things calmed down after this latest scandal with the minister's wife, he decided he would let her save him. Maybe this was exactly what he needed, too.

He'd fallen into a creative fugue, too. The dark subject he was handling with the docuseries could be the reason. And yet, he couldn't lie to himself. His work was beginning to be tainted by his self-imposed isolation. By his growing disillusionment with the world. By the distance he'd created between himself and the very essence of life—attachment and love and affection.

Being angry with the world took a whole lot of energy out of a man. He laughed at the irony of it. Zara's proposal couldn't have come at a better time. If nothing else, he would have fun needling the perfect composure she wore as a mask, and maybe stealing one or two more kisses.

And this time, he knew who and what he was dealing with.

It was a little past midnight but the party was still in full swing, showing no signs of dying down. Virat found Zara in one of the private nooks scattered over the palace, on the second floor, with a perfect view of the dance floor that had been set up at the center of the open courtyard.

A lazy quiet dwelled on this floor as there were no guest suites up here.

Up above, the dark sky glittered with twinkling stars and a soft breeze carried the scent of the sweetly pungent jasmine creeper that covered one entire wall of the hotel.

Virat stood still for a moment and stared at her through the open archway. She looked like a beautiful prisoner of some jealous maharaja in this setting, hidden away from covetous eyes.

They'd already paraded themselves in front of the wedding guests. Already answered enough probing questions for today. Looked at each other as if they couldn't bear to be apart. Not that they had to manufacture the soft hum of attraction that threatened to simmer over every time they touched.

That kiss was like a constant peal in his body. Both taunting him and mocking him for how easily he could fall apart when he was near her.

He shouldn't seek her out like this. Clearly, she was desperate for a break.

Except for the haunted look she'd worn all day. That flash of vulnerability was what had tugged him here.

With the colorful array of fat pillows and hand-sewn quilts sitting atop plump divans, the wall still retaining the original, hand-painted art, and small, dimly lit electric *diyas* placed artistically in tiny, hand-carved grooves in the rust-colored walls, it was a cozy, darkened escape from the madness below. The beats from the fusion hip-hop, Bollywood music pumping through the dance floor provided a background score.

He had to admit that with every step he moved toward her, his own heart matched the bop-bop of that dance beat. He was still that damned twenty-year-old when it came to her.

Attraction was different from affection, he reassured himself. Attraction could be worked out of one's system. Attraction didn't make you vulnerable.

Leaning his arm against the entry archway, he studied her.

Zara was reclining against one pillow, her knees demurely tucked sideways, her skirt spread around her in a circle as if someone had posed her like that. She had wrapped a silky shawl around her bare shoulders. From the *lehenga-choli* in the morning to the white crop top and blue skirt she'd changed into for the dance party, her transformation was seamless.

She wasn't slender or petite. Her statuesque form, the high forehead and the wide eyes all defied conventional definitions of beauty. And yet, in the last decade, the beauty he'd seen back then had only matured and sharpened. There was no doubt that Zara had come into her own.

And this bold, fierce woman who could go toe to toe with him was even more irresistible than the quiet, timid thing she'd been back then.

"Are you hiding, Zara?" he asked, genuinely curious.

"Maybe. I don't know," she replied, not looking away from her examination of the stars.

"I noticed you haven't been off your feet for a moment since all the rituals began at dawn."

Surprise painted over her face that he'd even noticed.

He shrugged. He didn't need to articulate that he was, as always, obsessed with her.

"I take my role as the naive bride's champion very seriously. It hasn't been easy to shield her from the World War III her stepmother and your mother—" she hesitated and surveyed him quickly "—want to begin. Naina's determined to satisfy everyone around her. To keep everyone harmonious. Even though Vikram has told her more than once that this wedding is all about her. So it falls to me to be the one who stands up to them."

He walked into the nook and she stood up fluidly. "You're a good friend to Naina."

A flash of anger flared in her eyes before she chased it away. "Don't sound so surprised, Virat. Like I told you, I'm not some one-dimensional vampy villainess." She continued on before he could respond, her chest rising and falling with anger. "What is really strange is that you of all men want to box me into one category. Aren't you the brilliant genius known for his three-dimensional portrayal of women? Hmm…is she a murderer or a sweet homemaker? No, she's both!"

It was this bold way she had of calling him out on his own preconceptions that drew him to her. She was right. He did keep trying to box her in. But the alternative was that she'd continue to consume him. And that was unacceptable.

Virat leaned forward to meet her eyes. "I don't think you're a vampy villainess, whatever that means." The truth of her statement lay heavy between them in the dark silence. He hated being wrong. And yet, he had a feeling he was continually putting his foot wrong with Zara. "It's not a huge leap to think there might be awkwardness between you and Bhai's newfound love. After all, you and he have been linked…"

"There has never been a whisper of physical attraction between me and Vikram. We let the media make more of our friendship than there really was because it served our purpose." The words fell into the silence with the force of a gale.

Virat felt as if he'd been smacked in the face. Not because of the clarification she provided after all these years but at the relief that poured through him like a gushing river. He hadn't realized how much bitterness he still nursed inside that Zara had chosen Bhai over him because Vikram could give her career a boost unlike anything Virat could have done for her at that time. But had she chosen Vikram, truly?

There was a clear disconnect between his version and her version of the past. Suddenly, the entire foundation he'd been standing on for a decade seemed full of holes.

This time, her anger wasn't hidden at all. It blazed out of her eyes and the twist of her mouth. "If you think I just swapped you for Vikram when I got bored or…"

He had no idea what he saw in his face but the fight deflated out of her. She blinked, as if fighting tears, her hand slightly trembling as she pulled her hair away with both hands in an incredibly graceful movement. "Of course. That's exactly what you thought. It's how little you think of me."

Before he could blink, she was moving away. "I can't take this, not today."

He wrapped his fingers around her arm, stopping her. "Zara, wait!" She turned her face away from him and he let her. Something in him rebelled at the idea of hurting her. Of being the reason for a strong woman like her to be brought low. "I didn't mean to hound you out of here. To throw recriminations at you."

Her fury only increased. "No, for ten years, you have simply looked through me. As if I didn't exist. As if our entire history together was erased. I would have welcomed recriminations, because at least that meant you were giving me a chance to explain. But I didn't deserve even that much in your eyes, did I?"

"You were the one who left, Zara," he said gently, as if that small fact hadn't rocked his life like an earthquake. "You accepted a movie offer from Bhai and left."

"Because I was trying to build a career and you—"

"Ms. Khan, is that you?" interrupted a soft female voice from outside the arched doorway. Zara's breath fell on his cheek in a soft stroke and Virat barely held his temper in check. The last thing he wanted right now was to deal with gushing girls who thought his and Zara's romance was a sparkly fairy tale they all could take part in.

"Oh, Ms. Khan, I don't know how to thank you for inviting me. I've already met so many people," the woman continued, stepping into the dimly lit nook. And then her gaze fell on Virat and his hand around Zara's arm and their heads tilted together. "I... Oh... Oh, I'm so sorry, Mr. Raawal. I didn't see you there or I'd have never—"

"Don't worry, Meera." Her fingers on his wrist, Zara

pulled his hand away from her arm. Her gaze held Virat's with a bold challenge that made his spirit sing. As he watched, she pushed away the naked hurt on her face until there was nothing but sweet charm. "I forgot what an important man my fiancé is and was bothering him with the most inconsequential thing from a long time ago," she said, looping their arms together and turning them around to face the woman.

After she'd left him, he'd no choice but to pretend she didn't exist. He'd used her betrayal as fuel to push him to reach for ever greater heights. His anger with her had felt so justified.

But Virat wasn't sure about anything anymore. Except the fact that with each moment they spent together, he wanted this Zara with a desire that defied explanation.

Zara felt the swift rise of Virat's irritation in the very stillness that came over him. If he had the reputation of being a demanding bastard on the set, he had zero tolerance when it came to the tabloid media. It stemmed from being used as evergreen scandal material every time his mother or their family or his movies came up in the news.

The whole "Was he a Raawal or was he Vandana's illegitimate son?" debate was a piece of news that had been cycled over and over again for its shock value.

"Mr. Raawal is delighted for your interruption. Aren't you, *jaan*?" she said, pouring flirty charm into her voice, clasping his jaw with her palm.

The endearment made his jaw tight like tar packed into a road, and delight bloomed in her chest. It was like pawing a predator who was only playing nice for a limited time.

Oh, God, how had she forgotten what fun it was to tease and taunt him? He had given her a kind of leeway he didn't allow anyone else. Then or now. And she was a pathetic puppy who was still counting the crumbs he threw at her.

He rubbed his nose against hers in a tender gesture that made her pull away. "What would I do if you weren't here to tame me, *shahzadi*?"

Zara snorted—he really was the devil—and turned back to the woman watching them with avid interest. "Did you settle in all right, Meera? Have you been shown to a proper room? Vikram knows you're on my guest list. If you need anything…"

"Oh, it's been perfect, Ms. Khan. Everyone's been really nice," the woman said, her gaze shifting nervously from Virat. For a man who could charm the panties off married women, he could give off a cold frost like no one's business when he wasn't interested. "I just wanted to thank you for getting me the invite to the wedding. It's been like witnessing a fairy tale. Thank you for convincing Vikram sir that our organization is the real thing. He wouldn't have given us a chance if not for your recommendation."

"What have you roped Bhai into, love?"

It was Meera that spoke up. "My sister and I run a shelter for women fleeing abusive relationships in Mumbai. We aim to empower them by matching them with the right career training and Zara ma'am has been our staunchest supporter from the beginning. Unlike most celebrities who just write us a check, Ma'am donates her time and network to find suitable jobs for the women. One of our members is an aspiring actress, and Vikram sir gave her a chance to audition for a small part in a different project. Zara ma'am set up the whole thing," she finished, beaming at her.

Virat studied Zara with such intensity that a warm trickle of sensation filled her every limb. "You're apparently a paragon of virtue, *jaan*. A patroness of arts, a charity doyenne… A true queen, then." But there was a hint of curiosity in his tone that promised a discussion later.

"Meera's exaggerating," Zara quipped. "I simply didn't forget what it is to start from nothing. And I want to pay it forward." She turned to him and nuzzled her face into the side of his neck, anger still coursing through her. "Does it make my ambition more palatable now? Does that make me more deserving of everything I've gained, Virat? Of you?"

She noted the slight flinch of his mouth with faint satisfaction. Nothing like holding a mirror up to a supposed man of principles. "You know that's not me and—"

But in that moment, Zara discovered she was petty and she didn't want to let go of the anger at his assumptions. She also knew that her ire was nothing but a shield against the hurt he could heap on her, given half the chance. "Meera also writes for *SuperWomen*. She's doing a feature on me for the next month's issue," she added for his sake.

Settling back down again on a divan, she invited the young woman to start her interview. During the first few questions, Virat stayed quiet, walking behind and around Zara, his gaze never leaving her face.

"Can I ask you some questions about your relationship now?" said Meera, her tone tentative, as if afraid Virat might cancel her invitation and send her packing.

"What kind of questions?" Virat said instantly, pinning the poor woman with his gaze.

Meera tilted her chin up. "Our audience would love

to know about the man who's swept Zara ma'am off her feet. They want to know if you deserve her."

Zara smiled at the sudden gleam of respect in Virat's eyes.

"That's something I'm still figuring out," he replied, with a slick charm that had Meera blushing.

Zara didn't miss the intention behind the statement. She sat back as he took the reins of the interview, smoothly bypassing most of Meera's probing questions about their relationship and bringing the focus back to the biopic and their working together. He gave just enough to satisfy Meera's curiosity without revealing anything he didn't want to. It was like watching a master manipulator at work and Zara was glad he was on her side.

"Do you want an official picture of us together?" he added silkily, just as the interview was wrapping up.

Before Zara could blink, Meera pulled out a professional-grade, high-end camera out of her bag, and she and Virat were discussing lighting, angles and the best pose that would show off Zara and him together. She was still trying to wrap her mind about how she had lost control of the conversation when he lifted her easily—she was by no means a small woman—and neatly placed her sideways into his lap, with one of her arms going around his neck, her other hand on his chest. Leaving her face dipping down into his, intimately close.

His arm went around her waist, his broad palm sliding into place over her belly. The other hand, he left on her knee. He smelled of aftershave and the cigar he smoked when he was stressed, and something that was so essentially him—a cocktail that she was so familiar with that her nerves went haywire.

Zara's heart started a thump-thump so loud that she was afraid the entire wedding party would hear it. Except in front of the camera, she hadn't been this close to a man for so long. Oh, she'd toyed with the idea of a casual affair once or twice but it had only remained a fantasy. It seemed the wounds she'd sustained during her marriage were too deep to let her guard down with anyone other than Virat.

She wanted to blame her body's absurdly needy reaction to his closeness on the drought she'd put herself through. Suppressing her natural desires wasn't healthy. And yet, she knew that would be a lie. Only Virat had ever managed to make her forget her wariness. Only Virat who tempted her, even now.

She didn't have to hold the pose for too long as Meera pronounced them done in no more than a few minutes. When she then asked for a selfie with Zara—the poor woman still seemed to be in awe of Virat—the blasted man dismissed her with a charming "I'd like to be alone with my Queen before the hordes find us."

If he asked nicely, Zara was sure the woman would have burned the place down. Zara knew she would. Meera left after a cheerful wave in Zara's direction and a grin that could be seen from her main office in Delhi.

A sudden silence descended in the cozy nook, weaving an intimacy around them. For the first time in years, Zara felt the thread of desire in her belly trump fear and doubts. Subsume everything except awareness of this man.

"Thank you for being nice to her," she said into the gathering quiet. Unwilling to run away.

"You know I would never deny someone starting from the ground up." His long fingers squeezed her knee. "You're doing good work, Zara."

There was no mockery or teasing in this. His compliment was genuine. Zara felt warmth filling her chest.

She didn't need his validation but she liked it anyway. This was a man whose good opinion would always matter to her. She'd already made her peace with that. "Thank you," she whispered huskily. His fingers on her belly felt like a heated brand on her bare skin even though the thin cotton of her crop top provided a barrier.

"Zara, it's clear we have different impressions of—"

Zara pressed her palm over his mouth and shook her head. "I don't want to discuss the past anymore. Not today, please. It's already beaten me down."

When he spoke, his words painted her palm with a warmth she desperately needed to feel elsewhere. Everywhere. All over. She wanted to inhale the warmth of this man and have him heat up the parts of her that had frozen with fear over the years. She needed him. "I know that, *shahzadi*."

She raised a questioning gaze to his.

He shrugged. "Let's just say I have a radar when it comes to these things. Or maybe I'm just tuned into you. You've been the perfect best friend, a charming actress and a loving fiancée all day. But there's been a haunted look in your gaze, too."

Zara wasn't surprised by his perceptiveness. The gentleness in his tone threatened to knock down all the barriers she'd pulled up around her heart. Shatter the concrete she'd built to keep out the guilt and joy and pain of this particular day. "I… A long time ago, my husband died on this day. It's difficult for me to talk about… Please don't ask me any more about it now," she added, on a wave of that same guilt and pain roping together.

But it was unnecessary. Because even back then, Virat had never probed. Never asked her for more than she was willing to give.

"Then I won't," he said with that easy acceptance she

adored. She loved everything about him then, the tensile strength of his arms around her, the warm, male scent filling every empty space inside her. "We'll simply sit here for as long as you want."

"Why?" she asked, suddenly desperate for more.

"Because I want to, *shahzadi*. Because we've ended up here in this moment again. Forget the past, Zara, and forget the future. Here, right now, you're safe."

And just like that, he made Zara crave more from him. More from this moment. Not the future. Not an uncertain tomorrow. Now. Just now.

"I want more, then," she said, the whispers in her head turning into words on her lips with an easy familiarity that colored their every interaction. "Something more from you."

He didn't move or speak or blink and yet a stillness came over him.

He waited, without giving her empty reassurances. And Zara realized he knew. And that he was waiting for her to ask. That this had been inevitable from the moment she'd wrangled him into acting as her lover at the magazine launch.

"Make love to me, Virat. I desperately need something real today to anchor me here. I want to feel. Not think."

CHAPTER FIVE

VIRAT SCANNED HIS brain for all the reasons he should be saying no to this. In the few days since they'd been reacquainted with each other, Zara had proved to him that he didn't know her at all. And yet, as he inhaled the scent of her skin and felt the sweet slide of her body against his, he knew he wouldn't say no. The taste of his defeat when it came to her was wholly exciting.

Despite what the world liked to believe, he wasn't indiscriminate when it came to his sex partners. He had however always been able to separate the emotional realm from mutual chemistry. Only with Zara had those lines blurred. But he wasn't that reckless twenty-year-old anymore.

And this Zara was a wholly different woman. This Zara knew what she wanted and had no hesitation asking for it. This Zara had seen a problem and tackled it head on. This Zara was fierce when it came to protecting the ones she loved. This Zara…damn it, he had seen the flashes of this Zara before. She'd always been there beneath the surface, waiting to break free.

This Zara was the one who could topple him all over again. And it was that very prospect that fired his blood. Conventional wisdom had never worked for him. The very idea of having this bold Zara—willing and wanton—in his arms, at his mercy, made the beast inside him roar.

He calmed the urgency in his blood, giving her his standard warning. Making it clear, as he always did. "This can be nothing more than sex. Nothing else. It can't—"

She bent her head and rubbed her lips against his stubbled jaw in a raspy whisper that tightened every muscle in his body. "I want nothing but to feel you inside me. I want…you, Virat. I don't think I've ever stopped." Those words came in a breathless rush as if she hadn't been meaning to say them. The flash of dismay in her gaze told him as much. But they were real, and knowing that, Virat lost what little control he had over this situation and of himself.

He sank his fingers into her hair and brought her mouth to his, unraveling at a level he couldn't fathom. With most women in his life, he played a part—the rebel, the scion of Bollywood royalty, the director who held someone's career in his palm, the bastard…but Zara seemed to so easily peel away all those masks he'd worn. Until she found the core of him. The kiss that followed was a war for control and yet they were both victors. It was a very different kiss from the first one in the pub. There was no polite finesse or soft exploration. It was all frenzy and fierceness, their bodies sliding against each other, limbs tangling and untangling in a wild search for more. And better.

Their lips and tongues and teeth met in a tug of want and heat. She was warm and soft in his lap, her tongue licking into his mouth as if she couldn't survive another second without his taste.

Harsh breaths fell into the silence as he let them up for air. He ran his palms up her back, his fingers tangling in the myriad colorful strings that held her blouse together. "These flimsy strings have been taunting me all day, *shahzadi*." He gently grazed his knuckles over her breasts and she shivered and pressed herself into his touch. Her head thrown back, her eyes closed, she was the most beautiful thing he had ever seen. "One hard tug and everything unravels. Will you unravel, too, Zara? For me?"

"Yes," she whispered and pressed another hungry kiss against his lips before she moved out of his lap. The door to the nook closed with a soft thud, and the bolt clicked into place. With the light from the portico cut off, little illumination remained in the nook. Just enough from the tiny lanterns to make out the determined tilt of Zara's chin and the rise and fall of her chest.

Desire uncoiled in his veins with the energy of a lightning bolt. "Here?" he asked softly, tracing the outline of her body in the dark with his hungry gaze.

"Here. Now," she said, slowly coming away from the door. "I'm protected. Are you clean?"

"Yes," he said, pushing off the divan and covering the distance between them. "But the window can still carry sounds down."

"It's past midnight and they're all half-drunk anyway. I don't want to go back to my room and discover all the thousand reasons why this might not be a good idea."

"Doubts already, *shahzadi*?" His fingers landed on her waist and he twirled her toward him, loving the soft gasp that fell from her mouth when he wrapped his arms around her from behind. The taut swells of her buttock pressed against his groin, sending his libido into overdrive.

"Not doubts so much as worry that ghosts of the past might rear their ugly heads again."

"The dark doesn't hide the truth, Zara."

"Not wanting to face up to your weakness is not the same as hiding from the truth."

He buried his nose in the crook of her shoulder, breathing in the wild, wanton scent of her. "So I'm a weakness, then?"

She placed her palms on his arms and leaned back into his body, as if she meant to burrow under his skin. Her husky laughter—as he gently grazed his teeth against her collarbone, was like listening to his favorite old ghazal. She sent her hands into his hair and tugged. "You're not a weakness. How you make my knees go weak is the problem. You're like a rich dessert, Virat. And I can only indulge in you for so long."

He laughed and sent his own hands questing up her body. Her breath hitched on a quiet gasp when he filled his hands with her breasts. Memory was a strangely erotic thing. He remembered how sensitive she was to any caress there, how she responded to the slightest touch. And in this, nothing had changed. The moment he found the aching buds and rubbed them between his fingers, she grew taut against him with a throaty moan. His own throat grew dry as she pressed her buttocks into his groin and ground herself against him.

And then there was nothing to do but tug the strings at the back of her blouse. The fabric came loose and he drew it off, the first contact of his fingers on her silky skin making rivulets of pleasure run through him. He cupped the generous globes and tweaked the sensitive tips.

She turned her head and reached for his mouth with a hungry whimper that made him groan, too. Fingers tugging in his hair, she plundered his mouth with a savage ferocity that threatened to undo him. Her obvious need for him was as much an aphrodisiac as anything else.

"Against the wall?" he murmured against her mouth.

Another light switched off somewhere and the darkness was even thicker, amplifying every hitch in her breathing. He loved the scent of her—of jasmine and warm skin—and the lushness of the dips and swells of her body.

"The entire palace will hear us," she whispered back. He felt the wide curving of her lips rather than see her smile.

"Bent over the divan?" he asked next.

The funky hip-hop music died, and in its place began the soft beat of a slow song. Hands at her waist, Virat whirled her around in the darkness and had the reward of her delighted laughter. The tiny bells hanging from a cord at her skirt tinkled along with her laughter.

He felt her nails scraping his chest before he heard the pop of buttons flying around. And then her hands were everywhere. Slightly cool against his heated skin. She traced his pectorals, her fingers pulling at his chest hair and then down to his abdomen in a maddening journey. Every time she reached the seam of his trousers, she lingered for a few seconds longer than the last time.

He felt like a man who was being tormented with a drop of ambrosia that would never touch his tongue.

"Too impersonal," she finally whispered, her voice carrying a conviction he couldn't unhear. A moment's hesitation gripped him.

"Zara, this is—"

"It's not a quiet screw in the darkness of the night with some stranger, Virat. Not that there's anything wrong with that. But that's not what I want.

"I want the warmth of a man I desire in return. I want to look into your eyes when you let go inside me. I want to be reminded how good it can be between two people who want nothing but each other's pleasure. Is that asking for too much?"

"Of course it's not," he said, only then realizing that she'd neatly propelled him back toward the plush divan. At the last moment, he flipped them around and she was the one falling back.

As if guided by his specific instructions, she created a cradle between her legs and Virat let himself fall there with a gentle thud that made her laugh again. He kept his weight off her by propping himself on his elbows. With his shirt and her blouse discarded, the slide of his bare chest against her naked breasts had them both groaning in bliss.

He dipped his head down and kissed her again. Slowly this time. With languorous strokes of his tongue and sweet nips of her lips, letting the frenzy between them heat up again. Her hands roamed his chest lazily, but she never went past his belly.

Virat noted the infinitesimal hesitation every time her hands were about to reach him. There was something about it that tugged at his heart. "Everything okay, *shahzadi*?" he whispered, dropping a kiss against her temple.

"Perfect. Just perfect," she said, her gaze not shying from his.

He saw the shadow of something in there but decided not to push. This was a hookup. Nothing else. They didn't mean anything to each other whatever she said. There was the comforting familiarity of an old lover, yes. The ease of no strings. But nothing more. "I'm going to touch you here," he said, bringing his palm to her groin. The skirt was bunched up against her thighs but still intact at her waist, providing a barrier between his palm and her flesh.

She nodded. "Yes, please. Now."

He laughed at the alacrity with which she said that.

"You're welcome to do the same, Zara," he added with a cheeky grin.

And he knew, even in the darkness, that she was blushing fiercely. Just as she'd done back then.

Then, slowly, softly, she traced the shape of his erection through his trousers with one finger. An almost there but gone contact that had him aching for more.

"Like this?" she whispered, watching his expression. Always watching him from afar. From nearby, too. Through a decade of him pretending that she didn't exist, that she was beneath his notice, Virat had always been aware of her watching him with this same hunger in her eyes.

With a longing that she hadn't always kept quite hidden. And he'd always wondered if she'd felt remorse over her decision. If she'd been sorry that she'd used their relationship to level up her burgeoning career in the industry.

"Yes," he said through a throat full of desire.

"Show me."

His head jerked up. "What?"

"Tell me what you'd like. Show me." When he didn't respond, she pulled up on her elbows and licked his lower lip. "Please."

"I'd like more," Virat said, and he could feel her resolve in the way she nodded.

"Okay, more like this?" she said, her one finger turning into her entire palm over his shaft.

"More like your hand wrapped around me without my damn trousers on," he said on a harsh exhale. Losing any semblance of control when her breasts pressed up against his chest.

The hiss of his trouser zipper was music to his ears. And then her hand was wrapped firmly around his shaft and Virat let out a filthy curse that should've woken up even the most inebriated party guest sleeping on the lower floors.

She laughed and her fingers turned into a fist, and she pumped him hesitantly and Virat thought he might have died and gone to heaven.

He lowered himself down, letting her feel his weight. His fingers wrapped around hers on his shaft, trapped between their bodies. He pressed open-mouthed kisses into the crook of her neck and shoulders and he loved how her body molded to his and how she looked at him at that moment and something shattered between them.

They were kissing again, but there was a difference to this kiss. It seemed every kiss of theirs had a different flavor, a new taste, a totally novel experience again and again. This one was full of a strange sort of harmony, even as excitement built in his lower belly. When she gently rubbed the tip of his shaft with her thumb, Virat threw his head back and let out a guttural groan.

"I love it when you do that," Zara said instantly, her mouth pressed into the hollow of his throat, breathing in and out, as if she didn't want to miss even a bit of him.

"When I do what, *shahzadi*?"

"When you let go," she answered instantly.

"I don't curtail myself for anyone, Zara. Isn't that exactly what landed me here?"

"That might work on the rest of the world but not me."

He frowned. "What do you mean?"

"The world thinks you have no control. That you give in to every urge and impulse. Then, of course, it forgives you for most transgressions—as it does most powerful men, because you create such brilliant pieces of work."

He couldn't help it. Virat laughed at her dry delivery and kissed her with a tenderness he couldn't hide. "Ah... cynicism suits you, *shahzadi*," he said.

"Oh, thank God! What a refreshing thing it is to meet a man who doesn't expect me to always smile and pander to his mood."

He laughed some more and ran his tongue between the valley of her breasts. Her long exhale was a breeze against his cheek. "Oh, you beast, I'm almost distracted," she said with a gasp.

"Almost is not good enough," he said, and blew slightly over one puckered nipple. He rubbed his stubble against one soft globe and she jerked as if she'd received an electric shock. Zara was writhing under his touch now, barely holding on. "But the world says, 'Oh, it's his uncontrollable impulses and urges that make him brilliant, so creative.' But I know it's all a sham."

Virat stilled. "What is a sham, Zara?"

She gazed into his eyes, hers challenging, even under the cloud of desire. "You're the most controlled man in any situation. Every impulse you give in to, every urge that you satisfy, nothing is done unless you're in complete control. Nothing is simply a lark. Nothing gets past the cynical shell you've carefully built around yourself."

The silence in the wake of her words was filled with Virat's shock.

Zara fell back onto the mattress and studied him with a wariness she couldn't hide. As if she was afraid she'd crossed a line. As if she was afraid he'd call a halt to the entire thing. Her perceptiveness did make him pause but not enough to forgo this pleasure.

"You think way too much, *shahzadi*," he said lightly, and gathered her closer to him. "I know the best way to get you to stop all that unnecessary thinking."

Without waiting for her response, he sent his palm up her toned calf and knee and past the silky-smooth skin of her inner thigh. Her panties were a flimsy barrier against his probing fingers. She almost came away from the divan as he delved his fingers into her soft folds.

"Oh…" Her pink mouth fell open.

Virat watched her with a hunger that only seemed to grow. Every hitch and gasp of her breath stoked his own need higher. He played with her clit, and she dug her fingers into his bicep. He thrust a finger into her wet heat and her reaction to that—more than anything—interrupted the mindless want that had taken over most of his rational mind.

"Zara?" he said, not sure what question to ask. There was the usual wariness within him since he'd never asked personal questions of a lover before. And he definitely didn't want to start now.

But then Zara had always made him forget his own damned rules.

"More please." She opened her mouth against his chest, the tips of her teeth digging gently into his pecs. "More, Virat." She demanded it this time when he didn't respond.

Virat stuck up a rhythm with his fingers and she pushed into his touch with a soft groan. He kept her there—at that cliff and then worked her back down again, until she was sobbing with want. Dipping his head, he kissed the taut nipple of one breast and then closed his mouth around it.

Zara writhed under him, her hands in his hair holding him there. Moving his hand away from her inviting heat—despite her husky protest and breathy warning, Virat pushed down his trousers and then reached for her skirt. The voluminous thing grated at the little patience he had left. Her toned thighs trembling, Zara lifted up her hips as he gathered her skirt and pulled it away.

Their gazes met and held, each challenging the other

to make this less than it was. Each searching for the other to make it more. Virat was the one to look away first and it felt as if he'd lost something in a battle he hadn't signed up for.

At last, there was no barrier between his flesh and hers. Pushing her thighs wider, Virat entered her in one smooth thrust. The sensation of her clamping him tight was so incredible that for a few seconds he didn't realize that she had stiffened under him. Her palms were on his hips, he realized through the fog of pleasure, her nails digging in.

Her head turned away from his, and he saw the sweep of her eyelashes cast shadows onto her cheekbones. She looked achingly vulnerable then, her body betraying a secret he didn't want to know. The last thing he wanted was to be the bearer of someone's secrets.

Especially hers.

"Zara?" he said then, his own voice a croaky whisper, his body humming at him to move. To see this through. But despite his best intentions, it was hard to treat this woman he'd once known so well as a stranger. He nuzzled his nose into her temple gently, gathering her to him. "We can stop if that's what you want, *shahzadi*."

She turned back then and he could see the Zara that held the world at bay had returned. "But I didn't even climax," she said, with a mock pout.

He smiled, even though a part of him was perversely displeased that the moment of vulnerability was over.

"Continue, please," she said with all the grave austerity of a queen ordering her knight to do her bidding.

"As you wish, *shahzadi*," he said against her lips, before sending his mouth on a foray down her soft cheek, to the madly fluttering pulse at her throat. He trailed kisses lower until he captured one taut nipple with his mouth and licked it until she was trembling under him.

"Slow or fast?" he asked with a smile, remembering how he'd teased her once.

"Slow and deep or hard and fast... I don't care," she said on a breathy whisper. "I just want..."

Virat tilted her pelvis and pulled out and then thrust in deep. Every muscle in his lower belly rubbed against hers. She was so snug around him he knew he wasn't going to last long. Every stroke sent him hurtling toward his own climax, the upward tilt of her hips every time he moved setting fire to his nerve endings.

"Please, Virat, now," she whispered.

He snuck his other hand in between their bodies and rubbed her expertly in exactly the right place.

She came like fireworks in the sky with a soft moan and his name on her lips. The spasms of her flesh sent tremors running up and down his legs. Pushing his free hand into her hair, Virat thrust in and out, in a series of shallow movements that lit up every muscle. That unraveled the knot in his lower belly even faster.

Then he took her fast and deep, chasing his own ecstasy with an urgency that had no finesse. The litany of his name on her lips only added to his satisfaction. His climax still roaring through his body, Virat buried his face in her neck.

The scent of sweat and sex was a powerful cocktail in the air around them, but instead of feeling the urgent need to extricate himself, all Virat felt was the opposite.

He wanted to linger in this languorous moment. Even that, however, wasn't a warning to his rational mind. Because sleeping with Zara was the easy part. Their chemistry was still a powerfully rare thing, but the intimacy it forced on them...

Slowly, without pulling out of her, he raised himself up on his elbows and studied her.

Her head to the side, her eyes closed, her breaths were shallow and fast. A bead of sweat lazily rolled down her neck and onto her chest. Virat waited and then licked it up just as it began its descent between her breasts.

She moaned, her entire body trembling under him.

He immediately went half hard inside her again.

"I thought you'd have outgrown that by now," she said, a wicked smile curving her mouth, carving that gorgeous dimple on one side that every man and woman oohed and aahed over.

When he went to pull away, she stopped him. Her gaze met his, full of a naughtiness that he barely saw flashes of anymore. "I'm not complaining."

He ran a thumb over the shadows under her eyes. Shadows that she never let anyone see. "You look tired. I should take you back to your room."

"I've been up for around twenty hours now, I think." She poked him in the chest. "And you don't have to find excuses to say you're not interested in a repeat performance. I can take it."

"Can you, Zara? Because—"

"Of course I can."

He went on as if she hadn't interrupted. "Every time I think I have you figured out, you throw another piece of the puzzle at me."

"I have no idea what you're talking about."

His knuckles tapped at her chin gently, his gaze not that of the wicked lover anymore. "Ah…*shahzadi*. I think you know exactly what I'm talking about."

And in that moment, Virat realized that in this room, in the darkness, she'd let him see a part of her that no one else ever saw. The vulnerable part of her. The part that had successfully held all other men at bay for so long.

And his brother, of course, had been the most convenient excuse to do so. He racked his mind back over the decade only to realize that except for the constant rumors surrounding her low-key relationship with his brother, she hadn't been linked to anyone else at all.

Suddenly, he had a feeling that he didn't know her at all. That there was something important she was hiding. That more than one piece of the puzzle was still missing.

A cold sweat claimed Virat, dispelling all the heat and want of the previous moment. Because, damn it, he hated puzzles. Thanks to his mother and father, his entire life had been one. The constant lies, the drama, the hold it gave people on others' lives…it was the last thing he wanted to embroil himself in.

Without meeting her gaze, Virat pulled out of her body. He heard her soft gasp but forced himself to ignore it. Ignored his own body's protest and demand for more. This was supposed to be a hookup, nothing more. Nothing less.

He didn't want to be interested in this woman. Or be curious about the organizations she supported, the shelter she'd set up, the farce she'd played out for ten years using his brother as a shield against relationships or even why she'd chosen Virat, of all men, to make love to her.

Something he was sure she hadn't asked lightly.

Zara knew the second that she'd lost Virat. Even before he'd pulled away from her physically. She felt his retreat like a cold slap against her bare flesh. Slowly, she straightened from the divan—not liking her prone position while he'd pulled on his trousers. She yanked her panties back on, feeling the weight and hardness of him like an aching echo at her sex.

Her body felt strangely awkward and beautifully limber at the same time, her muscles still reeling from the new kind of exertion. For a few seconds, she allowed herself to revel in every ache and twinge, every little imprint he'd left on her skin. She ran her hands over the bumps his stubble had left on the side of her breast, the faint pink impressions his fingers had left on one hip—and her whole body still shimmered with the pleasure of her climax.

Gathering her voluminous skirt from the floor, she glanced a look at Virat. His black trousers now hanging loose on his lean hips, he was staring out of the window into the dark sky. Zara felt the most overwhelming urge to run her lips over the smooth, muscled planes of his back. To walk over to him and wrap her hands around him, and let them run riot over his chest and hard belly to her heart's content.

She stemmed the impulse but couldn't stop the dam of thoughts encroaching. Her mind ran in a hundred directions, going back over everything she'd said and done. Mulling over what had gone wrong.

Had she been too clingy? Had she not been enough in some way? Had she…

No, stop!

It was a bad habit left over from her first marriage—this immediate impulse to look inward and find faults. Before she'd even met Virat on the set of her first movie as the heroine's best friend who, of course, died a gruesome death at the hands of the villain. A habit that she wasn't going to take up again because the only man she'd ever trusted completely was now behaving as if she hadn't met the mark of whatever he'd expected from this...evening.

With a deep breath, she consciously reordered her thoughts. She'd needed him tonight. And she'd had him. No regrets. No recriminations. If there was a part of her that was crushed because she wanted more and he clearly wasn't interested, then Zara neatly stowed it away.

She zipped her skirt back on. Her blouse, however, was a different matter. She pushed her arms through the blouse and went to him.

He turned before she said a word. As if he had sensed her presence in the very air around them.

Wordlessly, Zara presented her back to him. Her skin tingled as his fingers made short work of tying the strings together. Her breasts ached as the blouse became tighter, the fabric rasping silkily against her sensitive nipples. The memory of his tongue stroking them earlier sent a fresh tingle of sensation through her sex. But when she'd have moved away from him—she was not a pushover, she reminded herself—he stilled her with his hands on her shoulders.

He leaned his forehead against the back of her head, a pulsating energy radiating from him despite his stillness. "I've done a bad job of this."

"Of acting like a man who's so full of regrets that he clams up before the woman's even left the room? No, I'd say you're doing a very good job." Thank God she sounded angry rather than hurt. The last thing she wanted was his bloody pity.

He laughed then, and it filled the achingly lonely places inside of her. "No. I meant of these strings." His fingers slithered through the knots, as if they were chords on a guitar playing on her skin. "They're all tangled up now, *shahzadi*. Like you and me. You won't be able to take your blouse off when you get to your room."

"I will manage somehow," she said, moving away to dislodge his hands from her shoulders. She looked around the darkness to locate her sandals.

"Zara… I'm not regretting anything."

Zara stilled. The damn shoes were nowhere to be found, either. "We don't need a postmortem, Virat."

He was in front of her then, his eyes searching hers with an intensity she wanted to run away from. "I…you haven't been with anyone else since our last time together, have you?"

Zara's face flamed. Now she wished she'd politely thanked him and hightailed it out of the room. Instead, she was standing here, looking like a fool that was fixated on him. She let the cool poise she was known for fill her voice. "Wow, I thought you of all men wouldn't require a case-by-case recap of my sexual history. That you wouldn't decide a woman's worth by how many sexual partners she's had. Please don't turn out to have clay feet, Virat. My heart can only take so much."

He looked shocked for a moment. "I've never judged a woman for having the same needs as I do, never. You know that." He smiled then and it gleamed in the darkness. "You really know how to push my buttons, don't you, Zara?"

"I wish I believed that."

"Oh, believe it, *shahzadi*. You see far too much."

"I've learned that from you."

His arms casually came around her waist and Zara felt a sense of elation at the casual touch. God, she had it bad!

"Make sure to mention that at our next interview, please."

"Mention what?" he asked.

"How good I am at pushing your buttons. I'm sure my female fan base would love to hear of all the delightful ways Virat Raawal can be made to behave."

"Zara, why haven't you been with anyone else? Why use Bhai as a shield to hide the fact that you have no life?"

"I resent the implication that love and sex and marriage have to be the center of my existence just because I'm a woman."

He raised his hands and studied her, his mouth twitching. "I never said any of that."

Zara swallowed and looked away. He wasn't going to let up without her answering the question and truthfully at that. She wondered what she would truly lose if she told him this one truth. If she let him see a part of what made her Zara Khan.

But she suddenly couldn't bear it if he saw her as a victim. If he...treated her differently. If he thought she was too weak. Which meant she could reveal very little. She shrugged, and filled her voice with a breezy nonchalance that was hard to come by just then. "Success is a double-edged sword. Especially for women. After you and I parted ways I was too busy building a career. For a long time, I didn't want a man in my life.

"And then, once I had reached a certain level of success, my specifications for what I needed in a man grew, too. It was easier to battle loneliness than invite someone into my life who didn't make the grade. Than trust someone new."

"Ah...so I get extra points for—"

She pressed a hand to his mouth and glared at him. "You are familiar and convenient, yes." She scoffed when he made a hurt sound. "But I also knew that you'd make this easy and good for me and—" she shrugged when he caught her gaze with his "—you will not think you have a right to ask me unnecessary questions afterward."

With that, Zara walked away before the dratted man could see into her soul. And if he followed her to her suite and stood motionless outside it for a few minutes, while she did the same on the opposite side of the double doors with her hand pressed to her heart and her knees trembling beneath her, she told herself it was only because the sex had been that good.

That and nothing else.

CHAPTER SIX

"IF YOU CAN'T drag your sorry backside away from your
new bride for a couple of hours to learn your lines for
one measly scene, and if you don't stop grinning at her
from across the room like some…teenage Romeo, then
we might as well pack up and go home, Bhai!"

Her mouth dropping open, Zara stared at the unfolding
scene between the two brothers with alarmed fascination
like the rest of the production crew. She suddenly had a
better understanding of what her high school headmis-
tress had meant when she said pin-drop silence.

Having never been even offered a chance to audition
for one of his acclaimed projects before this one, she'd
never seen Virat in action on a set before. With her cal-
endar in conflict, she was the last one to come onto the
production.

Of course, his reputation as a strange combination of
a pit bull and a brilliant wizard who drew out stellar performances from the most average actor or actress was
widespread. The man's capability for diving deep into
his work was well known throughout the industry. And
yet, it left Zara feeling as if she were as memorable as
the cigars he sometimes smoked.

He'd forced his brother and Naina to cut their honeymoon short to just one week in the Swiss Alps.

So here they were, installed at a luxury resort two kilometers from the thousand-acre studio complex for more rehearsals before they began shooting Zara's main scenes.

Zara blinked and looked away, the harsh midday sun making her feel tired again. But not even under pain of death was she going to admit to Virat or anyone else on the team that she wasn't feeling a hundred percent. She was damned if she gave Virat an excuse to lay into her for being unprofessional or weak or something else. The man was a brutal taskmaster, surviving on little sleep and constantly on the go, and expecting the rest of the team to do the same.

The first few days on set had been eye-opening for them all. If anyone had expected Virat Raawal to give his beautiful fiancée special treatment for even a few minutes of the day, they were all grossly disappointed. If Zara didn't go to bed each night with the thought of his delicious weight pressing down on her and wake up every morning craving more of his expert, possessive kisses, she could have convinced herself that their time together at Vikram's wedding two weeks ago had been nothing but a feverish dream concocted by her horny body and hungry mind.

Not by one prolonged glance or look sent in her direction did Virat betray himself. In fact, Zara had no trouble believing that he'd shelved the entire evening as a completed task in his mind's diary. Not only had he vanished the next morning from the wedding, he'd been MIA for at least a week before he'd called the production team ahead of schedule for more rehearsals.

And she'd gone over a million scenarios about what—and particularly who—he might have been doing during the week that he'd been gone. But she wasn't going to ask,

Zara reminded herself fiercely. She wasn't going to act the part of a clingy, insecure fiancée, even though that was exactly who she seemed to be channeling these days.

This morning, however, Virat had been in an even worse mood than usual. He'd already bitten the camera crew's head off for some faulty angle, yelled at the makeup artist's assistant and was now laying into the one man the entire team had assumed was untouchable by their demanding director.

His brother, Vikram.

Vikram and Zara had been running the same scene over and over, all morning, with Virat's criticism spiraling. Pleading the beginnings of a headache, which was a full-on, real thing now, she'd gulped down a glass of fresh mango juice.

The overly sweet juice had only ended up aggravating her headache.

She'd been rifling through her scene notes and chatting with Richard Iyer, the British Indian actor whose mistress she was supposed to be playing on-screen.

The man was full of flirtatious charm and a dry wit that even Zara couldn't resist. His interesting background on stage paired with his clever questions about hers meant she'd been distracted instead of paying attention to Virat's comments after her last scene.

Honestly, she'd welcomed the distraction of the Brit's attention. The last thing she wanted to focus on were the complex emotions swirling through her since that evening. Or the quick spurt of joy that had filled her when Virat had asked the team to assemble a week earlier at the luxury resort for more rehearsals.

All the time wondering where he'd disappeared to only made her admit that the evening had been a highlight in her lonely life. She wanted that excitement again.

She wanted that feeling of being wanted. By him. She wanted him. As a lover. As a friend. For more than just a few hours.

The realization terrified Zara on a soul-racking level.

No, she couldn't. She couldn't even think in this direction. Couldn't continue indulging in that kind of silly daydream. Not about Virat, of all men.

Maybe she was simply exhausted.

Yes, that had to be it. She was weaving where she stood from lack of sleep in over a week. For the first time in her life, there was a restlessness inching under her skin. There was this disturbing feeling of having missed out on something more meaningful. This role, the most prestigious and meaty of her entire career, should have been consuming her. She should have been channeling the badass prostitute spy heroine juggling three men during India's independence movement, instead of moping around like a schoolgirl whose first crush had dumped her.

If nothing else, the four hours of dance practice with her kathak master at 4:00 a.m.—because of course at the last rehearsal Virat had called her performance awkward and clumsy—and then two hours getting into her elaborate makeup and costume on shoot days, in addition to six hours on the set, should have had her so tired at the end of the day that she should have passed out in sheer exhaustion the minute her head touched the pillow.

Maybe it was the fact that she was thirty-five now.

Maybe it was all the talk of marriage and love and the aching subject of loneliness she'd had with her mother two days ago.

Her mother only had a very vague idea of all that had transpired during Zara's first marriage. But she did know her daughter very well. Within moments of Zara calling her—for the third time in a week when she was usually so busy—she had quietly put a stop to all the incessant chatter Zara had been spouting and asked her if she was simply lonely.

Her soft whisper saying that it was okay to admit that. To do something about it. That one's career, however hard one had worked to build it, could not be everything. "Be strong where it matters, Zara," she had said when Zara had fallen silent on the line.

"What does that mean, Mama?"

"You fund shelters, you help women get back on their feet, you take on the big, bad men of the industry to fight for women's rights, but do you take risks with your own heart, Zara?" A lump in her throat, Zara had to swallow hard to not break into tears. And she wasn't a pretty crier. "Strength doesn't lie in caging one's heart, darling. I'd hate for you to miss out on happiness because you're afraid."

As always, her wise English teacher mother had given her a lot to think about.

Was that it? Was seeing her best friend, Vikram, leaping happily into matrimony after all these years of companionship affecting her more than she'd realized? Was it her stupid biological clock that was blaring suddenly? Or was this pining in her heart for only one particular man who challenged her with his wicked smiles and perceptive questions?

The answer was there for Zara to read, but instead she was playing hide-and-seek with it. Whoever said ignorance was bliss was a genius.

Virat blew out a breath and pressed the heel of his palm to his temple, in a gesture she was fast recognizing indicated an oncoming explosion. Or was that when he was praying for patience? She could live a thousand years and this man would fascinate her endlessly.

"You said you'd prep for this during your time off," he demanded of his brother, who'd come to stand by Zara.

The Raawal brothers together on the set was in itself a monumental moment. Their frequent arguments about the direction of Raawal House were infamous throughout the industry and had led to them never doing a project together until now.

But to see Virat cut the uncrowned king of Bollywood down to size had the entire staff freezing in their spots. Every one waited on tenterhooks for the explosion from Vikram. To everyone's amazement, he pushed a hand through his hair, his grin sheepish as he grinned at his new wife standing next to Virat's chair.

"That was before you cut short my honeymoon," Vikram said softly, with what seemed to Zara to be an almost entreating voice.

Her riotous curls framing her fiercely blushing face, Naina stiffened at Virat's impatient stare and then smiled at her husband's clearly adoring expression.

"If you don't stop mooning at Naina, I'm going to have her thrown off the set. I will send her back to Mumbai," Virat growled.

Vikram glared at him. "She won't leave me. Or Zara," he added as an afterthought. After all, it was Naina's position as Zara's personal assistant that enabled her to stay on set day after day. "And she's contractually bound to Zara for two more months."

Virat's expression said he was going for the kill. Zara's mouth twitched. There were very few in the industry that could naysay Vikram Raawal and survive for long.

Except his younger brother.

Zara had always found it fascinating that for all their

creative differences, both brothers were conscientious about not exploiting the power and privilege that rested in their hands.

"Naina will fly away in a moment if I tell her someone I know is interested in her latest film script. And Zara won't stand in the way of something that would launch Naina's career. Will you?" Virat said, turning that fiery gaze toward her.

Zara sat up in her seat and looked at both brothers, feeling as if there was no way she'd win here. But her answer, as the rogue had guessed, was clear. "Of course, I wouldn't stop Naina pursuing her dreams."

"Of course you're taking your fiancé's side in this," Vikram complained and Zara laughed at his disgruntled expression. "Even though he treats you no better than the rest of us on set. Even though he's been nothing but a disgruntled bastard from the moment he laid eyes on you and—"

"That's enough, Bhai," Virat roared, cutting him off. She didn't miss the flush scoring his cheekbones, however.

Instead of looking chastened, Vikram's grin widened. "And to think I doubted my lovely wife for a second," he said cryptically.

Zara looked at Virat and found his gaze unnervingly intense on her. "Well, his integrity's one of the reasons I adore him, Vikram," she said, trying to lighten the mood. "That and his ability to keep me supplied in…" Her words trailed off as Virat pinned her with his eyes.

"Keep you supplied in what, *shahzadi*?"

"Chocolates, I meant chocolates," Zara said, feeling her cheeks heat up.

Vikram howled with laughter and watched them with

a curious fascination that made Zara extra aware of the tension between her and Virat.

"I have it on good authority," Virat continued, "that Zara's the one who twisted this producer's arm to get him to take a look at Naina's script."

Zara wanted to look away from the curiosity in Virat's gaze, but damn it, she was far too interested in what he was saying. A few feet away, palpable excitement had Naina rocking on her feet. "So you're going to take it on?" Zara asked him.

Virat shook his head. "I recommended a female director I know. She's young and full of fire but she'll do it justice," he said by way of placating her. "I love that it centers on the female gaze completely. It's not my place to tell that story."

"Is it one of your numerous ex-girlfriends?" Zara asked before she could curb the reply.

"No," Virat said, arching an eyebrow.

Zara remembered all the pairs of eyes watching them and swallowed. "Thanks for the recommendation."

Virat shrugged. "Naina's script speaks for itself. You knew that." Then he turned to his brother, who'd been watching them with avid curiosity. Zara had no doubt that Vikram didn't completely buy their engagement. But thanks to whatever Naina had told him, he'd left the subject alone.

Plus the man was head over heels in love with his wife and it showed in how much he didn't give a damn about anything else.

"So unless you behave," Virat said to his brother, "I'll have that guy set up an immediate sit-down with Naina to discuss it, and unless you were totally heartless, you wouldn't demand your wife stay and make eyes at you when she could be advancing her own career."

Vikram stared at his wife as though suddenly wondering if she'd choose him or her script. Naina let a slow smile curve her mouth and his own mouth curved wide in response. The unspoken communication in that quiet moment between the couple was full of such raw emotion that Zara felt like a covetous voyeur and looked away. Her belly was full of a raw longing she couldn't misunderstand.

This is what you're missing, a voice whispered in her ear. *This is what you've been hiding from all these years.*

The realization felt like a fist hitting her chest, and Zara's gaze immediately searched for Virat. As if seeking…what? Why did it have to be this man who unlocked things she'd been happy to forgo for ten long years? What was it about him that twisted her into knots so easily?

When she turned, she found Virat's gaze on her, something flitting in and out of his eyes before she could properly understand it. But she'd no doubt that he'd witnessed the pure longing in her face, the dismay that she'd become so good at hiding her own desires from herself and the unadulterated panic of a second that she'd lost her chance at that kind of love. That she'd let her own fears, which she'd fought for so long, defeat her before she'd even tried.

"Fine," Vikram said, glaring at Virat. "I'll stick my head into that scene and see why I'm messing it up. And then I will accompany Naina to that meeting. She's not going to meet some unknown producer by herself," he added with a dangerous resolve coating his soft words.

Virat simply nodded. As if realizing he'd pushed his brother far enough. And then his attention turned to Zara.

Zara stayed glued to her chair as his gaze took her in with a thoroughly possessive heat. Tension sparked into life around them, stretching like an arc, as if one of the spot boys had set up a live wire to crackle between them.

Present meshed with past, sensations poured through into her limbs—him grinding his hips into her in a wicked rhythm that her body craved, the hard weight of his body holding down hers however he liked it, the bristle of his beard against the ultrasensitive skin of her breasts, and the thoroughly male noises he'd made when he'd climaxed inside her.

If someone had shot their lovemaking in the darkness of the nook that night and played it like a reel in front of her eyes, Zara would've been no less aroused than she was now. She wondered if every person present could read her thoughts. Could see the rising heat in her skin as his gaze held hers.

He blinked and a shutter came down over those eyes. As effortlessly as if he'd called for a curtain to drop. For the shot to end.

The tension dissipated, the not so quiet atmosphere of the set slamming back into her awareness as if someone had turned the sound system on again.

Zara blinked and looked around, wondering if she'd imagined that seconds-long instant connection between them. If the sun and whatever else was wrong with her was making her hallucinate—albeit wickedly erotic things—in the middle of the day.

His long stride ate up the distance between them in two steps and then Virat was hovering over her, forcing her to look up at him. In khaki shorts and a thin white linen shirt that hung loose on his frame and yet gave her a perfect view of the thick slab of muscles in his chest and abdomen, he looked like a tall glass of cold water that she wanted to pour all over herself.

"What shall I do with you, Ms. Khan?"

A shiver warmed her spine as Zara tried not to fidget in her chair. Something in his tone told Zara she hadn't imagined that sudden flare of intense connection. And that it hadn't been all on her side.

"What will you do with me, Virat sir?" she retorted, imbuing her tone with the syrupy obedience she'd seen some of the junior artists use when they approached him. It hadn't escaped her notice that the production manager's junior assistant—a pretty, peppy girl with wide brown eyes—had been hanging onto his every word and command like he were the God she'd been looking for.

His nostrils flared, but he didn't betray himself in any other way. "You've grown bolder," he said, a thoughtfulness in his expression.

"You mean after the other night or after all these years?" she taunted.

"Doesn't matter. I'm just pleasantly surprised by it."

Zara shrugged. "Apparently, it's the only way I can keep my errant fiancé's attention. If I need to be bold and brazen to keep my man from flitting away, then that's what I'll be doing."

A flare of heat licked into life on his face. For an infinitesimal second, his gaze took in the wide swoop of her blouse's neckline, her long legs in cotton shorts. Like a possessive lover. Like a man who couldn't wait to touch all he saw.

"How about you bring that boldness into this scene, Ms. Khan?" He didn't give Zara a second to respond. "You're freezing up every time you deliver your speech. Your accent…slips sometimes and sounds far too cultured for a *baazaari* woman who grew up on the streets. That final confrontation scene is your time to shine, Zara.

Either Bhai or Richard's stealing the show. You're not pulling your weight at all. Don't forget that your character is the one yanking on the thread that unravels everything. For all she looks like she's powerlessly caught between the two men.

"I thought you said you'd rehearsed the intonation before?"

"I'm doing my best, darling," she replied with a mock pout, knowing that the entire team was still watching. His criticism was justified—she *was* slipping up. Maybe because for the first time in her life, Zara's attention was not on immersing herself in the part.

But on the man who made her feel so much. Too much, it seemed.

She and Virat as a couple were still a source of great fascination to the world. Especially since some of the trashier cable channels had taken to calling the news of their engagement a twisted love triangle featuring Vikram and Zara and Virat.

While that had only brought renewed interest in the biopic—Vikram and Naina, secure in their love, had found it hilarious. But knowing Virat had initially thought she'd swapped one for the other ten years ago made Zara feel tacky and gross.

"Are you, though?" Virat demanded, looking down at her in her chair from his great height. His brown eyes devoured her face, as if he meant to see into her heart.

And Zara realized he was...*angry*. About something to do with her.

Maybe because she hadn't simply answered his probing questions that night as he'd demanded. Maybe because the brilliant Virat Raawal couldn't figure her out. Because, she knew, as well as her heart beating in her chest right now, that he liked people to be predictable and easy to catalog. It worked two ways for him—because it helped him understand human nature and bring it onto the screen in all its myriad forms, and also because it enabled him to maintain a carefully created distance between himself and everyone else.

Satisfaction coursed through Zara, like a cool stream drenching her. He couldn't pin her down and it was getting to him. She wanted to remain a mystery to him. She wanted to torment him as much as he was doing it to her.

She let her gaze fall to his mouth as he glowered at her, and licked her own lips. Not that she had to fake being all hot and bothered with him around. "I'm just… distracted, *jaanu*." She placed her palm on his chest and fluttered her eyelashes.

"That's clear, Zara. Your mind's not here. *You're* not here."

"That might be right. Can I tell you something utterly unprofessional?" she murmured in a voice no one else could hear.

His jaw hardened and he let out a pained breath. "What?"

"You were right that night."

"About what?"

"It had been a long time. Very long. But see, the thing is…" She drew a line from his jaw, down his Adam's apple to where his white cotton shirt was unbuttoned. "I've now realized what I've been missing. And I have decided…"

"That you want to have a repeat performance?"

"That I don't want to wait another ten years to carpe the diem or whatever."

"Is that what you're doing here, *shahzadi*? Picking your next lover on my set instead of focusing on your scene?"

Zara shrugged, loving that this giant of a man was indeed truly, horribly jealous. While his criticism of her and Vikram's performance was justified, it had been underscored by this emotion that was gripping him. But he would never admit it to her.

But she…she was done playing games. She knew what and who she wanted.

"I want you, Virat. No one else." The words fell into the silence between them as if a tractor had razed the entire set. She hadn't meant to say it. But her mother's words had been digging a hole through her head and her heart was pining away for this man who was so close, who was her fiancé as far as the world cared, and Zara was done fighting it.

His head jerked up.

"For as long as this charade continues," Zara qualified, blushing to the roots of her hair.

She tilted her chin, refusing to let the vulnerability she felt in every cell show up on her face. This was who she'd wanted to be for so long—a woman who didn't hide from her own wants and desires.

The pad of his thumb moved over her soft cheek. "There's that boldness again, tempting me."

"But?" Zara added, feeling some small part of her shatter.

Some unknown emotion flared in his eyes. And Zara felt as if she should brace herself for a blow that was coming.

Virat brought that thumb to her lips and Zara knew he was seriously tempted. Knew he wanted her with the same inexplicable hunger that she did him. Knew that he wasn't going to simply give in because she was available and willing.

"What?" she said, turning that dismay into a mocking taunt.

"I think we already burnt out the fun part of whatever this is that evening at Bhai's wedding. Now this feels like too much work. Too much like a relationship."

"The playboy is only a role. A partial truth you put out for the world to see," she said, refusing to bow out. "And if you were so shallow that having sex with me in the dark counts as too much work…then you're lying. To me and more importantly to yourself."

"Fine. I haven't stopped thinking about that night. About us. About you."

"Then why are you denying us?"

"Because I can't forget, *shahzadi*…" his voice was full of self-mockery "…that when you did have me, you traded me in for something better. Your career. Turns out I'm just as much of a resentful bastard as the man who refuses to admit that I'm his son." His fingers squeezed her shoulder as if he was reassuring her rather than rejecting her. "That's why this is too much work, Zara. Remember all those principles you used to tease me about? I still have them. And I don't like the man I become around you."

"No," she said, her tummy rolling in on itself. "No. You don't like that I make you feel something genuine, Virat. You don't like that you can't pretend that I'm just another one of the women you specifically choose exactly because they make you feel nothing. You don't like that you can't fit me into a box and put me aside. That you can't continue ignoring me anymore as you did for ten years.

"You don't like that it's not an itch that you thought you could scratch and it would have gone away by now."

He stilled for a moment and Zara readied herself for

whatever he'd throw at her. She didn't give a damn that everyone was staring at them. Or that they'd been obviously arguing, albeit very quietly, when they were supposed to be crawling all over each other.

But the thing was she'd never felt so fiercely alive. Fighting with Virat was more exciting than jumping off a cliff. Probably. Most definitely.

He stared at her for a long second but said nothing.

With a disgusted sound that Zara was sure was directed at himself, Virat threw the scene sheet he'd been holding into the air, called for a break and stormed out.

"Thank God," someone whispered.

It was as if the entire team took a collective breath in Virat's absence. However short-lived it might be.

Her hands were still trembling as Zara gathered her water bottle and her phone when someone tapped on her shoulder. For a few foolish seconds, hope leaped in Zara's chest and she thought maybe Virat had returned.

She turned to find Vikram regarding her with a thoughtful gaze. Naina was nowhere to be seen and most of the team had scurried away as soon as the big, bad lion had told them to get lost.

"Hey," he said, arms folded across his chest.

Zara took a sip of her water, just to give herself a couple more minutes before she had to face him. She put the cap back on and raised her eyebrows suggestively. "Why aren't you chasing your wife?"

"She ran after my angry bear of a brother, trying to learn more about the interest in her script. And abandoned me."

"Yeah, right," Zara said, laughing, despite herself.

Vikram tangled his arm through Zara's, steering her toward the cool marble lounge. "I thought we could catch up. I haven't talked to you in a while."

"Yeah?" Zara said, knowing that in trying to sound extra cheerful, she sounded awful.

"Should I say congratulations now and welcome you to the family?"

Zara hesitated for a fraction of a second before realizing he was fishing. "Of course you should."

"Welcome to the family, then, Zara." He said and embraced her so tightly that Zara felt tears prickle behind her eyes. She felt him press a kiss to her temple. Then he slowly put her away from him and examined her face with a thoroughness that reminded her of Virat. "Is everything okay with you two?"

"Have you talked to your brother about us?" she quipped back, knowing that the last thing she could do was to confide in Vikram. While the industry and sometimes even Virat called Vikram a sellout for making his commercial blockbusters, her best friend had always been a man of integrity. The last thing he needed to know was that his brother had thought Zara had dumped him for Vikram.

It would only make him come to her defense and fight with Virat.

"He'll have my head if he thinks I'm interfering between you two." He raised his hands, palms out.

"So don't," Zara said automatically and then regretted her words.

Vikram smiled, taking no offense. "Clearly there was something between you two all these years. Now I feel like a fool for—"

Zara cut his words off. "You don't know how much your friendship has meant to me. What Virat and I have is something altogether different."

Vikram snorted. "That's clear to anyone that's seen you together for more than five minutes. I thought I'd be surprised to see you with him but…"

"But what?" Zara asked, now curious.

"It's him I'm more shocked by. He's...different with you. I mean, he's always been intense and passionate about everything in life but I've never seen him like that with a woman. Jealous of every look you give your co-star on set."

Zara tried to not let those words mean anything more than the fact that while he preferred being behind the camera, Virat was clearly just as talented at acting as the rest of his family. "Remember that first movie you and I worked on together all those years ago?"

The memory made Vikram groan. "God, yes. According to my memory, the best part of that entire thing was getting to know you."

"Did you hire me for that because your mother recommended me for the role?"

Vikram's gaze turned thoughtful. "No. I gave you a chance to do the screen test because she mentioned your name. After I looked at your audition tape, which was smashing. I was looking for a fresh face. You earned the role because of your talent, whoever brought you to my attention."

She nodded, another small part of the puzzle falling into piece.

"Zara, why are you asking me about that now?" Vikram probed.

She made some nonanswer and hurried back to the hotel. Virat's resentment that she'd left him for Vikram might have been unfounded, but it hadn't been borne in a vacuum. And Zara loathed the very idea of him thinking the worst of her.

She showed up outside Virat's suite that night, knuckles at the ready to rap. Laughter from inside the suite—female laughter at that—sent her scurrying away from his door like a scared little mouse.

Once she'd reached her own suite, she called herself a hundred names.

What was the matter with her?

Why was she forgetting that she had no real claim on Virat, for all the drama they were putting on for the world? Why did she keep thinking that one evening of incredible pleasure with her meant he would come knocking for more? Why was she acting like a hyped-up, hormonal teenager because Vikram had said that Virat might be jealous of all the time she'd spent with Richard on set?

While the actual fact was that he hadn't even greeted her properly since arriving. If not for the crew avidly watching them every chance they got, she was sure he wouldn't have even acknowledged her existence.

This panicky, scrambled behavior was not her. This creeping through the corridors at night—even if the man was her fiancé in the eyes of the world—was not her.

Was she hoping Virat would somehow make their relationship permanent? She couldn't be so foolish as to fall for a man who hadn't even called her after their evening together, was she? A man who was already turning her upside down in a pretend relationship.

No, she couldn't. She couldn't let him have this much control over her emotions.

If he was determined to see her as nothing but a convenient lay—and that was what she had suggested when she'd begged him to make love to her—then that was how she'd have to treat him, too. She wasn't going to run after him, begging him to acknowledge her presence. To let her explain about the past.

She would be professional if it killed her. She was going to lock away all these confusing emotions in a box, bury them under the ocean and focus on her role.

Work was the only thing she could trust. Work was the only thing that would never let her down.

CHAPTER SEVEN

TWO DAYS LATER, Virat found himself strolling into the vast dance studio on the lower floor of the luxury hotel where Vikram and Zara and three more of their other stars had been staying, just as the clock in the expansive lounge of the hotel struck 6:00 a.m. The rest of the team were bunking down in the rooms provided at the thousand-acre studio, where they were shooting.

One of the dance numbers from the biopic blared out of the speakers as Zara and six background dancers practiced a long, fast number. Virat leaned against the far wall, loath to distract her attention.

In a pink tank top and black leggings, with *ghungroo* tied at her ankles, her hair in a messy bun on top of her head, Zara looked just as beautiful as she'd done last night at the team dinner, all dolled up in a yellow sundress that showed off so much of her smooth, silky skin that he'd felt permanently singed standing there with his arm around her.

They'd both performed the part of engaged lovers to perfection last night. But the tension in her body, the wary resignation when she looked at him... Virat felt like an absolute heel. Behaving like a spoiled jackass who was blowing hot and cold with the woman he desperately wanted left a foul taste in his mouth.

So here he was…with no particular plan. It had been easy to pretend she didn't exist for ten years. But now that he was getting to know Zara again, now that he found himself admiring the woman she'd become…he couldn't stay away.

While he also had a suite here at the hotel, he preferred to stay on the ground at the studio. He liked having instant access to any and all of the team members. Like last night, when he'd needed their costume designer—which was his sister—to make some last-minute changes to one of Zara's outfits. Having finished the designs almost six months ago, Anya hadn't been happy with his "unreasonable" demands, as she called them.

But since the outfit—something Zara had to dance in for this particularly fast number—had ended up being far too heavy for her to move in comfortably, Anya had relented and gone back to her drawing board. Or her sketchbook.

Staying at the studio also gave him a convenient excuse to not share his lovely fiancée's suite here at the hotel. The way he was feeling, he had no doubt he'd end up in her bed, all common sense gone. There was something about Zara that made him wary, that made him think too much. Feel too much.

The wooden floor thrummed with the energy of the fast number that it had taken his friend and the film's music director, AJ Kumar, two months to perfect.

As he watched Zara and the other dancers move across the vast ballroom in complicated twirls and impossibly difficult-looking poses, so many reflections of her in the floor-to-ceiling mirrors that covered the four walls of the studio, a jolt of satisfaction filled his veins.

Zara looked as if she'd been dancing kathak all her life. But it wasn't just the technicality of her steps or the poses she'd finally mastered. Or the grace she imbued into those steps.

No, this was Zara shutting up any critic who might have suggested Virat should have picked a younger actress to play this role. This was Zara fulfilling the promise he'd seen in her even in those first days when they'd met on a movie set, both of them desperately looking for a place to belong.

God, she'd been sweet and funny and fragile and had him utterly twisted in knots. She'd been the first and only woman to have made him look inward, that made him want to be better at everything. That made him want to change the world.

He'd been second assistant to the cinematographer—a glorified errand boy position he'd gained on his own merit. At least, that was what he'd told himself until he'd discovered years later that his mother had demanded the man take him on. Because she'd overheard Virat in an argument with his brother that the only man he'd ever even consider working for would be that cinematographer.

Leaning back against one of the mirrors, Virat groaned now. His mother had always interfered in his life in those days. Still tried to, today.

To compensate for her guilt, he had no doubt, and for her inability to stop his father from blatantly treating him differently from Vikram and Anya. Even back then, Virat had never blamed her if she'd taken a lover during one of their spectacular breakups. For seeking haven from a husband who'd resented her talent and her success while his own career had faltered and flickered out.

What he'd always been unable to forgive was her inability to walk away from a man who'd thoroughly traumatized his children.

The cinematographer, one of the few people Virat still

respected in the industry to this day, had told his mother in no uncertain terms that all Virat was good for right then was to bring him cups of chai and clean his equipment.

Virat hadn't minded at all—he'd always wanted to forge his own path.

The memory of his first meeting with Zara burst into his mind like a showreel he'd resolutely packed away for ten years but still shone like yesterday in front of his eyes, now he'd finally given it the light of day.

Zara had had the role of the heroine's best friend—a young woman who appeared in two scenes with no lines.

He'd noticed her on set before, wide-eyed and quiet and stunningly beautiful. A little wary around men. She'd had a presence even then, almost stealing the show whenever she appeared with the bland heroine in their scenes together.

They'd finally met standing in line for coffee. When he'd asked how her day was going, she'd quietly told him that the director had just bitten her head off for acting too much.

"How can you act too much in a dying scene," Virat had asked between howls of laughter.

"You're Raawal sir's brother. You are Virat Raawal," she'd said then, a sudden wariness claiming her expression. Stepping back from him.

Virat had morosely murmured yes. If it was an open wound that the world perceived him as a Raawal only when it pleased it, being known purely as the brother of the successful, beloved older son and protector of the family legacy was like throwing salt into that festering wound.

His brother had already built a name for delivering commercial blockbusters with mass appeal.

"I'm the cinematographer's second assistant," he'd said, full of pride, even though so far the closest he'd gotten to some of the equipment had been to make sure it was all in order when they packed up for the night.

"You mean your brother and mother aren't already planning a multi-star film to launch your acting career?" she'd asked then, before her soft gaze had taken in his features. Then that gaze had swept up the breadth of his shoulders and his tall frame, and she'd swallowed. That one furtive glance she'd sent his way had been enough to tell him that she'd felt it, too—that spark of attraction between them. The sudden tension in the air around them. "Why all this pretense of toiling behind the camera? You look good enough to be a hero," she'd muttered quietly to herself.

But he'd heard it.

Smiling goofily, his twenty-year-old self had strutted around the set for the rest of the day after that. He'd already had three girlfriends—daughters of his family's friends or acquaintances—all girls who'd come from the same class and privilege as his family. Girls whose only concerns were clothes and cars. Girls who thought his name and the notoriety of his birth made him "romantically tormented," as one of them had called it. As if the reality of his life was a drama to be played out, so that his girlfriend could play the heroine and "save" him from his loveless existence.

But then he'd realized after meeting Zara that his disillusionment and contempt for the girls he'd dated was his own fault. He had, after all, sought out a particular type.

Leaning against the wall now and watching Zara perform the dance, Virat rubbed a hand over his face at the realization that stuck in his throat uncomfortably. In fact, both before and after Zara, he'd always sought women who didn't even scratch beneath the surface of who he was.

It was galling to realize that while he'd pretended that she didn't exist, his life had irrevocably changed course because of Zara.

He'd shrugged and said to her, "I'm only working with the cinematographer for the summer." His brother had neatly manipulated him into it when Virat had, after another fight with their father, packed up his backpack, ready to walk out. "I'm not interested in anything to do with the fake industry of cinema. And anyway, I'd rather tell a story than being told how my little role in life should play out."

"So you're a control freak, then?" she'd said, and he remembered being taken aback for a second. And then he'd realized that she was the first person who'd so clearly seen through his charming, useless-rogue facade. "A rebel among the Raawals?"

"I don't need the Raawal name to build myself into anything," he'd claimed, determined that this woman with big beautiful eyes and perceptive opinions would see the real him.

He groaned at the memory. God, he'd been so full of himself back then, walking around like a festering sore, his bitterness and anger spewing on everything and everyone around him. He'd been a rebel without a cause, a talented young man, yes, but without direction or focus.

He'd constantly criticized his brother for being a sell-out when all Vikram had done was to choose to preserve his grandfather's legacy in whatever way had been possible.

Virat had gone about vowing that he would walk out of their lives one fine day, turning his back on the bloody Raawal legacy forever.

Zara had snorted when he'd told her that, a sound so full of scorn that he'd scowled at her and demanded to know what she'd meant.

"Never mind, Pretty Boy," she'd said then. If she'd thought he'd be offended by that, she had no idea.

He'd laughed, paid for both their coffees and said, so earnestly that even then he'd understood how much he wanted her good opinion, "Why did you laugh like that? I would like to know, please."

She'd nodded. And he'd stuck his scrawny chest out as if he'd won the first battle. "It's not something you can simply shed, is it? Your privilege... To think it doesn't carry weight wherever you go, to believe your face itself isn't a calling card, is not only foolish but insulting to the rest of us." He had no idea what she'd seen in his face, but she'd blinked and sighed. "I'm sorry. I don't know you. Please don't get me into trouble."

He'd jerked away, even hating the insinuation that he'd go telling on her to his superstar brother or his music director friend or any of the other big names he was on first-name terms with on set. Realizing that careers like hers, especially of women, could be made and destroyed on the whims of powerful men like his father, his brother and *even* him.

That...it *was* foolish to pretend that he didn't have all the privilege of being a Raawal, even though the industry and the media regularly liked to debate if his dissolute father was the true source of his genetic material or not.

His grandparents, his mother and brother and his sister, even Papa for all his own insecurities when dealing with Virat, had never deprived him of any kind of material comfort. Only he kept throwing it all in their faces.

It was the first time Virat had met a woman who'd

effortlessly showed him that ideals were often the cachet of the rich and powerful.

"You're right," he'd said then, determined that he would gain her respect one of these days. That surface attraction he'd felt for her ever since he'd set eyes on her had instantly solidified into something more in that moment. "That was a stupid thing to say. And I'd never do something so nasty as to get you fired."

She'd barely smiled. "It wasn't my place anyway. I'm a little rattled today, that's all."

"My idealism and principles may look like posturing to you, but they come from the right place. But you're right that I should acknowledge my privilege."

"Exactly. Better to embrace it and use it to do good. It's not like the rest of us can open our mouths and disagree with the powers that be without getting fired."

"You think you'll get fired for arguing with the director?" he'd asked then, not at all liking the prospect.

Sudden tears had filled her eyes and she'd looked away.

"Sit with me, please," he'd said, desperate to learn more about her. Even then, he'd known there was something special about her. "We don't have to talk."

She had let him walk her to a bench in the very same garden where her character got killed. They sipped their coffees in quiet and he had found more than a measure of satisfaction that she'd let him share the moment.

"I refused to let my skirt blow up when I fall to my death here," she said finally, lifting her head and looking at the concrete slab where she'd fallen earlier for practice, "flashing my underwear to the entire world. Isn't it enough that the girl's death is nothing but gratuitous violence to create shock and sympathy, to justify the hero's violence toward the villain? Do we also have to add the indignity of my bare thighs and pink underwear to it?"

That night, Virat had asked a favor of his brother for the first time in his life. And to give him credit, Bhai had listened when Virat had said it looked incredibly gross to have the victim's bare limbs and underwear splashed about in that scene, just to cater to the audience's baser instincts.

Since it was a movie being produced by Raawal House, Vikram's word to the director had held sway.

The next morning, after the shoot, Zara had come to see him. Hugged him just long enough for him to feel the warm imprint of her body on his, and whispered, "Thanks."

He'd told her she owed him coffee this time and she'd smiled so gloriously back at him that Virat had felt like a hero. Had felt as if for the first time in his life he could be something more, something other than a stain on the Raawal legacy.

Zara had always had the uncanny knack of bringing out the best in him. Of making him give voice to the dreams he'd denied admitting to himself. Of giving him the safe space he'd needed by listening to all the many story ideas that had been building up inside him for so long.

She had helped him see that for all that he'd mocked the film industry, his heart and soul were already deeply entrenched in it.

Now he knew he'd simply been lacking the kind of affection and acceptance Zara had shown him, all his life. She'd been the first one to see and acknowledge him as a man with potential.

"I know the entire world thinks your brother is your grandfather's true legacy. But I see it in you," she'd said once after he'd related an idea he'd had for a movie. "Storytelling is in your blood, Virat. Why run away from it?"

They had been together for three months, even after that movie had wrapped up, but they'd not seen as much of each other as Zara traveled around, attending more and more auditions.

Other than mentioning the fact that her husband had died the previous year, she hadn't wanted to speak about her past. And while he had been thirsty for knowledge of her, he'd never pressed, because he hadn't wanted to hurt her. The fact that she'd begged him to keep their association private had grated on him.

With her meager funds running low, she'd been desperate for something other than a role that gave her more than a minute's screen time.

And he...he had fallen for her—hard and fast—his emotions centering almost unhealthily around her. Only now did Virat realize that he'd used their clandestine relationship as an anchor in his life. But even then he'd had the sense to not pour his feelings out to her. To not let her see how much she affected him.

He'd continued partying with his usual fast and loose crowd, keeping up the appearance of being the useless scion of the Raawal family. Gathering interest and investors for a low-budget slapstick comedy he'd written himself.

Until one day...he'd heard that Zara had landed a role as the heroine in Vikram's next multi-star intergenerational saga. That she'd already left the country for a shoot.

And his mother had been the messenger.

Not seven months later, she'd been linked romantically with his own brother.

The burst of applause from the dance master and his assistants pulled him out of the spiral of the past.

Virat stared, transfixed at the lovely smile on Zara's face as the kathak master and his team gave her and the dancers an uproarious applause. And then, he asked himself the question he should have ten years ago. The question he'd even been incapable of seeing because he'd simply thought Zara was rejecting him.

In the three months they'd spent with each other, Zara hadn't, not once, asked him to help her land a role. Not once had she pried information from him about his brother—whose productions had already started raking in money at the box office—or his upcoming projects. Never even hinted for an introduction to his powerful family or their numerous contacts.

Even a small nudge from his brother would have saved her months of heartache at losing out to another star's sister or daughter or cousin.

She could have asked, knowing that Virat absolutely would have done anything for her.

She hadn't.

Then why use their relationship to move up in the world? Why make a bargain with his mother of all people, knowing what a contentious relationship he had with the woman? Had she thought he'd hate to be used for his influence? Had she…?

Thoughts crowded inside his head as Virat stayed against the wall. For so many years, he'd shut the past off. He'd made himself chase after shallow women and relationships with a limited shelf life, convinced more than anything that Zara had betrayed him.

But now, now that they were working together again on this biopic, now that he'd kissed and held and made love to her, he wasn't sure of anything that he'd thought had happened in the past.

Did the past even matter anymore?

He wasn't that emotional, rebellious youth who didn't know what he wanted from life. He was Virat Raawal now—a man who'd built his reputation and wealth outside of the umbrella of his family's reputation and power. He'd invested every rupee he'd made into real estate and luxury hotels and multiplied it until he could fund his own projects.

He'd come far from that man-child she'd once known. And the man he was now was more than a match for her.

It was that man that Zara was interested in. That man she'd so openly admitted to wanting. And the last thing he was going to do was deny himself.

As if pulled toward him, Zara looked up at that exact moment. Sweat shimmered on her brow, her chest falling and rising with fast breaths.

Heat arced between them across the room, amid dancers laughing. She was the one to break the contact and look away. The stubbornly tense set of her shoulders betrayed her awareness of him, however.

Virat smiled, the challenge in her stance riling something awake in him. He wanted to walk up to her in the midst of all the gaggle and press his mouth to the curve where her neck met her shoulder. He wanted to gather her up against him until all that icy fire melted and she pressed into him with that wanton need that made him crazy.

A grimace crossed her face as she straightened her legs from the complicated ground pose she had to strike at the end of the dance. The choreographer's assistant, a young man clearly besotted with Zara and possessing the sort of unending energy that made Virat feel a hundred years old, offered her a hand, and she pushed herself up. Zara thanked him with a bright smile but the young scamp didn't let go of her hand. He was complimenting her, clearly, as the color in her already pink cheeks deepened. Then he spread his arms wide and Zara pointed to herself, telling him that she was sweaty, Virat guessed, but the man shook his head and off she went into his embrace.

You're so possessive of her that you glare at any man who looks at her or smiles at her or generally moves in her direction. They're all terrified of you biting their head off just because they might have looked at Zara for too long.

His brother had looked deeply amused while he'd explained why one of the spot boys always dropped whatever he was holding anytime Virat was close by.

"Jealousy's a good color on you, Virat," he'd muttered before grinning, as if there was nothing more gleeful than seeing his younger brother make a fool of himself over his fiancée.

And Virat knew Bhai had spoken the absolute truth. While it had been easy to reject Zara's quietly spoken words in a moment of childish anger—she'd clearly been as surprised as him at her own admission—he hadn't been able to stop thinking about her. Of how much he wanted to take her up on her offer to make love to her again. How much he simply...wanted her.

And he was tired of fighting it.

He'd behaved like a grumpy bastard, throwing his accusation at her when she'd openly admitted that she'd wanted him. And he knew it hadn't been easy for her. She'd been vulnerable and he'd hurt her. Either he forgave her for the past and moved on, or he walked away now.

But the thought of never touching Zara again, of never bandying words with her again, was unthinkable.

Tormenting a woman because he was incapable of controlling his own emotions was something his father had excelled at. And Virat had spent an entire lifetime molding himself to be anyone but the man who could hold a lifetime's grudge toward his wife and an innocent little boy.

There was nothing to do but make amends to Zara.

CHAPTER EIGHT

"Can I have my fiancée back now?"

The gravelly voice at her back made Zara's spine tingle. Sensation washed over her skin, as if her every cell recognized the warmth emanating from the man behind her.

Apparently, her errant fiancé didn't even have to touch her for her body to start melting into a wanton puddle.

The choreographer's assistant froze. Even as she tried to control it, her mouth twitched at the man's horrified expression that he'd been caught mooning over their grumpy director's fiancée. Virat took another mostly non-menacing step, and the younger man let go of her so fast that she stumbled back, her legs nothing more than mush after three hours of dance practice.

His arm reaching out around her waist, Virat caught her easily. As if seeing the mother ship, her body fell neatly against his, sending all kinds of happy signals to her brain. Her heart thudded in her chest, her entire body trembling for a completely different reason now. Zara knew she should step away from the warm weight of his fingers over the bare skin of her waist.

Being near him and not having him, and pretending like she had him while he rejected her and went off to play with his numerous exes was already driving her bonkers.

But the greedy sponge that she was, she couldn't. Her shoulder leaning into his chest, his hard thigh pressed against hers. He was a thoroughly masculine presence she wanted to drown in.

God, where was this chemistry when she'd wanted it with another man? Why did she react like this to, of all people, the one complicated man she didn't understand? The one man who felt he was beyond her reach forever?

The poor assistant's face stayed in an awkward smile and then he backed away from both of them without turning. As if presenting Virat with his back might be an unnecessary risk.

Zara picked up a fresh towel and pressed it to her face. The coolness of the wet towel felt like heaven against her flushed face. But nothing could help corral the fluttering butterflies in her belly. Or the heightened anticipation that prickled across every inch of her skin.

She wasn't going to act like a clingy fiancée. She wasn't going to behave like a hormonal teenager whose teenage crush had turned out to be a total flop. She wasn't going to…

"I'm not going to disappear if you simply mutter things under that towel, *shahzadi*."

Zara mumbled, "Go away," before she realized she was doing exactly what he'd said. She pulled the towel away and redid her lopsided bun on top of her head. Virat's gaze swept over her in a quick survey, and when it met hers, it was warm and made something gooey erupt in her belly.

Dear God, wasn't she a little old for gooey things to happen anywhere in her body?

His white linen shirt, unbuttoned halfway down as if

just for her, gave her a peek at those tight pecs and the sparse, soft chest hair she loved running her fingers over. His light blue jeans hung low on those lean hips. His hair looked all kinds of rumpled and he looked deliciously ruffled. Just how she liked him.

"Stop terrifying everyone on set," she said, adopting a no-nonsense tone. "I don't want any of them to think they can't be honest with me because of your angry shadow hovering nearby. That young man you just scared away spent hours helping me get my posture and moves straight."

He looked behind him as if to check if the terrified man was still there. "But I haven't hovered around you at all. In fact, despite being the man you're happily engaged to, the man you should be…frolicking with, I never even get a chance to hover around you because there's always some guy taking my place and doing my job already."

Zara rolled her eyes, and bit her lip to stop smiling. "You're a workaholic. Do you even know how to frolic?" It had been like this between them once. She'd always taken herself and life far too seriously and he would come in like a storm and make her smile.

"Ah, now you're just hurting me, Zara. As you very well know, professional frolicking was a career choice I considered seriously back in the day. But coming back to everyone on the set, I agree, it's not your fault that you're so beautiful and lovely that they all want to be near you. I didn't realize until now you're one of those people who make everyone else want to be better, do better."

"Beautiful and lovely?" Zara threw back, even as her heart was doing somersaults in her chest. On the surface, those weren't compliments she needed. But Virat had always had high standards. The fool she was, she felt as if she'd won some kind of medal because he approved of her. "All these compliments when you've barely looked at me these past weeks on set, I feel like the sacrificial goat. You're here to fire me, aren't you?"

"Then I'll have a mutiny on my hands, no? You and Bhai are doing such a good job of keeping everyone calm when I terrify them."

It always came back to Vikram and her, for him, Zara realized suddenly. Not because Virat mistrusted his brother. But because for his entire life, Virat had been measured against Vikram by their father and found wanting.

Her actions ten years ago had hurt him. Very badly. That much was becoming clear. It didn't matter whether she'd done it on purpose or not. To him, she'd been the only woman he'd let close and yet, she'd ended up being the one who'd betrayed him.

"Well, it would be nice if you didn't bark orders at the staff and glower at anyone who looked at me. You're doing a really good job of making them think you're gaga over me."

He scowled. "Has anyone been bothering you because they can't take it out on me?"

"Of course not," Zara said, reminding herself that his concern over her was not romantic. More of a basic human decency kind of thing that he'd always been good at. "I don't want to be…associated with the grumpy bear that they all call you."

"Ah, but it's too late to break off your association with me, *shahzadi*."

Zara raised a brow. "I'm not the one breaking our agreement already. But I guess I have to give you points for discretion. For not making a joke out of me."

He frowned. "I have no idea what you're talking about."

Sheer frustration made Zara throw the towel at him. Which he caught deftly and threw into the neat little basket nearby. The thud-thud of her heart made Zara realize that the dance studio was suddenly empty.

Everyone had quietly filed out at one look from him. The man had too much power on set, but she refused to be one of the people who were so overwhelmed by his talent that they let him walk all over them. Overwhelmed by the sheer force of the masculinity he was focusing on her right now, though...yes.

"What do you want, Virat?" She checked her watch and frowned. "In fact, how are you still awake? It's barely six a.m. and you're a nocturnal creature that doesn't rise until noon on off-shoot days."

"I didn't go to bed at all."

Zara looked away, a swooping feeling in her belly. First he'd ignored her. Then he had some woman in his room. And yet, she had no right to complain. No right to demand anything from him.

But she wanted more.

The niggling demand was only a whisper in her heart right now. Soon, it was going to turn into a roar and she had no idea how to arrest it. Or how to pretend for another decade that Virat Raawal would always be the man who brought her to life with just one look.

But of course, the blasted man surprised her in this, too. "Ask me, Zara."

"Ask you what, Virat?" she said on a soft whisper that took everything she had to form.

"Anything. Whatever you want."

The past hovered between them, like a specter they would never be rid of.

You traded me in…

His words from earlier poked at her. Taunted her. And yet, the last thing Zara wanted right now was to fracture this truce he was offering. Clearly, he'd decided to leave the past where it belonged.

Should she make an effort to leave it, too, when this fake engagement was nothing but temporary?

Should she leave behind the niggling discomfort that if they didn't address the past, Virat would always look at her as if she'd betrayed him? She should look him in the eye and explain why she'd done what she'd done. He'd understand, wouldn't he?

But Zara didn't have the energy to fight with him right now. More important, she didn't want to lose the chance to be with him, for however brief a time. Maybe she'd always be a coward, then.

Tugged as if by some rope, Zara found herself caught in his gaze. This close, she could see two days' worth of beard on his cheek. The tiredness in his gaze. The deep grooves around his mouth.

"You look exhausted," she said, reaching out with a finger toward the line of his jaw.

"So do you, Zara. I've been a beast to you, haven't I?"

"You mean, you've treated me like you'd treat any other actress, demanding impossible standards of achievement so that I can pull off the performance of a lifetime in your film? Yes."

He laughed.

She pulled away as soon as the pad of her finger touched his skin. But he caught her wrist and pressed his face into her palm and something burst open wide in her chest. Some feeling she couldn't cage anymore.

Take the risk, Zara. Ask for what you demand from

life. From him, a voice whispered in her head, and Zara took the plunge.

"I came by the other night to talk to you. There was a woman laughing inside your suite. Vikram told me he saw you sneak the minister's wife out early the next morning."

His expression didn't change at all. He looked just as unfazed. "Ah…so that's why Naina's been working so hard to keep Bhai away from me. He wants to have a go at me because he's worried I'm a cheating bastard who doesn't deserve you."

"Everything's a game to you, isn't it?"

"And here I thought you were the only woman who understood my tormented soul, *shahzadi*."

He looked down and Zara knew he saw the wet sheen in her eyes. But she didn't give a damn anymore. Pretending like she wasn't affected by what he did had always been simply a sop to her ego. A pretense. But she was tired of acting as if he didn't matter to her.

Only a quiet stillness in his body betrayed his tension at her expression. He bent forward and his nose pressed into the crook of her neck and Zara felt electrified by the touch. "I'd rather see you punch my lights out than cry because of me. I'm not worth your tears, Zara."

"No man is worth my tears. I've always tried to tell myself that."

"That's my Queen, then."

Zara took in a rough breath and closed her eyes.

She opened them to find him caging her body with his broad one. Her breath was filled with the scent of him, infusing every little corner. Her fingers crawled into his hair and she tugged roughly, wanting him closer, needing to burrow into him. It was a strange thing that she'd seek comfort from him, when he could become the very thing that might truly break her.

"Why was she in your room, Virat?"

"She was scared. I've been doing a docuseries on powerful men and all the abuse they heap on women under their very protection. My supposed affair with her was nothing but a cover for our frequent meetings. She gives me information on the various women in his life he exerts that power over and I provide her with a much-needed dose of courage and motivation to leave the man."

"A docuseries? Against powerful men?" Fear was an acidic thing in her throat.

"Hmm. So far, I have a high court judge and the minister."

"And you plan to do what? Expose these men?"

He shrugged. "Something like that. She's in a fragile place right now. I told her you'll reach out to her. I know it's an imposition but if you can take her under your wing and help her understand that her life is only beginning…"

Zara tucked her fingers under his chin and tilted it up, to look into his eyes. "Not even Vikram knows what you're really up to, does he?"

"Bhai has enough on his plate without me becoming another liability. This project will be under my own banner. Not Raawal House's."

"Because you think he wouldn't approve?"

He smiled then, a soft light awakening in his eyes. "Because it's a risk. In many ways. Bhai has earned the freedom to not have to deal with any more problems created by the rest of us."

"But you trust me enough to look after this girl?" Zara asked, hope fluttering like a persistently stubborn thing in her chest.

"Why wouldn't I? You're clearly experienced and interested in helping out these women."

Zara nodded and looked away, afraid that if she even let one tear out, there'd be no stopping the rest. She'd no idea why she was feeling this emotional. But she was.

With his perceptive gaze, Virat noted her state. But thankfully, he said nothing about it. "Shall we get to the most relevant thing in all of this? I know the world thinks I'm totally uncaring but I do have standards, *shahzadi*."

"You and she have never…then?"

Distaste etched around his mouth. "She's caught in an unhappy, powerless marriage with an abusive husband. The last thing I'd do is take advantage of her."

"And she showed up here at the hotel, in your suite that night. I'm guessing to confront you about the news of our engagement."

His eyes were intent on her face. "How do you know that?"

"She's fixated on you as her way out of an unhealthy relationship. Probably even believes that she loves you."

He regarded her with an intensity that made Zara feel naked to her soul. "How do you understand her so well? If I didn't know you better, I'd have thought you'd overheard our conversation."

Zara felt as if she was teetering right on the precipice of something. But she pushed the feeling away with a shrug. "Never mind how I know. I hope you let her down easy, Virat."

"Such little faith in me, Zara?" Zara didn't know what he saw in her eyes but when he spoke again, there was no such mockery in his voice anymore. "He married her when she was nineteen. The girl has no idea what freedom feels like. I told her the last thing she needs is another control freak like me in her life. Then she said something about you."

"What?"

"She said she felt sorry for you."

Zara raised a brow. "Why?"

"Because you have to deal with me, I suppose." He nuzzled into her neck and Zara thought she might melt right there. "And I told her you had me so thoroughly wrapped up around your little finger that she should worry about me. That you're the strongest woman I've ever met. I had her barely out the door when Anya showed up after an early morning flight. We had to finalize your new costume and then I had a meeting with the set designer."

Her gaze rested on the blue shadows under his eyes, and yet, there was no dimming the vitality the man gave off by just occupying a space. "So I was wrong about you, then."

"About what?"

"I thought you'd agreed so easily to our fake engagement because it would give you the perfect chance to torment me."

"But?"

"But you did it because your alleged affair with this woman was bringing you too much attention. You didn't dare risk exposure about the docuseries. And there I was ready to fall into your lap with the perfect reason to make the minister let down his guard again."

"But not every woman would have roped me into a fake romance that easily, Zara. Only the one I've never stopped panting over."

Zara touched him then. Not touching him at this point was akin to trying not to breathe. She clasped his cheek with one hand, fisted his hair with her other and pulled him for a kiss.

Head bowed, mouth open, he let her have her way with him. He tasted of whiskey and warmth that Zara knew she was never going to get enough of. Soft, eager lips met hers in hard kisses and sweet nips. She rubbed her cheek against his bristle, dug her teeth into his lower lip. The kiss made her dizzy with want.

She pressed her lips against his, moaning into his mouth.

"Come to bed, *shahzadi*. I'd rather not faint like a Victorian virgin while you kiss me like that. Think of all the rumors on the set. *Virat Raawal faints at the feet of his fierce fiancée, unable to withstand the heat of her kiss*."

Zara giggled and his nostrils flared. He traced an abrasive finger under her eyes. "I know I've been driving you like the beast that I am. So let's give ourselves a rest and then—"

"Wait, what?" she said, sounding breathy. "You're asking me to sleep...like actually sleep with you?"

He rubbed his eyes with the heels of his palms and pushed a hand through his hair tiredly. "I mean, I'm not going to be of much use to you until I get some sleep in me, since I have been awake for...about forty-eight hours but—" his gaze shone with a wickedly naked hunger "—I was thinking it would be nice to have you right there when I wake up and we can get right down to it. Without wasting any more time.

"Also, my suite is the only place where we won't be disturbed. There're about a thousand people who want a piece of me right now. The last thing I want to do is wake up and come looking for you, only to be surrounded by your fans again."

"You're having trouble falling asleep again, aren't you?"

He thrust his fingers through his hair. Only now did

Zara see how desperately he needed to sleep. "You remember then?"

"Of course I do. You work like a demon, skate the line of burnout and then you get into a spiral of sleeplessness. A long bout of hot sex with a willing woman is your usual answer, but—"

"But I don't want to take a strange woman to my bed."

Her smile was so wide that Zara thought her muscles might break. "Breaking patterns, are we?"

"Finding comfort in old playthings."

Zara gasped and went at him with two fists. She barely landed one on his bicep before he caught her. Firm fingers pulled her arms behind her and Zara moaned at how good the stretch felt on her muscles when he did that.

"You're far too tight here, Zara," Virat added, his fingers weaving magic on the tight knots in her shoulders.

"Hmm…" Zara said, with a smile. It felt as if her heart was bursting with a feverish, giddy joy.

Gathering her against him, Virat crushed her mouth with his. Zara could feel his heart thumping against her. Could feel the faint outline of his arousal teasing against her belly. The strength of his powerfully corded thighs anchoring hers as she trembled at the onslaught of pleasure. Hard and warm, he was exactly what she wanted right now. "Come to bed with me, *shahzadi*," he whispered in her ear. "I'll give you an apology for barking at you in front of everyone, at least three orgasms before the day is out and a little direction as to why you and Bhai are botching that scene."

"No wonder they call you a hard taskmaster."

"Well, I do have a lot of items on the agenda I want to do with you," he added with a wicked grin.

Zara followed him when he tugged her, feeling as if

she'd follow this man anywhere. If living in the moment meant pushing away the clamor of questions she had for him and take everything he was willing to give her right now, then she was going to do it.

She was going to take the biggest risk of her life if that meant the man she'd always wanted would be hers, even if only temporarily.

CHAPTER NINE

IF VIRAT THOUGHT the intimacy of spending two entire days with Zara would somehow descend into awkwardness, he'd have been completely wrong. If he'd thought drowning himself in her company and her body and her wit and laughter would somehow get her out of his system, then he'd have failed utterly.

But since all he'd wanted was to indulge himself very thoroughly with a woman he was finding increasingly irresistible on more than one level, he'd succeeded.

As long as Zara and he kept the past where it belonged, as long as he could quiet the resentful niggle that she'd chosen him this time around because now he was successful and powerful and independently wealthy, the easy connection they'd once shared came kicking back into life.

He suited her this time around. That was the only explanation he had for how effortlessly they'd found the camaraderie and connection that had once sparked so easily between them.

The off day he'd forced the both of them to take had been one of his better ideas. Zara had fallen asleep even before he had, and the warmth of her body next to his—the woman he hadn't stopped wanting for ten long years—had knocked him into a dreamless slumber.

And then to wake up and find those silky limbs tangled all around him…it had been even more deliciously decadent than he'd imagined. Just the memory of how hard and fast they'd gone at each other sent a shiver through his muscles. Of how equally fierce her own need had been for him would forever be etched into his brain.

He smiled at the thought now, as Zara and he lazed on a sofa in her suite. She was stretched out along its length, with her feet in his lap while she went over her lines for the final scene they were going to start shooting tomorrow.

One more week and the shoot would be wrapped up. He would begin postproduction work with his team and Zara would go back to Mumbai and start whatever other job she had lined up next.

As he sat there with his head thrown back and thinking of all that was waiting for him as soon as this small interlude was over, Virat felt a strange sense of peace that had been missing for some time now. Was it because he had been avoiding any deep connections—whether romantically or otherwise—for so long?

Or was it simply because for ten years he'd worked round the clock and he'd been in a rut? The docuseries and the biopic were the most important projects he'd ever tackled, and yet, he couldn't lie to himself that it was seeing Zara, teasing and taunting her, having her to himself that had got his blood pumping these past few weeks.

The idea of walking away from this, from her, and going back to his old life held no appeal. And yet, there was no future for them together. Not with a woman he could never fully trust.

It was the very finiteness of this thing between them, he was sure, that made it so powerfully raw at the moment.

"You have a very serious look about you right now," Zara said softly, her face hidden behind the script pages.

Virat tensed. Zara had a way of seeing through to his innermost thoughts that he found more than a little uncomfortable. "I'm going to leave a little earlier than planned once the shoot wraps up," he blurted out, surprising even himself.

She didn't lower the pages. Her feet stilled in his hands. "Okay." After a beat of silence, she said, "I have a long stretch of vacation after we wrap this up. I've been pushing myself too much recently. If you let me know what your schedule looks like, I'll come see you. As and when you're available."

"Look at me, Zara," he demanded.

She lowered the papers with a sigh. The rust-colored sleeveless blouse she wore brought out the warm golden tones of her skin. Her hair was a silky mess since he had plunged his fingers and messed it up when she'd walked out of her shower wrapped in a white towel that he'd unwrapped as if she was his very own present.

But as lovely as she looked, there were dark shadows under those big eyes. There was also a taut, drawn look to her face. He suddenly remembered the costume designer's two assistants working all night because Zara's outfits had to be taken in again before the shoot next morning.

"There's the audio release party and a couple more events that we have to attend together anyway," she said casually.

Of course, they'd continue this charade until the release of the biopic. He always forgot how efficiently she could manage this weird melding of their professional and personal lives. How effortless and easy she made it for him to indulge in this with her, with barely any demands on him.

But then, Zara never asked you for anything even back then, a voice whispered in his ear.

"Is that what you meant just now?" he taunted her, shutting away the disquiet in his own mind. He was forever pushing her. Forever wanting to see her vulnerable with him. Forever asking her for more than he was willing to give.

As if it was a toll she had to pay again and again for her past actions.

God, he was so unforgiving.

But if he thought she'd back down or hide away behind excuses, he was wrong once again. The more he challenged his own conceptions, the lines between them and what he demanded of her—with some strange need to see her back down from this, from them—the more Zara pushed back without balking, without even blinking an eyelid.

He wanted to see how far he could push her before she backed away.

"No," she said, her gaze steady. "Yes, there are some social events we'd have to smile and laugh and coo over each other at. But I meant that I want to come see you. Outside of the drama we're enacting. Outside of the biopic's demands.

"At your flat. My bungalow. Wherever possible."

He wanted to say some cold and awful thing like, "I might have moved on by then," or "I can't give you any guarantee that I'll still want you," or some such nonsense. Instead, his heart raced and desire twisted his belly into tight knots. His fingers tightened over her calf and his other hand cupped her hip, and the ever-present current of heat between them filled his skin with a restless hum.

He traced his fingers wordlessly over her belly, tucking them under the loose band of her shorts. Raising his gaze to hers, he stilled his hand there, seeking her answer.

Color scoured her cheeks, filling the pale canvas of her skin. "Yes."

One word. But it rang between them like a clanging bell. Like some unchangeable truth. He wanted to ask how many more times or for how much longer she'd keep saying yes to him.

But in the face of the open desire in her eyes, his rational questions lost out. His seeking fingers pushed inside her soft cotton shorts. A groan ripped from him when he found her velvet folds damp and ready for him. Hips tilting up, Zara dug her teeth into her lower lip. Neck thrown back, eyes closed, breasts falling and rising, she looked achingly beautiful.

Within moments, Virat disposed of her flimsy shorts and filled his greedy hands with the soft skin of her thighs.

"Open your eyes, Zara," he said, playing with her intimate flesh the way he knew she liked.

Dark, desire-smudged eyes held his. "What do you want, *shahzadi*?" he asked, needing to know. Always needing to know with her. Always needing to hear her desire given voice on those lips.

"You. This. Now."

"Then come closer," he whispered, bending his head and pressing a soft kiss to the skin right above her knee.

Her breath hitched. "Closer?" she whispered, pink seeping up her neck now.

"Yes," Virat said, letting her see his desire in his eyes. "I want to put my mouth on you, Zara. I want the taste of you on my lips. Can I?"

The moment suspended between them—an agony of

hope and desire and something else passing like shadows on her face. He cupped her knee and pressed another soft kiss to her calf. "Only if you want it, *shahzadi*. No rules between—"

"Lovers. Only pleasure," she finished for him.

Her shoulders jutting out, she propped herself up on her elbows. A bead of sweat dripped down her temple into the valley between her breasts. "Will I be allowed to return the pleasure?" the minx demanded, swiping the tip of her tongue over her lower lip.

His erection twitched against his upper belly, demanding release. To take what she was offering so boldly. When the very idea of either of them doing this very thing had made her shy away from him once upon a time. But there was something about this intimacy between them—something that was raw and honest and incredibly fulfilling—that Virat was beginning to fear and crave at the same time. "It's not a transaction, Zara."

Scooting down on the sofa, she raised her head just enough to reach his mouth. Her lips and tongue were eager and warm and soft and tasted like honey. Her little pants when he let them breathe and her mewl of pleasure when he nipped her lower lip ignited pockets of pleasure all over his body. The kiss was a taking. Rough and fast, it sizzled right down to his bones. "Ten years have meant nothing when it is you, Virat. Do you still doubt me? Doubt this?"

Her eyes shone with a glittering resolve. "I want all the pleasure you can give me this time around. And I want to be the adventurous, bold lover I couldn't be ten years ago."

There it was. Virat wrapped his fingers around her neck and held her to him. He nuzzled into her cheek, that tenderness overflowing within him. "Zara, you were perfect then. Why would you think—"

"I wasn't. I was afraid that someone would find out about us. I was afraid that I'd disappoint you. I was afraid that you'd realize that I was nothing but trouble..." She trailed off then added, "I was afraid of my own desires. We only got close at all because you were irresistible and kind and patient with me," she whispered, a fierceness in her voice that made his gaze jerk to hers.

What he saw swimming in her eyes made his chest tight. Made him question all his assumptions of her all over again. She brought his palm to her mouth and pressed a sweet kiss to it. Dug her teeth into the rough pad of his palm. When he rubbed that lower lip that was beginning to haunt his dreams with one finger, she licked the tip. Her tongue wrapped itself around his digit. Her eyes holding his, she sucked on it as if it was her favorite lollipop and then released it.

He lengthened against her thigh and the smile she shot him was sheer perfection tempered with a flash of naughtiness that he wanted no other man to ever see. A little rumpled, a little undone, she looked like a siren. And with an artist's eye, he saw that this was the promise he'd seen in the woman back then. She'd always been destined to be a queen. "This time, I demand everything you can give me," she announced.

"Then shall I taste you, *shahzadi*?"

"Yes," she said, letting her thighs fall open.

His erection notched into the cradle of her sex and Virat thrust his hips into that warm, inviting heat, unable to resist, and they both moaned. "God, you'll have me dry-humping you like it's our first time together, *shahzadi*," he said, looking up, and she laughed. God, she felt perfect and he was insatiable.

His breath hitched at the poignant beauty in her face. It wasn't just pleasure and beauty but some indescribable joy that lit her up from within. "I didn't know sex could ever be such a warm, funny, raw experience until that first time the both of us made such a mess."

Her laughter rang around them but he saw the shadows of pain beneath it. And Virat wanted every part of her— both the good and the bad, everything that had made her the woman she was today.

"Zara…"

"Not now, Virat," she said. "Please, not here."

She bent forward and pressed a soft kiss to his mouth. Pleading and begging, it was the sweetest kiss he'd ever tasted. Raw with longing and something he wasn't even sure he could return. "Now, what about what you promised? Because more than anything, I need you inside me. Now."

He ran his mouth in a trail from her neck to the curve of her breast and the tight knot of her nipple exposed by the thin top. He tugged at the neckline roughly and it tore with a rasp. He tongued the plump nipple and then sucked it into his mouth, and Zara thrust her hips upward into his erection, seeking him.

He treated the other breast to the same treatment, the taste of her skin making him harder, crazier for all of her. Burying his face in the valley between her breasts, he peppered kisses all over her damp skin.

Fast fingers pulled away her top when he reached her belly, and he laughed and pressed his mouth into the soft curve there. And then he moved lower and breathed in the musky scent of her, licking the wetness waiting for him in a slow, soft stroke of his tongue.

Zara came off the sofa but he anchored her there with his hand on her belly and then added his fingers. Her fingers in his hair tightened and her moans grew in urgency and her thighs clutched him harder but Virat didn't stop until she fractured against his tongue and his name was a litany on her lips.

He looked up and caught the one tear that had trailed down her cheek with his finger. *"Shahzadi?"* he whispered, afraid that he'd hurt her. But beneath that thin thread sat a much larger, uncomfortable truth. That he was never going to get enough of her.

She looked down at him and breathed in a long rasp. Nimble fingers undid his zipper and then clasped his erection. Her fingers were bolder and surer around him now as she pumped him hard and fast, just as he'd shown her he liked. "Inside me, now," she said, on a husky demand, and Virat complied.

Pushing her legs back on either side of him, he entered her in one long thrust. The backs of his thighs tingled, every muscle ached with need, greedy for relief as he took her ruthlessly.

As his climax threatened to undo him, Virat wondered if there would ever be a time when he would look at Zara and not want her.

The setting sun limned Zara's bare limbs with a golden glow as her lashes fluttered awake. Virat ran a finger over the delicate lines of her collarbone. He hadn't missed how quickly she'd fallen asleep again when they'd moved to the bed or how drawn her face looked even after two days of R and R.

He pressed a kiss to her shoulder, unable to resist. "Have you lost weight since Bhai's wedding?"

She frowned. "Why do you ask?"

He shrugged. "You looked as if you needed the break more than I did. And two days of special Virat Raawal treatment later—" she let out an outraged gasp and pressed her foot into his chest "—you still look pale, *shahzadi*."

"Maybe because these two days didn't officially count as a break for me."

His curse reverberated in the room. "Damn it, Zara. You should have told me you were still rehearsing—"

"What I want is to not be treated as if I'm fragile or breakable. I wanted to make love in all the positions we've tried. According to some research groups in Sweden, women hit their sexual peak at thirty-five. I bet you're only saying this to cover the fact that you can't keep up with my demands."

He laughed and her gaze hungrily ate him up. He bent and ran a finger over her cheek. "You're beginning to look almost gaunt, Zara."

She scrunched her nose in that cute way of hers that made him smile. "I haven't been eating well. And yes, my nutritionist and personal trainer are both a little worried that I'm losing muscle. But, as I reminded them, I have been dancing for three hours a day for the last three weeks. That's more cardio than at any other time in my life."

"That's true," Virat said, sitting up and leaning against the headboard.

Her hair in glorious disarray, Zara held the edge of the soft duvet against her chest and looked around for her clothes. Virat gave the duvet a swift tug on his side and it slipped between her fingers.

Her bare breasts rose and fell, the plump light brown nipples puckering up. His arousal lengthened, his muscles tightening with a desperate need that didn't look like it would ever be sated.

She huffed and pulled on the T-shirt he'd thrown away

in a hurry earlier. He pouted and she sighed. "I do want to get through the scene with you. The last thing I need is a fresh rumor that Zara Khan has lost whatever little acting talent she possessed because she can't get enough of her fiancé's hot body."

He folded his arms behind his head. And her greedy gaze traced his muscular arms, his hard chest and everything in between. He grinned and sighed. "Fine. Let's go back into the sitting room."

"Don't worry, Virat. I can take the shift from sexy lover to demanding director."

She sat down on an armchair opposite the bed with a blue pen and the script in hand, and looked at him. He sighed. "Fine. Your monologue sounds preachy. Like something you learned by heart to just regurgitate in front of the camera. You're not able to get a handle on her character in this scene. Especially Mayavati's final decision," he added, mentioning the name of the prostitute spy Zara was playing.

Surprise painted over her features. "How did you know I don't like the final scene?"

He shrugged, glad to know he'd hit the nail on its head. "It's my job to figure out what's blocking you. My job is to get you to connect with the character, to help you immerse yourself in it.

"What exactly is bothering you about her, Zara?"

"I struggle with how Mayavati plays such cunning games with not one or two but three different men—the budding actor who goes on to establish the biggest studio house that becomes the foundation of Bollywood later, the British general and the solider turned manservant.

"She constantly puts her life on the line for the first, plays dangerous games with the second and takes advantage of the third's quiet devotion. All three men adore her and yet…she's far too fickle with her affections. I don't…understand how any woman could be so…outrageous and cunning and…" she whispered the last word "…brave."

"I thought her interesting background would give you a better understanding of her," he prompted. "That you would connect with her better than, say, a…twenty-year-old actress whose biggest accomplishment is that she's convinced her powerful daddy to sink a few crores into launching her career because she can act."

"I did think you'd go with a fresh face. Not that I doubt my own talent."

"Mayavati, despite being the underdog, despite being a prostitute on the lowest rungs of society, knows how to play the game. Knows how to make all the men around give her her due."

Her head jerked up, a sudden tension around her mouth. She looked down and then back up at him. "Is that how you see me? As someone who plays games?"

A few weeks ago, Virat didn't know what his answer would have been. But now there was a certainty in him. "I see you as someone who wins despite the odds. When you started your career doing Bhai's masala popcorn mass blockbusters, I didn't think you'd last long. For a while, you played nothing but a glamorous sidekick at best, a one-dimensional accessory at worst."

"Ouch," Zara said, knowing that he was absolutely right.

"Until you produced and released that series of short films for TV. You… I was stunned by the breadth of acting you showed in those."

"You watched them?"

A smile lingered around his lips. "At the first chance I could get. That was a first-class move. You shut up most of your critics. You pivoted your career at the exact right moment. You…made us all sit up and take note of you."

"Thank you," Zara said, her heart bursting with pride and pleasure and something more. "Your praise means a lot to me."

"Because I've criticized you and Bhai more than once?"

Zara shook her head. "Because even ten years ago, you were full of raw talent. I've always respected your opinion, Virat."

He stared back at her, something in his eyes that Zara couldn't recognize. She'd complimented him, but the moment became weighted with something else.

"Tell me what you like about Mayavati," she asked to break the mounting tension.

For a second, she thought he wouldn't answer. Then he said, "She's the most complex female character I've ever handled—they are thin on the ground to begin with. Wily and cunning and stubborn. Even with all the pressures society puts on her, even with all the demands the first two men make on her, Mayavati lives only for herself. By her own rules.

"But it's her final decision that shows us how truly complex she is.

"Her choice in the end to spend the rest of her life with the manservant—the one man who truly loves her despite knowing everything she is—instead of the general who could give her riches, or the visionary Vijay Raawal who promises to launch her as an actress, tells the audience that Mayavati is, at the end of it all, desperate to be loved. To be accepted for who she is.

"And *that* is a universal emotion."

He held her gaze, a flash of something in his own. "Maybe you're struggling because you can't see why she'd make such a selfless choice? Why she'd walk away from the chance of being a wealthy actress with my grandfather's character or the call to adventure with the general?"

There it was, at the core of it all, the shadow of the resentment she'd always spied in his eyes. "You think I'm not able to connect with her because I don't see why she values love and acceptance before everything else." It wasn't even a question anymore.

Without answering her, Virat leaped from the bed, as if she'd caged him for too long. His sweatpants hung low on his lean lips as he turned away from her.

And Zara knew then. Two things hit her in the face. Hard and fast. Almost crushing her under their weight. "You don't trust me at all, do you? After everything we've said and done the past few weeks? After all this time? At least have the guts to say it to my face, Virat."

He turned then and she saw the truth in his eyes. "Let's talk about the scene, Zara."

Zara threw away the pages in her hand, with a fervor that her character, Mayavati, would have admired. "No, Virat. Let's talk about the one thing we've both avoided for long enough. Let's talk about why it's so hard to fathom for your brilliant brain that you're one of only two men I can absolutely trust in this world? That my friendship with your brother has eaten away at you for ten long years?"

"Don't, Zara," he said, a slow fury awakening in his eyes. It etched itself onto his features, and even then, Zara's heart only marveled at how beautiful he was in the moment. How so very breathtaking he was, how deeply he could feel…how much she wanted to hold him and press her face into that warm chest. How much she never wanted to let him go.

"Don't what, Virat?"

"Don't talk about trust as if this was a remotely normal relationship. As if this is anything more than a convenient fling for both of us," he gritted out.

"It started as that, yes, but I was just kidding myself. This is the first relationship I've had in ten years. Ten long years where I didn't lack for interest from men. Good men, even. I've already made my peace with the fact that you're the only man I can let my guard down with. That you're the only one I can let close, even if it's just nothing but a fling.

"And that I can't stand for you to look at me with that same contempt you show the entire world."

"I don't."

"Yes, you do. I told you, Virat. I know you better than anyone else. I know how deeply you feel things. I know you're nothing like the superficial playboy you show the world. I…know you, Virat."

"Leave it alone, Zara."

"I can't. I'd rather you call me the vilest names you can think of to my face than blow hot and cold with me. I can't take it when you look at me as if I'm a stranger to you."

He closed his eyes and looked away. "Because you are."

"No, I'm not." And then Zara asked the question she'd wanted to from the first moment he'd taunted her. "Why do you think I traded you for Vikram, as you called it?"

"Damn it, Zara! Because you did. You built your entire career on the back of your relationship with me, using me to get to him. I tried to…" He pushed his fingers through his hair roughly. "I understand how hard it is to get traction in this industry. I…know that.

I expected that kind of behavior from everyone else.

I grew up amid it. But you…" He looked at her then and Zara gasped at the pain etched deep into those familiar features. "I thought the world of you. I…but you simply cashed it all in."

Zara felt his words like a slap. She'd pushed him to this, she'd foolishly wanted to break down the barrier that their past had left between them. She'd wanted more. And yet, his accusation stole the ground from under her. She wished she could simply walk away from this. From him. From the past.

But she couldn't. She wouldn't sleep a wink or function like a normal human being while he thought the worst of her. She was done fighting the power this man had over her. Done questioning why her heart beat a thousand times louder near him. Why he meant so much to her.

She folded her arms, bracing herself for more. "Is that what you think I did?"

"Please don't pretend. I can forgive you anything except the pretense that you didn't take money from my mother to leave me. And that she didn't pull a number of strings behind the scenes to land you that role with Bhai—the one that launched your career, the one that started your friendship with Bhai, as a bonus payment for leaving me."

Zara had no idea how she managed to stay upright. How she didn't launch herself at him, screaming that it was all lies. Big, fat lies. That there were reasons why she'd left him but they had nothing to do with money or her relationship with Vikram. That Virat was the only man who brought her alive. Who made her take risk after risk with her battered heart. "And you know this how?" she asked calmly, already knowing the answer.

"Mama told me that you'd struck a deal with her. That

when she approached you, all you could talk about was how much you'd wanted to land a role in Bhai's movie. How desperate you were that your career wasn't going anywhere…"

She flinched but fired back, "You knew what my career meant to me, Virat. So is it my ambition that you're holding against me? Because, if it is, it makes you worse than all the other men floating around."

"No, *shahzadi*," he said, and Zara wondered if he even realized how he was addressing her. "Don't lay that sin at my feet. You thinking Bhai was a better bet for your career…skewered me, yes. But that was the truth back then. I was nothing and he was everything.

"But what bothers me, as much as I try to get over it, is the fact that you used our relationship to do it, Zara. It was your bargaining chip with my mother. It turned everything into a transaction. It tainted everything we had.

"It was worse than losing you…to him."

"He never had me, Virat. Don't you get that?"

"I know that, Zara. Now. But I was an angry twenty-year-old who thought you were rejecting me for him."

"But that's not true. Don't you understand that there's a reason I found my way back to you again?"

"The resentful bastard in me says it's because I'm me now. A powerful man in his own right."

Zara flopped onto the settee behind her, her knees shaking beneath her. "Wow, so you think I came back to you because now you are of use to me again?"

"No. I don't." He pressed the heels of his palms to his eyes. "You have nothing but my respect, Zara. But the past…" an angry groan fell from his chest "…is like an angry shadow that haunts me."

"Then maybe you've become the very man you've hated your entire life," Zara said softly. "Maybe you're more like your father than you realize—a man who's so caught up in the past that he ruins his own future."

If she thought he'd mock her that she wasn't part of his future, he didn't. His gaze shifted away from her but not before she saw him flinch. His words when he spoke felt like they were wrenched from him. As if the very thought had haunted him. "You think that possibility hasn't occurred to me? You think I'm not trying every moment to let the past go?"

And that was what these two days of respite had been. Zara knew he was trying to let things be. Knew she had pushed him into that place of hurt and irrationality. Knew that…he'd always tried to live his life guided by those very principles that had drawn him to her.

Frustration raked its nails through her at the specter of past always coming between them. She believed him that he wanted to get past it. But he never might. And that broke her heart a little.

Of course, Vandana Raawal had lied about Zara's reasons for leaving. She'd spun the entire thing to make herself look better to her rebellious son. She had used the opportunity to get closer to the son she'd already hurt beyond repair.

After all, the absolute truth was Vandana had picked Zara's audition tape from hundreds and put it in front of Vikram.

In a twisted world, she could even understand the desperate woman's motivations. After all, when Vandana had approached Zara, she'd thought she'd been doing the right thing for her son. She had thought Zara wasn't good enough for him.

But for Virat to have believed that Zara had taken money from his mother to leave him, that she'd been out to get everything she could, that their relationship hadn't meant the world to her, that it hadn't nearly broken her to walk away from the one man who'd made her feel alive again...that hurt.

The truth was, she hadn't been ready for another serious relationship after her travesty of a marriage and her husband's death. She didn't even know who she'd been back then.

He came to her then, his long fingers falling on her shoulders gently. Her skin tingled with awareness. Every inch of her body prickled with that mixture of excitement and anticipation. A quiet joy that her mind would always associate with the very scent of this man.

"Zara," he whispered, his breath coating her temple. "I'm not a small man who begrudges you the career you've made for yourself. I..." his jaw tightened "...don't want to be..."

Zara pushed his hands away and stepped back.

She'd vowed to herself a long time ago that no man was ever going to make her feel small again. No man was ever going to control her happiness again. And she couldn't let Virat do it to her, either, she thought bitterly. Even though there was a part of her that now understood how shattered he must have been to think she'd left him for money and to get a role in Vikram's film.

"I'm ever so grateful that you slept with me even though this is what you think of me, Virat. I can't tell you how—"

"Stop, Zara. I've tried to forget the past. I've forgiven you. I realize I was an idealistic prig back then. It doesn't matter what I thought of you, of us. After ten years, I can see it as less of a betrayal and more as a powerless woman using everything she had to get ahead in an industry that rewards connections and power."

"Wow, so you forgive me, do you?" Zara retorted,

sheer fury pushing away the hurt that he'd think that of her. "Then let me tell you that you're still an idealistic prig. You... You're right. This was never going to be easy or fun or just a fling." She looked away from him, feeling as if she was saying goodbye to him all over again.

She felt his chin rest on her head, his fingers tightening around her shoulders. Felt his harsh exhale stroke the skin of her neck. She desperately wanted to lean back into his hard body, to let him enfold her in those strong arms.

He was waiting for her to do just that. She knew. Letting her decide the course of this. Letting her know with that voluble silence of his that he still wanted her. That they could just bury the past here in this moment, thorns and all.

That they could continue this thing between them for as long as she pleased. That he wanted her, despite what he thought she might have done. Every inch of her wanted to lean back into him, to cover the distance.

She took a bracing breath instead and said, "I swore to myself a long time ago that I'd never cry again in front of a man. Please leave, Virat."

The sudden cold kissing her spine told her he had left. And now that he was gone, she perversely wanted him back. Wanted him to hold her and kiss her and make love to her until she was too trembling and sated to think straight.

Zara didn't cry. Exhaustion and that same nausea she'd been battling for weeks now began to set in, leaving her body sore and achy. But as she flopped down onto the bed and buried her face in the scent of the man she missed like an ache already, she wondered why she hadn't simply told him the truth. Why she hadn't simply defended herself.

Vandana Raawal had lied to her son. Outright, completely lied that Zara had taken money from her as payment to walk away from Virat. She'd not only convinced Zara that she wasn't good enough for her son, that she was ruining Virat's bright future back then, but she'd also broken her son's heart with her own hands. Ruined his trust in Zara.

Even worse, she'd broken his trust in himself.

But however she looked at it, Zara knew she'd had a hand in it, too. Her inability to trust him back then, her fears about how her last marriage had turned out and her uncertainty about the future—hers and Virat's—had made her run away from him. Had made her choose the easy way out, convincing herself it was the best thing for them both.

Was she willing to do the same thing again or was it time to finally tell him the truth about her past and about what his mother had done? She fell asleep, pondering the answer to that question, desperately missing Virat in her bed and in her heart.

CHAPTER TEN

ZARA ARRIVED AT the audio release party being held at a sprawling luxury resort, another property that Virat had invested in, her belly full of fluttering butterflies.

Since Virat was flying in at the last minute from God knows where, there hadn't been a need for them to arrive together. Instead, she happily joined Vikram and Naina, even though the both of them kept stealing glances at her face. That she had fainted the other afternoon was news she couldn't have kept to herself.

The only mitigating factor had been that Virat had already left. She'd had a reprieve to deal with everything. Before she had to face him again.

She'd seen him on set for the last week of the shoot, and for the impromptu wrap-up party Vikram had arranged for the team. Thanks to their crazy schedules, she and Virat hadn't had the time or the need to act all lovey-dovey in front of others.

Ten days after their argument, she was less hurt with his impression of her and the past, and more...angry at herself. Not explaining about her marriage and its aftermath, and then running away from what he'd made her feel the last time around was what had caused all this. She'd opened the door to allow in Vandana's manipulation and lies.

Not that he was without fault. But then, Zara also knew how deep old wounds could run. How they twisted and corrupted everything that was good in life.

She was done running. From him or herself. Especially now.

She was pregnant. With Virat's child.

Nearly six weeks along. And thanks to the intense cardio regimen and sixteen-hour workdays, she'd been completely unaware of the changes in her own body. At least, the lack of hunger and the exhaustion all made sense now.

Three days later, she still couldn't manage her emotions at what her blood test had finally confirmed. Elation sent her swinging high one moment, and then the idea of confronting Virat with the truth sending her mood dipping low the next.

Like a coward, she'd even indulged in the idea of skipping this release party in its entirety. She could have claimed she was feeling unwell and it wouldn't have been a complete lie.

But she also knew she had to face Virat soon. She was wary of his reaction, yes, but this wasn't something she wanted to hide from him. No more evasions, no more lies between them.

No expectations. She kept whispering that as her mantra. Whatever his reaction, she wasn't going to be surprised by it.

The last thing she wanted was to force him into a role he wasn't ready for, to somehow ingratiate herself into his life in this way. But she did want to share it with him first. She wanted to share everything she was feeling, she wanted to…

No, Zara! No expectations, remember?

The audio release was the first in a chain of PR events that were still to come, to build the buzz for the film's release in three months. While the schedule had over-whelmed her, Zara was glad of the extended leave she'd scheduled for herself at the end of the biopic's production.

Today's event also constituted the first look at the stills from the film and a trailer. It had exceeded even the stir that Virat and Vikram had hoped to cause. She couldn't remember the number of people—both familiar and un-familiar—that she had smiled at, or shaken hands with, or accepted congratulations from. The movie trailer had spurred such an applause from the audience that it was still ringing in her ears.

Even though she'd been present for the last week of filming as Virat had pushed and pushed both Vikram and her to do better, the trailer was still a shock. Her performance, even in the forty-five seconds she had in the trailer, was breath-stealing.

Her gaze had automatically sought his in the darkened auditorium as if tugged toward him.

There was no smile on his lips as he held her gaze. Not after they'd had to embrace and laugh and kiss each other on stage, to please the crowd. Not when within mo-ments of touching, they'd lost themselves in each other.

Not when the possibility of something real and raw danced into life every time their eyes met. When it was clear that for all their arguments, nothing had changed between them.

And yet everything had changed.

Zara sat back into her chair and closed her eyes. Pray-ing to God for composure for just a little longer.

The lights came back on, and onstage, Vikram talked about how the project was a culmination of years of thought and effort—a homage to his grandfather Vijay Raawal. A continuation of the prestigious Raawal legacy.

Zara felt a sudden flush claim her skin and she laid a

hand on her still-flat belly. Her child would now also be a part of that legacy. Her child would be…

When Virat arrived on the stage, there was a feverish anticipation in the crowd. And while he thanked his brother for giving him the opportunity to direct such a masterpiece, and said Vijay Raawal was an inspiration to everyone in the film industry, he didn't mention the Raawal family or his place in the legacy at all.

Making Zara wonder yet again how he would take her news after all. Reminding her that she'd tangled with a man who'd always forged his own path.

But before he left the stage, Virat thanked each and every technician and staff member for putting up with him.

Zara clapped the hardest, feeling a profound gratitude and a strange pride in him. As if he belonged to her.

Even now, as she circulated among the glitterati who had been fortunate enough to get the first glimpse of the magnum opus of the Raawal House of Cinema, she couldn't believe what she had seen with her own eyes.

Vikram had always had a magnetic presence on screen, and his portrayal of his grandfather had been truly sensational. But she…she had shone. Virat had been absolutely right—it was her chance to steal the scene from her leading man and she had done it. In just a matter of a few weeks, she felt as if she had learned a lifetime's worth of skills under Virat's direction.

The man was truly a genius behind the camera at what he could wring out of the actors on the screen. And in real life, he was a man who'd built an island around himself. A man who used the camera as a shield between himself and the world.

Picking up a glass of sparkling water from a passing waiter, she drank it in one go, hoping it would settle her stomach. It was more than three hours now and all she wanted was to take Virat's hand and disappear.

As if summoned, he was there on the next blink. She felt him at her back, the warmth of his wiry body beckoning her closer. The hair on the nape of her neck prickled with awareness.

"You fainted as soon as I left? Did you miss me that much, *shahzadi*?" His words were a raspy whisper against the rim of her ear.

Zara knew he was teasing her and yet the truth of that thought struck her still.

She felt him lean down. His fingers landed gently on her shoulders and squeezed, even as a photographer captured them from the other side. Neither did she miss the curious glances, from family members and friends to the press and other media moguls.

Zara gritted her teeth against the self-indulgent anger that rose through her. She was beginning to hate the very charade she'd started. She wanted his raw intensity, the real man, and not this polite, attentive lover he played in front of the world.

When he'd have retreated, Zara kept her hand clasped around his neck.

"More posturing, *shahzadi*? If I'm to hold you and kiss you and touch you for public consumption, then I'm going to demand the same in private," he whispered, bending down to rub his unshaven cheek against hers.

She looked into his eyes, the naked want in his tone finding an echo in her. "Don't mock this. Whatever you might think of the past, if you mock what I feel for you…"

He raised his hands, palms up. "No mockery, Zara. The entire world be damned, I refuse to continue this charade in public and then go to my bed alone. I want you, *shahzadi.* I can't sleep without you by my side. I admit that I want to see where this will take us."

Excitement thumped so hard in her chest that it filled her ears. She desperately wanted to take what he was offering. Especially now. If she weren't pregnant, if she were free to take risk after risk…

"Are you going to practice forgiveness afresh every morning then?" Zara couldn't help taunting back.

Deep grooves formed around his mouth as he considered her. "I've never said I was perfect, Zara. But I'm trying to let things be."

Zara shook her head, wondering why she was pushing this again. When there were bigger, life-changing matters waiting ahead for them to discuss. "I've already done the whole vicious cycle of having a man heap abuse on me the previous night and then pledge a fresh start the next morning, in my last marriage. For three long years. By the end of it, I was completely twisted up, inside out. I lost myself."

Stillness enveloped him, and when he spoke, shock pervaded his every word. "Really, Zara, now? You choose to tell me this now?"

Zara regretted the words instantly. It was as if there was no filter left anymore within her. "That was a cheap shot." She held onto him when he'd have stepped back. "I'm sorry. It was unfair to compare you to…him. I… I don't want to do this, Virat. I don't want this to be our default setting."

His forearm came around her back and he held her so gently that for the first time in years, Zara thought she might break. "No, Zara. Don't apologize."

A sudden shiver took over her body. "I don't want this poison to fester, Virat. Not between you and me. I can't stand the thought of that. Whatever the future holds, I don't want us to part like this."

"Shh…*shahzadi*. Shh… Nothing like that is going to happen to us. I've got you, Zara. I'm…so—"

The last thing Zara wanted from him was an apology. Not like this. Never like this.

Throwing every warning to the wind, she snuck her fingers into his hair and pulled him down until his mouth met hers. She was hungry for him, for his warmth, for his kiss, for the strength of his arms around her. She felt his shock for maybe a second.

Then he took the kiss over, and every muscle in Zara's body sighed in shuddering relief. It felt like coming home after years and years of being away.

He explored her mouth with a wondrous gentleness that brought tears to her eyes. This was no rough possession. This felt like escape and invitation, all blended together into a soft storm. Like a new beginning between them, washing away the pain of the past.

This felt like retreating into a world in which only they both existed. He kissed her as if he had been waiting for her to make the move again. Even as she drowned in the warm cavern of his mouth, Zara couldn't help but demand more. Want more.

"I'm not going to apologize for doing that," she whispered against his cheek, keeping her fingers in his hair. "Nor am I going to pretend that it was for someone else's benefit."

He raised a brow, challenge glinting in his eyes. "No?"

"No. I needed that kiss."

He laughed, sending vibrations into her mouth and the rest of her body. She tightened her fingers in his hair, punishing him for the taunt. Desperate for the anchoring of his taste, she clung to him, her breaths suddenly shallow.

His fingers gently clasped her face as he studied her. "Something's bothering you, Zara. You're not yourself."

She looked into his eyes and there was no laughter there. He knew. Just like that. Rubbing a finger over her lips, she nodded. "We need to talk. I've been waiting for you to get back."

He frowned, his gaze studying her intently. "We'll leave immediately." He pushed onto his feet and took her hand in his. "Are you unwell?"

"Yes. No. I mean, I know why I haven't been feeling completely okay."

Her statement shocked him, she knew. But his expression remained steady. And that was what Zara needed. "I have a suite on the thirty-fifth floor. We'll talk there."

Zara looked around and noted that their departure was already making waves. "Vikram will kill me for dragging you away," she muttered.

"Bhai knows this is not where I naturally shine, Zara. This is his arena."

When she still looked doubtful, he wrapped his arm around her waist and pulled her. "Come, *shahzadi*. Your career won't sink if you bunk off being on show for one evening."

It felt as if it took no longer than a blink of an eye before the lift pinged and they were walking through the white marbled foyer into the sitting lounge. Beautiful teak furnishings gave the room a warm glow. Greenery draped from ceilings and climbed along the white walls, giving the expansive space a very cozy feel.

Zara knew Virat was watching her. Waiting for her to speak. And that she was only postponing the inevitable. She took a bracing breath and turned around.

He'd already thrown his jacket away and undone the cuffs of his linen shirt. Dark and broad and unfailingly male, he made Zara's pulse dance in her chest. She swallowed and looked away.

He came close and whispered her name, a thousand questions in it. "Zara?"

Zara looked at him, and blurted it out. "I'm pregnant. I'm about six weeks along." She had to take a long breath at the end of that statement. And when he didn't move or even blink, she whispered inanely, "It's yours, Virat. The baby's yours."

Virat laughed. Or at least he'd thought he'd laughed. But the sound that emerged was a hollow, lackluster mockery of the real thing. "I didn't think otherwise, Zara. But thank you for the clarification."

"Oh, I didn't mean to say that you doubted me. I'm sorry I have no template for how to do this and I shouldn't have just blurted it out like that—"

"Don't. God. Please stop apologizing." He pressed a hand to his temple and let out another laugh. "There's no speech you could give that could prepare me for that revelation, is there? So yeah, don't worry about your delivery."

She didn't move. Just looked at him steadily. Ever the poised woman. As if waiting patiently to let him process it all.

For a few seconds, he wondered if he was in some sort of a strange feverish dream he usually had when he was sleep-deprived. When the rest and peace he desperately wanted eluded him.

But that wasn't possible. Because he didn't want to tie himself down to Zara, did he? Not when he still didn't completely trust her, when he didn't like that she continued to haunt his every waking thought.

Not when she was beginning to matter too much.

No. The last thing he should want, or dream about, was that Zara was pregnant with his child. With *his* child.

A girl or a boy who might look up to him. A totally innocent child who would be affected by his every word, gesture or action. Or by the very lack of word, gesture or action from him.

Virat thought he might throw up without the benefit of alcohol for the first time in his life.

"Virat?" Zara asked, her eyes wide, her stance both challenging and yet defensive. As if she was ready for anything he might throw at her. When it was she who'd been turning his life upside down from the minute she'd walked back into it.

"You're determined to pull me under, aren't you, *shahzadi*?" he asked then. The words came automatically, as if his brain could send mechanical responses while his heart…his heart tackled the avalanche of emotions that threatened to drown him. If he let them…

"Pull you under?" she said, coming closer tentatively.

"First you blurt out to me that you…that your marriage was a…" He rubbed his hand over his face, unable to even form the words. The outrage that filled him at the pain he'd seen in her eyes defied words.

God, he'd been so blind. The signs of an abusive marriage had all been there. When they'd met back then, she'd been so wary of him in the beginning. Of any man who might have been even a little friendly. Constantly on alert as if she was afraid he might steal something she didn't want to give. Needlessly second-guessing her every small decision.

Her wonder at the silliest of sights. Her sudden alertness as if someone might have been watching and gauging her every word and action. The silent tears she'd cried when he'd taken her on a tour of the city at night.

And now, after all these years, the simple admission that she hadn't taken a lover in ten years. That she couldn't let her guard down with anyone else. With any other man but him. He considered himself a good judge of human character, a master of human nature, and yet he'd been so blind to it.

"Virat… I shouldn't have mentioned it at all. Not like that and not tonight of all nights."

"You should have told me a long time ago, *shahzadi*," he added, and regretted the demanding words immediately. The last thing he wanted was to heap more accusations on her, to make this all about him. "Zara, the last thing I want is to hurt you. Even before you told me about this. That's why I made myself stay away."

"I know that. I do. It's just that if I had told you about what a disaster my first marriage had been, how long it has taken me to gain my confidence back, you'd look at me as you're doing now. As if you had to weigh every word you say to me. As if I was nothing more than a victim." Frustration painted her face. "I've earned the right to be seen as more than a sum of my past. Don't take that away from me now, Virat. I couldn't bear it if you…looked at me like that."

"No one can take that away from you, Zara." He understood her perfectly in that moment. And all he felt was that same inadequacy that had haunted him since she'd asked him to leave the bedroom ten days ago. He chose his words carefully. "I won't ask you to talk about it," he said. "Not tonight. Not ever if you don't want to. But, Zara, I would like to know. When you're ready. When you think I've earned the right to share that episode of your life."

"Yes, okay," she said, clearly eager to get away from the subject. "Now can we talk about the…baby?"

He pushed a hand through his hair, a knot of uncomfortable sensations sitting like a damned weight on his chest. God, there was so much to unpack, so much waiting to drown him. But the wariness in her eyes gave him the anchor he needed right now.

This wasn't about him or the ground being pulled away from under him, or whether he wanted to be a father or not. This was about Zara and what she needed from him now. What she wanted from him. And that was what he should focus on.

He went to her then and took her hand in his. Gently squeezed the long fingers. There was still a fragility about the fine angles of her face but also a quiet spark of resolve that made him relax. Clearly, she was handling this better than him. "You have decided to keep the baby, haven't you?"

"Yes, I have." She sighed. "I've never thought of myself as a mother but…it's strange how right it felt once it sank in. If there's one thing I've learned, it's that life never works out the way we expect.

"I met Saleem at a wedding and fell in love overnight. I went against my parents' warnings that we were too young and married him. I had so many plans for my life with him. And then…a few days into our married life, he changed. He refused to let me pursue acting. Even though he knew it was my passion. He…knocked my confidence in everything.

"Since he passed, I've learned to count my blessings as they come to me, Virat. Ten years ago, it was meeting you in line for coffee.

"Now, it's this chance to be a mother when I didn't even plan for it.

"I choose to see this as a good thing. Can you understand that?"

There was such sheer confidence and joy in her words

that Virat had no words, for a few seconds. And he knew without doubt that his child was indeed fortunate. That Zara would be a wonderful mother.

And the clarity of her vision began to clear his own doubts.

"How do you feel?"

She smiled. "Good. Now that I know the reason for the strange headaches and the lethargy, really relieved. I… I've never fainted before in my life and it took everything I had to get Vikram and Naina to leave me alone so that I could talk to the doctor."

"And she said everything…with the…" he cleared his throat "…baby is good?"

That smile in her eyes again. "Yes. In excellent health. I…" she sighed "…I told her I'd never missed the pill, not one single day. But I did do a round of antibiotics when I caught something while I was traveling just before Vikram's wedding, and she said…"

He cupped her cheek. "You don't owe me an explanation as to why or how it happened, Zara."

"I know. It's just that I've known for three days, and there's so much to talk about…and I was worried that we'd left things in such a bad place. But I…" Her hesitation made his rollicking thoughts come to a halt.

"What, Zara? Tell me what you're thinking."

"I'm glad…you see that this is my decision. I'm the one taking on this responsibility and…you don't have to…" Virat didn't know what she saw in his face because that wariness came back again. "I want to make it clear that there's no pressure on you at all. You…you can decide how much of a role you want to play in the child's life. You can…"

Virat stood up, a restless energy crawling under his

skin. A strange anger was coiling around his limbs and he didn't even understand at what, or why.

He looked out into the night, his emotions just as dark and unruly. All his life, he'd possessed a thorough awareness of his dreams and fears. Even as a child, he'd had to develop the sort of emotional intelligence to deal with his father's cold distance.

And yet, suddenly it felt as if he didn't know himself at all. As if there was a hungry cavern inside of him that wanted what it wanted. "I don't want any child of mine to go through what I did. I don't want him or her to ever doubt its roots, its family, its very existence. That's non-negotiable, Zara."

"Of course. I wouldn't dream of denying our child that knowledge. Or you of whatever relationship you wanted with her or him.

"You know what calmed me down when the magnitude of this hit me? When I thought, *Oh, my God, I'm going to be a mother and I don't know the first thing about it*?"

"What?"

He felt her move behind him. Her arms came around his waist, as if she knew that the calm persona he was showing her right now was nothing but a facade. Her breasts pressed up against his back, her cheek against his shoulder, she draped herself all over him.

"You…the thought of *you* calmed me down. That whatever way we do this, however I bring up this child, our child, that I will have your support in every decision. That…we will somehow muddle through this together."

He scoffed. "You have a lot more trust in me than I do in myself right now, *shahzadi*. I know next to nothing about bringing up a child."

She laughed then and he felt the vibrations of her laughter sink into his skin. And Virat knew, in that moment, that this was his chance to do it right. His chance to build everything he'd been denied his entire life. "Neither do I. And what I have trust in is *us* together. I trust that whatever the past, and the future, we both will always want and do the best for this baby."

He turned and took her mouth in a kiss that was more necessary than breath itself. She moaned into his mouth, just as eager as him, cementing the decision that was gaining momentum inside him.

He wrapped an arm around her waist and pulled her closer. The other hand, he sent on a foray, needing the feel of her soft curves to calm the furor in his blood. The more he touched her and kissed her, the more Virat felt the rightness of his decision.

He pulled away and leaned his forehead against hers, his breaths just as shallow as hers.

"Shall I tell you what I want, then, Zara? How I want this to play out?"

"Yes," she whispered. "I just don't want any more shadows between us, Virat. No more things that can fester."

"A fresh start, then, *shahzadi*?"

She smiled, and her face lit up with a glorious kind of joy. "Yes, exactly. We will start a new scene. Draw a line under the past."

"Then let's turn our engagement into the real thing. Let's get married."

She jerked away from him, just as he'd expected. But Virat didn't release his hold on her. She was soft and solid and real in his arms—more real than anything he'd ever beheld in his life. "What?"

Virat led with logic, knowing that that was the only way to appeal to Zara. "We're knee-deep in an engagement that will continue for at least another three months. At least until the release of the biopic, is what we said, right? And by then… I assume you're going to be showing."

"Yes," she said, her eyes full of that wariness. "But—"

"Do you want to split up then, Zara? Do you want to put yourself through the stress of going through a separation that's splashed all over the press? Do you want me to play the role of the heartless bastard who dumped his pregnant fiancée?

"Do you want to start our future together as parents like that?"

"But—"

"Or do you want to start as a married couple who want to do the right thing by their child? A couple who know exactly what to expect from each other? Is there a better foundation to begin our life together?"

"And you won't care about giving up your bachelorhood? Tying yourself to me permanently?"

"Like you said, we're already tied together, Zara. This baby has already changed everything. I'm just streamlining the process and trying to make everything official."

She laughed and he held her close, and Virat knew that this was the right thing to do. For the first time in years, he felt a strange sort of peace fill him. And he didn't worry over how easy and effortless this felt. How…right it felt.

But then, as he'd learned in the last ten years, when it came to his personal life, decisions made with his head rather than his heart, always worked out.

And maybe that made him a fraud, but he knew that life was nowhere near as logical or neat or even sane, as the most chaotic piece of it captured as a piece of art.

CHAPTER ELEVEN

ZARA HAD NEVER imagined planning the wedding—especially her wedding—could be this much fun. Of course, this time she wasn't planning to run away with a man she barely knew, against her parents' wishes. Wasn't young and impulsive and looking for a way out of her mundane life.

It also helped that she had the wealth this time to properly plan the wedding. Even though she'd had to naysay her groom again and again when he insisted that first she let him pay, and second, she pick a wedding planner and take it easy.

She'd commissioned Anya Raawal to create a custom-designed *lehenga* and a sari for the two ceremonies, and the brilliant girl had accepted, her gaze bright with joy. Anya had simply said, "He seems so happy, Ms. Khan. I've never seen my brother like that."

Of course, Zara had immediately told her to call her Bhaabi, like she did Naina.

It didn't matter that what she was planning was for a small, intimate wedding of no more than ten that constituted her closest family and friends. And even in that, half of the guest list comprised the Raawal family. The thought of coming face-to-face with Vandana Raawal had made her more than a little anxious, but Zara had decided that Vandana was unlikely to confess to Virat what she'd done to him ten years ago, and that nothing, not even her deceitful future mother-in-law and her obsession with her younger son, was going to mar the pleasure she was discovering in all the details that were going into planning two different ceremonies.

Her mother had been quite insistent that Zara should have a proper *nikaah* this time, and Zara had heartily agreed. In a twist that even she hadn't seen coming, Virat had, of course, charmed the pants off her strict English teacher mother by visiting her without Zara's knowledge. "He didn't say he was going to make you happy, Zara. He knows you well, *beta*. He simply said he'd do his best to keep up with my powerhouse daughter." Zara had closed her eyes, fighting the tears that threatened to overflow. The man did know her well. Her mother's fluttery "He's so…handsome and…sexy, Zara," at the end of the phone call had sent her into paroxysms of laughter.

"You've chosen well, *beta*," she had added softly. And Zara's heart had felt full to bursting. "He seems like a very thoughtful young man."

It had been a month since their fake engagement had turned into a real one. The night he'd proposed, Virat had simply asked her to consider his proposal without rejecting it outright. Had stayed with her all night long and made love to her in such a tender, gentle way that she'd ended up crying in his arms.

She'd woken up in the early hours of the morning to find his palm on her belly and a sort of wonder etched into his face. His gaze had been somewhere else, until Zara had clasped his cheek and kissed him. She'd seen something there, then—a wretched sort of loneliness that she understood very well. "Whatever you decide, Zara, we'll be a family. Of our own making."

She had nodded and demanded that he hold her. Desperate to have him back, away from the shadows of the painful past that glimmered in his face. And she'd known then that she'd already made her decision.

Happiness was a choice, and Zara wanted to spend the rest of her life building on the magic that was already there between them. Not that Virat had taken her acceptance for granted.

No, he'd waged a weeklong seduction campaign that Zara had been all too happy to succumb to. If he wasn't bringing her her favorite desserts from all around the world, he was bringing her old gramophone records of artists from a long-gone era. He'd cooked for her, gone over possible scripts with her that she might consider in the future, and found new and adventurous ways to make love to her.

Just thinking of the last time he had taken her to bed sent heat flushing through Zara. What had begun as an innocent massage of her feet when she'd complained of exhaustion had somehow turned into the wicked man going on his knees in front of the sofa where she'd been sitting, and burying his face between her thighs.

Zara still had no idea how he made sex so raw and intimate.

How one night, they'd communicate with greedy fingers and throaty gasps and the damp slide of their bodies in the darkness. And the next, they would be watching some cheesy movie in bed for research, laughing, taunting each other. And amid that laughter he would strip her and slowly slide into her ready heat, and her laughter would transform into desperate need.

One evening, she'd opened a safe sex box from one of the rural outreach projects she was overseeing, and out had popped a tube of lube. Of course, the wicked man had immediately suggested they test the product and they'd lost track of time and had arrived flushed and late to a dinner with Vikram and Naina.

If she'd been hovering over the threshold before, now she was completely, irrevocably in love with him. She loved how he didn't hesitate to discuss their future. How he bossed her around when he thought she was unnecessarily tiring herself.

How he spoiled her rotten when the mood took him. How he could go from demanding and insatiable to a gentle lover who wanted nothing more than to hold her through the night.

"I'm so happy for you both, Zara," Naina had said, when Zara had informed them that the wedding was imminent. Vikram had looked relieved and hugged Zara so tight for so long that Virat had growled and pulled her away. Leaving Naina in a fit of giggles at his jealous behavior.

Zara had felt a strange reluctance to share the news of their pregnancy, even with her best friend and his wife. And Virat had understood her reluctance without her having to spell it out. Only then did Zara realize that he was a very private man. Especially when it came to things that mattered the most to him.

That even with his brother—with whom he shared a true bond despite their creative differences and career trajectories—there was a shield he maintained. As if he didn't dare let anyone close. As if he'd become an island so that no one could hurt him.

And yet he'd let her in, Zara knew. He'd let her see the true Virat, despite what he thought she'd done to him. The man who loved and hurt and felt things so deeply.

Despite that, she didn't have a single doubt in her head that her pregnancy was the primary reason he had proposed marriage. She did want her child to know her father, but sometimes she woke up in the middle of the night feeling as if she had lost him once again, and reached for him.

His bare back warm to her touch, his muscles solid and real, he was always there. She blinked at the realization that in the weeks since they had been engaged—the real engagement—he'd spent almost every evening with her. It was as if he had decided, just as she had, that he was going to give this everything.

When Zara had asked him if they should have the wedding the morning before the release of the movie, he had sent her an almost forbidding look. Not that it scared her one bit.

"Don't glare at me," she'd said, wrapping her arms around him and pressing her cheek to his chest. Outside of having him inside her, making sweet love to her, this was Zara's favorite thing to do. She'd realized he wasn't given to overt displays of affection but she didn't care. He was big and solid and hers, and she had already spent so many years denying what she felt for him, battling loneliness. The thud of his heart against her ear made her feel safe and warm and alive. "It's an option I'm exploring, that's all," she'd said, pressing her finger to the ferocious scowl he wore. "Your schedule is crazy bonkers and that's one of the days where everyone is available and—"

"I don't care if it ends up being just you and me, Zara. And your mother, of course. I don't want to face your mother's wrath if she can't attend." His sudden grin and warmth reminded her of when she'd met him for the first time. "But I don't want even a hint of PR spin about our wedding. If Bhai tries to convince you that the idea of us appearing as a married couple on the eve of the premiere after some top secret, romantic wedding that morning—*because we just couldn't wait,*" he said in a mocking, high voice, "will skyrocket the ratings for the movie and create even more interest, then I'll throw the punch that he deserved to get the other night at dinner when he kept hugging you."

Zara's mouth twitched and his scowl turned into an outright glower. "Let's not get crazy, darling," she said, pressing her lips to his. "That's the last thing we need when the tale of our supposedly twisted love triangle has finally died down. I'll tell your brother that he's not invited to the wedding, how about that?"

"Are you managing me, *shahzadi*?" he'd said then, his eyes blazing with mock severity.

"Manage the most brilliant director of our generation? Me, I wouldn't dare," she'd said, going on her toes, ruffling his hair. She undid the tie he'd just spent ages putting on and slid her greedy hands under his shirt to find the warm, smooth skin of his pecs. She kissed him again, deep and long, uncaring what they'd been talking about, and he let her, knowing very well that she was trying to do exactly that.

It was quite a while before both of them made their way back to the discussion at hand. He looked rumpled from her kisses and Zara decided she liked him like that best.

"I want our marriage, our child, our lives, our entire future," he said, putting on his Italian handmade shoes, "to be separate from the lives we lead on-screen. No performances for the media.

"No public avowals of affection. No discussing our private lives in front of the camera for someone else's titillation. Not even for one of your numerous charity projects and empowerment efforts or anything else. Not even in front of Bhai and my mother will we talk about our life together." He finally looked up. "Is that clear, Zara?"

Zara had simply nodded, knowing where the words were coming from. "I understand, Virat."

"I don't want to have to send our child away to boarding school at some far-off destination, but if that's what it takes to keep the drama of our public lives away from him or her, we will do it. I can't stand the idea of anything or anyone hurting the…baby, even through words."

Zara had gone to him then and hugged him tight, letting him know that she understood perfectly. That he could dictate to her about this until the end of time and she would only agree with him. That their life together would be real and have none of the glittering artificiality his parents had embraced.

He'd simply nodded and left. And for a few seconds, Zara had wondered at the deep wounds still pulsing below the surface of the man he showed the world. At the shadows she saw in his eyes whenever the subject of the Raawals came up. And wished so hard that she hadn't played a part—even unwittingly—in transforming him from that spontaneous, full-of-life twenty-year-old into this hard man who refused to look into his own heart.

And the fact that she was irrevocably in love with even this incarnation of him was simply a fact she was going to have to get used to.

She had just finished talking to her mom on the phone when Virat walked into their sunroom where she had been lounging about, taste-testing different samples of desserts a caterer had sent her to pick from.

She was definitely going to have to order the *gulab jamun* for their reception. The syrupy, gooey goodness had melted on her tongue. "Will you be mad at me if I tell the caterer you've demanded to taste the *gulab jamun* before we put in an order and then I eat all of your share when they come in?" she said, wiping her fingers on a napkin and looking up.

It only took one look at his face to know something was very wrong. A prickle of nervous apprehension ran down her spine.

"What is it, Virat? What's happened?" She said, looking up from the cozy armchair where she'd been reclining and watching a rerun of an old movie.

He didn't answer her but paced the expansive room, a restless energy radiating from him.

For a few seconds, Zara simply took in how the afternoon sun kissed the rigid line of his jaw, lovingly traced the breath of his wide shoulders. The dark denim clung to his hips and buttocks, and she had to swallow the instant need to touch him, claiming him for herself.

"You said no more lies, Zara."

She jerked her gaze to his and the fury she saw there sent a tendril of fear to blossom in her belly. "I didn't even know you were back in town," she said, buying for time. "I thought you were flying in tomorrow morning."

He shook his head, seeing through her ploy. "Don't play games with me, Zara."

"I am not," she said defensively.

He sighed and sat down on the armchair far away from where she was sitting. Zara hated the distance he was imposing between them. And knew he'd done it on purpose. For all the control he exerted on himself, Virat's fury was something to see.

He buried his face in his hands, and a long, harsh groan escaped his mouth. Though the sound was muffled by his hands, Zara heard the anger and frustration in it. It made her want to hold him, more than anything else, but she also knew he didn't want to be touched right now. His body language made that much clear.

"I wanted to surprise you tonight, with an engagement party." He checked the time on the Rolex she'd bought him not two weeks ago, and rubbed his face again.

"Your mother's supposed be flying in in an hour. Bhai was going to bring her to my grandmother's house. Naina helped me plan it."

Zara stared blankly, having had no idea about it. She leaped up from the chair and reached him, laughing. She thought she might burst with joy.

But something in his gaze stopped her at the last moment, just as she was about to touch him. Something so hard and flat and so resigned that her heart kicked in her chest.

"I invited my mother and father, too. What you said the last time we talked…about our child growing up as a part of a family, it stayed with me. Despite all the drama my parents created, my grandparents and Bhai and Anya saved me. They…kept me sane and going. I wanted that future for our child.

"So I decided, in that magnanimous way of mine—" his laugh was full of scorn "—to at least try and forget the past, even if I couldn't completely forgive it. I decided that it didn't matter if my mother had a hand in you leaving me. If my father continued to reject me as his son to his dying breath.

"I was a Raawal in all the ways that mattered. So I'd give my child the pride and belonging I had always deserved but was denied. I'd start a fresh slate with my mother, too. She was, of course, overjoyed and couldn't stop singing your praises all morning.

"Then she announced—in that melodramatic way of hers—that admitting to all her sins would absolve her and my father of years of dysfunctional parenting. Would undo all the damage they'd wrought on Bhai and me and Anya."

Zara felt as if a lead weight was sitting on her chest. She knew now where this was going. Her stomach turned over.

"As part of this new awareness," Virat continued, his tone dripping with contempt, "she told me that she had lied to me ten years ago. About you. That she had driven you away. Because, of course, in her twisted mind, driving away the only woman who saw me for who I was, the woman who made me see myself in a new light, was an act of motherly love. Because, in her opinion, you weren't the right woman for me.

"Because she was looking out for me. Because she wanted me to have a wonderful future. Forget all the early childhood trauma she put me through by staying with a man who continually rejected his own child."

"Virat, please listen to me—"

"Apparently, she got rid of a pesky brother-in-law for you, who was determined to prove you were a murderer."

Zara felt as if she was caught in a nightmare of her own making. "Saleem, my first husband, killed himself after I finally worked up the courage to tell him I was leaving him. His controlling behavior had spiraled until he was locking me in my room and refusing to let me out. Yet his younger brother decided I was responsible for his brother's death and was going all out to punish me for it, even if he had to lie to do it.

"Your mother offered to use her power and reach to make the case he was going to lodge against me disappear. I knew that if any of it came out in the press, the chance of me pursuing a career in acting and landing decent roles with that sullied reputation would be nil. And if Saleem's brother had his way, I might even have ended up in prison.

"So yes, I accepted her help. But I thought it had been offered in good faith! I didn't know that she was going to lie to you about it, make me out to be the villain."

He still didn't look at her. His head was cradled in his hands, and Zara knew that she had hurt him again. By hiding this.

"Why didn't you tell me any of this before?"

"Because you were only twenty and bright and brilliant and had your entire future ahead of you…" Her voice broke but Zara continued, "You have to realize that I was a widow, newly out of an abusive marriage, afraid of her own shadow, guilty about the freedom I suddenly had and facing a possible murder charge. What kind of future would you have had with me? I didn't want to drag you down with me, Virat, if it all went wrong."

"You were the first real thing in my life. You stood outside of my prestigious family. Outside of the industry I was surrounded by. Our relationship was something I had chosen for myself."

"And that very intensity of your emotions…that terrified me so much." Zara knelt in front of him, her hands on his knees, her head bent. "It wasn't you that I didn't trust, Virat.

"It was me. I was petrified of how you made me feel, frightened that someone would find out, terrified that you would see who I really was."

"And what would that have been?"

"Nothing. I thought I was nothing. An imposter not worthy of your attention. All I had were empty dreams. Three years with Saleem had dented my confidence in myself, in my decisions. His death damaged my ability to even trust myself, and then his brother accused me of killing him.

"I was already worrying about where we were going,

Virat. It felt like we were getting way ahead of ourselves. You even started talking of maybe leaving the industry behind, of starting fresh somewhere else, in a new country. And I… I was scared of leaving you but also terrified of leaving behind everything that was familiar.

"So when your mother approached me and asked me where I saw our affair going, pointed out that I was no good for you, I let her convince me that you were better off without me. That you were just infatuated with me, and if I left, you'd quickly get over me. I let her use her influence to stop Saleem's brother from pursuing the case against me.

"But I thought she was trying to help me. I promise you I didn't cash in on our relationship. I simply walked away from you. When the screen test for it landed in my lap, it was completely coincidental, but I took it as a sign. That I was better off with a career than with a man who deserved so much more than I could ever give him."

Virat looked up and Zara thought she might break into a thousand pieces if he didn't take her into his arms. "Then why lie to me when I blamed you for her actions? Why not tell me the truth then, Zara? God, you know how much I hate lies."

Zara sat back on her heels, guilt clawing at her. How had she made such a bad judgment call? "Because more than anything, I didn't want to hurt you any more by revealing her actions. I knew your relationship with her was already shaky. And I admit that I struggled to tell you what a coward I'd been back then."

He didn't open his eyes and Zara pushed herself between his legs and took his face in her hands. She put every ounce of feeling into her words, trembling with the need to tell him. The words came easily, fluttering onto her lips as if waiting to be released. "Because despite believing the worst of me, you still came back to me.

"You…gave me a chance. You tried to forgive me even when you thought I'd been paid off by your mother. You needed me just as much as I did you. And that, more than anything, convinced me that you and I belong together. This time, I have the guts to stand here and admit that—"

He looked into her eyes then. And the blankness she saw there made her chest hurt. "Don't, Zara."

"I'm in love with you. You make me laugh. I feel… alive even when I'm fighting with you and you pass out one of your dictates. Every time I reached out to you, you've given me more than I could ever ask." She took his hand and placed it on her belly. "Including this baby that neither of us expected."

"Zara—"

But she didn't stop. She wanted to give words to the wonder in her chest. "I have never stopped loving you. Even ten years ago, when you swept me off my feet. Yes, I was scared, but you also made me see myself in a new light. You…made me laugh and find joy in new things. Ultimately, you…helped me heal, even though I didn't realize it until it was too late.

"And now, I'm so much stronger. I love you and I know I can stand by your side and weather anything. As long as we're together—"

He recoiled. "No, Zara, stop." He pushed onto his feet and moved away from her, as if he couldn't bear to be near her. "I can't do this. I'm sorry. I thought I could. But I can't."

The emptiness she'd always been so scared of came barreling at her, and still, Zara tried to hold it off. "You can't do what? Marry me? Build the family that we both want? We've already agreed to draw a line under the past, so at least, look at me and tell me why."

He turned and there was such raw anguish in his eyes that she flinched. Any other man would have given in to the emotions radiating from him. But not Virat. Not when he had had to harden himself against pain and hurt, again and again. "I proposed we get married because I wanted my child to have everything I didn't. Because I thought we both knew what to expect from each other. But…love, Zara…it complicates everything. I didn't sign up for that.

"My mother and father ruined each other's lives and ours in a futile pursuit of love."

"We're not them, Virat," Zara said, trying not to lose patience. Lose hope. "Don't you still get that? We went through the worst, we avoided each other for a decade but we found our way back to each other." She laughed and the sound was a little broken. "I have no expectations of you today that I didn't have yesterday. Nothing has changed."

He pressed a hand to his temple. As if he couldn't take any more. As if hearing her say she loved him was his worst nightmare. "Everything has changed. Your love… if I accept it, will only make me weak. It will suck me in and then…when it's taken away again…"

"It will not be. I'll never stop loving you. Trust this, please. Trust me," she said, reaching out with her hands. Beseeching him to forgive her truly this time. To want her just one more time. To choose her one more time.

Instead, he walked away, leaving Zara standing there alone.

CHAPTER TWELVE

ZARA ARRIVED AT the first premiere of the biopic to a select audience of critics and industry pundits after two months on an uncommonly cold spring night in an off-white, sleeveless silk blouse and a beautiful handwoven silk sari in the same white shade, with a beautiful red border in contrast. The best part, however, had been that the sari had come pre-stitched—as if the designer had known that a four-and-a-half-months pregnant woman would have to manage it. So all Zara had had to do was to pull it on and one of her friends, Anna—who had sung the soundtrack for the movie—had easily pinned it over Zara's shoulder.

Her hair had been braided and dressed in a beautiful knot, and a white jasmine *gajra* wound around the knot.

The PR person had delivered, along with the sari and the blouse, a heavy pearl necklace intertwined with shimmering rubies in an antique Hyderabadi design and matching *jhumkas*. She knew the color scheme would be coordinated with Vikram's clothes as they were appearing together at the premiere and at the after-party tonight.

Zara had always loved the simple and stunning beauty of a sari. But this sari—so close in shade and texture to the one she'd picked for her and Virat's Hindu wedding ceremony, draped beautifully, even around her rounding belly. It felt as if it was made of clouds, and floated with Zara as she moved.

For a few seconds after Anna had left, Zara had stood staring at herself in the full-length mirror in her bedroom.

Until today, Zara had worn mostly loose, free-flowing dresses at the few PR events she'd attended. With her statuesque frame and long legs, it had been very easy to hide her pregnancy. Even though it had been Virat who had decided it, Zara had also loathed the very idea of talking about their relationship or the pregnancy or anything else to the press.

Only Mama, Naina and her friend Anna knew about the baby, because when Zara had told them they were postponing the wedding date, they'd all simply showed up one evening demanding to know everything and wouldn't leave until she'd told them at least part of it.

The whole truth about what had happened felt intimate and private and something that only belonged to both her and Virat. Since she'd had a scheduled vacation anyway, she'd mostly laid low.

Tonight would be her first public appearance with her small belly showing clearly. She knew it was going to create more than just waves. But she wasn't going to hide it anymore, either.

Their relationship, it seemed, was in limbo.

Virat hadn't announced to the world that he had dumped his pregnant fiancée because she had admitted she was in love with him. And Zara had left it alone, too. She wasn't the one who'd walked away. If he wanted to tell the world that they were done, then he was welcome to do it himself.

At first, she'd been so unbelievably crushed that if not for her mother's opportune arrival for the blasted party that Virat had arranged, she would have walked around her bungalow like some ghostly apparition singing mournfully about the true love who'd deserted her for a richer, prettier woman.

Like the very scene she loved so much from a slapstick comedy/thriller Virat had written and directed a few years ago. The shimmering ghost woman, turns out to have killed her lover before the movie begins, and in a brilliant reversal, it is the man that turns out to be the ghost.

With its masterful visual effects and immersive storytelling, the movie was an ode to his talent.

As her chauffeur maneuvered the Mercedes around the bustling square and traffic to the newly renovated centuries-old theater—where Vijay Raawal had released his first movie years ago, Zara had a flash of complete empathy with the heroine of Virat's movie.

She would have very much liked to bash his stubborn head against something hard until he saw sense. She took in a long breath as the car came to a halt around a courtyard, and saw reporters and media persons being pushed behind lines by uniformed constables.

The door opened before her chauffeur had even moved. Expecting Vikram, Zara put on a wide smile and stepped out of the car.

Instead, it was the man who'd always held her heart in the palm of his hand.

Zara's smile fell, and she felt a swooping sensation in her belly—the ache from two months ago just as acute and fresh as if it had been yesterday that he'd left her. A small part of her wanted to get back into the car and drive away. To never see him again.

A large part of her urged her to throw herself at him and demand that he come back to her. That he take her in his arms and kiss her and hold her, only as he could.

Somehow, Zara managed to suppress both of those voices inside her head and gave her hand into his outstretched one. "I was expecting Vikram," she said softly, even as she could hear the pop of a hundred flashes going off in every direction around them. "You know, the man who doesn't keep disappearing from my life for long stretches of time."

She heard the whispered hiss of his indrawn breath, and felt a savage satisfaction. "You know where to hit me to hurt me the most, don't you, *shahzadi*?"

"Do I?" she said fluttering her lashes. To the world, they looked like lovers, with their fingers laced together. Their gazes greedily drinking in each other after a long drought. Zara was sure it was desperation she spied in his eyes. Naked hunger. Raw longing. Because for two months, she'd seen the same emotions in her own eyes when she looked at the mirror, morning, noon or night.

Who the hell was he punishing? she wanted to ask.

"And since you disappeared to God knows where for two months without a word, and it was Vikram who kept an eye on me, it's not that much of a stretch, is it?"

Draping his arm around her shoulders, he subtly adjusted their bodies until he could bend and kiss her cheek. Her skin felt as if it would catch on fire from the simple contact. "I don't begrudge your friendship with him. And he's always been a good brother to me. Even when I was calling him names. He agreed to keep an eye on you, without asking me exactly how I'd mucked up everything."

Her gaze jerked to his. "What?" Zara saw the truth in his eyes. Truth that gave her hope. Hope she suppressed by embracing anger instead. "I don't need you to appoint a keeper to look after me. I'm very capable of looking after myself."

"I have no doubt about that, *shahzadi*. Whatever I did was for my own peace of mind. I had to leave for Switzerland immediately and I couldn't get out of it. Bhai, I knew, you wouldn't refuse."

"I take back everything I said about parenting this baby together. You can't flit in and out of my life whenever you feel like it—"

"I knew I was wrong the moment I left you, Zara. That I was making the biggest mistake of my life."

Zara's heart thundered in her chest. "And it took you two months to say this to me?"

"By the time Bhai found me looking at the bloopers from the movie, like a drunken Devdas raving about his lost lover and I'd recovered from the hangover, I was already late for the flight to Switzerland. And once I was there… I couldn't leave until I finished the postproduction work on my docuseries.

"I only arrived back home a few hours ago. Zara—"

She had no idea what he'd been about to say, because an avalanche of reporters descended on them and Zara forced a smile and walked up the path with him, arm in arm.

The premiere of the biopic showed to rave reviews. Zara and Vikram's performances were off the charts and Virat was being lauded once again as the most brilliant director of their generation. The movie was already being touted as one of those once-in-a-century intersections of commercial and creative storytelling.

It was the biggest night of Virat's life. And yet, it had nothing to do with the movie. In fact, he'd found his attention wandering again and again to the woman sitting next to him in the dark theater, the scent of jasmine in her hair winding through him.

All day, he'd felt jittery. He'd thought he'd calm down once he saw her.

When she'd stepped out of her car, that beautiful silk sari draping perfectly around her growing belly, he'd nearly fallen to his knees. He'd wanted to beg her right there and then for forgiveness. For acting like a thick-skulled fool.

But that wasn't him. What he wanted to share with Zara was private and intimate and bound his very soul to hers. The three hours of the movie, and the two hours on top of that, meeting and greeting critics and reviewers and peers alike, had felt like torture.

And now, with her head lolling around on his shoulder in the moving car, the drive toward his grandparents' old bungalow felt like the longest of his entire life.

Zara came awake slowly when her head lolled onto a hard shoulder. First, she closed her mouth since she knew she must have fallen asleep with it open, like a fish. This falling asleep whenever and wherever was really one of her least favorite things about being pregnant.

This and the feverish dream she'd had that the scent filling her nostrils and lungs was Virat's. It was there now, too—a deliciously familiar cocktail of sandalwood and the cigar he smoked when he was nervous—filling her with that achingly desperate longing.

She fluttered her eyelashes open and found his dark eyes looking into hers. There was that look that she loved—as if she was his past, present and future. The look he gave her only when he made love to her. Or when he thought she wasn't looking.

"You fell asleep in the car."

Zara nodded. "Yeah, I sleep about sixteen hours a day

now," she said, just to say something. He was carrying her, she realized, her other senses slowly coming awake.

Carrying her over the threshold of a huge bungalow she'd visited only once. Or twice.

His grandparents' bungalow. And it looked all dressed up. There were strings of lights over the arched entrance and flower garlands hanging everywhere. Strains of *shehnai* came next and Zara fidgeted in his arms. "Put me down, Virat," she barked, feeling as if she was walking through her favorite dream.

Or her worst nightmare, if one looked at it in a certain way.

"Almost there, *shahzadi*," he whispered, and then they were in the inner courtyard where there was a small raised dais in the center. All dressed up with lights and more flowers, like a wedding *mandap*.

And there were people standing around, watching them with curious eyes. Vikram and Naina—with expressions almost like trepidation in their eyes—and Virat's grandmother, with a soft smile, and Anya Raawal next to her. On the other side stood Virat's best friend, AJ, and his wife, Zara's friend Anna. And beaming at her was her mother in front of the *mandap*, with Virat's parents a little distance away. Avidly gazing at both of them.

It was the wedding party she'd planned for. On closer inspection, Zara realized there were exactly the same flowers and music and decorations she'd picked. She looked down at herself and realized it was, of course, the same sari that she and Naina had chosen from a designer's catalog.

Zara's heart might have catapulted out of her chest if Virat hadn't gently brought her down to her feet and enveloped her in his arms. As though shielding her from prying eyes. She felt the tension in him when he embraced her tighter. Almost as if he were a tuning fork vibrating to someone else's frequency.

Hers, she realized slowly.

"Will you marry me, *shahzadi*? Today? Now?" he said and Zara felt as if she might burst into tears.

"Why?" she muttered through a sob half-ready to erupt from her chest.

Virat went on his knees and pressed his face into her belly. When he looked up at her, shock and wonder and so many emotions filled his eyes that Zara had tears in her own. "Because I can't live without you. Because you were always the woman for me. Because I never stopped loving you.

"You were right, Zara. I was a coward. I didn't trust you. And I didn't trust myself, either. I...thought becoming successful in my own right would prove to you and myself that I was enough. But you showed me that I was already enough.

"You bring out the best in me, *shahzadi*. I understand exactly why you felt you had to leave me ten years ago, and even when you did, you still gave me direction in life. Let me show you how much I love you now, Zara. Let me be the father of our child. Let me be the man my Queen deserves."

Zara buried her hands in his hair, tears falling freely onto her cheeks. "Why wait two months to tell me, Virat? Why... I thought you'd really abandoned me. I thought you were punishing me for leaving you ten years ago."

"God, no, Zara. This was about me needing to face up to my own insecurities. My own cowardice. I had a lot to work through...needed to take a long, hard look at myself. I needed to be sure that I would never hurt you like that again. That I wouldn't repeat past mistakes.

"Say yes, Zara. I will spend the rest of our lives showing you how much I love you. How much I deserve you."

When Zara would have flopped onto her knees to join him, he leaped to his feet and held her. "You already have me, Virat. You've always had me."

And then he was kissing her and Zara thought her heart might burst with happiness.

As they walked toward the *mandap*, she tucked her arm through his and leaned close to whisper, "It's a boy," and the joy that filled his eyes was so raw and real that Zara stopped him and stole another kiss.

Whoops and laughter surrounded them as she clung to Virat breathlessly. "What do you think of living here?" he asked then and Zara looked around in surprise.

"But Daadiji lives here," she said, looking at his grandmother.

"Daadi has decided to move back in with Mama and Papa. Since Vikram took the ring that my Daadu gave her, I asked her if we could have this bungalow."

"And?"

He grinned. "She laughed and said she'd been waiting forever for me to ask her. That they'd talked when Daadu had been alive and he wanted me to have the house. She told me it has always been mine.

"It was just waiting for me to claim it."

Zara squeezed his hand and he smiled ruefully. There was a wealth of pain and regret in his eyes but there was a new kind of joy, too. As if he'd released a burden that had claimed him for too long. "Isn't it weird how I always had her and Vikram and Anya and Daadu's love and support, and yet I craved the acceptance of the one man who was too small to give it?"

She nodded. But she knew old wounds didn't heal that easily. That people were wired to want what they didn't have. For months after seeing Saleem's true colors, she'd still gone on believing his empty promises that he would do better next time. That he wouldn't fly into jealous rages and threaten her. That he would control himself better. In the end, Zara had hated his quiet, loving moods even worse than the angry rants that always followed. Because the latter had been the reality of the man. And the former had just filled her full of a poisonous, false hope that crushed her every time he didn't keep his promises.

"Daadu used to call me Choté Raawal Sahib, you know. I forgot about it until Daadi and Vikram reminded me two days ago. I kept them at a distance, too, when all I had to do was to show them how much it hurt. How much I craved to be a part of all this. So many good things I suppressed under bitterness...

"It took you to give me that courage to reach out and ask for what I needed, Zara. It took you to make me see I already had everything I needed. That I was a Raawal where it mattered.

"In my heart."

Zara pressed her face to his chest then, and he held her tight.

"My grandfather built this house for my grandmother," he said, enfolding her in those strong arms. "It represents everything I loved about him, everything he taught me a Raawal man should have—loyalty and kindness and, above all, love. Daadu told me stories, made sagas about love. Because he said it trumps everything else.

"They were married for fifty-seven years, Zara. Can you imagine loving an entire lifetime together like that?"

And there was the romantic man she'd fallen in love with. His heart in his eyes. His love in his words.

Zara simply said yes.

"And the cool shadow of their marriage is what saved

Bhai, me and Anya in the end from the toxic heat of our parents' relationship. It taught us how powerful true love can be. I want that kind of marriage, Zara. I want to believe that we will last a hundred years."

There was need and love in those words but Zara realized he was asking her to lend him a little faith, too. And she had it in tons. She had enough to last them a few lifetimes together.

Zara nodded, tears forming a lump in her throat again. She raised his hand to her mouth, kissed the back of it and whispered, "To a hundred years together. To forever."

And then the wedding party took over, pulling her away from her groom, and Zara blew him a kiss, knowing this time their separation would only last a few minutes.

Because forever was waiting for them.

* * * * *

THE WORLD'S MOST NOTORIOUS GREEK

JACKIE ASHENDEN

This one is for Damerel and Venetia.

CHAPTER ONE

WILLOW HALL HAD never seen a naked man before. Or at least, not one that wasn't on her computer screen when she'd inadvertently looked up the wrong thing on the internet. And definitely not coming boldly out of the lake he'd been swimming in only moments before, as if he didn't much care if there was anyone around to see him or not.

Of course, given the fact that the lake was on the Thornhaven estate's grounds and therefore private property, he probably wouldn't expect there to be someone lurking in the undergrowth at the lake's edge watching him.

Then again, this *was* private property and, even though Thornhaven had been vacant for the past few months following the old owner's death, it was clear that he was trespassing.

Not that it made her invasion of his privacy any less egregious, and not that she was technically any less a trespasser than he was, but still. She lived next door to the estate and had been walking the grounds for years, had played in the woods nearby as a child, had loved the overgrown, rambling nature of the estate ever since she could remember, and, even though it wasn't actually her property, she viewed it as such.

She'd certainly never expected to come across someone

swimming in the lake when she'd set out blackberry picking this morning, still less swimming *naked*.

She should really do the right thing and move on. Visit the groundskeeper and tell him that there was a stranger in the lake. She really shouldn't be standing here peering through the trees like some pervert in an anorak.

Yet she didn't move.

Something held her rooted to the spot. Because the water was cascading over his naked body as he stepped from the lake, the late morning summer sun gilding his already golden skin, making an art form of every chiselled muscle. He was tall, with broad shoulders and lean hips. Long, powerfully muscled legs. His chest and stomach looked as if they'd been carved from marble as an example of the perfect masculine form, all hard planes and perfect hollows.

His hair was black, slick as a seal's, and as he walked slowly out of the water he lifted his hands and pushed it back from his forehead, biceps flexing with the movement.

Oh, lord…

Willow's mouth went dry, an inexplicable heat creeping through her, making her cheeks burn. This was very wrong. It wasn't the kind of thing she did at all. Maybe once, back when she'd been a teenager and much more prone to the vagaries of curiosity and her own wild passions, she wouldn't have thought twice about it, but certainly not now.

She was twenty-five, for God's sake, and she'd put those days behind her.

Yet somehow her feet wouldn't move, and she found she was clutching on to her basket full of blackberries, her fingers itching with the unfamiliar need to touch him, to trace the lines of all those intriguing muscles just to make sure he was real, because surely someone that beautiful couldn't be. She'd certainly never seen a man like this one, still less met anyone who looked the way he did, not in the cafe where she worked in Thornhaven village, or indeed anywhere in the village, full stop.

This man was like one of the Greek sculptures in her father's books on art history, the very pinnacle of male beauty, except all that travertine marble had been made flesh.

She didn't move, forgetting to breathe, the sunlight lovingly following every flex and release of his muscles as he bent over the small pile of clothes lying on the gravelly beach. He picked up a dark blue T-shirt then, as he straightened, Willow's heart beat even faster as he began to towel himself roughly off.

Her gaze drifted lower, over his lean hips and muscled thighs, to that most male part of him…

Her cheeks were so hot they felt scalded.

She should definitely *not* be looking at that.

What she should be doing was getting back to the cottage she lived in with her father, because she didn't like to leave him for too long. He'd had a stroke nine years ago that had left him extremely physically limited and very much dependent on her. Which he hated. But there was nothing either of them could do about that since there was no one else to look after him. She was his sole caregiver and it was a duty she took extremely seriously.

So she needed to stop staring and move on.

He'd started wiping down that incredible chest, his head bent, his profile as perfect as the rest of him. High forehead and straight nose. Cheekbones to die for and a strong, square jaw. His mouth was beautifully shaped and sensual, curving slightly, as if he knew something very wicked and utterly delightful…

Curiosity tightened inside her and she wanted very much to know what that something was.

Weren't you supposed to move on?

Yes, that was exactly what she'd been going to do. And she would. Right now.

'You'll get a better view from over there,' the man said casually, nodding at the bank directly in front of him.

Willow froze. His voice was as deep and rich as textured velvet, his accent aristocratic and yet with a lilt that suggested he'd spent a lot of time in places other than England. It tugged at something inside her, something she hadn't known was there.

She ignored the sensation, staying very still. He couldn't be talking to her, surely? She was hidden by the bushes and there was no way he could have spotted her. He hadn't even looked in her direction.

Perhaps he was talking to someone else. Someone she hadn't seen. Or maybe he was talking on his phone. But no, that was stupid. He'd just come out of the lake and, given his current level of nakedness, it was very obvious he wasn't carrying a phone.

'It was your hair, by the way,' he went on, unhurriedly bending once again to the small pile of clothes and picking up a pair of plain black boxer shorts. 'If you were wondering what gave you away. It's very bright. I would suggest covering it with a scarf or hat next time you want to hide in the bushes and spy on someone.'

Oh, dear. He *was* talking to her.

A tide of intense embarrassment washed over her, heating her entire body in a way she hadn't felt for years. It made her feel as if she were a kid again, helpless shame filling her as her father spoke to her in that cold, quiet voice. The voice he only used when she'd done something wrong.

You have done something wrong. You intruded on this man's privacy.

A quick, bright anger at herself flickered inside her, and she caught her breath at the unexpected heat of it. But no. She wasn't going to get angry. That wouldn't help. Her emotions were dangerous things and she needed to keep her distance from them.

What she had to do now was own up to her indiscretion, give him an apology, then promise that it would never happen again.

Willow took a silent breath, forcing down the hot tangle of unwanted emotion that sat in her gut, then stepped out from behind the bush.

The beautiful man straightened, still naked, T-shirt in one hand, his underwear in the other. He didn't seem at all embarrassed or self-conscious. Then again, he had nothing to be self-conscious or embarrassed about.

He was quite simply the most magnificent thing Willow had ever seen in her entire life.

His eyes were a deep, dark, midnight blue and the instant his gaze met hers she felt an almost physical impact, like a short, sharp electric shock. All the air left her lungs and her mind went utterly blank.

Then he smiled and she forgot where she was. She forgot *who* she was. Because that smile was warm and wicked and sensual all at the same time, and it made her feel hot and oddly feverish, though she had no idea why. She had no idea why a simple smile could do all those things to her.

He's dangerous.

The thought came out of nowhere, instinctive, though it didn't make any sense. Because he wasn't being threatening and she wasn't getting any strange vibes off him. He was simply standing there, smiling at her.

'Would you like to keep on looking?' Amusement glittered in his deep blue eyes. 'Or shall I dress?'

Willow struggled to get her brain working, her thought processes sluggish, as if they were mired in melted toffee. 'I do apologise,' she said in a scratchy voice. 'I heard the sounds of splashing and came to see what was happening.' Then, because, after all, he shouldn't be here, she added, 'You are aware that this is private property?'

The amusement in his eyes seemed to deepen. 'Oh, yes, I'm aware. That is the whole point of trespassing, isn't it?'

So…this was deliberate? That didn't make any sense. Why would he deliberately break the law? Wasn't he worried that she would report him? But he didn't look worried. He didn't look worried about anything at all, which didn't seem fair. Especially when she felt as if she'd been struck by lightning.

She drew herself up to her not inconsiderable height, aware in the same moment that he was very much taller than she was, which didn't help her irritation. It didn't help either that he made not the slightest effort to cover himself or even dress.

'Well,' she said coolly, 'I suggest that you stop trespassing, get dressed, and leave the property. The groundskeeper here isn't very welcoming and he might decide to call the police.'

'Noted,' the man said, dry as dust. 'Are you the owner perhaps?'

'No. I'm the neighbour. I have permission.' Which was true. Her father and the previous owner of Thornhaven—the late Duke of Audley—used to be friends before the Duke had become a recluse, and they'd had an understanding about Willow's childhood rambles. It had suited her father to have her out of the house, because he found her a disruption.

'I see.' The man tilted his head, his eyes gleaming with an oddly wicked light. 'So have you finished looking?'

Willow's blush returned, though she ignored it as fixedly as she'd ignored it the first time. If he could be perfectly calm about this, then so could she.

'Yes, I believe so.' She threw him a disapproving look. 'There's not much to look at after all.'

She expected him to be annoyed or even a little chagrined. He was not.

Instead, he laughed, and the sound hit her like a shock, wrapping around her, deep and dark as melted chocolate. And all she could think was that she'd never heard anyone laugh like that. In fact, it had been a long time since she'd heard anyone laugh at all.

'Far be it from me to disagree,' he said, 'but the blush in your cheeks would seem to indicate otherwise.'

Oh, yes, he's very dangerous.

That laugh of his was still resounding through her entire body, like she was a tuning fork he'd just struck, and she couldn't understand why. She couldn't understand her response to him at all. She only knew that some instinct inside her was urging her to get away from him and as quickly as possible.

However, Willow had given up listening to her instincts, because they were always wrong. And besides, running away would be to acknowledge that this man had got to her in some way, and she could never allow that.

'The blush in my cheeks has more to do with being suddenly accosted by a naked stranger than anything else,' she said. 'You could put on your shorts, you know.'

He raised one straight dark brow. 'You could also turn around.'

Willow ignored the burning in her cheeks. 'It's a bit late for that now, isn't it?'

'Indeed.' The glitter of amusement in his eyes changed, shifting into something else, something more intense. 'In that case you won't mind if I take my time about it.' He tilted his head again and, though his gaze didn't move from her face, she felt as if he'd scanned every inch of her body. 'Feel free to resume blackberry picking. Or you could stay and watch me dress. Either isn't a problem for me.'

She opened her mouth to tell him that she certainly wouldn't be staying, but he didn't wait for her to respond, instead turning and going over to where a pair of black running shorts and expensive-looking running shoes sat. Then he began to dress in an unhurried fashion.

His movements had an athletic grace to them that held her oddly mesmerised and she realised after a couple of moments that, far from resuming her blackberry picking as she'd fully intended, she was in fact standing there doing exactly the opposite.

This was ridiculous.

'I'm going now,' she announced, both to herself and to him.

He didn't respond, bending to tie the laces of his running shoes, black hair gleaming in the sun.

Yet her feet wouldn't move. It was as if her body had a mind of its own and what it wanted was to stay near him, which made no sense whatsoever. She'd had a couple of crushes on boys back in high school, but not since. She didn't have either the time or the inclination for such things, not when her primary focus was looking after her father and earning enough money to cover their expenses. That was far more important than mooning over some man, so why she was still here, fascinated by this particular man, she had no idea.

He rose again, his T-shirt still in one hand. He made no

move to put it on and when he turned to face her, his incredible golden body still mostly on show, he didn't smile.

And all of a sudden Willow was certain that the danger she'd sensed from him before was about to make itself known and bizarrely, instead of fear, a sensation that felt a lot like excitement curled through her.

You know this is wrong. Walk away.

But the air between them was thickening with the strangest kind of tension. Hot and electric, like the atmosphere just before a summer storm.

She needed to leave, get away from him and his disturbing presence. Get away from the rush of what should not be excitement that crowded in her throat and from the fluttering in her stomach that felt like the wings of a thousand butterflies all beating at once. Get away from this physical response that she knew was wrong and bad for her, yet could not ignore, no matter how hard she tried.

But she didn't move. She stayed exactly where she was.

He started towards her like a great panther stalking its prey, moving with purpose, approaching her without any hesitation, coming so close that she could see drops of water glistening on his skin where he hadn't finished drying himself. She could smell, too, the fresh scent of the lake on him, undercut with something warmer, spicier and deeply masculine.

Her breath caught. Did men always smell this good or was it just him?

He was so tall she had to tilt her head back to look at him, which she couldn't recall ever having to do with anyone before.

'Look at you.' His deep voice was soft and warm with a familiarity that held her rooted to the spot. 'You have leaves in your hair.' He reached up and she was powerless to stop him as he casually extracted something from the tangle down her back. 'You also look like Diana, the huntress—did you know that?' He extracted another leaf. 'What were you hunting, Diana? Was it me, hmm? Well, you can stop your hunt now. You've caught me.' Then without any hesitation he slid the fingers of one hand into her hair and closed them into a fist, holding her firmly but very gently, the slight pressure making her tilt her head back ever further.

Willow was absolutely transfixed, her heartbeat so loud she couldn't hear anything else. Couldn't see anything else but the midnight blue of his eyes.

She'd never been touched like that before. Never had a man stand so close she could feel his heat, smell his warm, spicy scent. Never had strong fingers in her hair, carefully securing her.

Hunger rose inside her, forbidden and hot and desperate, though for what she had absolutely no idea.

But he seemed to know. Because he murmured, 'Time to take your trophy, my huntress.' Then leaned down and covered her mouth with his.

Achilles Templeton, Seventh Duke of Audley and known throughout the gossip columns of the world simply as Temple, was used to kissing women he didn't know.

He'd done it many times before, and it was always a pleasure. Women in general were always a pleasure and he made very sure they also thought the same of him. But he generally kept his attentions to socialites and party girls, experienced women who knew exactly who he was and what they were getting themselves into with him.

Not complete strangers wandering his estate grounds with leaves in their hair after being caught spying on him swimming.

In fact, he wasn't sure what had made him kiss this particular stranger.

If she'd caught him while running, he might have blamed it on the adrenaline high. But he hadn't been on an adrenaline high as he'd come out of the water. No, if anything he'd been cold as ice. It was his usual state, his cool control firmly in place, as it had been since he'd arrived at Thornhaven early that morning to tidy up his father's affairs.

But there were a lot of old ghosts in the old manor house and so he'd decided on exercise to get rid of them, going out for a run almost as soon as he'd arrived. But even twenty miles and a swim in Thornhaven's icy lake hadn't done a single thing to shift the dread inside him, the dread that had gripped him the minute he'd crossed the threshold. A dread that even cool distance couldn't shift.

It had only been the woman who'd provided the distraction he'd craved.

He'd caught a glimpse of her bright hair as he'd come out of the water and had been amused at how she'd tried to stay hidden. Because there was no hiding that brilliant shade of gold, not in amongst all that green.

Then all his amusement had vanished as she'd stepped out from behind the trees.

Tall, statuesque, her hair hanging down her back in a tangle all the shades of blonde and tawny, burnt toffee and gold, gilt and even a few streaks of silver. Her face was vivid, her features a mesmerising combination of sensual and girl-next-door, and her eyes were the intense golden brown of fine topaz. What she was wearing, he afterwards couldn't recall.

What he did know was that she was a golden goddess of a woman and the way she was looking at him was as if she'd never seen anything like him in all her life, as if she was dying of heat and thirst, and he was icy cold water...

Women looked at him all the time with varying degrees of desire and avarice, but he couldn't remember being looked at with wonder and that had hit him like a punch to the gut.

It had melted the dread clean away.

He'd only meant to take the leaves out of her hair. At least, that was what he'd told himself as he'd stridden towards her, the chemistry between them crackling and snapping like fresh green logs on a roaring fire.

He hadn't meant to slide his fingers into that glorious tangle of hair. He hadn't meant to bend his head and cover that beautiful mouth with his.

By rights, she should have slapped his face and called the police. But she hadn't.

She hadn't even moved. She'd just looked up at him, a hunger burning in her eyes and a question she probably didn't even know she was asking.

So he'd given her the answer. Without a single thought.

Her mouth was warm under his, but he could feel her tension. Could sense her shock. So he remained still, his lips gently resting on hers, his fingers curled around the silky mass of her hair. Waiting for her to either push him away or take it deeper.

A shudder went through her, as if she'd been fighting some internal battle and a part of her had surrendered. And her mouth softened under his, opening to let him in.

His fingers tightened in her hair as he tasted the tartness of blackberries and then something sweeter, like honey. Desire reached up inside him, gripping him by the throat, and he'd deepened the kiss before he was even conscious of doing so, exploring her mouth, chasing that delicious sweet yet tart taste.

She made a soft sound and he felt her fingers brush lightly, hesitantly over his chest. It felt as if a star had fallen and come to rest on his skin.

Theos, it burned. The touch centred him, grounded him, got rid of the creeping sense of unreality that coming back to Thornhaven always seemed to inspire in him. The feeling of fading into nothing, becoming a ghost…

Suddenly the warm touch of her hand changed and it was no longer resting on his chest but pushing hard. Pushing him away.

He didn't want to let her go, because he knew if he did that feeling of fading away would return, but he'd never forced himself on anyone who didn't want him, so he made himself open his hands and let himself be pushed.

The glint in her eyes had gone molten, like liquid gold in the sunlight, and her cheeks were flushed. Her mouth was full and red, and he could see the fast beat of her pulse at the base of her throat.

'I…' she began in that rich, smoky voice, a thread of heat running through it. 'I…don't know… I can't…' She fell silent, breathing fast, staring at him.

Then before he could say anything she abruptly picked up the basket she'd dropped, turned and fled down the path that led around the lake.

Achilles stood very still, fighting the urge to go after her, catch her. Take her down on the forest floor and distract himself, ground himself in her lithe, strong body.

But his urges were always controlled and he didn't like how uncontrolled this one felt. Anyway, he never chased women, not when they came so easily to him, and so he wasn't about to start, no matter how much the idea appealed to him.

The neighbour, she'd said she was. Well, it wouldn't

do to start off his tenure at Thornhaven by distressing the neighbour, now, would it?

He waited, breathing deeply, the hunger receding. He didn't know what he'd been thinking to kiss her like that. Clearly he'd let being back here at his family's estate get to him.

It wouldn't happen again, that was for sure.

He might be famous for his appetites, but his appetites were always controlled. He never let them rule him. He was the one who brought a woman to her knees, never vice versa.

Feeling more like his usual self, Achilles continued with his run back to the manor house.

Maybe he'd call up one of his favourite lovers and invite her to spend a weekend in the wild Yorkshire countryside. She probably wouldn't want to—Jess was a city girl through and through—but she did like having sex with him and that was a considerable inducement.

He was, after all, very, very good at it.

He'd nearly reached the house when his mobile went off. He didn't like to answer it when he was out running, but the sixth sense for trouble that had proved itself useful in his business life kicked in, so he stopped and pulled out his phone, glancing down at the screen.

It was Jane, his very efficient PA. Which meant it was probably something he needed to deal with.

He hit the answer button. 'What is it?'

'There's a problem with the will,' she said crisply, getting straight to the point, which was what he liked about her.

Of course there was a problem with the will. When had his father ever given him anything but problems?

He stared out at the woods and moors that surrounded the manor house. 'Explain.'

'The lawyers have just got back to me. Apparently your ownership of the house is an issue. There are certain… codicils in the will that were overlooked.'

This was not a surprise. Even in death Andrew Templeton was still making sure to torture him.

'What are they?' he asked, part of him knowing already if not what those exact codicils would be, then certainly the intent of them.

'You must be married,' Jane said and then, uncharacteristically, hesitated.

Everything inside Achilles tensed. 'And?' he bit out.

Jane's voice when she spoke was quiet. 'And you must also have a son.'

CHAPTER TWO

A WEEK LATER, Willow was upstairs in her father's office giving it a good dusting. It was a small but cosy space at the back of the house, overlooking the little rose garden that she tried to maintain herself since her father hadn't been able to care for it following his stroke. It didn't look like much of a garden now, as she knew next to nothing about caring for roses. But she couldn't afford to employ a gardener, so it was that or nothing.

The straggly nature of the garden offended her sense of order, so she stopped looking out of the window, paying attention to the already dustless shelves of the office instead. Her father couldn't deal with stairs, meaning he was barely ever in here, which made dusting pointless, but she didn't like to see his office look unused so she kept it clean just in case.

Besides, she liked looking at his collection of books. Not so much his medical textbooks as the ones he had on botany that he kept for interest's sake. The woods outside had always held a fascination for her and so she liked reading about plants, or anything to do with the natural world. She had dreams every so often, of going to university and doing a science degree, studying Biology and Natural Sciences, but of course that was impossible.

Not when she barely earned enough to cover her and her

father's existing expenses and maintenance for the old cottage, let alone for university fees. And then there was the ongoing issue of care for him. She could leave him alone for the day while she worked, but not longer than that.

She definitely wasn't able to leave him while she undertook a degree, though study by distance might be an option. But still there was the issue of fees.

It was a situation that both her and her father were unhappy with, but both of them were trapped in it and there wasn't much to be done.

She couldn't leave him alone. He was her father, and she owed it to him. Not only because he'd had to give up his career as a surgeon after his stroke, but also because he'd brought her up after her mother died, and that hadn't been easy. She'd been a difficult child, hard to manage even for the nannies he'd employed. Eventually he'd been forced to bring her up himself, which had greatly impacted on the career he'd wanted for himself—as he'd never ceased to point out to her.

It wasn't his fault that they had no money and the cottage was falling down around their ears. It wasn't his fault that he was limited in what he could do because she wasn't able to help him physically the way he needed her to.

It wasn't his fault that she'd basically ruined his life.

Willow knew all that. Just as she knew it was her job to fix it.

She frowned ferociously at her duster, her brain sorting through various money-making scenarios.

The extra shifts she'd picked up at the cafe would help, but they weren't a good long-term solution. No, she was going to have to think of something else.

Her phone in her jeans pocket buzzed.

She took it out and glanced at the screen, and saw a text from her father:

Come down to the sitting room.

Since his stroke had left him unable to walk with any ease, he'd taken to texting her when he needed her to do something for him. It was a system that worked very well, except when she was in the middle of doing something and he was impatient. But luckily those instances were few and far between.

Clarence Hall was where he usually was, sitting in his old armchair near the brick fireplace when she got downstairs, his handsome face drooping slightly on one side due to the effects of the stroke. He'd always been a stern, serious man who'd never had much time for humour, and today he seemed even more serious than usual.

'Sit down, Willow,' he said in sententious tones.

Willow checked—surreptitiously, because he hated it when she fussed—that he had what he needed on the table beside his chair, then sat in the armchair opposite. 'What is it, Dad?'

'I have some news.' He pulled at the edge of the checked woollen rug that covered his knees, seemingly agitated, which was very unlike him. 'Something that I haven't told you and should have.'

A curl of foreboding tightened inside her, but she ignored it. If her father hated her fussing, he hated her worrying more. In fact, he hated all excess emotion, and so Willow had spent many years curbing her wayward feelings and getting them under control.

She knew all too well the dangers when she let them run riot.

'That sounds portentous.' With the ease of long practice she schooled her brain into focus, because it tended to go off on tangents when she was supposed to be listening and her father got very annoyed when he thought she wasn't paying attention.

'That's because it is.' Her father gave her his usual repressive stare, as if he expected her to start screaming or weeping or performing any other such unwanted emotional display.

But Willow's last show of anger had been when she was sixteen and she had kept her feelings under perfect control since then, so she simply gave her father the same cool stare back.

He gave an approving nod. 'Well, you recall Audley, don't you? Who died a couple of months ago?'

Audley referred to the Duke of Audley, who owned Thornhaven and with whom her father had once been friends years earlier. He'd been a virtual recluse for nearly as long as Willow had been alive and that, coupled with her father's physical limitations, had meant it was a friendship very much in the past tense even before he'd died.

Reminded suddenly of Thornhaven, Willow caught her breath as yet again the memory of what had happened just over a week ago rushed to fill her head. Of the beautiful man coming out of the lake and of that kiss he'd given her.

Heat crept into her cheeks and she had to pretend she was examining a loose thread on the edge of the sofa cushion to hide it.

The memory of that wretched encounter kept creeping up on her whenever she least expected it, no matter that she'd put the entire incident from her mind the instant she'd fled. And there should be no reason to think of it now. None at all.

Briefly she'd debated contacting the groundskeeper to tell him she'd seen someone trespassing, but then the thought of being questioned about said trespasser made her feel uncomfortable and so she'd dismissed the idea.

If that…person ever trespassed again, the groundskeeper would soon catch him, that was for sure.

'Yes, I remember Audley,' she said, forcing the memory away and trying to bring her attention back to her father. 'I don't think I met him though, did I?'

'No, you were too young. But the Duke and I talked often, or rather we used to. He became a recluse about ten years ago and I didn't see him at all after that.'

'That's probably why I didn't meet him then. Why do you want to know?'

Her father's dark eyes were still sharp and they gave her a very direct look. 'We made a certain…gentleman's agreement one night. It was a long time ago and I forgot about it. Especially when he broke off all contact. However…' Uncharacteristically, her father paused, seeming hesitant. 'I got a letter yesterday from the Duke's office, reminding me of the agreement and asking me to honour it.'

Willow frowned, unsure of where her father was going with this. 'What agreement? Please don't say it concerns money, because you know—'

'It's not about money,' Clarence interrupted, his voice flat.

The foreboding that she'd forced away earlier crept back, though she fought it down. 'Then what is it about?'

Her father's fingers picked at the edge of his blanket, yet more signs of an agitation that wasn't like him at all.

What have you done now?

The foreboding gripped her tighter, even though she hadn't done anything that would cause her father grief, not recently at least.

That kiss maybe?

She swallowed. No, surely not? Who would have told him? No one else had been at the lake, she was sure of it.

And anyway, what did that kiss have to do with the Duke of Audley?

'Audley and I went to university together,' her father said. 'This was before I married, but he'd just come home from Greece with his new wife, and she was pregnant. They knew it was a boy. We were celebrating his impending fatherhood and he suggested that if I was to ever have a daughter, then she could marry his son. I…confess I'd had more than a couple of pints and I was a little worse for wear. I agreed that it was a fine idea and so we shook on it. He never mentioned it again and neither did I, and soon I forgot about it.'

Willow blinked in surprise. She couldn't imagine her father drinking let alone being 'a little worse for wear'. He was famously abstemious and hated rowdiness of any kind. He also wasn't the type to indulge in drunken gentlemen's agreements either.

'I see,' she said, puzzled. 'So why are you mentioning this to me now?'

'Because the Duke of Audley's son, now the *current* Duke of Audley, has asked me to make good on my promise.'

Willow's surprise deepened. An arranged betrothal between the children of two friends lost in the mists of time? The idea was so ridiculous, so utterly preposterous, it had to be a joke. 'Dad, are you sure this isn't a scam? Is the letter legitimate?'

'Yes, of course it's legitimate and I know a scam when I see one.' His mouth thinned. 'The Duke wishes to see you tomorrow night at Thornhaven so he can put his proposal to you.'

She opened her mouth. Shut it again. She didn't know whether to laugh at the insanity of the situation or be outraged by it. But, since she didn't display any extremes of emotion these days, she settled on a tight smile. 'I appreciate the invitation obviously, but he can't possibly think that I'm going to agree to it.'

But Clarence only stared at her. 'He has offered certain…financial incentives.'

Oh. No wonder her father was taking this so seriously.

She was very conscious all of a sudden that her palms were damp and her heartbeat had quickened. 'What kind of financial incentives?' she asked, pleased by how level she sounded.

'I don't know,' her father said, his gaze still sharp and direct. 'His letter was very brief. I assume he'll tell you more when you meet him.'

She stiffened. 'What do you mean, "when"? I'm not going to Thornhaven—'

'I want you to hear him out, Willow,' Clarence said flatly. 'We can't keep going on the way we have.'

'But I've taken on extra shifts—'

'That's not going to help either of us and you know it.' Her father's expression became hard, the way it always did when he thought she was disobeying him. 'The house needs to have money spent on it, or we need to sell it. I've been looking into treatment for myself too. There are a couple of options that would improve my quality of life immensely, but they're expensive. And I'm tired of waiting. This could be the answer, Willow.'

It was true. Depending on what kind of 'financial incentives' the Duke was offering, it could mean the solution to all their difficulties.

And all she'd have to do was marry a complete stranger.

You wanted to fix this. You're the reason you're in this mess in the first place, after all.

That was also true. Her father might have been a world-renowned surgeon if her mother hadn't wanted a baby and hadn't talked her father into it; he hadn't been keen on the idea. And if her mother hadn't then died six months later in a car accident, leaving her grieving father to bring up a child he hadn't wanted in the first place. An overly emotional, stubborn and headstrong child, whom her reserved and self-contained father had no idea what to do with. And whose behaviour had been a contributing factor in the stress that had triggered his stroke.

She swallowed down the guilt, forced it aside along with all the other unwanted emotions that still seethed inside her, no matter how many years she'd spent ignoring them. Once, she'd thought that they'd go away altogether, or at least she wouldn't feel them so very deeply, but that day hadn't come yet.

When she'd been very young and her father's disapproval and cold distance had been too much for her, she'd used to escape into the woods and the Thornhaven estate, where she could shout and sing and even scream to herself and no one would tell her to be quiet or to go away, or that she was a damn nuisance.

But she didn't go into the woods often these days, because these days she was much better at controlling herself. She wasn't that difficult child any more.

'In that case,' she said without inflection, 'Of course I'll see him.'

Her father gave her another of his sharp, assessing looks, as if he'd somehow picked up a note of protest in her tone, though there hadn't been even the faintest hint of one. 'You don't have to marry him, Willow. No one's going to force you. It's not the Middle Ages after all. But the logical thing to do is to get all the information so you can make an informed decision.'

She didn't know how he'd managed to pick up on her reluctance, not when she'd barely acknowledged it herself.

Or perhaps it wasn't reluctance, only surprise due to the unusual nature of the request.

Whatever, her father was right. She needed to gather all the information before making a decision, in which case accepting the Duke's invitation was the logical thing to do.

Really, she was viewing this with far too much emotion, especially when she didn't even know what kind of proposal the Duke was going to put forward.

It clearly wasn't going to be a real marriage, not when they'd never met. Perhaps it was because of some legal difficulty? Not that it mattered. Marriage—whenever she thought of it, which she seldom did—seemed to work well for some people, but it required a certain amount of emotional involvement that she wasn't willing to give.

She would have to inform the Duke of that when they met so he was clear. She certainly wouldn't want to mislead anyone.

'No, you're right,' she said in the same cool tone. 'You can tell the Duke that I'd be happy to accept his invitation.'

Her father was pleased, she could tell, and that gave her a certain satisfaction. And, since she wasn't going to get anything done if she thought about it too much, she put it out of her mind.

At least until the next day rolled around and she couldn't put it out of her mind any longer.

She told herself that she wasn't in the least bit nervous as she surveyed her very meagre wardrobe, trying to decide on what to wear. She never went out anywhere, so she didn't have any nice dresses apart from a summery cotton thing in white. She liked the dress, but putting it on made her feel as though she was making an effort and some stubborn part of her didn't want to be seen to be making an effort.

The same stubborn part of her that had refused to look

up anything about the current Duke of Audley on the web. There was bound to be something about him—some photos at least—to give her an idea about what to expect, but something inside her absolutely refused.

She knew that giving in to her stubborn streak wasn't a good idea, since it had caused her problems in the past, but she rationalised it, by telling herself that she didn't want to go to Thornhaven with any preconceived ideas.

Besides, she'd find out about him soon enough, and there was always the possibility that the whole ridiculous situation was a joke. Or something her father had misunderstood, or some other easily explicable thing that would become apparent the moment she arrived.

It wouldn't have anything to do with her actually marrying some man she'd never met, and a duke at that.

So she didn't make an effort. She wore jeans and a serviceable shirt in plain white and she didn't even touch her very likely out-of-date make-up. She made sure her father had everything he needed for the evening, double-checked his phone was within reach so he could call her if he had to, and then she stepped outside and walked across the lawn to the little path that would take her to Thornhaven.

It was a beautiful evening, the long summer twilight lying over the moors beyond the woods lighting the grey stone of the large, Georgian manor house. Ivy covered the walls, softening the stark, square lines and the austere front entrance.

While Willow loved Thornhaven's grounds—its wild wood and large ornate gardens—she'd never actually been in the house itself.

But she'd always been curious about it. When she'd been much younger and wilder, she'd made up stories in her head about the reclusive Duke who lived there, fairy tales where the Duke became a dark and dangerous prince who was rescued and led to redemption by the girl who lived next door, who was also a princess with super-powers.

Those were ridiculous stories though, and ones she'd left behind long ago.

Now as she approached the front entrance, her footsteps crunching over the gravel of the driveway, she wasn't thinking about fairy tales, but why the old Duke had been a recluse. And why his son hadn't visited him. Why that son had been in touch with her father to call in this ridiculous gentleman's agreement. Not to mention why he hadn't contacted her directly.

Nerves fluttered inside her as she stopped in front of the big front door and pressed an incongruously modern-looking button for the doorbell set in the door frame.

The door was immediately opened by a slightly cadaverous-looking man who was clearly one of the Duke's staff. He greeted her, requested that she follow him, then, without waiting for a response, stalked off, leaving Willow no choice but to do what he said.

She wasn't given time to look around, though she caught a glimpse of high ceilings and ornate plasterwork, and paintings in heavy gilded frames. The floor was worn parquet and her footsteps scuffed as she hurried after the staff member who was obviously doing butler duties.

He opened a door to her left and ushered her into a very comfortable sitting room with a huge fireplace down one end, where a collection of couches and armchairs were arranged in front of it. Bookshelves stood against the white panelled walls, piled high and untidily with vast amounts of books. There were occasional tables scattered about and littered with various knickknacks, piles of papers, more abandoned books, plus a few cups and saucers. Old silk rugs covered the floor, softening the stark feel of the place, but nothing could mask the faint smell of must and

damp. The scent of an old, neglected house that had been
shut up and abandoned for far too long.

Despite that, the sitting room gave the impression of a
room well lived-in, and it was warm, and Willow found
herself relaxing somewhat.

'The Duke will be with you directly,' the man said and
left without another word, closing the door behind him.

Willow stood a moment, the silence of the house settling around her. Out of the corner of her eye she spotted
a small painting near the fire that looked suspiciously like
a Degas, but surely couldn't have been. And she was just
starting towards it to have a closer look, when she heard
the door open again behind her, then close just as quietly.

And all the hairs on the back of her neck lifted in a kind
of primitive awareness.

'Hello Diana,' a deep, rich and very familiar male voice
said.

Willow Hall, daughter of his father's old friend Clarence
Hall, stood near the fireplace with her back to him, her
hair flowing down her spine just as wild and glorious as
it had it been beside the lake the week before.

Though this time there were less leaves in it.

Achilles waited, anticipation gathering tightly inside
him.

After Jane had informed him of the will bombshell, he'd
spent an intense and very expensive couple of days with
his legal team examining every inch of the document and
its codicils, trying to find any loopholes. But there were
none. His father had left nothing to chance. The Thornhaven estate could only legally be owned by him if he
married and had a son.

Really, he should have expected more hoops to jump
through, but he'd thought his father would have long since

forgotten his existence, since Achilles had purposely forgotten his. A stupid thought, clearly. Or perhaps his father expected him to be grateful?

Regardless, he'd spent the past fifteen years of his life making sure the world and everyone in it knew that Achilles Templeton was his own man and had nothing to do with his historic lineage. That he was vastly successful and a force to be reckoned with, in his own right.

He'd built a billion-dollar high-risk venture-capital firm from nothing, using only his excellent brain and his business skills and, not only that, but was the scourge of the elite party circuit as well. He worked hard, played harder, and if his life was one of excess, it was an excess he'd earned.

And if he took a great amount of satisfaction that the name 'Templeton' had become synonymous with a certain dissolute lifestyle, then what of it? Achilles didn't care. His father certainly wouldn't, because his father had never cared what Achilles did.

But apparently his father had cared. In the last few years of his life he'd somehow remembered he had a son and that said son was going to inherit the title when he died, so naturally enough, in a last, spiteful gesture, old Andrew Templeton had made sure that inheritance was as difficult for Achilles to get his hands on as possible.

Because of course, in his father's eyes, it wasn't Achilles' inheritance at all.

It was his brother's. Who'd died years ago.

Perhaps the old man was expecting Achilles to give up and let him have the last laugh. Achilles certainly didn't need the money or the title, or the austere, gloomy manor house that went with it. He'd bought property in Greece, his mother's country, and spent most of his time going from one country to another, following his business interests and the parties that went along with them, and certainly didn't have any ties to his father's country. He had no loyalty to the title, felt no need to settle down and continue the bloodline. Domestic bliss was the last thing he wanted. And there was a comfortable, reassuring emptiness in his heart where sensations of an emotional nature should have been, and weren't, that he was in no hurry to fill.

Yet the moment Achilles heard about the will's requirements, it was as if someone had flicked a switch on inside him. That emptiness in his heart had rippled and shifted, currents moving inside him, and he realised that yes, he in fact *did* care about this. And no, his father would *not* have the last laugh.

The house and the title were his and he would have both, and if his father thought that marriage and fatherhood would be enough to put him off, the old bastard was wrong.

Then after the codicil had been discovered, his lawyers had found something else in amongst his father's documents.

Written down on a very old piece of paper and signed by both parties was an agreement that promised the Seventh Duke of Audley, one year and two months old at the time, to the yet-to-be-born oldest daughter of Dr Clarence Hall. The agreement was dated long enough in the past that it was clear the Seventh Duke of Audley was, in fact, Achilles' dead older brother, Ulysses, who'd died of meningitis when he was fifteen.

His older brother who somehow in death was more alive than Achilles had ever been in life.

It was clear from the will that his father hadn't wanted Achilles to inherit everything that should have been Ulysses'. Which meant, of course, that Achilles had to do everything in his power to take what should have been his older brother's and make it his own.

Including Ulysses' intended bride.

His father would have turned in his grave if he knew Achilles was intended to step into precious Ulysses' shoes, but Achilles didn't care. That was what he wanted. The old man had denied him everything as a child and he could pretend that didn't matter to him now, that he was long since over the neglect and pain caused by both his parents. But it did matter. He was over the pain, but maybe the anger was still there.

So he'd got his legal team to look into the document and to research this Clarence Hall, and, sure enough, they'd turned up a daughter. Except she'd been born many years after Ulysses' death and a good ten years after his own birth, too. Clearly his father had forgotten about the agreement and had done nothing about it since, but it appeared that the girl—or rather woman now—lived with her father and had remained unmarried.

Which had been all to the good. And then his team had handed him a photo of Miss Willow Hall, and it had felt as if he'd been struck by lightning.

Because it turned out that the woman he'd kissed by the lake the week before was the same woman.

Which made everything crystallise in his head.

That lovely, lovely woman would be his wife and together they would make the most beautiful child. He would have the inheritance his father had denied him, and she would make it a pleasure to do so.

Ulysses' intended bride would be his, the final repudiation of everything his father stood for.

The old Duke had thought to leave him a curse, but instead he'd given Achilles a gift.

So he took it.

He'd pored over the information his team had provided for him, investigating every aspect of Willow Hall's life.

Which wasn't much. She worked at the cafe in the village while caring for her father, who'd had a stroke nine years earlier. Her finances—because of course he investigated those—were in a terrible state, since she didn't get paid much and obviously couldn't get work elsewhere because of her father's health.

She was in dire straits and, as he was a man who'd built his business empire by taking advantage of every opportunity that came his way, he would take advantage of this one too.

Money would be the lever he'd pull in order to get her to do what he wanted, since money he had in abundance. Sex too was a lever, as he knew after that encounter down by the lake that she wanted him. Not that it would be any hardship; there was nothing he liked more than making a woman burn for him.

No, he'd always come second to the dead brother he'd never met, but he wouldn't any longer. Ulysses was dead, but Achilles wasn't, and he would have what was rightfully his.

Willow had gone very still, like a deer catching a predator's scent.

He'd thought she'd have researched him before she'd arrived the way he had with her, and would already know that he was the man she'd met by the lake. But it was clear from her stiff posture and sudden tension that she hadn't known. Not until he'd spoken.

He stared at her elegant back, conscious of desire stirring to life almost instantly inside him.

Ah yes, he remembered that feeling, not to mention his own uneasiness with the ferocity of it. But he could manage that. It was only physical desire, and he knew, if anyone did, that desire only meant what you wanted it to mean. Which to him was only pleasure, nothing more.

There was nothing emotional about it. Emotions he avoided like the plague.

So he let himself look at her, let the desire rise inside him, because she was tall and sleek, and her figure was accentuated by the plain jeans and white shirt she wore. And her blonde hair was falling down her back in a simple ponytail caught at the nape of her neck, and she was still every bit the wild goddess she'd been in the woods that day.

She would be a perfect wife for him, at least for a time. And the perfect mother for their child. It was as if she'd been intended for him all along, and their intense chemistry only proved it.

'Except your name isn't Diana, is it?' he murmured into the silence. 'It's Willow. Willow Hall.'

She turned around abruptly, her gaze the same brilliant golden brown as he remembered, and just as full of shock.

Then the sexual tension hit, a sharp jolt of electricity that had him catching his breath.

Colour rose into her cheeks, making it clear that she felt it too, though he knew that already. He'd tasted her desire for him along with the tart hint of blackberry.

'You,' she breathed.

Achilles inclined his head. 'Yes. It is indeed. The naked man you kissed beside the lake last week.'

'You're...you're the Duke?'

'Achilles Templeton, Seventh Duke of Audley. My friends call me Temple.' He gazed at her vivid, passionate face. 'But I suppose you're probably wanting to call me "that bastard".'

'That's why you were swimming,' she said, ignoring him. 'You weren't trespassing.'

'No.' He shook his head slowly. 'I was out for a run and decided to cool off in the lake. *My* lake.'

She kept on staring, her eyes wide. Then the shock

drained away and a thousand angry golden sparks glittered suddenly in her gaze. She strode forward, closing the space between them without hesitation until she stood only inches away.

The expression on her face now blazed with outrage and anger. A goddess who'd been wronged and who was now looking to punish some poor worshipper for their transgression.

Theos, but she was magnificent. So tall he barely had to tilt his head to meet her gaze, and her anger had brought the most beautiful flush to her golden skin.

There were very few people who confronted him in this way these days. He covered his single-mindedness and the icy streak of ruthlessness that ran through him with a veneer of dry amusement to put people at ease, which was useful when it came to both business and pleasure. But that veneer was thin. And when people sensed it, they were intimidated.

But she was not intimidated. She was not afraid. She looked at him as if she wanted to strike him for his temerity and he found that he almost wanted her to try. He would enjoy a fight with this woman. Anger was a potent fuel when it came to generating pleasure.

'How dare you?' She sounded shaken and furious, her eyes gone a smoky, molten gold. 'How dare you not even say one single word to me? You should have told me who you were, not let me assume. And how dare you let me come here not knowing—?'

'I didn't *let* you do anything,' he interrupted coolly, though cool was the last thing he felt. 'I assumed that you would have done the most basic internet search. Research, Diana. Isn't that what intelligent people do?'

He knew saying that would be like throwing a lighted

match into a pool of spilled petrol, but he wanted to see her blaze. And she did. She went up like a torch.

He saw the moment her temper snapped, the moment her hand lifted, and so he was ready, grabbing her wrist calmly before her palm could connect with his cheek, the sound of his heartbeat roaring in his head.

You fool. What do you think you're doing, provoking her like this?

Maybe he was a fool. But now her skin was warm against his fingertips and her furious golden gaze was on his, staring right at him. And he realised he'd never felt more alive than he did in this moment. In this old house he hated, that somehow still managed to make him feel like a ghost in the walls, even all these years later.

A taut, crackling second passed.

Her skin was warm and silky, and he could feel the tension in her arm. Outrage and fury poured off her. She was like the sun during a solar flare, flames leaping in her eyes, a fire burning under her skin.

It made him want to take that fire in his hands and coax it higher, make it burn brighter. Turn it into a bonfire. And only when it was blazing as high as it would go would he step into the flames and have them consume them both.

Careful. She could have you on your knees.

No, she wouldn't. He'd never let anyone have power enough to put him on his knees and he certainly wasn't going to start with this woman, no matter how lovely she was.

In fact, maybe he should prove it. Both to himself and her.

Achilles firmed his grip on her wrist, then slid his other hand around the back of her neck, cupping her nape. Then he pulled her in and took her mouth.

She didn't pull away, didn't protest. A low moan escaped her instead that sounded a lot like relief, as a shudder coursed the length of her body. Her lips parted beneath his. She tasted of melted honey and wild heat, and before he knew what he was doing he'd deepened the kiss, his tongue exploring her mouth, his hand on the back of her neck holding her still.

Dimly, a part of him was appalled, because this wasn't how he'd intended this meeting to go. He was supposed to present her with his proposal, lay out his terms. Give her the details of her financial recompense, offer her some refreshments and then possibly, depending, offer her some sexual inducements as well. Not a full seduction, not yet, but certainly a reminder of their chemistry. Just enough to pique her hunger.

He was not supposed to kiss her again within seconds of being in her presence.

So much for her not having any power over you. You're about to take her right here and now.

The thought registered, a bright shock in his head. No, that was ridiculous. He was the one in control here.

Forcing away his desire, Achilles lifted his head. But he kept his grip on her wrist and his hand on the back of her neck, holding her where he wanted her. Testing his control still further, because obviously he needed the reminder.

Her eyes were molten honey, her mouth full and red. The pulse at the base of her throat raced and the pretty flush that stained her cheeks now extended down her neck and beneath her shirt.

She looked as dazed and as hungry as he felt.

'I would not advise getting close to me again.' He tried to make the warning sound casual and offhand, but his voice was rougher than he wanted it to be. 'Not if you don't want to end this with you on the floor and me inside you.'

She blinked, as if coming back to herself. Then just like

that the hunger in her eyes vanished, the golden flames of her fury flooding back.

This time though she'd learned her lesson, because she jerked herself out of his grip and strode back to the fireplace then stopped, keeping her back to him.

The silence seethed and crackled, the tension drawn so tight it was almost a living presence.

But he had himself well in hand now and he didn't move.

'I apologise,' she said at last, her voice slightly shaky-sounding, her whole figure stiff with tension. 'I shouldn't... have done that.'

An apology? He wasn't expecting that. How...interesting.

Achilles put his hands in his pockets and studied her obdurate back. 'Shouldn't it be me apologising? I'm the one who kissed you. Which I'm not sorry for, by the way.'

'I'm not talking about the k-kiss. I was...going to hit you.'

Ah.

'Yes. I know you were.'

She turned around sharply, and for a second he saw real distress glittering in her eyes. 'I lost my temper and I shouldn't have.'

A slight discomfort twisted in his chest. He didn't like distressing a woman, especially a woman he was attracted to, and, though he didn't concern himself overmuch with other people's feelings, he wasn't a man who got pleasure out of pain.

'It wasn't entirely without provocation,' he allowed.

'But you're right.' She lifted her chin. 'I should have done my research. I should have at least prepared myself by looking up your name and I didn't.'

This was not going the way he had thought it would. He

should have been pleased with her apology and then her admission, yet he felt vaguely…dissatisfied in some way. Almost as if he'd wanted her to fight more.

Not a good idea considering what just nearly happened.

No. Perhaps not.

'So why didn't you?' he asked.

'Because I…didn't want to.' The distress had disappeared, along with her anger, a certain cool dignity gathering about her. 'I'm only here because of that letter you wrote to my father and he thought I should hear you out.' Her gaze narrowed. 'Though I think you should know that I have no intention of marrying you.'

Achilles smiled. Because there were many things she didn't know about him, the most important being that he always got his way.

'Well,' he said mildly. 'Let's see if I can change your mind.'

CHAPTER THREE

HE WAS NOT going to change her mind, Willow had already decided that. There was nothing he could do, nothing he could say.

Not after she'd lost her temper and nearly slapped him.

Not after he'd answered that with a kiss that had made her forget everything, even her own name. A kiss she'd let him take, because she hadn't been able to help herself.

She was a fool. The minute she'd heard him speak, she should have walked out of the room. But she hadn't.

Instead, she'd heard his voice and turned around and seen him, the beautiful man from the lake. And, just like that moment a week earlier, she hadn't been able to move.

He'd been dressed this time, but that in no way had lessened his sheer physical impact. He wore a dark blue business shirt open at the neck that deepened the colour of his eyes and enhanced the breadth of his shoulders, as well as black suit trousers that emphasised his lean waist and powerful thighs.

And the very second he'd locked his intense blue gaze on her an electric pulse of desire had gone through her, shaking her down to her soul. Making her realise that her week of telling herself she'd forgotten all about him was a lie. That the memory of the kiss he'd stolen from her was seared into her brain. And worse: she wanted more.

And just as she was processing all of that, she'd become aware that he'd called her Diana before she'd turned around. Which meant he'd known who she was before she'd arrived.

Willow had thought she had her temper well under control these days. She hadn't lost it in years. But right then her grip on it had faltered and a wave of righteous fury had filled her, partly fuelled by shock at his presence and the fact that he'd known who she was, and partly by the shame of her own physical response.

So she'd stormed up to him, ready to give him a piece of her mind, and then he'd said that thing about intelligent people doing research, sounding so much like her father at his most dismissive that what little grip she had left on her temper failed completely.

Thoughtlessly she'd raised her hand, ready to slap his arrogant, handsome face, to do harm to another person. Then he'd grabbed her wrist and stopped her, kissing her, and all her anger had abruptly found a new path: desire.

She'd let herself get lost in that kiss, let it carry her away. Because for some inexplicable reason the way he held her, contained her, made her feel safe. As if she could rage inside the circle of his arms, push against him, fight him, and he would remain immovable.

She had no idea why she'd felt that way. She only knew that when he'd pulled away, all her anger had come rushing back and she'd had to jerk herself out of his arms and put as much distance between them as she could. Because he was right: getting close to him was dangerous.

You cannot marry him.

No, there was no way. Not when his very presence threatened her hard-won control over herself and her emotions. She couldn't allow herself to go back to the girl she'd been before her father's stroke, angry and stubborn and rebellious. Who made life difficult for everyone around her. Who hurt those she loved.

She trembled as the splinter of an old guilt tugged at her heart, but she forced it away. Forced *all* those terrible, awful emotions away.

She couldn't lose her temper again. She wouldn't.

The Duke was standing in the middle of the room, his hands in his pockets, his head tilted to one side. It was a relaxed, casual pose, and yet the way he looked at her was anything but casual. The deep midnight of his eyes burned and he radiated a subtle, sensual energy that made the air around him crackle.

He looked like a man who'd never heard the word 'no' in all his life.

Unluckily for him, 'no' was the only word she had.

'I'm not going to change my mind.' She clasped her shaking hands together in an effort to still them. 'I'm not marrying you.'

His gaze flickered, his mouth curving slightly, and she had the disturbing thought that far from putting him off, her insistence was only inciting him further.

'But you haven't heard my proposal yet,' he said mildly. 'Isn't that why you're here?'

'I don't need to hear it. I already know that my answer will be no.'

'Of course. But you can hardly tell your father that you heard me out when you haven't, in fact, heard me out.'

Oh, that was right, her father. The money. Treatments…

Willow swallowed, fighting a sudden wave of stupid panic. This was madness. Logic was the answer to this mess, not the wild swing of her emotions. She had to get herself under control and stop listening to her gut.

'Fair enough.' She tried to sound as level as possible. 'Let's hear your proposal, then.'

He didn't say anything though, his gaze holding hers, and she could feel the air between them thicken again, a charge building like static.

Why was it that every time she looked at him, all she could think about was how he tasted? How hot his mouth had been on hers? How wild and hungry for him she was…?

He smiled lazily, as if he could read her every thought. 'Some refreshments first, I think.'

Willow opened her mouth to tell him that she didn't want any refreshments, but he'd already turned to the door, moving over to it with that easy, athletic grace that she found hard not to notice. Pulling it open, he stepped outside for a couple of moments, and she heard him murmur something to someone outside.

Then he returned, shutting the door behind him.

'I was just going to say that I don't want anything,' she said.

'You're assuming the refreshments are for you.' He strolled closer, loose and easy as a panther on the prowl. 'Perhaps they're for me. Perhaps I need some liquid courage in order to ask you to be my wife.'

A man less in need of liquid courage she couldn't imagine.

Her fingers curled into fists at her sides as he came even closer, stalking her, and her heartbeat was rocketing around in her chest like a bird desperate to find its way out of its cage. She was afraid. Of him and what he could unleash in her. What he'd *already* unleashed in her. If he got any closer…

Stop. You're letting your emotions do your thinking for you. Again.

Willow gritted her teeth and ignored her frantic heartbeat, shoved away her fear. She was cool, collected and in control. She was *not* the girl who'd hurt her father. She was the woman who would fix him.

'Your Grace...' she began, pleased with how uninflected her voice was.

'Oh, no, not "Your Grace".' Mercifully he stopped a couple of paces away from her. 'My father liked an honorific, but I'm not one for formality.' His smile reminded her of a very wicked, very hungry wolf. 'As you've probably noticed by now.'

His shirt was open at the neck, exposing the strong, tanned column of his throat, and found herself wondering what his skin would taste like if she kissed him there. And what he would do if she did...

'I don't care what you'd prefer to be called,' she said. 'I'd prefer not to call you anything at all. Just say what you have to say and then I can go home.'

He stared at her a moment longer, like a predator deciding whether or not to pounce, and her pulse started to climb, excitement and a strange, fearful anticipation winding tightly around her.

But just then a knock came on the door, mercifully catching the Duke's attention, and as he turned and moved to open it Willow felt as if she'd earned a reprieve of some kind.

A member of staff came in carrying a tray in one hand and a bottle in the other. He deposited the tray on the coffee table by the couch, put the bottle beside it, then left. The tray contained a selection of cheeses and crackers, two long-stemmed glasses, and a steaming cup of tea.

The Duke moved over to the tray and picked up the tea. 'There is champagne, of course, but I thought you might prefer something a little more calming.' He carried it over to the small table that stood next to the armchair closest to the fireplace and set it down. 'Please. Sit.'

She didn't want to sit. And she didn't want tea. What she wanted was to walk out of the door and flee back to the safety of her home, or anywhere really as long it was away from his disturbing presence. But that would be to admit he affected her, and, since he'd already overwhelmed her control twice already, she decided there would not be a third time.

She was stronger than that.

So she moved over to the armchair and sat down, pointedly ignoring the tea.

He gave her an amused look, as if he'd expected exactly that, then sat down in the armchair opposite, long legs stretched out in front of him.

'So,' he said. 'My proposal. Thornhaven, as you know, is my family estate and, as I'm the only child, it should automatically come to me following my father's death. However, a couple of codicils in his will have come to light and it has become apparent that I can only inherit after two stipulations have been fulfilled. The first being that I must be married.'

Willow studied him. He didn't seem all that cut up about his father's quite recent death, which was puzzling. Perhaps they hadn't got on. 'That seems very…'

'Old-fashioned?' the Duke finished. 'Yes. Remarkably so. My father was a very old-fashioned kind of man, not to mention vindictive. But that's another story.'

It certainly sounded like a story. But not one she was interested in, sadly for him.

'What has this got to do with me marrying you?'

'My personal assistant found a note in my father's papers signed by your father, promising a marriage between the Seventh Duke of Audley and your father's eldest and yet unborn daughter.' He gave her that predator's smile again. 'I am the Seventh Duke of Audley and you, I believe, are your father's eldest daughter.'

Willow smoothed her already smooth jeans then clasped her fidgeting hands in her lap. 'Yes, but my father said it was a gentleman's agreement. A handshake that they both then forgot about.'

'He certainly forgot about the note, yet that is indeed in existence.'

'You think I'm going to agree to marry you because of some note?'

'Of course not.' Blue gleamed from beneath thick black lashes. 'I'm not a fool, Diana.'

Heat rose in her face. She was letting him get to her again, wasn't she?

Glancing away, she found herself staring at the cup full of tea. She could smell its faint, slightly citrusy scent. It looked to be her favourite kind too, Earl Grey with a slice of lemon. 'I'm not sure why you think I'm going to marry you based entirely on some long-forgotten agreement your father had with mine. It's nonsense.'

His laugh was soft and deep and sexy, and she remembered that too. He'd laughed down by the lake and she'd been shocked by it, since she'd never heard such a warm sound. It shocked and transfixed her now.

'You're right,' he said, as if he had no idea the effect his amusement had on her. 'It is nonsense. But I can make it nonsense that is very much worth your while.'

'And how are you going to do that?'

The gleam in his eyes intensified. 'With money, of course.'

'You mean you'll pay me to marry you?'

'Exactly. It's not a love match, obviously. I prefer to think of it as a business arrangement. You allow me to marry you and I pay you for the privilege of having your name on the marriage certificate.'

Loath as she was to admit it, there was a certain cool logic to the idea. And the calm, dispassionate way he talked about it, calling it a 'business arrangement', helped too.

Perhaps there was merit in it. Her father would at last be able to get the help he needed and she would finally be able to go to university.

She met his gaze. 'How much are we talking about here?'

'I take it you're interested?'

'In the money, certainly.' A sudden suspicion gripped her. 'But you knew that, didn't you?'

He didn't even blink. 'Yes, I knew that. *I* did my research.'

She could feel herself flush again, but ignored it. 'Give me a figure.'

He leaned back in his chair in a lazy movement. Giving every impression of being at his leisure, and yet his eyes gleamed hot. 'How much? How does this sound?' And he named a price that stole her breath entirely away.

It was a lot of money. A *lot* of money. Enough for the expensive treatments her father had wanted. Enough for an entirely new house that would enable him to live more independently than he was doing now. And definitely more than enough for her live comfortably while she studied.

'You're joking.' Her voice was breathless with shock.

He didn't seem at all bothered. 'Oh, I assure you I'm not.'

'But that kind of money? Purely to get married?'

'Yes, well, you remember I said that there were two stipulations?'

Willow's gut lurched. 'And what is the other?'

He gazed at her steadily from beneath his lashes, that wicked smile playing around his beautiful mouth. 'I must also have a son.'

Her eyes went wide, her mouth opening slightly.

Poor Diana. This was not at all what she'd been expecting, was it?

Achilles didn't move, keeping his posture relaxed. He would have to go carefully here, because yes, this would be shocking to her. And her instinct would be to refuse. Which meant he'd have to walk a very thin line.

She'd already revealed herself to be passionate and that she had a temper. And he could see, too, a certain stubbornness in the firm line of her jaw and the tilt of her chin. A woman who did not like being told what to do. And really, why should she?

If his research was correct, she'd spent the last nine years caring and providing for her father, which meant that, although she might be relatively young, she had a certain maturity. He could not simply fling some money at her and expect her to fall at his feet. Nor, he suspected, would simple charm work. At least, not to tempt her into motherhood.

He would need a more complex plan.

'So let me get this straight,' she said at last, her voice flat. 'Not only do you want me to marry you, but you want me to have your child too.'

'Yes.'

'That's…madness.'

Achilles spread his hands. 'What can I say? When I told you my father was old-fashioned, I meant it.'

'Why?' She was sitting bolt upright in the armchair, the tea he'd brought her untouched. He hadn't really expected her to drink it, but he had seen her glance longingly at it, and he filed the information away for future reference. 'Why on earth would he make those stipulations?'

'Because he's a vindictive old bastard? Who knows? But I assure you I went over that will with a fine-toothed comb. There are no loopholes.' He could tell her about Ulysses now, but what would be the point? She didn't need to know.

She put her hands on the arm of the chair. 'You can't be serious.'

'Oh, but I am. Deadly serious.' He tilted his head, watching her. 'However, I agree it's a big ask. Hence the amount of money I'm willing to pay in recompense.'

'You can't possibly think I'll agree to it.'

'Actually, people agree to the strangest things when money is involved.' He gave her another smile, non-threatening and pleasant. 'But I can see you're not convinced. Well, that's fine. I thought it wouldn't hurt to try.' Pushing himself out of the armchair, he rose to his feet. 'Don't fret, Diana. I have other options.'

She blinked, clearly surprised. 'So...that's it?'

'What did you expect? That I would march you at gunpoint to the altar? Of course not. That would be far too mediaeval of me. Well, don't let me keep you.' Achilles turned and strolled casually to the door, pulling it open. 'You probably have a lot to do and I don't want to take up any more of your valuable time.'

He'd unbalanced her, that was clear. Which was all part of his plan. If she didn't like being told what to do, he wouldn't tell her. He would coax her into it, seduce her. She was probably wise to a bit of reverse psychology, but he guessed that she wouldn't be able to help questioning him all the same. She needed that money and desperately.

Sure enough, she said, 'But I thought you needed a wife?'

'And I do. Not to mention a son. But as I said, I have a

number of other options.' He raised a brow. 'Did you think you were the only one I was considering?'

Her lovely mouth opened, then shut, a certain amount of bewilderment flickering over her face. 'If you have other options, then why ask me?'

'I told you. The agreement between our fathers. I thought it was polite to ask you first.'

'Polite,' she echoed, as if she didn't understand the word.

'Yes.' He nodded towards the door. 'Please, don't stay any longer than you need to on my account.'

But she was now looking at him fixedly and he felt the kick of satisfaction deep inside. The hook was baited and she'd had a taste of it. All he had to do was reel her in, but again, he'd need to be careful. It wouldn't do to rush this.

'So what exactly are you expecting from a marriage?' she asked. 'Apart from a child?'

He let none of his satisfaction show. Now was the time to lay out what he wanted and there was no point holding back or making it seem less than it was. There was a time for honesty in business and there was a time for subterfuge, and now was the time for honesty.

He didn't want anything to come back to bite him when she finally agreed, because she would agree. Of that he had no doubt.

'If you're thinking it would be marriage in name only then you would be wrong.' He looked straight at her, let her see that he was giving her the pure, unvarnished truth. 'Considering our chemistry, I would very much like to conceive a child naturally. However, until that happens, our lives will remain separate. There is no need for you to live with me, for example. And once the child is born, we can get an amicable divorce and you can go on your way. You'll have access to the child, if you wish, but it will stay with me.' Now was the time to add the sweetener. 'If you agree, I will pay you the amount of money I specified, plus see to any other needs you may have. Your father may continue to live in his home with a caregiver, though I hear there are some excellent treatment facilities in the south of France, which I would be happy to pay for. Certainly the weather there is better.'

At first, he'd considered a marriage in name only and the conception of the child via medical assistance. His father's will hadn't stipulated any other requirements such as living together or being a proper family. He would of course raise the child himself, since there was no way he'd risk the chance of any child of his having the kind of upbringing he'd had.

But all those initial ideas had changed over the course of this meeting, coalescing into a single, bright, shining whole.

He would have her. And why not? He wanted her and she wanted him, which meant the sex would be phenomenal. And it would make conception extremely pleasurable into the bargain. And once that was accomplished, they could go their separate ways. Of course, a child needed their mother—his own mother had left when he was ten and so he knew how that felt—and he wouldn't deny her access if she wanted it.

But it wouldn't be a permanent arrangement between them, not when he had no idea what kind of mother Willow would be. And after his own experiences, the last thing he wanted was to expose a child to a parent who didn't care.

People said that love was infinite, but people were liars. Love had a shelf life. It was limited. And when it ran out, there was no more to be had. Certainly his parents' supply had been exhausted by the time he was born and Willow's could very well be the same.

Regardless, he couldn't risk it, which meant the child would remain with him. Of course, his own heart had been burned out long ago, but he could pretend. He'd certainly make damn sure the child never felt the lack of care and attention. No child of his would ever feel like a ghost.

Yes, it all made perfect sense to him and he would get what he wanted in the end.

He always did.

She blinked and he could see her mind working, going over the possibilities of what he'd said.

He smiled. 'Well, I can see you're not interested, that's clear.'

Her gaze abruptly focused on him. 'You think anyone will be?'

'Oh, I know of many women who will be.' He allowed just a hint of heat into his eyes. 'Like I said, I have many options when it comes to choosing a wife. And some of them wouldn't even require any financial recompense. In fact, for some, just having access to my bed would be more than enough.'

Willow made a sceptical sound, but he could see the blush that tinged her cheeks. She was already imagining herself in his bed, he'd lay money on it.

'However, it's not for you, I can see that,' he murmured, because now that he'd piqued her interest it was time to send her on her way to think about it. 'Your father must be waiting for you. Please don't allow me to keep you.'

She stared at him for a long moment, her eyes narrowing. Some part of her might be aware that he was playing her, but, since he wasn't forcing her into anything, she wouldn't be able to tell how.

But he couldn't force this anyway. It would have to be her choice.

And if she doesn't choose you?

She would choose him. It was inevitable. He'd weighted the dice and they would fall in his favour.

He would make sure of it.

After a second's hesitation, Willow pushed herself out of the armchair and walked hesitantly to the door of the room. He didn't take his eyes off her, watching her the whole way, allowing some of the heat their chemistry generated to flood the space between them in case she needed a reminder that it wasn't only money he could give her.

She paused beside him, no sign of a flush in her cheeks now. Her eyes had lost that smoky, molten look, glittering like hard little jewels. She'd cooled, a volcano gone dormant.

'I'm sorry,' she said, not sounding sorry in the least. 'But I can't give you what you want.'

'I understand. Like I said, I have plenty of options.' He held out his hand to her. 'Thank you for coming.'

After a moment's hesitation, she gave it to him, which was a mistake she'd surely kick herself for later. Because he took it in his and turned it over, laying a kiss in the middle of her palm.

Her breath caught, sparks flickering in her eyes.

So, the volcano wasn't quite as dormant as he thought.

He was tempted to lengthen the moment, intensify it. But everything was so finely balanced that he didn't want to push, and already the kiss might have been a step too far.

So he let go of her hand before she'd even opened her mouth to protest. 'Goodbye, Diana,' he said, and stepped back.

She looked as if she wanted to say something, but then, clearly thinking better of it, she only murmured, 'Goodbye,' and went out.

Achilles closed the door behind her.

And smiled.

CHAPTER FOUR

WILLOW STOOD IN front of the dusty fireplace in the living room, unclasping then re-clasping her hands, trying to stay calm. She hadn't thought this would be so hard, and yet with her father sitting there in his usual chair, the tea she'd made him sitting on the table beside him untouched, that disapproving, cold stare on his face, she found it was more difficult than she'd expected.

She'd just finished telling him about her meeting with the Duke the night before, and what the offer had been. And then how she'd flatly refused, because she'd had to. Of course she had to. Because it wasn't a 'business arrangement' after all. No, the Duke wanted them to conceive his child naturally, and she couldn't do that. She just…couldn't.

Especially not after reading everything that had turned up in the internet search she'd done the night before as soon as she'd got home.

Achilles 'Temple' Templeton, the Seventh Duke of Audley, appeared to be one of the most notorious playboys in Europe, if not the entire world, and had the reputation to prove it. Which, remembering him from the night before, did not surprise her.

That he was also the head of a worldwide, high-risk venture-capital firm did. She knew next to nothing about playboys, but had always assumed that they cared more about parties than they did about business, though it seemed that the Duke of Audley was an exception.

Then again, given his behaviour the night before and what she knew about him now, that shouldn't be a surprise either. He was clearly a man used to negotiation, used to driving a hard bargain, and being utterly ruthless about it. He was certainly a man used to getting his own way.

He'd used those business tactics on her and she'd been well aware of it at the time. Letting her know that she was his first choice, and yet being clear that he had other options. Before putting her off-balance by ending the meeting before she was ready.

A little reverse psychology, of course. If she'd been thinking straight, she would have given him a dose of his own medicine. But she hadn't been thinking straight. She'd been shocked and angry and overwhelmed, and he'd taken advantage of that shamelessly.

It made her want to refuse him out of sheer principle.

But that her father would never understand. She hoped he'd understand her caveats about the 'natural conception' proposal, but, judging from the way he was looking at her, it was clear he didn't understand that either.

'What exactly is the nature of the problem, Willow?' he asked coldly. 'Is it the…physical interaction?'

Heat burned in her cheeks. She didn't want to be having this discussion with her father, but there was no help for it. He'd been in bed by the time she'd got home the night before, which had given her a brief reprieve, but this morning the first thing he'd wanted to know was how it had gone. And now, why she'd refused.

'Dad, please,' she said repressively. 'Do I really need to go into detail?'

But her father's sharp, dark stare was unavoidable.

'You're assigning emotion to what is essentially a bodily function, Willow. There's no need for embarrassment, just as there's no need to make a fuss about it. It's also no reason to refuse his very generous offer.'

Her heart was beating very fast and her palms were sweaty, and she felt the almost-impossible-to-ignore urge to move, to pace up and down, get this agitation out somehow. It reminded her of being a little girl again, full of that insatiable, hungry energy that made it very difficult for her to sit still. That little girl who felt everything so deeply—too deeply. The little girl whose demands used to annoy her father so much he would lock her out of the house for the entire day.

No wonder he was looking at her with such disapproval.

Willow's jaw ached with the effort it took to force away her agitation, to stiffen herself into rigidity so she wouldn't fidget.

It was the Duke's fault, of course. All of this was *his* fault. If he hadn't been the man who'd kissed her beside the lake, the man who'd made her lose her temper and nearly slap him, and who'd kissed her a second time in front of the fireplace in Thornhaven…

If he hadn't been that man, then none of this would have been a problem.

She would have accepted his proposal without if not a second thought, then at least a third thought.

But he was that man and so she couldn't risk it.

It's not him that's the issue. It's you.

Her jaw got even tighter and she was conscious of her father's gaze on her, cold and disapproving. How could she explain to him what the issue was? That she was afraid of being in the Duke's presence because twice now he'd made her forget herself? That even the touch of his hand and a glance from his relentless blue gaze made her feel shaky with anger and desperate with a hunger she didn't understand?

Yes, it was true. It wasn't the Duke himself she was afraid of but of his effect on her. Her reminded her of how she had used to be, wild and uncontained and at the mercy of her own emotions. Of how demanding and difficult she'd been, a howling whirlwind of rage that had culminated in the tantrum that had led to her father collapsing on the floor at her feet as the stroke had taken him.

She didn't want to be that girl again.

'It's not that simple, Dad,' she said flatly, not wanting to go into it.

'Yes, it is,' her father disagreed. 'Be logical for once in your life. The money will enable me to be more independent and you to do whatever you want to do. I don't understand why you're even hesitating.'

No, he didn't understand, as she'd suspected he wouldn't. For her father logic was everything, while emotions were suspect and weren't to be trusted. And he had reason, she knew that. He'd loved her mother passionately and had been devastated by her death, and the only way to ease the pain had been to cut it entirely out of his heart.

So he had.

But he was right, though. Refusing the money that would give them a much better quality of life simply because she was scared of how the Duke made her feel was utterly ridiculous. Her emotional responses were always suspect, so why was she even taking any notice of them?

She let out a breath, rubbed her palms down her jeans, ignoring the old urge to run into the woods the way she had used to as a child.

'He wants a son, Dad,' she said. 'You did hear that, didn't you?'

Clarence shrugged. 'Then give him one. He'd look after

it, you said? If so, then that shouldn't be a problem. It's nothing that people haven't done before. And it's probably better to do it sooner rather than later, when you have a career.'

The offhand way he said it stabbed at something deep inside her. He hadn't wanted her, and he'd told her that on more than one occasion. He'd only agreed to have her because her mother had wanted a baby and he'd loved her mother, not out of any desire for a child himself.

And this would be the same, wouldn't it? She hadn't wanted children, not after her own experience of growing up, and certainly the emotional commitment it took to be a parent wasn't something she could do.

Then again, the Duke had said that the child would stay with him. She wouldn't have to be involved in the process of bringing it up.

History would repeat itself.

A lump rose in her throat. She stared down at the threadbare carpet and forced it away. No, it wouldn't be history repeating itself. It wouldn't be having a child she didn't want for someone else, condemning them to be brought up by a mother who hadn't wanted them in the first place.

The Duke had said he would keep the child and she would have access to it, if she wanted. He was rich. The child would live in luxury and have every opportunity. And he'd no doubt be a much more stable and steady parent than she would ever be. She was, after all, quite volatile and impatient, both of which weren't great traits for a mother.

But would he be able to give a child love?

Good question. The Duke wasn't exactly a family man by all accounts. And yet what was the alternative? If she didn't marry the Duke, her father would be stuck here in this half-life, where he couldn't do the things he wanted because the house couldn't accommodate him. Because she was too physically weak to provide him with the support he needed. And there was the constant struggle for money and all the bills that needed paying that her wages from the cafe barely covered...

If you don't do this, he'll blame you even more than he already does.

The lump in her throat became larger. She'd ruined his life; how could she ruin it any more?

'What if I...want to be in the child's life?' she asked, even though she hadn't meant to.

Her father lifted a shaking hand. Once those hands had been rock steady, able to cut and stitch even the smallest arteries. Now he could barely manage to lift his teacup. 'You won't,' he said tersely. 'Children are hard work.' His hand must have been shaking harder than normal, because although he managed to get it to his mouth for a sip, when he put it back down it clipped the side of the saucer and fell over, spilling hot tea everywhere.

Instantly Willow dashed to the kitchen, grabbing a cloth to mop it up, her father sitting there in stony silence.

His was a cold anger, diamond hard and bright, full of sharp edges that sometimes felt like knives against her skin. She could feel those knives now, cutting into her, leaving her in no doubt as to who he blamed for the spill. Not his shaking hand, but her.

She was the reason he'd lost his career and his health, his independence.

Her and her anger.

You can't refuse the Duke. Not if it means leaving your father like this.

No, it was true. They needed the money too urgently. Her father needed better care and, since she was the reason he was sitting in this chair, his career—his whole life—in ruins, then it made only logical sense for her to be the one to fix it.

But she wasn't going to give the Duke everything. She had to draw the line somewhere to protect herself too.

She would marry him, but she wouldn't sleep with him. And she'd give him the child he wanted, but only via medical assistance. Her father would find her reasoning flawed, but then, her father wasn't the one who had to do this. She did. And she could tell herself all she liked that the Duke didn't affect her, that she was stronger than the chemistry that leapt between them, but twice was enough to tell her what lies those were.

Better to be intelligent about it and nip temptation in the bud before it had a chance to grow.

The Duke would no doubt argue, since he was clearly a man used to getting his own way, but he could find other women for his bed. He didn't need her.

Willow gave her father a last mop up with the cloth and then went back into the kitchen, dumping it in the sink before coming back out again.

'You're right,' she said flatly. 'I'll do it. I'll marry him.'

Her father's expression lost a little of that hard, cold edge. 'I knew you'd come to your senses eventually.' He nodded approvingly. 'Good girl.'

She ignored the little glow in her chest his good opinion always gave her. Cut it away.

She was doing this for duty's sake, nothing more.

Achilles gave her two days. If she hadn't come back to him after that, then he'd have to reassess his plan, but she'd come back to him, he was certain.

The money would make an attractive package, and, though she'd balked at the idea of sleeping with him, he'd seen the hunger in her eyes. Had tasted it too in her kiss.

She was passionate and she wanted him, and if she agreed to his plan he would make sure she wouldn't regret it.

He thought about staying in Yorkshire until she'd made a decision, but he hated being at Thornhaven and, since he never waited on someone else's pleasure, he took a helicopter down to London for a few days, giving his staff strict instructions that, should Willow Hall make contact, he was to be told immediately.

He was in the top-floor meeting room of his building in the City, in the middle of a discussion with some top execs from an Italian tech company, when Jane knocked on the door then put her head around it.

Achilles didn't like to be disturbed or interrupted while he was conducting business, but Jane never did so if it wasn't urgent, so all he did was raise an enquiring eyebrow.

'Sorry to interrupt,' she said briskly, 'but I thought you'd want to know that I have Willow Hall on the line.'

A pulse of the most intense electricity went through him, deep satisfaction following behind it.

Of course she would come back to him. There had never been any doubt.

'Thank you, Jane,' he said calmly, allowing none of that satisfaction to show on his face. Then he looked back at the execs sitting around the meeting-room table. 'Ladies and gentlemen, I'm afraid I have an urgent matter to attend to. I'm sure you won't mind if we adjourn this till tomorrow.'

Naturally, nobody minded. Or if they did, they didn't dare say.

He got Jane to put Willow through to his mobile phone immediately, then turned his chair to face the window, looking out over London shimmering in the summer heat. He waited a moment then said, 'Miss Hall? This is a surprise.'

There was a slight pause.

'Is it?' Her voice, sweet and husky, held a hint of asperity.

'Of course.' He leaned back in his chair. 'You were very clear that you wanted no part of my offer.'

'Yes, about that…' She sounded very cool and yet he could hear the uncertainty beneath it. 'I've had a chance to think about what you offered me a couple of days ago, and on reflection… Well, I might have been a bit too hasty in refusing.'

'I see.' He let no hint of triumph colour his voice. 'Have you had a change of heart, then?'

'Possibly. If your offer is still open, of course.'

He rested one foot on the opposite knee, gazing at the light glittering off the windows of the city below him. 'I have been pursuing other options, as I mentioned in our interview,' he lied smoothly, because it wouldn't do to let her know he'd been doing nothing but waiting for her. 'But I haven't settled on anyone yet, if that's what you're asking.'

'Oh.' Another slight pause before she went on. 'In that case you should know that I've changed my mind. I would like to accept your offer.'

Satisfaction twisted hard in his chest, his smile reflected back from the windows in front of him sharp and white as a tiger's.

So, he would have it. His brother's inheritance. His brother's title and his house, and his wife. Except it wouldn't be his brother's any longer.

It would be his.

Idly, he wondered whether his father was spinning in his grave yet.

'There is just one condition,' Willow said.

For a second, too lost in his own triumph, Achilles didn't hear her.

Then he did.

He frowned. 'A condition?'

'Yes.' Now she was very cool and collected, no trace of uncertainty. 'It's just a small thing.'

Achilles was not in the habit of granting conditions. However, he wasn't an unreasonable man and he knew what he was asking from her was a lot.

'And what thing would that be?' he asked, keeping the question casual.

'That the marriage will be in name only.' Her voice was firm, unwavering. 'And that the child should be conceived with medical assistance.'

Achilles went very still. 'That was not the offer I made.'

'I realise that. However, you did say it was a business arrangement. In which case you should consider this a counter-offer.'

He stared at his own reflection in the windows opposite him, the tiger's smile vanishing, the intensity of his disappointment surprising him.

Did you really expect her to agree to everything?

Yes. Yes, he had. She was passionate and she wanted him, that had been obvious to him the moment he'd first spotted her watching him swimming in the lake.

He didn't think he'd been wrong. He knew when a woman desired him. She'd certainly kissed him as if she was dying for him, and he was certain it hadn't been an act. So what was the problem?

Good question. One you could ask yourself.

Denial had never bothered him before, not that it happened very often, but still. So her refusal shouldn't be an issue. And yet it was. And he had a sneaking suspicion he knew why. That it was about how she'd made him feel out there beside the lake and in the sitting room of Thornhaven, the fire of her passion lighting him up, chasing away the ghosts of his past. Making him feel alive.

And which in turn made him uneasy. He didn't like

acceding her any power and yet there was no denying that she had some. Otherwise why would he be feeling so annoyed about it?

'Can I ask why?' He made sure he sounded as calm and as cool as she did. That he was not disappointed in any way. 'You seemed to enjoy the kisses we shared. Or did I overstep?'

'No,' she said quietly. 'You didn't overstep. And yes, I… enjoyed them. But you're a stranger to me. And I'm afraid I don't know you well enough to sleep with you.'

'You don't have to know anyone well in order to sleep with them, Diana,' he said before he could stop himself. 'In fact, sometimes it's better if you don't.'

'That might be the way you do things, but it's not the way I do them. I don't sleep with people I don't know.'

Annoyance sank claws into him, but he fought it down, because that wasn't going to help. No, it wasn't about her or what she gave him, it was about what she represented.

If he didn't claim her as his wife in the most basic way, then she could hardly be his, could she? Then again, in order for her to be his, he only needed to have one night with her. They didn't have to keep sleeping together.

He stayed silent a moment, turning the thought over in his head.

She was clearly a woman who knew her own mind and would not be pushed. In which case he wouldn't push.

'Very well,' he said coolly. 'So, how did you imagine this business arrangement would progress?'

'Obviously to where we'd lead separate lives. I'll live at the cottage and you can live…wherever you like.' She paused briefly. 'I won't expect you to be faithful. As long as you're discreet, I'm sure it won't be a problem for you to take lovers.'

Part of him was outraged that she'd somehow managed to take control and start offering conditions as if the whole thing had been her idea, while another part of him was amused and not a little admiring of her audacity, not to mention her intelligence.

'Discreet?' he couldn't help saying. 'You did do your research about me, didn't you?'

'Yes, I'm aware of your reputation. But I'm sure that will change once you have a family to consider.'

He nearly laughed at her cool certainty that he'd do exactly what she asked, despite the fact that it was something he'd already decided to do himself.

'Of course,' he murmured. 'And I'm sure you will do the same when it comes to lovers.'

'I will not be having lovers,' she said crisply. 'I'll be too busy attending university. But, as I said, if you want them then I won't mind.'

University, hmm? Interesting.

'That's very gracious of you,' he drawled. 'But somehow I fail to see how a woman as passionate as yourself can go years without having sex at least once. Or are you planning on taking your vows?'

'That's really none of your business. But I've managed very well so far and I don't see that changing any time soon.'

Surprise rippled through him, though, on reflection, it shouldn't. 'You're a virgin?'

'Well… I… I mean… I don't think…' She stopped, sounding flustered. 'So? What if I am? It doesn't matter anyway.'

It shouldn't matter. He preferred not to deal with virgins. He preferred women who knew what they were doing.

Yet somehow it did matter.

She will be completely yours.

That thought made the blood pump hard in his veins,

a primitive, almost Neanderthal reaction. But it was true. She would be his in a way that Thornhaven would never be. That the title would never be. Because they were all things that Ulysses had once had.

But Ulysses had never had her.

Achilles didn't think. The idea was already in his head and so he said, 'In that case, I have a condition to your condition.'

There was a small silence.

'Oh?' She sounded wary now. 'What condition?'

The tiger's smile was back, the reflection in the mirror looking hungry. He wanted this and he would have it. He was *owed*. For all the years of neglect. For all the years of feeling as if he was the ghost, not his brother. For all the years of anguish, trying so very hard to be the boy his parents had lost so they would love him too.

Never realising that they had had no love left to give him.

'I want a wedding night,' he said in a voice that didn't sound like his. That wasn't either lazy or seductive. That was stripped to bare bones.

'Excuse me?'

She didn't sound quite so cool now and that was just as well. Time she learned that this was his show, not hers.

'I think you heard me.' He swung the chair gently back and forth on its pivot. 'I am happy for you to have a separate life and do whatever you choose. Go to university, see whomever you want, or not, as the case may be. But I want a wedding night.'

'Why?' Her voice was sharp. 'If it's just sex you want you can get that from any woman.'

It was true, he could. But it wasn't just sex that he wanted.

It was sex with her. With the woman who should have been his brother's.

'But it's not just sex that I want, Diana.' He couldn't give her the whole story, but he could give her some of it. It would admit her some power, yet he knew, as he had back at Thornhaven, that now was the time for honesty. And that he wouldn't get what he wanted unless he gave it to her. 'I want sex with *you*.'

'Me?' This time she sounded shocked. 'But... I...why should that matter?'

'You have passion. And I am a connoisseur of passion. I want yours and I think that perhaps you want mine too.'

She said nothing.

And suddenly he found himself on the edge of his seat, tension gripping him, every part of him focused on the phone in his hand and on the woman on the other end of the line.

'One night,' he said in that bare-bones voice, all his seductive techniques deserting him, leaving only demand left. 'That's all I will ever ask of you. Just one. And I can tell you this with absolute confidence, that if you want to enjoy your first time with a man then I am the man you should enjoy it with.'

More silence.

'That's the most arrogant thing I've ever heard anyone say,' she said at last.

He wanted to smile, but not because he was amused. 'I have never pretended to be anything other than what I am. And yes, I can be arrogant at times. But if you know my reputation then you will also know that women do not go away from my bed unsatisfied.' He felt himself wound tight as a spring. 'I will make it a night to remember, I promise you.'

Yet more silence, longer this time.

You sound as if you're begging. Since when did you ever beg?

He didn't like that thought. Didn't like that thought at all. It made him feel the way he had with his father, constantly hoping that one day it would happen. That his father would see the son he had right in front of him instead of being obsessed with the one he had lost.

Theos, why had he said anything? Why had he granted her even this modicum of power over him?

Too late to regret it now.

'Just one night?' she said at last. 'One night and that's all?'

He didn't move. 'Yes. One night and that's all.'

The silence this time felt like the longest stretch of time he'd ever experienced.

'All right.' Her voice was breathless. 'You can have a wedding night.'

Then she disconnected the call.

CHAPTER FIVE

THE DUKE MOVED with unsurprising efficiency.

The next day a courier arrived on Willow's doorstep with a thick-looking folder of legal documents that proved to be a contract cementing her agreement to marriage and a child legally. Which stood to reason. This was a business agreement after all.

So she sat down and spent the entire day combing through it, making sure she understood everything. It was clear and unequivocal and there were no loopholes of any kind. The Duke's ruthless business reputation was obviously well earned.

You'll soon find out if his other reputation was also well earned.

The thought wound through her head, the words of the contract blurring in front of her as the memory of the previous night's conversation abruptly hit.

'I want a wedding night.'

Willow's heartbeat sped up, the throb of some deep and inexplicable ache gathering inside her.

She still wasn't sure quite why she'd agreed to a wedding night when she'd been so sure that she wasn't going to sleep with him. Or how she'd somehow let slip that she was a virgin.

The latter, because she'd wanted to shock him maybe. But the former...

He'd told her he wanted her passion, and after that his voice had gone deeper, rough, no longer quite so lazy or seductive. Almost as if he was desperate, which a part of her had liked far too much.

She, the little virgin from Yorkshire, had the world's most notorious playboy begging her for a wedding night.

She'd said yes before she'd thought twice about it.

He wanted her. And more than that, he wanted her passion, and no one had wanted that in so very long. She also couldn't deny that she wanted him in return.

It was probably a mistake, probably a sign of her general lack of control, but surely one night wouldn't hurt? Just one. Her wedding night. And after all, he'd basically insisted. She really couldn't say no, could she?

Dismissing the thoughts of the wedding night, Willow read on, the terms for the child giving her another lurch of doubt. It was strange seeing it in black and white, her agreement to provide him with a son. A big undertaking, especially when she'd never thought about having children herself. And most especially considering the child would live with the Duke and not with her.

Yet, as she'd thought earlier, that would be the best thing for the child. She wasn't motherhood material after all. She could visit though, the Duke had promised her that, and she would. A child should know its mother, even if that mother wasn't a particularly good one.

That all of these were rationalisations she knew deep in her heart, but she decided it was better not to think about them too deeply. The most important thing was that she and her father got the money that the Duke promised them.

Sure enough, after she'd signed the contract and sent it away, the money landed in her bank account. Then a car and a nurse arrived to take her father to a renowned stroke specialist for an assessment and some recommendations for further treatments at her father's preferred facility in the south of France. It was horrifically expensive, but the Duke agreed to cover the cost without hesitation and soon arranged for her father to travel there after the wedding.

Willow had expected some registry-office ceremony, conducted swiftly and without much fanfare, since it wasn't as if they were making vows of love in front of friends and family. But apparently that was not what the Duke wanted.

A small ceremony with a 'few hundred' of his closest friends was what the Duke wanted, though she wasn't sure why he seemed so set on making a big deal out of it.

He also wanted to discuss it with her, suggesting she join him in London at her earliest convenience. She didn't particularly want to discuss it with him, since she didn't much care about the wedding itself, but, as refusing to go just because she found his presence threatening would be admitting far too much, and her father now had a full-time caregiver, she felt she had no choice but to agree.

And so a few days later she found herself on a helicopter flying south, a building nervousness along with a strange sense of anticipation collecting inside of her.

She tried to ignore both sensations by watching the unrolling green of the countryside below her and attempting to enjoy the novelty of flying, since she'd never been in any kind of aircraft before, let alone a helicopter.

But all too soon they were approaching London and once again she was faced with the reality of having to be in the Duke's disturbing, compelling and dangerous presence. The thought made her heart beat fast and her palms feel sweaty.

The helicopter circled around the City of London before zeroing in on a particular building. The Duke had told her that he'd fly her directly to his office where they could chat in peace and this was clearly it.

Willow gripped tightly to her usual distance as the helicopter came in to land on the building's rooftop helipad, and when she got out she was instantly surrounded by people.

A no-nonsense, businesslike woman who introduced herself as Jane, Temple's PA, whisked her down to the waiting room outside the Duke's office.

It was the most luxurious waiting room Willow had ever seen, with thick, pale, silvery carpet and black leather furniture. Black and white abstract photographs on the walls. Clean and minimalist and looking extraordinarily expensive.

Willow's heart began to beat even faster and she had to resist wiping her palms down on the light summer dress she wore. When she'd put it on in her bedroom earlier she hadn't given it much thought, since she wasn't used to fussing around with her appearance. It had been cool, and that was the extent of her thinking.

Now, in amongst all this sophistication and quiet luxury, about to meet the man who unbalanced her so completely, she felt underdressed and shabby, as though she'd gone to a ball in her nightgown by mistake.

It made her temper shift, the veneer of her thin control cracking, and she had to grit her teeth hard to hold on to it and not let it escape. Because bad things happened when she lost her temper. Very bad things.

Jane led her to the big double doors of the Duke's office and then pushed them open, ushering her inside.

The Duke himself was standing by the floor-to-ceiling windows that looked out over the city. It was the most magnificent view, though it wasn't the view that immediately drew the eye. How could a mere view compete with the man who stood there as if he owned it?

Dressed in a dark charcoal suit that highlighted the width of his powerful shoulders and lean waist, he was a commanding, magnetic presence as he talked on the phone to someone. That deep, rich, melted-chocolate voice filled the room, whispering over her skin and making her shiver. He wasn't speaking English but some language she didn't recognise—Greek maybe?—and the musical sound of it was a delight that held her unexpectedly mesmerised.

She wasn't aware of when Jane backed out silently. She didn't notice the doors shutting behind her. She even forgot about her temper.

All she was aware of was the man by the windows, the taut electricity of his presence surrounding her and stealing all her breath.

Who are you kidding? You couldn't resist a wedding night and you know it. And now you don't have to.

Something inside her gave a strange little twist and then relaxed, as if she'd had her hair in an overly tight bun the whole day and then had let it down.

Perhaps it was being away from the cottage and Yorkshire, away from her father, that was affecting her, because all of a sudden a loose, easy feeling flooded through her, the tension in her muscles gradually unwinding.

She'd agreed to marry him. She'd signed a legally binding contract and there was no escaping it. She'd also agreed to a wedding night, one that he'd argued for, because he'd wanted her. And not just her; he wanted her passion too.

So what was the point in resisting him? What was the point in controlling herself?

Perhaps you should give him a taste of who you really are...

Willow took a silent, shaken breath as the idea took hold, a combination of excitement and trepidation gripping her. And why not? He'd wanted that passion, had told her he couldn't get it from anyone else, and so really she was duty bound to give it to him. Of course, once he found out who she truly was, he'd probably realise, as her father had, that she was too much trouble to bother with. Not that she cared.

She had her university plans and no doubt they'd soon be starting the procedure for having a child. His opinion of her was the least of her worries.

Willow waited for him as he finished up the call and then a silence fell as he slid the phone into his pocket and turned, his midnight-blue eyes meeting hers.

She didn't look away. Couldn't, if truth was told. The sheer masculine beauty of him and his electrifying presence held her hypnotised. The air crackled between them, a shifting, twisting static charge, and her breath stopped in her throat. And for a second she thought he might stride straight across the space between them and take her in his arms. She wouldn't be sorry if he did, not at all.

But, of course, he didn't.

Instead he moved over to the great black slab of a desk that stood near the windows and leaned back against it, folding his arms, studying her.

'You really are quite the virgin sacrifice, aren't you?' he murmured.

For a second, Willow had no idea what he was talking about. Then she realised. 'Oh, you mean the white dress?' She kept her voice as cool as his. 'It was the first thing that came to hand.'

'I see.' His long, beautiful mouth curved. 'It's very appropriate.'

'I didn't wear it because it was appropriate. I wore it because it was too hot for jeans.'

He tilted his head, watching her. 'Is that a fact? Nothing at all to do with me, then?'

'Why would it have anything to do with you?'

'It's a lovely dress.' His smile took on a wicked edge. 'I can see right through it.'

Oh, dear. She hadn't thought of that, because it wasn't something she'd ever thought to check. She wore black trousers and a black T-shirt to work in the cafe, and she made sure they were clean when she dressed, but she'd never thought about whether her dresses were see-through or not.

Her cheeks heated, the spark of her temper igniting, and her instinct was to quell it and force it down. But, since she'd decided to give him a taste of the passion he said he wanted, for the first time in a long time Willow let it burn.

She met his gaze, held it, let him see her annoyance. 'Then perhaps you shouldn't be looking.'

The smile on his face slowly changed, losing its practised wickedness, and then he gave a genuine-sounding laugh. 'You're quite a contrary beast, aren't you, Diana?'

Contrary. Yes, she'd been told that many times, but usually in far more unflattering terms, such as oppositional and demanding, and difficult. And most often accompanied by a cold stare that made her feel small and stupid, as if there was something wrong with her.

But the Duke wasn't looking at her as if there was something wrong with her. He was looking at her as if he found her being contrary utterly delightful. And that didn't make her feel either small or stupid. It made her feel good.

It was an unfamiliar feeling and she didn't quite know

how to deal with it, so she only shrugged. 'I'm not a beast and you can stop calling me Diana. My name is Willow.'

'Willow,' he echoed, as if tasting the sound of it and finding it delicious. 'It's a beautiful name, though you're not at all willow-like if I may say.' His gaze dropped slowly down the line of her figure, taking in every inch of her, a trail of sparks scorching her right through. 'You're far too fiery and strong for that.'

There was no doubt that he thought those were good things and that he liked them very much. It was clear in the heat in his eyes as they met hers.

That unfamiliar feeling in her chest, a kind of warmth, spread outwards, but she still didn't know how to deal with it, so she tried hard to ignore it. 'I'm nothing of the kind,' she said coolly. 'You wanted to discuss the wedding?'

'Straight to the point, aren't we?'

'I have some things I need to get back to.' Which was a lie. She had nothing at all to get back to.

He gave her a very direct look, which she met head-on, challenging him to call her out on it. And for a second she thought he might, but he only gestured to the long, low, black leather couch that stood near the desk. 'Please, take a seat.'

Willow moved over to the couch and sat, smoothing her dress over her knees.

'Would you care for coffee or tea?' he asked, all politeness. 'Or maybe even something a little more exciting? Champagne perhaps to toast our engagement?'

She blinked in surprise. 'Engagement?'

'Well, I can hardly marry you without an engagement,' he said as if it were self-evident. 'That wouldn't be proper at all.'

'I didn't think you cared about propriety.'

'Perhaps I've changed my mind.' He gave her a look from

beneath his thick black lashes. 'Perhaps I do care about it after all, especially now I've decided to settle down.'

Willow found the conversation oddly discomforting, though she didn't know why. 'But you're not really settling down, are you?' she pointed out. 'You're paying me to be a wife and to have your child.'

His mouth curved in one of those sensual smiles that she was starting to see were quite practised. 'Yes, when you put it like that, it is rather cold and clinical. Perhaps that's why I'd like an engagement and a proper wedding. In a church. Perhaps I'd like people to think that it's real.'

She stared at him, trying to read the expression on his beautiful face. Trying to understand why he wanted all these things. Because they hadn't been in the contract she'd signed.

Why do you even care? What does it matter to you?

That was a good point. She didn't care if he wanted an engagement, or if he wanted a wedding in a church. Those things had no particular meaning for her. She was never going to have them anyway, since a real family and marriage wasn't on the cards.

So why the thought of them made something inside her ache a little she had no idea.

'Fine,' she said levelly, trying to sound disinterested. 'It doesn't matter to me.'

He frowned. 'You're very biddable all of a sudden, Diana. Why is that?'

A little shock went through her that he'd noticed. Then again, those eyes of his seemed to miss nothing.

She smoothed her dress again, not wanting to admit that the thought of an engagement and wedding made her uneasy, because she couldn't explain it even to herself, let alone him. 'Because you're clearly going to do whatever you want to do. Me arguing with you isn't going to change your mind.'

He lifted a brow. 'Do you want an engagement and wedding?'

'Surely it doesn't matter what I want?'

'Why would it not?'

She glared at him. 'Stop answering questions with questions.'

That much warmer, more genuine smile flickered around his mouth again. 'You're not at all afraid of me, are you?'

'Why would I be afraid of you?'

'Now who's answering questions with questions?'

She felt breathless all of a sudden, that smile touching something deep inside her. Something hot that she'd covered in a cold, hard shell.

'No,' she said. 'I'm not afraid of you.'

And his smile widened, as if that was something he liked, too. 'You should be, you know. I'm very rich and very powerful.' His voice deepened, taking on a sensual edge. 'And I'm also extremely notorious when it comes to women.'

Yes, he was. She'd read everything about him that she could lay her hands on. Research, of course. It wasn't at all because she found him unexpectedly fascinating.

'So I've heard.' She clasped her hands together to stop them from fidgeting. 'Again, nothing that would make me afraid of you. I do wonder, though, why you haven't answered my question. You're marrying because of a will, so why do you need a wedding when a quick ceremony in a register office would do the trick?'

'An interesting question.' He was very still, his lean, powerful body perfectly at rest, which somehow relaxed her, easing her urge to fidget. 'The fact is, I'm a very busy man. I work hard and then I play hard, and in the past that hasn't left a lot of time for other things. I hadn't thought a family would be important to me, but I admit that after my father died, that changed. I am the only Templeton left, and so I want a son to carry on after me.' Something she didn't understand shifted in his eyes. 'Would you really blame me if I wanted wedding pictures of his parents to show him when he got older?'

It certainly sounded good. Almost as if he believed every word he'd said. And yet she couldn't quite shake the feeling that he was spinning her a story. Not lying, she didn't think. More as if he wasn't giving her the whole truth.

'Wedding pictures?' She didn't bother to hide her disbelief. 'This is really all about wedding pictures?'

His expression was guileless. 'Oh, don't get me wrong. I wouldn't mind announcing to the world that I'm getting married also. It's not real if it isn't talked about on the internet somewhere, after all.'

Now, *that* he meant, she could tell.

'But it's not real,' she felt compelled to point out. 'I'm not marrying you because I'm in love with you.'

'Why should love make a difference?' There was an odd note in his voice that she couldn't quite interpret. 'But that doesn't matter anyway. In the eyes of the law our marriage will be as real as it gets, and the wedding is just the icing on the cake.' He gave her a sidelong look. 'Don't you want to wear a pretty dress?'

She ignored the question, studying the perfect lines of his face, trying to read the undercurrents in his voice and interpret the shadows shifting in his blue eyes. She wasn't sure why she found his motivations so interesting. Perhaps it was because they weren't obvious. Certainly he was turning out to be more complicated than she had thought, and she wasn't sure if that was a good thing or not. Probably not.

She didn't want to find him complicated. She didn't want him to be interesting.

She didn't want to be drawn to the still way he stood or feel warmth when he smiled at her.

Physical attraction she could deal with. Anything else, no.

'Keep staring at me, Diana,' he said softly, eyes gleaming. 'I like it very much.'

Her breath caught, yet another blush rising in her cheeks. She hadn't meant to be quite so obvious with her study, but then again, he was far too observant.

He gave another soft laugh, and before she could say anything he pushed himself abruptly away from his desk. 'Let me find Jane and we'll get some champagne in here. I want to do this properly.'

Willow wanted to tell him that there was no need, but he'd already pulled open the door and given some instructions to his PA. And then five minutes later, Jane bustled in with a bottle of what was clearly outrageously priced champagne and a couple of glasses on a silver tray. She deposited them on the table in front of Willow then bustled out again.

The Duke went around the side of the desk, pulled open a drawer, retrieved something from it then came over to where Willow sat.

The look in his eyes was hot, a blue flame that made it impossible for her to think.

Then, much to her shock, he dropped down onto one knee in a sudden, graceful movement. 'Don't look so surprised.' His smile was wicked and slightly mischievous, wholly seductive. 'I told you I wanted to do this properly.' He held out his hand, opening his fingers to reveal a small box of deep blue velvet. 'Willow Hall,' he said formally, 'will you do me the honour of becoming my wife?'

Willow stared at him uncertainly and a bit of him was pleased at how he'd managed to surprise her, disturb that cool, sharp front that was so at odds with the fire he could sense burning inside her.

And it was still there, that fire. He hadn't imagined it. Hadn't built it up over the space of the time since he'd seen her face-to-face into something it wasn't.

A contrary beast, he'd called her, and she was. Even now, sitting there on the couch in the most delicious white dress, she looked cool and collected, and totally self-contained.

Yet that dress was floaty and sheer, had a few little buttons at the front that were undone, revealing her light gold skin, and he could see the faint shadows of her knickers and bra beneath the fabric. And there was a certain energy to her, something kinetic, as if she could hardly keep from pushing herself off the couch and start pacing around.

He found the contrasts in her unexpectedly fascinating. How cool and still on the surface she was and yet how fiery and restless she was underneath.

He'd been a quiet, studious child himself, back before he'd realised how little that had mattered to his father, and some lost part of him was inexplicably drawn to her restlessness. It was bright as a star, flickering like a firefly, and he wanted to put out his hand to try and catch it.

In fact, Miss Willow Hall herself was proving to be a whole lot more intriguing and desirable to him than he'd first thought, which was not a bad thing.

The moment she'd walked into his office, oblivious to how lovely she was, her beautiful golden hair still in that wild ponytail that fell down her back, all he could think about was what she'd promised him—a wedding night. And as her gaze had met his, he'd known that she was thinking the same thing.

He'd been very tempted to throw caution to the wind and seduce her right here, right now. But he'd decided even before she'd arrived that he wasn't going to touch her again before their marriage. He was going to do everything in the proper order. Not quite what he was used to, yet anticipation wouldn't hurt and would make the night they eventually shared even more spectacular.

She stared at him and then at the little box in his hand, then reached out for it.

But he pulled it away before she could take it. 'Uh-huh. You have to give me your answer first.' He was teasing, of course, yet only for the pleasure of seeing the heat of her temper flare.

Obligingly it did, those golden sparks flickering in her eyes, which he found deeply satisfying. 'Of course I'm going to marry you. I've already told you I will. I even signed that wretched contract.'

'No, "I even signed that wretched contract" is not the right answer. Say "Yes, I'd love to be your wife, Temple".'

Her straight golden brows drew down. 'Why "Temple"? Is it just easier?'

It was not the question he'd expected to be asked, not at this important moment.

'No,' he said, a little irritation creeping into his tone, before trotting out his standard reply. 'Achilles has a weakness. I do not.'

'I see.' Her gaze was very sharp all of a sudden, making him feel as if she'd somehow managed to prise off a piece of his armour to reveal the skin beneath it.

It was not a comfortable feeling and he wasn't sure how

she'd managed it. He was usually the one who discomfited people, not the other way around.

'Well?' he demanded when she didn't say anything more. 'I can wait here all day if I have to.'

He didn't actually want to remain on one knee in front of her all day, and the fact that he'd even done it at all was something he didn't want to think about. But he wasn't a man who backed down, and she needed to understand that.

For a long moment they simply stared at each other and he thought that perhaps he *would* have to be stuck here all day, when she suddenly said, 'In that case I'd love to be your wife… Achilles.'

He didn't miss the deliberate use of his name. Just as he didn't miss the jolt of electricity that arrowed down his spine as she said it. The name he hated, because, as his mother had often told him, it was Ulysses' second name and so they'd given it to him, another burden he had to carry.

But it didn't sound like a burden when Willow said it. Instead it sounded sensual and sexy, and it made him hard.

You're letting her get to you.

No, he wasn't. So he liked her saying his name? It didn't mean anything. And if it made him hard, then again, what of it? It was only going to make their wedding night even better.

He inclined his head in acknowledgement of his name, but gave her no other sign of how it affected him, because that was another bit of power he didn't want to give her.

Instead he allowed her to take the box out of his hand, waiting as she lifted the lid.

A ring sat in the midnight-blue velvet. A beautiful, clear yellow diamond in a heavy white gold band set with tiny smaller white diamonds.

He watched her face as she stared at the ring, conscious

of how the satisfaction inside him became heavier, settling down to lie deep in his bones, becoming a certainty.

The diamond was the exact shade of her eyes, just as he knew it would be.

The ring destined for his brother's bride.

'This is…beautiful,' she said huskily. 'I can't—'

'You can.' Because he would have this. 'It was my mother's engagement ring, and my grandmother's before her. All Audley brides wear it.'

'I…'

He took the box from her, discarding it on the floor as he extracted the ring. Then he reached for her hand and gently slid it onto her finger.

It fitted perfectly.

Her skin was warm on his and when she looked at him he felt another electric shock of desire go through him, along with an intense feeling of possession. As if he'd known all along, even from the moment he'd seen her by the lake, that this woman was destined to be his.

Perhaps it should have disturbed him, because he'd never once felt the slightest twinge of possessiveness over a woman before. He simply hadn't cared enough.

But he wasn't disturbed. It felt right. It felt as if it was meant to be.

Colour rose in her cheeks, a deep and pretty pink, as if she knew exactly what he was thinking. And he thought that might make her jerk her hand from his and walk straight out of his office.

But she didn't. Instead her gaze dropped to his mouth, and suddenly everything slowed down, time becoming thick and syrupy as honey.

Her gaze flicked up to hold his, golden as the diamond on her finger and just as full of glitter and sparks. Then she leaned forward and lightly, so lightly, as if testing, brushed her mouth over his.

He didn't move, didn't breathe. Her kiss went through him like light, like the dawn breaking over frozen-solid ground. A warm ray of sun, heating him up, melting him. And he almost moved. Almost reached for her and pulled her to the floor of his office, almost gave in to his own hunger, the depth of which he hadn't guessed at till now.

Almost.

But there was still a part of him that wouldn't countenance such a loss of control and so he remained on one knee, frozen where he was on the floor, his hands curled into fists as her lips brushed over his and then away.

Her gaze was molten, smoky with heat, and he thought that perhaps the kiss had pushed her to the edge, just as it had pushed him. And that maybe she wanted him to keep on pushing, because there was a distinct challenge in her eyes.

But no, he wasn't going to let her goad him into it. A wedding night he'd demanded and a wedding night he'd have. And that would happen when *he* wanted it to happen, not her.

So Achilles smiled at her, letting her know that he could see what she was trying to do, and that it wouldn't work. Then he rose to his feet and moved unhurriedly over to the coffee table where the champagne and glasses were.

She didn't say anything. Yet he could feel the pressure of her gaze on his back.

Had he made her hungrier? Made her mad? He hoped so. That fire in her burned so bright and he wanted it so very badly.

He grabbed the champagne bottle and popped the cork, forcing aside the desire that gripped him, concentrating instead on the feeling of satisfaction. Everything was going exactly according to his plan and that gave him an inordinate amount of pleasure.

Pouring out a couple of glasses, he then carried them over to where Willow sat and handed her one. She gave it a faintly suspicious glance, then took it.

He raised his own glass and tapped it against hers. 'Here's to our marriage.'

She gave a little nod then took a sip of the fizzing liquid. 'So, you wanted to discuss the wedding?'

'Indeed I did. I see no point in waiting, so the ceremony will take place next week at the church in Thornhaven village. Then we will honeymoon in Greece, at my villa on Heiros.'

She blinked. 'Next week?'

'You have a better time?'

'Oh, no, I just didn't expect it to be so soon.' She frowned. 'But...a honeymoon?'

Ah, he might have known he wouldn't be able to slip that one by her. She was too sharp for that.

He shoved one hand in his pocket and sipped at his champagne. 'Of course a honeymoon,' he said casually.

'Why would we need a honeymoon?'

'Don't you want to go to Greece?'

'Stop distracting me. That's not what I asked.'

He didn't particularly want to confess this part of his plan to her, but she would find out soon enough. Because yes, she was far too sharp not to guess his intentions. And it had been something that he'd been considering for the past couple of days as he'd taken charge of the wedding preparations.

'Very well.' He met her gaze head-on. 'I decided on a honeymoon because I fully intend to seduce you into extending our wedding night to at least a week.'

Her eyes widened, and her mouth opened, then shut.

So he went on, 'You want to conceive our child via medical assistance, but if we're going to have one night anyway, then we might as well use that to try for a baby. And if we're going to do that, then why not extend that to a week while we're away?' He smiled. 'It makes perfect logical sense, don't you see?'

At least, it had made perfect logical sense to him. One night wasn't going to be enough, not with the kind of heat they generated between them, and, since they had a child to conceive, they may as well make use of that heat to its fullest extent.

'Yes,' she said at last, her voice more than a touch hoarse. 'I do see.'

It was clear she was shocked and more than a little uneasy, and it made something tighten uncomfortably in his chest. What was it about sex that disturbed her so much? The kisses they'd shared earlier she'd enjoyed, she'd told him as much. And even just now, she'd kissed him and there had been clear desire in her eyes. So it wasn't him.

Had she had a bad experience with someone else, though? Was that why she'd remained a virgin?

Why are you so interested? What does it matter?

Perhaps it didn't matter. After all, they weren't going to stay married long. Yet the tightness in his chest intensified, a surge of something that felt like anger going through him. Whether it mattered or not, he didn't like the thought of her being hurt. He didn't like it at all.

'I won't force you,' he said with quiet emphasis. 'Understand that right now. I would never do that to you or to any woman. If you don't want me, you only need to say.'

More surprise flickered over her face and she looked away, clearly flustered. 'I'm…that's not what…' She trailed off and was silent a moment. Then she said, 'I said I would give you a wedding night and I meant it.'

'But you're reluctant.'

She said nothing, taking another sip of her drink.

'Why?' His own drink was forgotten as interest grabbed onto him. 'Did someone hurt you? Did someone—?'

'No.' The word was sharp. 'No, nothing like that. I just…' She stopped again. 'I haven't felt this way before. About anyone.'

The admission was hesitant and for a second he didn't understand it. 'You mean…desire?'

Slowly, she nodded. 'I haven't met anyone I wanted before. Not like this.' There was a brilliant flash of gold as she glanced at him. 'Not like…you.'

He didn't know why that hit him the way it did, like a short, sharp punch to the chest. Maybe it was because no one had ever said that to him before. Oh, women wanted him. Women went out of their way to make that very clear. But none of them had ever told him they'd never wanted anyone else but him.

It was only physical desire, he knew that. It didn't mean anything. And yet he felt as if it did all the same. Because for the first time in his entire life, someone wanted *him*. Not his money, not his power, not his reputation. Not even his skill in bed.

She hadn't known about any of those things when she'd seen him by the lake, and yet she'd wanted him.

You. Not Ulysses.

It shouldn't matter. It shouldn't have anything to do with Ulysses.

But it did matter. It mattered a lot.

'That frightens you?' he asked, watching her.

'No. It…it means that…' Her fingers around her glass were clenched, her other hand gripping the material of her dress. The restless energy to her seemed to increase, and he'd crossed the space between them before he could think better of it, taking the glass from her suddenly shaking hand and putting it down, then holding both her hands in his and instinctively squeezing gently to calm her.

Her gaze dropped, but she didn't pull away or stiffen up. She just looked at her hands in his and slowly her agitation began to ebb away.

'I'm difficult, Achilles,' she said in a low voice at last, her gaze still on their linked hands. 'I have a very bad temper as you probably saw last week, and I don't lose it very often, but when I do I can…hurt people.' The flush to her cheeks had become more intense, but this time he knew it wasn't hunger. It was shame. 'When I'm pushed or challenged, it gets worse, and it seems you have that unfortunate effect on me.' She looked up at him suddenly, a raw honesty in her eyes. 'I'll certainly try not to be difficult after we're married, but when I'm around you…well, I can't guarantee anything.'

He had not expected such candour. Hadn't expected his own reaction to it either, and it was clear from the look on her face that it had cost her.

But he couldn't imagine her hurting anyone. Yes, she was fiery and yes, she'd lifted a hand to him, but he had provoked her. And the electricity between them surely hadn't helped. She didn't seem a woman liable to flying off the handle, though, not when she'd seemed very cool around him—when he wasn't provoking her, of course.

What had happened to make her think it was an issue? And why did she call herself difficult? She hadn't seemed difficult to him. A woman of deep passions, perhaps, but not difficult.

He wanted to ask her questions, find out why she thought these things about herself, but he didn't want to make her distressed or agitated more than she already was. Perhaps there would be some time later, when they were on honeymoon.

You don't need to know. Why would you want to?

Achilles shoved that thought away. 'Diana, I handle extremely difficult people every day. One fiery, passionate goddess is nothing.'

She frowned, even as the remaining tension in her seemed to die away. 'I'm not a goddess.'

'Let me be the judge of that.' He gave her fingers another squeeze then let them go. 'Now, let's discuss something less problematic for a change. What are your thoughts on wedding gowns?'

CHAPTER SIX

OVER THE COURSE of the next week, as arrangements for the wedding began in earnest, Willow wondered from time to time if her confession in Achilles' office had been a mistake. She'd never been so honest with another person before—she'd never had any kind of personal discussion with anyone before—and part of her had been very reluctant to confess to anything.

But she could tell that he wasn't going to let her reluctance go when it came to a physical relationship. He was too observant to lie to and too experienced for made-up excuses. He knew she wanted him, she'd as good as told him, and so of course her clear agitation about the thought of sex was going to make him curious.

She couldn't bear for him to assume things, either, or think that the issue was him when it wasn't. Or rather, it *was* him, but not for the reasons he thought.

So truth had seemed to be the best option.

She hadn't known what to expect when she'd told him about her terrible temper—some offhanded, casual comment perhaps. A shrug. Or maybe even distaste, because he didn't seem a man given to overly emotional displays himself.

What she hadn't expected at all was for him to put his wine down and come over to her and take her suddenly shaking hands in his. And she hadn't realised how agitated she'd been until that moment.

His hold had been warm and firm, feeling strangely like an anchor keeping her in place, and his attention had been wholly on her as she'd told him, his gaze direct yet without judgement. And it hadn't felt as hard to confess such a terrible weakness as she'd first thought.

She'd thought he might ask her whom she'd hurt in the past with her anger, and she hadn't wanted to tell him about her father, about the last precious photo of her mother that she'd torn up because she'd been so furious. Or about how her normally shut-down father had looked at her as if she'd stabbed him, and then clutched at his head and collapsed in front of her.

He'd nearly died that night. The doctors had told her that his stroke could have happened at any time, but she knew it was because of her. Because she'd ripped up the last photo he had of his beloved wife in a fury. Because she'd hurt him and had wanted to hurt him.

Luckily, though, Achilles hadn't asked her and so she at least hadn't had to confess that crime to him, and she'd been more than happy to move on to discussing gowns and other less fraught subjects.

He hadn't pursued the topic, clearly busy with wedding arrangements. He'd made various gracious invitations for her to join in with the decision-making process, which she just as graciously declined.

She didn't want to be involved in it. The whole thing was a pointless performance, though part of her was curious as to whom exactly he was performing for. She certainly didn't believe he'd suddenly decided on a formal engagement, complete with ring, plus a wedding and honeymoon, just for some photos.

No, it was about something more than that, but she

tried to put it out of her mind. The very last thing she wanted was to become curious about her notorious playboy husband-to-be.

He did have her try on numerous wedding dresses before finally approving some white silk and tulle concoction, accented with gilt thread, that Willow told herself she didn't care about. Yet at the same time, as she looked at herself in the mirror, she was conscious of a strange ache somewhere deep inside her.

She'd never thought a husband and children would be for her, and yet here she was, about to commit herself to both. That it wasn't real, she knew. But that didn't change the small ache inside her, the tug of longing for something...more.

But that was dangerous, so she ignored it.

In between wedding-dress fittings and investigating degree programmes at various universities, she found herself casually looking up Achilles on the internet, despite telling herself that she really didn't need to know anything about him.

Apparently though, some part of her was desperate for information, hungrily combing through search results for anything interesting.

There were lots of news reports of how he'd left home at sixteen with nothing and then made a lot of money in investment and venture capital. How he'd cut a swathe through the female population of Europe and then the States, apparently not caring one iota about his family or his reputation.

His father had publicly repudiated him from all accounts, not that it made any difference to Achilles; he was famously reported for saying, when asked about his father, 'Who?' That of course piqued Willow's curiosity.

The two had not got on, it was clear, and naturally she wanted to know why.

So she'd focused her research deeper, on Andrew Templeton and his lovely Greek wife, Katerina. They'd apparently had a perfect marriage and been deeply in love, and not long after their wedding they'd had a son they named Ulysses. There were lots of pictures of the happy family, the lovely wife, the handsome Duke and their adorable little boy.

And then she came across a news item that made her gut lurch.

Ulysses had contracted meningitis when he was fifteen and had died very quickly. The Duke and his Duchess had been devastated. And then a year after their first son's death, they'd had another child. Achilles.

Willow found that puzzling for reasons she couldn't quite pinpoint, the first son's death and then Achilles' birth so soon afterwards. Almost as if the Duke and Duchess had tried to replace the son they'd lost. Clearly whatever healing they'd attempted hadn't worked, because five years after Achilles' birth, his mother had divorced the Duke and returned to Athens, leaving her son behind, and had died a few years later.

It was obvious that neither the Duke nor the Duchess had got over the death of their first son, and it made her wonder what kind of childhood Achilles had had with that kind of shadow hanging over his head.

And then she thought about the wedding he was planning, the engagement with the family heirloom on her finger, the honeymoon in his mother's country…

It's definitely not for you.

The ache inside her, the one she told herself she didn't feel, deepened, though it shouldn't. Because she knew he wasn't marrying her for her. That it was all for whatever point he was trying to prove—and he was trying to prove a point, that was obvious. Though to whom, she didn't know.

Whatever, she needed not to feel the ache. Becoming emotionally invested was dangerous for her, and if she'd learned anything by now it was that.

She had to keep her distance. Shut herself off. Lock herself down.

And your wedding night? The honeymoon he wants from you?

She remembered back in his office how his presence had made her feel restless and wound up, and then not long after that how his touch had calmed her. There had been something still in him that had then stilled her, and she'd found it…restful.

It was strange that he could be both calming and arousing, but maybe that would help come their wedding night. Because the more she thought about it, the more she wanted it. Perhaps it would even help. It could be like a safety valve, helping her let off steam in the same way being in the woods had helped her let off steam as a child.

The day of the wedding arrived all too soon.

Willow found her little bedroom in the cottage full of make-up artists and stylists, people poking and prodding her until she finally emerged in the beautiful tulle and silk wedding gown, her face immaculate, her hair braided in a crown around her head and threaded through with flowers, a shimmering veil in gilt lace thrown over the top.

She barely had a moment to look at the stranger in the mirror before she was whisked downstairs and into the black limo that would take her from the cottage to the little church in Thornhaven village.

The church was historic, Norman age, and packed with people. The press waited outside, cameras at the ready as

Willow got out of the limo. They called her name as she went up the old church's steps, shouting questions at her as she went, but by that stage Achilles' PA, Jane, was there, helping her with her gown and flowers, whispering in her ear to just ignore them.

She tried, but it was all very strange. The whole situation was strange. Dressed in white and ready to marry a man she didn't love in front of a big crowd of people she didn't know, and all because she needed the money and her father taken care of.

A business arrangement, Achilles had assured her. Yet it didn't feel like a business arrangement any more. Not when there was a gown and an engagement ring, and a church. Not when there was a honeymoon.

All the trappings of love without the emotion.

A bit like your life, isn't it?

Willow clutched her bouquet, waiting for the music to start for her walk down the aisle. Conscious that the place at her side was empty. Because the place at her side, where her father should have been, was always empty.

He hadn't wanted to walk down the aisle with her because he wasn't physically steady enough, and he'd said it wasn't real anyway so it didn't matter that he wasn't there. He'd gone to Europe, to get the treatment paid for by the Duke.

He's never been a real father to you anyway. All the trappings without the emotion.

A lump rose in her throat. She'd loved her father, but he hadn't loved her. He'd never said it to her, hadn't ever demonstrated it to her. She'd been the baby he hadn't wanted, the child that had ruined his career. A lasting reminder of what his beloved wife had wanted and didn't survive long enough to have.

He'd done his duty by her, given her a roof over her head

and food on the table, ensured she had a decent education, and as soon as the Duke's money had arrived he'd left.

Perhaps he was right, though. Perhaps it didn't matter. Perhaps it was fine that this was all for show and that none of it was for her.

Nothing ever had been, after all.

Well, not quite nothing.

There was *one* thing that was for her and he waited for her by the altar, exquisitely dressed in a morning suit of dove grey. The man who might not love her, but did want her, and certainly enough to demand a wedding night from her.

That gave her some courage as she walked towards him, as did the look in his midnight eyes, full of a strangely intense satisfaction and fierce possessiveness that she didn't quite understand.

It might have been the look of a man desperately in love who was finally marrying the woman of his dreams. Except she knew that wasn't true, that he didn't dream about her. That all of this was simply a show that he was putting on, and she was merely part of it.

But then there was no time to think too deeply as the ceremony began, so she pushed it aside, concentrating instead on remembering the lines she had to say. And then before she knew it, Achilles' ring was on her finger and her veil was being pushed aside as he bent slightly to kiss her.

People were smiling and clapping as she walked out of the church on her new husband's arm, photographers clamouring, confetti in the air. She smiled reflexively at no one in particular as Achilles walked with her down the church steps to the long black limo that waited for them at the side of the road.

And then she was in the car, the door slamming shut

behind them like the vault of a crypt, and she was finally alone with Achilles.

She turned to look at him, but the moment he'd got in the car he'd pulled out his phone and was now talking to someone in liquid Greek.

Her husband.

She looked down at her hands clasped on the white silk of her gown, the yellow diamond sparkling, the heavy gold band of her wedding ring a perfect complement.

You're married.

Yes, she was. But it didn't mean anything. All that it meant was that now…

You get your wedding night.

Her breath caught, everything tightening inside her. She could still feel the warmth of his mouth as she'd leaned in to kiss him that day of their engagement, that ring heavy on her finger. Unable to stop herself. Drawn inexorably to him by the heat in his eyes and the hunger that she couldn't escape.

He'd been so still as her mouth had brushed over his and she'd wanted very much to make him move, to get him to reach for her, perhaps pull her down onto the carpet of his office and show her everything a man could do to a woman to give her pleasure.

But he hadn't.

As soon as she'd lifted her mouth from his, he'd risen to his feet and moved away as if nothing had happened. As if she hadn't shaken him as completely as he'd shaken her.

Perhaps tonight she'd rectify that.

Are you sure that's wise?

Well, maybe not. But then, she'd told him that she was difficult. He'd been warned. And he hadn't looked all that perturbed about it, either, telling her he dealt with difficult people every day, which was probably true, given his business dealings.

But were they more difficult than her? Had any of them nearly killed their father?

Achilles abruptly disconnected the call and pocketed his phone, turning his head and meeting her stare. And a familiar heat washed through her at the intense look in his blue gaze.

Yes, this was for her. *He* was for her.

The thought made a cold, hard knot in the centre of her chest loosen slightly.

'Don't worry, Diana.' His tone was lazy, at odds with the look in his eyes, and he reached for her hand, bringing it to his lips and brushing a kiss over the back of it. 'I'm not going to ravage you now, though believe me, I'm very tempted. I have other plans.'

She shivered at the light touch and at the heat curling through her. 'I assume a reception?'

'Oh, there's a reception, certainly. Except we will not be attending. We will be elsewhere.'

'I see. And where will we be?'

Achilles leaned back in his seat and smiled. 'We will be on our way to Greece.'

She lifted a brow. 'Honeymoon already?'

'Of course. I didn't want to wait. We're headed to the airport now and the jet will take us to Athens and then on to Heiros, a little island not too far from Santorini.' His eyes gleamed. 'I thought you might appreciate some sun.'

It struck her then, almost forcibly, that, while everything else might have been for show, the honeymoon wasn't. He didn't need it to fulfil the terms of the will. All he'd needed was her name on the marriage licence and eventually a child.

The honeymoon had been because he wanted her.

Not just anyone. *Her.*

There were so many reasons why she shouldn't let that matter to her, so many reasons why it shouldn't be important, but right now, with a ring that didn't mean anything on her finger and wearing a wedding gown that was just for show, it did feel important.

The hard, cold knot in her chest unravelled completely.

'Yes.' She smiled, something she hadn't done in far too long. 'I think I would appreciate that very much.'

They took a helicopter to London and, from there, Achilles' private jet to Athens. Somehow a passport had been got for her, as had several suitcases that apparently contained all she would need for a honeymoon in Greece.

No one batted an eyelid at her wedding gown as she boarded the jet, but by then she'd long got over any self-consciousness. There were too many other things to look at. The novelty of being on a plane, for example, and the excitement of take-off and landing. The view through the windows of the world beneath them and the glimmer and glint of cities as they soared over the continent.

Willow forgot about trying to be distant and cool, too busy alternately staring out of the window and leafing through a magazine about the Greek Islands, all the while firing questions at Achilles lounging opposite her. He looked ostensibly as lazy as a sleepy panther, but every so often, when he looked at her, she could see the glow of blue deep in his gaze. A hungry glow.

It was exciting. It made her want to get up and go to him herself, see what he'd do if she kissed him, if she laid her hands on him. But despite everything, she still felt a little shy, so she didn't.

A few hours later they landed in Athens, only to be taken to a helicopter that flew them straight out across the Aegean and to Heiros, Achilles' private island.

The villa was the most perfect house Willow had ever seen. It was built of white stone and perched high on a clifftop overlooking the sea, and walking into it felt like walking into the interior of a cloud. The inside was white, white walls and a white stone floor, nothing to compete with the views of the intense blue sea outside, the rocky cliffs and the deep green trees clinging to those cliffs. The couches and chairs were all deep and cushioned, covered with white linen, and colourful cushions were scattered here and there.

The outside of the villa was wrapped in ivy and there was a stone terrace that led straight out from the front living area, shaded by an ivy-covered pergola.

Willow, drawn by the view, stepped straight onto the terrace, looking down to see a path cut into the rocky cliffside that led to a pool that had also been cut into the cliffside. The water was as blue as the sea below it and incredibly inviting…

It was so different to Yorkshire, the house she'd grown up in and the forests around Thornhaven. This was all blue sea and rocky cliffs and heat, while Yorkshire was green and cold and rainy.

It was so beautiful. She wanted to stay here for ever.

In the villa behind her, she heard Achilles speaking to his staff as they carried in the last of the bags, and then the door closing behind them as they left.

There was no one else here, just her and Achilles.

Her mouth dried, her heartbeat suddenly picking up. The air around her was warm, smelling of salt from the sea, and she could hear the cry of the gulls in the air.

And then she felt his hands settle lightly on her hips, the heat of his body right behind her. 'And now, Diana,' Achilles murmured in her ear, 'I believe I owe you a wedding night.'

* * *

He'd been good the whole day. Right from the moment she'd stepped into the church and he'd watched her walk up the aisle to him, a vision in white and silver gilt.

The gown had been perfect, her hair a braided golden crown on her head, threaded through with flowers and covered by a silvery veil. His tall goddess now a fairy queen.

The cream of society had watched her marry him. In the church where his own parents had been married and where Ulysses had been christened. He'd been christened there too, but that had been before his parents had realised that he would never replace the boy they'd lost. That he didn't measure up. That he was faulty.

His father had told him the night of his sixteenth birthday, after Achilles had handed him the scholar's prize he'd won for his year, hoping to impress him, that it didn't matter what marks he got. It didn't matter how good at school he was, or how impressed his teachers were with him. None of that mattered. The only thing that did was that he was supposed to be Ulysses. Ulysses, who had been good at rugby and who'd loved going fishing with his father in the lake. Who had wanted to go hunting and who had already been learning how to use a rifle and was a crack shot.

Ulysses, who'd been good at everything that Achilles wasn't.

That was the night that his father had also mentioned that the only reason Achilles had been born was to replace the son they'd lost. Ulysses was the heir, Achilles the spare. And the spare was all he'd ever be, because the heir had gone and nothing could replace him.

And that was also the night that Achilles had left Thornhaven with nothing but the clothes on his back and his passport. He'd gone to Greece, but not to find his mother—

she'd died years earlier, and besides, it had been obvious what her choice had been the day she'd divorced his father and left without looking back. He'd wanted to get away from England, get away from his father and the constant hope that refused to die that one day his father would let Ulysses go. That Andrew Templeton would move on from his grief and love the son he had just as much as he loved the one who'd died.

But it was a hope that had never materialised and so he'd killed that hope stone dead.

He wanted to build his own life on his own terms, to not feel like a ghost haunting the rooms of his own house, pouring himself into filling a dead boy's shoes.

But things had changed now. His father's will had changed it, and now the woman meant for Ulysses was his, and he was going to make that true in every possible way there was.

He couldn't wait. He'd been dreaming of this the whole week, of having her to himself. Of taking her here to his island and unleashing her fire. He wanted to know what it would look like and how it would feel. Whether she'd be as difficult as she'd said she was, and oh, he hoped so. He was desperate to match himself against her, watch her ignite, watch her blaze. And for him. Just for him.

Gently he tugged her back against him, so that she was pressed against the length of his body. She was soft, the sweet scent of her winding around him. He had been fantasising about peeling that dress from her, then unbraiding the crown of golden hair on her head, the flowers woven into it scattering everywhere.

Greece was the territory he'd claimed for himself rather than the estate where he'd always felt like an interloper, and so bringing her here appealed to his sense of possessiveness. A good decision, he thought as the breeze from the sea stirred her veil, bringing the scent of salt and sunshine. There were no ghosts in Greece. Of course, there was his mother, but she was long gone, and anyway, she'd lived in Athens.

He felt Willow tremble slightly and then she turned around, looking up at him.

There was something in her expression he couldn't read. It reminded him of that day in his office, when she'd become so tense, and he'd taken hold of her hands, and she'd told him that he had to be careful of her.

'What is it?' he asked, cupping one cheek in his palm, her skin warm and silky to the touch. 'Are you afraid? I won't hurt you, Diana. I know what I'm doing when it comes to pleasure.'

She shook her head, yet he could feel the tension in her body. Could see it in her golden-brown eyes. She stared at him. 'This…this is for me, isn't it? The honeymoon. Because you wanted me.'

There was a raw edge to her voice, a glitter in those beautiful eyes. Wanting it to be true and yet…afraid that it wasn't.

He remembered that feeling. Every time he'd looked at his father, hoping that this would be the day that it wouldn't be Ulysses he saw when he looked at Achilles. That this would be the day he'd finally feel like his father's son and not the ghost he'd been made into.

But his father had never looked at him that way, and now he never would.

You'll always remain a ghost.

Achilles forced away the thought, stared down into the fear in Willow's eyes, and he knew that there was no part of him that could lie to her. Or to himself.

Of course this was for her. He could have bedded her in Thornhaven straight after the wedding if it had simply been about claiming her. If it had all been about taking his dead brother's promised wife.

But it wasn't just about that. It was about her. Willow. His golden goddess. About the chemistry that leapt between them. About the way she made him feel, as if there was fire inside of him too instead of only ashes and shadows.

And she was here because he wanted her to ignite him, just as he wanted to ignite her. It was about sex, yes. But he couldn't pretend it was only about that. If it had been, the master suite at Thornhaven would have sufficed. He wouldn't have brought her here, to the place where he felt the most alive, and for an entire week.

You cannot make this mean anything.

Achilles stroked his thumb over the satiny skin of her cheekbone. Oh, it wouldn't mean anything, no fear of that. Though it was perhaps a little deeper than purely physical, it wasn't much deeper.

His emotions, such as they were, were shallow things, and shallow was where they needed to stay.

'Yes,' he said, no seductiveness in his voice now. 'This is for you. Because I want you. But don't make it mean anything.' He stared down at her, watching the currents shift and turn in her eyes, knowing he had to say it. That he had to make it clear so there could be no misunderstandings. 'What is between us is physical only. Nothing more.'

Some fleeting emotion he couldn't read flickered through her gaze, then was gone. 'Yes.' Her voice sounded thick. 'I understand.'

'Good.' Achilles slid his thumb across her cheek again, brushing the corner of her lovely mouth. 'And I want a week, wife of mine. Not just one night. Will you give me that?'

She looked at him for one long, uncounted second. And

then she abruptly rose on her toes and pressed her mouth to his.

The smouldering fire inside him ignited.

The taste of blackberries and sunshine filled his head, a bright explosion of sweet and tart, and suddenly he couldn't think. It felt as if he'd been waiting half his life for this moment, for her mouth under his and the sweet taste of her on his tongue.

He wanted more. And he wanted it now.

Everything fell away. His father. His brother. His mother. All the pain in his heart that he told himself he didn't feel and all the anger underneath it. The creeping sense that he had sometimes that he was the one who had died, not Ulysses.

All of it was gone. There was only this. Only her. Her sweet mouth and the heat that leapt between them. And the hunger that followed hard on its heels.

He'd had plans for her. Plans to make this special, to go slow and take his time. Ease the trepidation he'd sensed in her the week before in his office. Gradually coax her flame high and hot, and only then would he take her.

But all those plans burned to ashes on the ground.

Fabric ripped as he clawed her gown from her, buttons scattering on the stone floor of the terrace. He wasn't seductive or sensual. He was a beast as he tore away the material and then pulled at the fragile lace of her underwear.

She didn't protest, her entire body shivering as he bared her, her mouth as hot and hungry as his, her arms tight around his neck as she pressed herself against him.

Yes, he'd had plans. A wide, soft bed upstairs strewn with rose petals, and champagne to toast their marriage.

Instead he barely had enough time to get her to the living room. He laid her down on the couch, her body long and lithe and a pale, creamy gold. Slender thighs and shapely hips. High, perfect breasts with the prettiest pink nipples. A soft nest of golden curls between her legs. Utterly and completely beautiful.

He didn't pause to look at her, to appreciate her the way he'd planned. He didn't stroke her to ease any nervousness she might have had. He didn't kiss his way down her body the way he should have, or murmur seductive praise as he did so.

Because she reached up to him and pulled him down, her mouth demanding on his, and then he was pushing her thighs apart while clawing at his zip. Getting his suit trousers undone and getting himself ready.

And then he positioned himself.

He should have waited then, should have tried to build even the smallest amount of anticipation.

But it was beyond him.

Then she wound her arms around his neck, arched her back, closed her legs around his waist and he was pushing inside her, and then there was nothing but fire.

She shuddered, gasping against his mouth, her hips lifting against his, trembling.

He kissed her harder, deeper, tasting her, exploring her. She felt so hot around him, so slick. Clasping him so tightly. Her body was a wonder, silky and smooth, and he felt his grip on reality loosen.

He began to move, an insistent, demanding rhythm, slipping a hand beneath the small of her back, guiding her to match him. And she did. Her kiss became feverish, her legs around his waist tightening.

He felt feverish himself, half-crazed. He moved harder, deeper, faster. Her scent was around him, sweet and musky, and somehow her hair had come down from its braided crown and was in his hands. There were flowers scattered all around them, crushed between them and scenting the air.

And, as he'd thought, she was fire in his hands and she was burning. And so was he. Fire and magic, and raw, intense pleasure. It was everything that had been missing from his life and he hadn't even known until this moment. Everything he had never thought he wanted.

Her passion made him real, somehow. Made him feel as if he existed, as if he was alive. Truly alive, not just going through the motions of it.

You want more than a week.

The thought was crystal in his brain, sharp edges and glittering planes.

And then she writhed beneath him, her teeth closing demandingly on his bottom lip, and the thought exploded into sparkling shards in his brain.

There was no thought any more, only the most primitive of physical responses and the pleasure that spun like molten mercury through every part of him, searing him straight through.

He moved inside her, driving them on, and there was no time to savour. No time for anticipation or for being lazy and easy. There was only the fire of her and her gasps of pleasure in his ear, the hoarse demands she made.

Her nails dug into him, and he had enough of himself left to ease a hand between them, down to where they were joined, giving her her pleasure first. And then as she cried his name, he took his own.

It came for him in a blaze of light, the bonfire of her rising up around him, consuming him. And he flung himself into the flames and burned himself to ash in her arms.

CHAPTER SEVEN

WILLOW LAY BENEATH ACHILLES, panting, feeling as if every part of her had shattered and then been put together in a strange and new and wonderful way.

Pleasure echoed through her like the tolling of some vast bell, a pulsing deep inside that made her shiver and shake. And for a second all she felt was wonder. His weight was heavy on her, but she didn't feel crushed. She could hear his breathing, as fast as hers, and she swore she could almost hear the thudding of his heart too.

She'd never been this close to anyone before, not physically, and the feeling of being surrounded and contained made her feel calm and safe, and relaxed for the first time in what felt like years.

So different to how she'd felt out on the terrace, where a sudden burst of fear had taken her. That somehow being here on this beautiful island was for show too, that she'd misunderstood, and that all of this wasn't for her after all. Even that he didn't want her as much as he'd implied.

She'd had to know. So she'd turned and looked up into his dark blue eyes, and asked him straight out. But the truth had been there in his gaze and in the heat of his body, in the stroke of his thumb across her cheek. Desire burned there and she knew it was for her.

This was only physical, he'd told her, but she didn't need anything more.

Right now, that was enough. Especially when she'd kissed him and the veneer of the lazy playboy had cracked apart completely, leaving a hungry panther in its place.

Oh, she'd wanted him so badly. His heat and his hands on her. Wanted the electricity that danced between them. Wanted his danger, his wicked edge. Wanted his hunger for her to consume him as much as she was consumed by her own.

And it had.

She'd loved him ripping her wedding gown from her and her lacy underwear too. Loved how he'd picked her up in his arms and carried her to the couch, laying her down on it. Loved how he hadn't even stopped to undress, before spreading her thighs, and thrusting deep inside her.

It hadn't hurt. It hadn't even felt strange. It had felt right and perfect, as if he was supposed to be there. As if they were supposed to be joined in this way, a raw, elemental meeting, creating magic between them.

Willow looked up at him, still dazed, meeting his eyes gone gas-flame blue. And she opened her mouth to tell him how amazing he was and how wonderful he'd made her feel, when he pushed himself off her abruptly and stepped out through the double doors that led to the terrace before she could say a word.

Willow blinked, a cold feeling shifting in her gut.

Had he not liked it? Had it been disappointing? Had she been too demanding? Too difficult? She'd forgotten herself since getting on the plane, hadn't she? She was supposed to be much more distant and self-contained, but she'd asked too many questions, had talked too much. And then she'd been demanding when she'd got here too. Had kissed him with too much hunger, been too needy.

You ruined it. Like you always do.

She'd tried that day, years ago. She'd worked hard for the marks she'd managed to get that summer, but school had always been tough for her, because she didn't like to sit still. She'd showed her father that she'd managed to get a B plus in Biology, and she'd thought he'd be pleased. That finally she'd done something right. But he'd told her it wasn't good enough, that he expected better and why hadn't she'd tried harder?

And that was the problem. She'd tried *so* hard and it still hadn't been good enough for him. Nothing she ever did had been good enough for him. So she'd lost her temper. She'd grabbed the photo of her mother that was on his desk, the only one he had of her and which he treasured. She'd ripped it out of its frame and torn it into pieces, because she'd wanted to hurt him as he'd hurt her. His cold veneer had cracked apart then as he'd rushed to the fireplace, futilely trying to grab at the pieces of the photograph. 'No…no…' he'd whispered hoarsely. 'Not that one… It's all I have left…'

She had hurt him. She'd hurt him badly.

Then he'd raised a hand to his head and collapsed.

It had been her temper that had caused the stroke, she had no doubt. If she hadn't ripped up the photograph, he wouldn't have been in such emotional pain and so perhaps wouldn't have collapsed.

Maybe it was the same here. Something had made Achilles leave suddenly, as if he couldn't wait to get away from her, and it was bound to be something she'd done wrong, because she always did something wrong.

Willow slowly got off the couch. Just before she'd felt as if someone had opened up a bottle of champagne inside her, the bubbles fizzing and filling her with effervescence and light. Now she felt raw and bruised and cold.

Perhaps she needed to go and have a shower or something, rather than to follow Achilles.

That's it, run into the forest the way you always do.

When her father had locked her out of the house, she'd always run into the woods around Thornhaven and disappeared into them, going where the trees didn't mind if she was loud or asked too many questions. The silence of the forest calmed her, though it had never made her feel less lonely. She'd used to make up all kinds of friends in the forest, a boy who would play chase with her and fight dragons with her. A boy who became a prince when she got older. She would sometimes be his knight or his friend. Sometimes she would be his princess and sometimes he saved her. Sometimes she saved him.

But he never told her to 'go away'. And he never told her to 'leave me alone'.

Except there were no forests here and running away wouldn't solve anything. She'd learned that the hard way.

The salty evening breeze came through the open double doors, carrying with it the heat of the day, and it wasn't cold. But still Willow shivered. She looked around for something to wrap around herself, since she was still naked, but her gown lay outside on the terrace where Achilles had stripped it from her.

Her veil though was on the tiled floor next to the couch, so she picked it up, shaking out the flowers that had fallen from her hair and wrapping the beautiful gilt lace around her. It wasn't much of a covering, but it was better than nothing.

Then she stepped out onto the terrace.

The sea lapped against the sheer cliffs below, the dark outline of Achilles' tall, broad figure set starkly against the blue sky. He had his back to her, his hands thrust in the pockets of his suit trousers.

He looked so unapproachable, so complete and self-contained that for a second she couldn't bear to disturb him. Her father had hated her doing that, after all. And besides, what did it matter what she'd done to make him walk away?

'If you think that constitutes a wedding night,' he said without turning around, his beautiful voice roughened, 'then you can think again.'

She hadn't made a sound, so she had no idea how he'd known she was there, and for a second she didn't understand what he'd said. Because he wanted more? Was that what he was saying?

'I'm sorry,' she began, her own voice not much better than his. 'I don't know what I did wrong, but I—'

'Why are you sorry?' He turned abruptly, his gaze meeting hers, rooting her to the spot. 'And you didn't do anything wrong.'

Willow tried to find her usual cool, but for some reason it had vanished. There was a hot, burning expression in his eyes, the lines of his perfect face taut. He was so still and yet there was a tension in that stillness; the panther ready either to pounce or to vanish back into the jungle.

She *had* done something wrong, though, hadn't she? He wouldn't have shoved himself off the couch so quickly otherwise, surely?

'But you left.' She clutched the lace of her veil more tightly around her. 'Why? Was it because I was too…d-demanding? I know I'm not—'

He cursed, something low and filthy in Greek, stopping the words in her throat.

Then he moved, crossing the space between them in a lithe, fluid movement that had her heart suddenly racing, making her very acutely aware that the only thing protecting her modesty was a length of hugely expensive lace.

He stopped in front of her, his gaze holding hers. 'It wasn't you, Willow.'

'Then…what?' She searched his face, looking for clues.

'I had plans when it came to you. And those plans did not include tearing your dress from you and taking you on the couch like a damn animal.' He lifted a hand and thrust it through his hair in an unfamiliar, agitated movement. 'That was not how your first time was supposed to go.' He cursed again, his gaze narrowing. Then he stepped forward, reaching out to her and drawing her close, searching her face. 'Are you all right? Did I hurt you?'

He was so warm, his hands gentle on her hips. But she remembered his intensity, remembered the hunger of his kiss, the raw demand of it. The way he'd thrust inside her without hesitation, possessive and rough.

It shook her with longing right down to her soul.

'No,' she said thickly. 'No, you didn't hurt me.'

He lifted both hands and cupped her face, frowning at her as if he couldn't quite believe her. 'Are you sure?' His thumbs stroked her cheekbones, a gentle, almost tender touch that made Willow shiver. 'You make me so hungry, Diana. And I thought I had better control over myself than that. But apparently not where you are concerned.'

So. He'd lost control and she, the woman who'd never been what anyone, not even her own father, had wanted, had made him lose it.

The cold inside her melted away.

She stared up at him, leaning into his palms and the gentle stroke of his thumbs. 'I don't care. And I lost a little bit of control myself, too, if you must know.'

His gaze was enigmatic, whatever thoughts he had locked securely away behind the walls in his eyes. And she could see those walls. They were metres thick. And of course her insatiable curiosity immediately wanted to know what was behind them, what he was hiding from her, even though she shouldn't.

She shouldn't want to know *anything* about her unexpectedly passionate husband and yet she did. Not that she didn't know things about him already, about his parents and his long dead older brother…

His thumb moved gently on her skin again and her thoughts scattered in a whirl of sparks.

'I'm sorry,' he said. 'I shouldn't have walked away like that. But you surprised me. You shocked me and I thought I was unshockable.'

She blinked. 'But…why?'

His thumbs paused, the look on his face intensifying. 'Because I have never wanted anyone as badly as I wanted you.'

Her pulse gathered speed, the muscular heat of his body warming her straight through. The lace of her veil was scratchy on her skin and she wanted his hands there instead.

And maybe he knew that. Maybe he could see, because one hand on her cheek spread out in a slow movement, sliding down over her jaw and her neck to rest in the hollow of her throat. The tips of his fingers pressed lightly against her pulse, measuring it. Feeling the pace of her desire.

The blue of his eyes had gone the deep, inky black of midnight, and just as dark and mysterious. 'Shall we try that again?' His voice had become darker too, roughened and hungry-sounding. 'Slower this time?'

'I don't need slow.' She was shivering again, leaning into the hard strength of his body. 'I just need you.'

But something in his gaze flared in response and one corner of his beautiful mouth turned up. 'In that case, you shall have me.'

He didn't grab her this time, though. Instead he picked

her up in his arms and went into the house, carrying her up the wide staircase and into a bedroom that had windows everywhere facing the sea and a huge white bed.

There was champagne on ice in a bucket near a low white sofa, and glasses on a low table near by. And rose petals glowing like rubies on the sheets.

Achilles laid her on the bed and then he stepped back, pulling his own clothes off until he was as naked as she was. As naked as he'd been that day beside the lake. She couldn't help herself then, shrugging off the lace of her veil and slipping off the bed, going to him.

The sunset poured through the windows, outlining every perfect muscle of him in brilliant gold, and when she put her hands on him he didn't move, allowing her to explore. To touch the wide, muscled plane of his chest and then the hard corrugations of his stomach. The powerful contours of his arms and the lean shape of his waist. His skin was golden and smooth and velvety, and when she pressed her mouth to it he tasted salty and delicious.

His fingers pushed into her hair, cupping the back of her head as she kissed down his chest, her hand stroking lower, finding the hard length of him hot and powerful. She touched him, stroked him, watching the flex and release of his muscles in response to her touch.

He was mesmerising. She wanted to go down on her knees and worship him, but he stopped her, pulling her close instead, his mouth hungry on hers. He didn't let her protest. Instead, he picked her up and carried her to the bed, laying her out on the mattress, then moving over her. He kissed her deeply, making her moan, and then his mouth went lower, to her throat, tasting her skin the way she'd tasted his.

Willow shut her eyes as he kissed down her chest to her breasts, his tongue on her nipple, teasing her. She gasped and arched up, her hands in his hair. 'Yes,' she sighed. 'Achilles.'

The heat of his mouth closed around her nipple, the pressure drawing a moan from her. She sighed again, arching higher. 'More, please, more.'

'If this is you being demanding then you'll have to do better than that, my Diana,' he murmured. 'Perhaps you need some more provocation. Allow me to provide it.' And before she could respond he moved to the other breast, his hot mouth covering her nipple and sucking lightly on it.

Another raw sound escaped her as sensation burst through her in a bright glitter, like sparks against her skin. And, though a reflexive concern rippled through her, she ignored it. Because she'd lost control of herself downstairs and it had been okay. He'd pushed away from her, but it hadn't been her fault.

It was because he wanted her. Who had ever wanted her the way he had?

No one.

So she did nothing as he moved down further, easing her thighs apart. And when his wicked tongue found the beating heart of her, she gave herself up to the sensation completely.

Pleasure glittered in her blood, sparks of electricity winding everywhere as his fingers spread her wider, his tongue exploring deeper. She moaned, arching her back and lifting her hips, forgetting herself. Forgetting herself utterly.

'Scream for me, Diana,' he whispered against her shivering flesh. 'I want to know exactly how much you like me doing this to you.'

All her concerns fell away, everything subsumed by the pleasure he was giving her. By the touch of his fingers and tongue. And then suddenly everything was drawing tight inside her and the climax hit her like an earthquake, and she did scream, his name echoing off the walls around them.

He didn't stop.

She was still shivering and half blind with the effects of her orgasm as he settled himself between her thighs. And when he pushed into her, there was only that sense of perfect rightness. Of a completion she'd only ever found in the woods, where she could be herself and be free.

His body on hers was a glory, the heat of him and the slight prickle of hair. His hardness against her softness. Everything about him different and yet the hunger in his eyes was the same as the hunger in hers.

She lifted her arms around him, arched against him, encouraging him. He slid deeper inside her.

'Every night,' he said in a low, rough voice, the intensity of him shivering through her. 'You and I just like this. Every night. Do you agree?'

She was lost in the pleasure, lost in him. And right in that moment she would have agreed to anything, especially when it concerned more of him.

'Yes,' she said huskily. 'I do.'

It could have been triumph that flickered across his beautiful face. Or it could have been pleasure. It was certainly satisfaction.

Then as he moved there was nothing but pleasure and the long fall that came after it.

Achilles had never spent much time with a lover and so he had nothing to compare being with Willow to. He'd thought they'd probably spend the entire week having sex and sleeping, sharing meals and then more sex, with a couple of swims thrown in for good measure.

He didn't think that there would be more.

After that first day, she wasn't shy and she didn't hold back. She made no secret of her hunger for his touch or that she enjoyed the pleasure he gave her. She was as passionate as he'd thought, the hot coal of that passion igniting every time he was around, which gratified him on basically every level there was.

And as the days passed and they spent them making love on every available surface, or eating delicious food that was brought in and left for them by his staff, or talking about nothing of consequence, he began to realise what he'd already suspected: that the cool, contained woman she'd been back in England was a lie.

That energy he'd sensed in her, bright and fizzing yet locked down, burst to the surface like champagne bubbles in a glass. She wanted to talk to him about a great many subjects and asked questions constantly, wanting to know his opinion and why and how he formed it. One day she wanted to walk around the entire island and hear about all the different kinds of trees and plants that grew on it, so he hired a local to answer her questions, since he didn't know the answers himself. The next day she wanted to explore the beach and the coast, again full of questions, and again he hired another local to answer them.

She liked to argue with him and, since he liked to argue too, they had a great many very vocal disagreements that both of them enjoyed, and which always ended the same way: with both of them naked and him inside her.

Her bright energy was fascinating to him. He'd been a serious, studious child, always with his head in a book, and he'd known that if he'd met her as a boy he would have been just as fascinated with her then as he was now. She would have dragged him from his books, would have taken him off for adventures in the woods, and he would have followed, helpless to do anything else. Drawn by her effervescent spark.

A few days later they were beside the pool built into the cliffside. Willow was naked, lying on her front on the sun lounger. He'd braided her lovely hair into a long plait down her back, weaving flowers into it, because he liked it when there were flowers in her hair. Her long, golden body was divine in the lazy, liquid heat of the late afternoon, her eyes molten as she gazed at him from the pillow on the white linen sun lounger.

She was a goddess like this. His goddess. A possessive thought and one he allowed himself because she *was* his now. In every way.

He leaned over, running a lazy hand down her elegant back, her skin silky and hot and slick with the sunscreen he'd put on it only a couple of minutes earlier.

'You're made for Greece,' he said. 'For sun and good food and sex. How did you ever survive the cold and rain of Yorkshire?'

She arched under his touch like a cat being stroked. It was strange how the electricity that leapt between them hadn't decreased in any way since they'd been together. He would have thought it would, but it hadn't. If anything it had become stronger, a deeper, more intense pull.

It had made him rethink his initial 'separate lives' idea. That maybe, when they returned home, they could spend more time together.

'Oh, it wasn't so bad.' Her voice was husky with sex and sun. 'Dad used to shut me out of the house, so I would always take off into the woods around Thornhaven. I made up a whole lot of friends to have adventures with.'

Achilles frowned as he stroked down her back again. 'He shut you out of the house?'

She sighed. 'Remember that I told you I was difficult?

Well, I was. Always asking questions, always wanting his attention. I was demanding and I hated it when he ignored me. I used to throw the most terrible temper tantrums.' Her golden lashes had drifted closed. 'So he'd shut me out of the house and wouldn't let me back inside until I was quiet. It was good in a way. I found the woods didn't care if I had a temper tantrum.'

There was amusement in her voice, but he didn't find it funny. He didn't like the sound of her as a bright, sparky little girl being locked out of the house for being 'difficult'. Because she was curious and passionate and fiery, yes, but he liked those things about her very much. In fact, he shared some of those qualities himself. She was also quick to laugh, quick to apologise, and had a huge amount of empathy. He suspected that she was a woman of deep emotions and perhaps her father hadn't appreciated exactly how deep.

And he knew himself what it felt like to be unappreciated. To be dismissed and rejected. His entire childhood had been that.

'You find that funny?' he asked quietly. 'That your father never wanted you around?'

Her eyes opened and she gazed at him, an expression he couldn't read in her eyes. 'No, it's not funny. But I wasn't what my father wanted. It was my mother who wanted a baby, but she died in a car accident a couple of months after I was born. Dad had to bring me up himself. He was a surgeon and, though he hired lots of nannies to look after me, they all left one after the other because I was a 'handful'. Anyway, Dad had to look after me himself in the end, and his career was severely impacted. I…' She hesitated. 'I ruined his career in a lot of ways.'

There was a note of pain in her voice and he could feel the muscles of her back tensing up. This was distressing for her clearly and no wonder. She'd been told her father hadn't wanted her.

Theos, he knew how that felt. He knew how that felt all too well.

Anger smouldered in his chest, but he fought it down, because this wasn't about him. Instead he followed his instinct and got up to sit on the lounger next to her, put his hands on her beautiful back and stroke her, massage away that tension.

He could feel her resist a second and then she let out a soft breath and relaxed beneath his touch.

'I was a quiet, studious boy,' he said, wanting to give her something more, something to make her feel good about herself rather than bad. 'I know it's hard to believe, but I was all about study and getting good marks. I didn't have many friends, because I didn't really like doing all the stuff other boys did. But I was curious and asked questions too, though I found a lot of answers in my father's library. I think I would have liked you, though.' He massaged out the hard knots he could feel in her upper back. 'I could have answered some of your questions, and you could have dragged me away from my studies to play games in the woods.'

Slowly she turned her head to the side, her muscles now relaxed completely under his hands. 'Quiet and studious? You?'

He smiled. 'I told you it was hard to believe.'

Her lashes drifted closed and her lovely, almost shy smile turned one corner of her mouth. 'When I played in the woods, those friends I made up, they weren't girls. I don't know why, but I always imagined my best friend as a boy. Sometimes he would save me from certain death. And sometimes…sometimes I would save him.'

He'd never thought he needed saving. He didn't think it

now. But he could imagine that if there came a time where he did, she would be the woman to do it.

'And did this boy ever become real?' he asked softly. 'Or was he only ever imaginary?'

'No, he was never real.' She sighed. 'Probably a good thing. Dad didn't like having other kids around. Said they were too loud.'

'You and I should have swapped fathers. Mine didn't care about marks or studying. He always wanted me to go shooting and hunting. And fishing. Playing rugby. All the things a proper English boy should like.' All the things that Ulysses had been good at.

She opened her eyes again, flicking him a look. 'And you didn't?'

'Well, I wasn't a proper English boy. I was half Greek. Not that Greek boys prefer reading books any more than English boys do, but certainly I did. Things in books always seemed more exciting.'

She turned her head a little. 'You never went out and explored the woods at Thornhaven?'

Something inside him hardened. He didn't want to talk about his childhood. He didn't want to feel like a ghost here, on his island, with her.

'Not often,' he said, running his fingers down her back again, lightly. 'So what happened with your father? He had a stroke and you became his caregiver, I take it?' He knew that already, because, after all, he'd done his research. But he wanted to hear the story from her.

A shadow passed over her vivid, expressive face. 'Yes. I had to stay with him after I left school, because we had no one else. I took a job in the village cafe, sometimes cleaned people's houses. I couldn't afford to get a job anywhere else, because that would have left Dad without anyone to look after him.'

It sounded like a miserable existence for someone like her. All her bright passion subsumed into looking after one old man, who from the sounds of it hadn't appreciated what he had. Had she had dreams of more? And if so, why had she stayed with a man who didn't deserve her care?

He certainly wouldn't have done the same with his own father.

'Forgive me, Diana,' he said, unable to help being angry on her behalf, 'but your father sounds like he didn't deserve you limiting your life just to look after him.'

Willow looked abruptly away from him, her muscles tightening once more. 'He's my father.'

He shouldn't push her, shouldn't make this personal. But he was angry for her. He didn't like how she'd locked such a vital, beautiful part of herself away and he wanted to know why.

Calmly, he began to knead her muscles, easing her tension again. 'Fathers have to earn respect just like anyone else. They're not automatically entitled to it. What did your father do to earn yours?'

She was silent. He could feel her tension, could sense her gathering herself to move away from him. But he pressed down a little harder, adding some more pressure, because she seemed to like being touched and being held.

Gradually, very gradually, she began to relax again.

'He didn't do anything to earn it,' she said after a long moment. 'But the stroke was my fault. Or rather, I feel it's my fault.'

That sounded like her.

He kept up the gentle massage. 'Tell me about it.'

'It's nothing.'

'It's something. Tell me.' He didn't pretend it wasn't an order, because sometimes she liked him being authoritative. It gave her something to rebel against, which he knew she liked also.

But apparently not today, because she let out a breath then said, 'He was a surgeon, like I said, and I wanted very much to do something that would make him proud of me. So I spent the whole of my sixteenth year paying attention to my studies. I…wasn't the best at school, but I tried very hard that year, because he liked me to. I got a B plus for Biology in the end, and I was very pleased. And I expected him to be impressed, but…he wasn't.' She turned her head slightly away, as if she didn't want him to see her face. 'He was disappointed I hadn't got an A, told me I needed to work harder and not to bother him for any less than an A minus. I was…furious. I don't know why it hit me so hard that night, it just did. I'd tried so hard for him—I always tried hard for him—but he just wasn't interested.' Her voice had become scratchy. 'I lost my temper. I wanted to hurt him the way he'd hurt me and so I grabbed my mother's picture off his desk and took it out of the frame. And then I ripped it up into pieces.' She didn't look at him, the setting sun gilding her lashes. 'It was very precious to him because it was the only photo he had of her and he'd loved her so much. He'd never got over her death and I knew that. It was my mother who'd wanted a child, not him, but then she died and he ended up with me, and I… I guess I ended up being a reminder of that.' She paused. 'He was so upset about the photo. I'd never seen him get so emotional about anything. And then he…just collapsed. I had to call an ambulance and they took him to hospital. He'd had a fairly serious stroke and, although they told me it wasn't my fault, I…'

'You still blamed yourself,' he finished gently.

Her lashes lowered again, the tension receding from her muscles as he kneaded her shoulder. 'Dad was always telling me I needed to control myself and he was right. I wanted to hurt him and I did.'

But no, he couldn't have her thinking that. Because it wasn't true. The only thing she was guilty of was loving deeply a father who couldn't love her in return. A father who was too busy grieving someone who was gone.

Like you.

No, not like him. Because it was apparent that Willow still cared, while his own heart remained empty. All his caring was gone. He'd used up the final dregs of it the day he'd left Thornhaven.

Achilles gripped her gently and turned her over on her back, so her pain-filled gaze looked straight up into his. She protested a little, trying to turn away, but he put one hand on the side of the lounger, leaning on it as he took her determined chin in his other hand, holding her still.

'Listen to me,' he said flatly. 'Yes, you were angry and yes, you lost your temper. Yes, you wanted to hurt him. But you were only sixteen and you can't take responsibility for his failings. You were his daughter. He should have loved you and accepted you for what you were, not blamed you for what you weren't.'

'But I—'

'No. You're not difficult and you're not a "handful". You're not demanding. And your temper is a beautiful storm. *You* are a beautiful storm, do you understand?' He said the words calmly, clearly, and with all the conviction in him, because they were true and he wanted her to know it. 'You're passionate and curious and you feel things deeply.' He leaned down, holding her chin firmly, and nipped at her bottom lip, making her breath catch. 'You're a goddess, my Diana. A bonfire.' Another nip. 'A solar flare.' He kissed her, taking his time, taking it deep, hot. 'You're stubborn and challenging and I like it.' Another nip, a little harder. 'I like you angry. I like you passionate. I like you wild. I like you the way you are and you don't ever have to be anything else for me.'

She was trembling, her gaze wide and smoky and dark. She didn't say a word, only reaching for him, bringing his mouth down on hers.

But that was all the response he needed, because he could taste her answer in the desperate, hungry kiss that she gave him, as bright and as passionate and as demanding as she was.

And there in the sunset he took the flame that she was and stoked it higher, turned her into a bonfire, a goddess blazing in her glory.

Then he let those flames of hers burn him to the ground too.

CHAPTER EIGHT

WILLOW SAT CURLED UP in the soft leather seat of the jet on the way back to England, reading a book Achilles had bought her on the flora and fauna of the Greek islands. She found it fascinating, but it was getting harder and harder to concentrate because Achilles was lounging in the seat opposite her, long legs outstretched, gazing at her very intently from underneath his long black lashes.

He was planning something, she could tell.

Anticipation coiled inside her, along with a certain heated excitement. She loved it when he looked at her like that, like a very hungry panther looking at her prey.

He'd done that a lot over the previous week in the white villa beside the sea. He'd done a lot of other things too, showing her all about how taking one's time could lead to the most delicious pleasure. Talking with her about any topic she wanted to discuss, his mind a storehouse of seemingly irrelevant yet fascinating facts that he was more than happy to share. Arguing with her—she especially loved that—about inconsequential things which always ended up with them in bed, who was right and who was wrong forgotten. Walking with her over the island and clearly reluctant to do so, yet willing to go along all the same, before taking her back to the villa's small library and going over some of the things they'd seen out on their walk in the pages of the books there.

Sometimes he was quiet, reading or working on his laptop, and then she'd like to sit and watch him, his stillness somehow calming and relaxing.

There was something steady about him in general that she liked, an anchor that kept her from floating away in the worst of the storms. Not that there had been many storms. Passion burned in her—she could feel it—and yet gradually she'd started to realise that it wasn't anything to be afraid of. Not when there was Achilles around to take it, channel it, and make it bloom like a firework in the night.

All the things she'd been afraid of in herself, he liked and actively encouraged.

'I like you wild,' he'd told her that day by the pool, when she'd confessed to him the terrible truth about herself and her temper. And she'd seen nothing but fierce acceptance in his blue eyes. He'd shown her then, with his hands and his mouth, exactly how accepting he was by stoking that wildness in her and letting it rage out of control. Showing her that there was nothing to be scared of, not with him.

You can't go thinking things like that. He might be your lover but he only married you because of a will. This marriage will be over as soon as you have his child, remember?

Oh, yes, she remembered. But that was fine. That was what she'd wanted after all.

'We haven't talked about what's going to happen when we get back to England,' Achilles said suddenly.

Slowly, she lowered her book. 'What do you mean? Aren't we going back to separate lives?'

'That's what we agreed, yes.' He leaned his head on his hand, his elbow resting on the arm of his chair, his long, powerful legs stretched out before him. He looked relaxed and yet the intensity in his eyes made a lie out of it. 'And my child is to be conceived via medical assistance. Though, to be fair, you could already be pregnant.'

A little electric shock pulsed through her. It was true, she could be. They hadn't used anything in the way of protection and to say they'd been having a lot of sex was an understatement.

She looked down at the book in her lap, feeling suddenly self-conscious. She hadn't been thinking about the child he'd wanted, not once while they'd been on Heiros. She hadn't thought about the future at all. She'd been too consumed with him and how he made her feel every time he touched her, smiled at her, laughed with her.

It's just a business arrangement, remember?

No, she hadn't remembered. She'd fulfilled one of his requests and now it was time to fulfil the other. Bear him a son. A little boy with blue eyes just like his...

Something in her chest gave a pulsing ache, an unexpected longing tugging at her deep inside.

She'd always thought children weren't for her, that she wouldn't make a good mother. Her temper was too wild, too volatile. And after what she'd put her father through, the thought that she might lash out at her own child in the same way made that decision a simple one.

And yet, Achilles had told her that she wasn't difficult or demanding. That her temper was a beautiful storm and that he liked it, so perhaps... Perhaps she wouldn't make such a bad mother after all.

But he'd said that their marriage wouldn't be a real one and that their child would stay with him, though she could have access to it.

You really didn't think that one through, did you?

That ache in her chest sank deeper and she found herself clutching the edges of the book. 'So what are you saying?'

He didn't answer for a long moment. Then abruptly he

shifted, leaning forward, his hands clasped, his elbows on his knees, the intensity in his face shocking the breath from her. 'I don't want us to have separate lives when we get back to Thornhaven. And I don't want to use medical assistance to conceive. I want us to live together, have a proper marriage.'

Shock pulsed through her. 'A...proper marriage?'

'Yes.' His gaze was like a laser beam boring into her. 'Living together as husband and wife. The same house, the same bed. Shared lives. At least until our child is born. Then we can reassess it.'

Long fingers folded around her heart and squeezed. 'But...that's not what you said earlier.'

'I know. But I've changed my mind. We're good together, my Diana, and I think you know it. And I don't want to give up what we had on Heiros when we get to England.'

It was strange, all the emotion tangled up inside her. Bright threads of joy and excitement wound around darker threads of uncertainty and doubt.

Because being on honeymoon was one thing but living together was quite another. And then there was the issue of the child...

'You said this was a business arrangement.' She tried to keep her voice level, to not let any of her doubt show in her voice. 'That doesn't sound very...businesslike to me.'

His intent gaze narrowed. 'What are you afraid of?'

That he'd bypassed her uncertainty and gone straight to the fear that lay underneath it wasn't surprising. She should have expected it really, because he was extremely observant. And so it was a pity she didn't have an answer.

You know why. You just don't want to admit it.

Willow ignored both the thought and his question. 'What made you change your mind?'

'The honeymoon. You. I don't want this to end.'

'A honeymoon always ends.'

'But the passion doesn't. Sleeping together doesn't.'

'What makes you think it will be the same once we're back in England?' She wasn't even sure why she was protesting. 'And once we have a child?'

He didn't answer immediately, simply staring at her. Then, slowly, he got to his feet and came over to where she sat, putting his hands on the arms of her seat on either side of her, leaning in, caging her with all his powerful, muscular heat.

Her breath caught at his nearness and the way he was looking at her, as if he wanted to ignite her right there in the chair.

'You didn't answer my question,' he said, his voice low and fierce. 'What are you afraid of, Willow?'

She stared up him, her heart beating hard, caught fast as she always was when he revealed the hunger at the heart of him. And it was that hunger she saw in his eyes and his expression. Hunger for her and the raw edge of desperation.

He wanted her to agree, that was what he wanted. And he wanted it desperately.

He'd given her so much over the past week. Shown her what her passion could be like when she wasn't fighting it, when she could be herself and not worry about being demanding or loud or difficult. And she couldn't deny that she very much wanted more of that for herself. She also wanted to give something to him in return.

So what did it matter if she felt a little uncertain and doubtful about continuing what they had on Heiros in England? There hadn't been anything bad about it. No, it had been the opposite. So there was no reason to let those doubts stop her, and there was no reason to be afraid. And after all, it had been a long time since she'd felt as happy as she was when she was with him.

She didn't have to give it up, not yet.

'I'm not afraid,' she said quietly.

'Yes, you were. I could see it in your eyes.'

'I was shocked. That's all.' She lifted a hand and touched the side of his face gently, his skin warm against her fingertips. 'And yes, I want that too.'

Blue fire leapt in his eyes. 'There will be no medical assistance when it comes to conceiving our child.'

'No,' she agreed. 'There won't.'

You want him so very much. It could become a problem.

It could. But she wouldn't let it. She might want him, but it was only sex. And sure, her experience with sex might be severely limited, but she knew her own mind. She knew her heart. And it wasn't involved. So where would be the harm?

'We will conceive our son naturally,' he insisted, as if she'd argued with him. 'You will be in my bed every night.'

There had been times on their honeymoon where he would get oddly intense and demanding like this. It was usually in bed, while they were having sex, and sometimes it felt as if he wanted something from her. Something she didn't understand and didn't know how to give. When that happened, she would open her arms and hold him, give herself up to him, and that would seem to satisfy him in the moment.

But she had the sense that it wasn't quite what he wanted.

His skin was warm beneath her fingertips and she let them trail along the curve of his finely carved mouth. 'I will,' she agreed.

'Do not fight me on this.' His gaze burned. 'I will have what I want.'

'I'm not fighting you, Achilles. I want what you want.'

Finally his gaze flickered, the intense blue glow in his eyes easing. He turned his head, his lips brushing against her palm. 'Good.'

She thought he might lean down and kiss her, but he didn't. Instead, he pushed himself away from her and strode down the length of the jet, taking out his phone and starting into a string of phone calls, pacing as he talked.

He was agitated, that was clear, which was unusual. She was the one who usually paced, not him. Was it going home that was getting to him? The honeymoon ending? What?

She wanted to ask him, but he remained on the phone for the rest of the flight.

They landed in London in the early evening and Willow thought they might stay the night in his city penthouse before returning to Yorkshire in the morning. But it soon became plain that wasn't the plan as he ushered them both into a waiting helicopter for another flight north.

It was raining and gloomy when they finally arrived at Thornhaven, but clearly Achilles' staff had spent a productive week airing out the house and freshening it up in preparation for their arrival.

She wanted some time to explore the manor, or maybe even a half-hour to recover from the journey, but Achilles ushered her straight up the sweeping staircase from the entrance and to the master suite.

It faced the rolling back gardens, the fountains and the woods, though long curtains in dark blue velvet had been drawn over the windows. A massive four-poster bed stood opposite the windows, freshly made up in white linens with a thick, dark blue velvet quilt thrown over the top.

A fire burned in the fireplace, giving the room a warm glow.

It wasn't Heiros, but it was cosy and welcoming, especially with the late-evening snack that had been prepared and was sitting on the coffee table before the fire, a couple of armchairs standing in front of it.

Achilles didn't seem to be interested in the snack, though.

His agitation hadn't eased since they'd arrived back in the country. If anything it seemed to have got worse.

As a staff member put down the last of their luggage, he paced back and forth in front of the windows, his hands in his pockets, a taut expression on his face.

She recognised that expression. She was tired and it was late, and yet still it made her breath catch.

As the staff member closed the door after him, sure enough, Achilles turned from the windows and came straight for her.

She was standing beside the bed and made no move to evade him as his hands settled on her hips and he drew her hard against his body. There was a strange, feral light in his eyes. Something was wrong.

She didn't want to make his agitation worse, so she didn't push him away, merely leaning into the hard, muscled heat of his torso instead, resting her hands on his chest. 'What do you need?' she asked quietly.

'You.' The word was rough and hard. 'Now.'

It was coming home, wasn't it? Being here, in this house. She wasn't sure how she knew, but she could feel it in the tightness of his muscles and in the hard strength of his grip on her hips. He was so tense.

It wasn't the right time to ask, but she didn't like that tension in him. It made her think that he was in pain, and she didn't like that thought either.

'What's wrong?' she asked.

He bared his teeth in what she thought was supposed

to be a smile. 'Nothing. Why would you think anything is wrong?'

'You're very tense and restless. You have been ever since we left Greece.'

His fingers firmed on her hips. 'Well, once you take your clothes off, I won't be tense any more.'

Willow debated giving in, letting him work out whatever was bothering him in the privacy and comfort of that big four-poster bed. But some part of her balked. It wanted to know what the matter was, because this man was different to the quiet, thoughtful man he'd been back on Heiros and it troubled her.

If he was in pain, she wanted to help him. Wasn't that what a wife did for her husband? She helped him when he was in pain and vice versa.

Except you're not a real wife.

No, that was wrong. She *was* a real wife. And she'd agreed that their lives wouldn't be separated. They may not be in love, but if they were going to be sleeping in the same bed and being intimate physically then that didn't mean she couldn't help him out emotionally when that was needed.

'Achilles,' she said quietly, looking up into his face, 'what is it?'

She was very warm and he could smell wild flowers—her scent. And her eyes were as golden bright as the flames in the hearth. There was a crease between her fair brows: she was worried. She was worried about him.

He wanted to tell her that there was nothing to worry about, that he was fine. More than fine. And he'd show her how fine he was, right now in fact, in that bed behind her, the bed where he'd probably been conceived.

But he wasn't fine and he knew it.

The difficulty had started back in Greece, as they'd got on the plane from Athens. Or no, maybe it had started before then, when he'd heard her fears about herself, and he'd told her that she was perfect the way she was. Then he had proved that to her, several times, before lying back on that sun lounger with her in his arms, his hands buried in her hair, realising that he couldn't give this up after the honeymoon was done. And not just couldn't. Wouldn't.

He wanted her in his bed every night. To be able to talk to her whenever he wanted. Argue with her if they were both so inclined. Read books together. Walk in the woods together. Share meals and ideas, and passions.

He'd never had that before with anyone and he couldn't see why he couldn't have it with her. Just until their child was conceived.

The desire for it felt so strong that he hadn't been able to sit still the way he normally would, couldn't put it from his mind to come back to later the way he would with any-thing else. Couldn't pretend it didn't matter to him, either.

And perhaps that was why he was so agitated about it. That it mattered to him. That he wanted her to say yes and couldn't bear the thought of her refusing.

That was a problem, when he wasn't supposed to care.

He didn't know when it had happened, when she'd crept beneath his guard and got inside him. Got him interested in her opinions, her thoughts, and her feelings. And he *was* interested, that was clear. They mattered to him and they shouldn't.

The whole situation had been exacerbated by coming back to Thornhaven, and the wash of memories that poured in on him every time he stepped over the threshold.

Memories of the sitting room where his mother had walked out without a backward glance, leaving his father standing there white-faced and grief-stricken. And he, standing by the door like the afterthought he'd always been. She hadn't even looked at him; she'd walked right by him as though he weren't even there.

Of the dark hallways he'd used to wander at night, feeling as if he were the ghost and his brother were real. Because there were pictures everywhere of Ulysses and none of him. Ulysses was the only one even worth mentioning, while his father barely had a word to say to him.

Of the room down the end of the other wing, a small room, that was his, because Ulysses' room had been a shrine and no one was allowed to go inside but his father. And how he had used to sit at his desk, throwing himself into his studies, because that was where *he* was real. That was where Ulysses couldn't touch him, because Ulysses had been better at sports and physical pursuits, not school work.

There were days when his own existence had felt precarious, as if if he didn't do something to ground himself in reality then he'd fade like smoke, like a dream his parents had once had. He could feel that sense of fading tugging at him even now. As if the house itself didn't believe he was real, that it wanted him just to disappear.

The replacement son. The spare.

The one who should have died.

He hated this place.

So why bother holding on to it? Why come back here at all? Why bother with all of this marriage nonsense for your inheritance in the first place?

Because he couldn't let it go. If he did, his father would win. His father had wanted him to disappear, to have not been born, and he couldn't have that. He would take his inheritance and he would make it his.

He would force the spirits of this place to acknowledge his existence once and for all.

'Achilles,' Willow murmured and gave a little hiss of pain.

And he realised he was standing there, holding on to her tightly. Too tightly.

Theos, he'd hurt her. What was wrong with him? Why was he letting this house get to him? All of that had happened years ago and he'd made his mark now. He'd forced the entire world to acknowledge his existence and they had. He'd become more than his brother would ever be, richer, more famous, more powerful, more notorious...

Forcing away the agitation took every ounce of strength he had, but he managed it, dropping his hands from her and stepping back.

'I'm sorry, *chriso mou*,' he said. 'I didn't mean to hurt you.'

But she was still frowning, still looking at him with some concern. 'What did you say?'

And he realised he'd spoken the whole thing in Greek. Another slip.

Perhaps it would be better if he slept alone tonight. He didn't want to disturb her and he certainly didn't want to hurt her. He didn't want her asking questions, either, because talking about Ulysses, conjuring up his brother's shade, was the last thing on earth he wanted to do.

So he gritted his teeth, forced himself to smile, to relax as if nothing at all was wrong. 'A slip of the tongue. I was apologising for hurting you.'

She shook her head as if that was negligible. 'You didn't really hurt me. It's okay. But you looked upset.' Her gaze searched his face, sympathy glowing there, as if she knew exactly what he was feeling and why. 'Is there anything I can do?'

It made him feel even more exposed than he already was, that look. And he didn't want to explain, because this agitation, this desperation was inexplicable. Even the things he could explain, such as Ulysses, he didn't want to.

He didn't want to have this discussion at all.

He was tired, that was the problem. They should have spent the night in London, but he'd wanted to get here. He'd thought being here with her would make a difference and yet it hadn't. Perhaps it would tomorrow. He was no fit company for anyone tonight, though.

'I'm not upset.' He knew he sounded cold, but there was no helping it. 'It might be better if I leave you to sleep alone tonight.' He made himself let her go and turn away, moving over to the door.

'Is it this house?'

Her voice was soft yet the question struck him like a blow, pinning him to the spot, his hand still on the door handle. His heartbeat echoed in his head, a loud pulse of sound. 'What did you say?' he asked, even thought he'd heard the question perfectly well.

There was a long pause and he heard her soft exhalation. 'I know about your brother, Achilles. This house must have…some bad memories for you.'

Electricity crackled the length of his body, his knuckles white where they gripped the door handle.

'How do you know about my brother?' His voice sounded strange in his head.

She met his gaze squarely. 'I did what you told me to do. Some research.'

Of course she would have done some research. The information was there on the internet for anyone to see. The reports of the loving marriage of the Duke of Audley and his beautiful Greek wife. The joy when they had their first child—a son. And then the tragedy of that son's death. The single report about Achilles' birth and then nothing but silence. No one spoke about him healing the hole that

Ulysses' death had left in that family. No one spoke about him bringing love back into his parents' lives.

No one spoke about him at all.

Because you don't exist. You never did.

His hand was cold where it gripped the door handle, his knuckles bone white, and he had to force himself to let it go. He should leave, get out while he had a chance, and yet he didn't.

He turned around instead.

Willow stood next to the bed, that terrible sympathetic expression still on her lovely, vivid face. Concern glittered in those beautiful golden eyes, as if she cared about how he felt.

He didn't understand why she would. After all, no one else had. And he didn't understand why she wanted to ask him about his past, either. About his brother.

Sullen anger burned inside him, a healing fire.

'Did you, now?' His voice had turned to ice and he made no attempt to adjust it. She had to learn that the subject of Ulysses was out of bounds. 'Then you'll know that the only reason my parents had me was to replace their dead son. He was the heir, I was the spare. And you might also know that it didn't work. That the disappointment when I turned out to be nothing like my brother essentially meant that I was a living reminder of the fact that he was dead.'

Emotions flickered over Willow's expressive face: sympathy, concern and even a touch of anger. And then she was coming across the space that separated them, and he found he'd taken a step back as if to put some distance between them, the door behind him preventing him from moving any further.

She stopped in front of him, that sympathetic gaze stripping him bare. Seeing his pain. Seeing his anguish. Seeing the lost, lonely boy he'd once been, desperate for love and attention, yet who'd been ignored so completely he'd started to question his own existence.

His heartbeat was drumming in his head, and when she reached out to him he flinched. But she only took his hand and held it gently, the warmth of her touch grounding him, keeping the edges of him solid.

'Come,' she said quietly, and tightened her grip, taking a step towards the fire.

He didn't know why he let her lead him from the door and over to the armchair by the fire. Why he let her push him gently down into the chair. Why he let her open the bottle of wine that was sitting on the coffee table and pour a couple of glasses. Why he let her put one in his hand and wrap his fingers around the stem of the wine glass. Why he damn well let her put some food on a plate and put it on the table beside his chair.

'What are you doing?' He couldn't make himself move.

'Looking after you,' she said matter-of-factly.

Then she grabbed her own glass, set it down on the floor beside his chair, then knelt at his feet. She put her hands on his knees, leaned forward and rested her chin on them, the sensation of the soft warmth of her body against his legs grounding him even further. She looked at him steadily and the fading feeling dissipated. He had the oddest sense that she made him real, somehow.

'Tell me,' she said quietly.

It wasn't a command; he didn't have to do it. But she was watching him and suddenly he had to get it out, to let someone know that sometimes he felt as if he was disappearing, like he'd been conjured out of the air, a god that vanished if no one worshipped him, if no one saw him. And perhaps if he told her, this desperation, this agitation, would go away.

'Ulysses died when he was fifteen,' he said roughly. 'Meningitis. It was very fast. One minute he had a headache, the next he was dead. I know all of this because my father would tell me about it over and over again, how my brother died and how quickly. How he blamed himself even though there was nothing they could do.' His fingers closed on the stem of his wine glass so tightly it hurt. But the pain grounded him. 'They told me a lot about my brother. What he was like and how loved he was. And how they had me to replace him, but I didn't turn out the way they wanted me to be. They wanted me to be him and I wasn't.'

She watched him, her topaz eyes glowing, no judgement in her face. 'Go on,' she said, as if she knew he hadn't finished, and that there was more, so much more to say.

So he did.

'Nothing I did was good enough. My very existence was like a slap in the face to them. Ulysses liked to shoot and hunt and fish with my father, while I liked to read books and look things up on the internet and play computer games. They had me because they thought I would heal the grief in their hearts. But I didn't. I only made it worse.' For some reason all his muscles had started to relax. Even though remembering all of this and uttering it was painful. But the warmth of her body pressing gently against him, the scent of her winding around him, made it easier somehow. 'My mother left my father eventually. She couldn't stand the grief. Couldn't stand being in this house where memories of Ulysses were. My father didn't want to leave for the same reason. So they separated. My mother didn't even look at me, didn't even say goodbye. She walked right past me as if I weren't even there. I was five.'

Willow's body pressed harder against him, her golden-eyed gaze intent. She didn't speak and she didn't look away, and neither did he.

'Dad completely ignored me,' he went on. 'I tried to make him proud—I was desperate to, you understand. But trying to be what my father wanted only made it more apparent how unlike Ulysses I was. So I worked hard at school, thinking that getting good marks and awards would make him see my worth. Make him see *me*. But they meant nothing to him. He didn't care about marks or awards, or how his son had graduated top of his class. I wasn't Ulysses and that was all that mattered to him.'

Willow's hands spread out on his knees, her fingers pressing down on him as if she knew instinctively that was what he needed; some sensation to make him feel as if he was part of the world. 'So what did you do?'

He picked up his wine glass and drank, tasting nothing, remembering the rage that had burned inside him. 'I got an acceptance from Oxford University years earlier than I should have and I thought that finally this might actually get him to take notice of the son that was right in front of him and not the one who was dead. But he looked at the letter and didn't say a word.' The anger inside him, hot all this time, leapt up again. 'He didn't care. So I yelled at him, told him that he had to stop living in the past, that he had to let Ulysses go. That he had a son right in front of him who was alive and who needed him...' Achilles stopped abruptly, gritting his teeth, hating the memory of how vulnerable he'd been in that moment and how his father had cut him off at the knees. 'But Papa said he had nothing to give to me, that Ulysses had taken it all. And that's when I realised how little I mattered to him. To either of them. They couldn't let him go. My dead brother was more important to them than I was.'

Willow's fingers abruptly dug into his knee, an expression of pain and sorrow flickering over her features. But again, she didn't speak, leaving him space to talk.

'So I left,' he went on, taking another sip of wine. 'I left my father to his grief, because that was better than constantly hoping he would change. That he'd miraculously find he had some love left to give me after all. So I went to Greece and set about making sure that the world knew who I was, that I was alive and Ulysses was dead. And that everyone would have to deal with it.' Which was what he'd done. He'd made the world acknowledge him, forced it to notice that he existed, and notice it had. Every woman he bedded and every company he helped make a success made him more real.

Willow didn't speak, but he could see the gleam of tears in her eyes, and instantly his heart contracted.

'I'm sorry,' he said roughly. 'I didn't mean to make you cry. That's not what—'

'No.' She shook her head. 'Keep going. It doesn't matter. I'm just sad for you and that's okay.'

Had anyone felt sad for him? Had anyone beyond his teachers noticed the lonely, ignored little boy he'd once been? Who should have been loved and adored by his parents if his older brother hadn't died? Or maybe they saw the truth? That there was nothing in him to love?

The cold wound through him, a creeping frost tugging at the edges of his existence, wanting to pull him apart, so he stared hard at her, stared into her topaz-gold eyes, feeling reality harden around him, anchoring him.

'Dad didn't leave me an inheritance,' Achilles said. 'He left me a final test. He knew I would never marry and settle down, never have a son. That's what he wanted for Ulysses, not me. This was his way of denying me, because he always denied me.' Achilles gritted his teeth. 'Did you know that you were intended for Ulysses? That's why I chose you, Willow. It wasn't because you were intended for me. You were intended for my brother all along.'

CHAPTER NINE

CLEARLY ACHILLES HAD said it expecting some kind of response, though what kind of response he thought he would get, she didn't know.

It didn't matter. He'd chosen her initially because of that agreement between her father and his, and it was that agreement that was important, not for whom she'd originally been intended. Could he even say she'd been intended for Ulysses when she hadn't even been born?

So she only lifted a shoulder and, holding his tortured blue gaze, said, 'So?'

Achilles laughed, a cracked sound devoid of humour. 'So? That's all you have to say?' His face had that taut look to it again, anger burning in his eyes, but now she knew what lay beneath that anger. A raw and agonising wound.

Just as she herself had been rejected by her father, he was a boy who'd never been accepted for himself. Who'd been brought into this world to take someone else's place and then had been rejected because he wasn't that person and could never be that person.

A boy who'd been hurt and hurt deeply by the people who were supposed to have loved him. She could see the pain that caused, it was there in his eyes, though he tried to cover it with rage. He'd tried to be what they wanted and then, when that hadn't worked, he'd tried to be himself, and that hadn't worked either.

It was all such a terrible situation. His parents had clearly been grief-stricken and had never managed to move past the death of their oldest son, and her heart hurt for them. Yet grief could make people selfish—her father, for example—and it seemed as if it had made Achilles' parents selfish too. And that angered Willow.

They'd had a caring little boy right in front of them. A little boy who only wanted to love them, to heal them, and yet they'd been too mired in grief to notice.

So they'd ignored him.

It hurt her. It caused her actual, physical pain. Because she knew what it was to be ignored by the only people who were supposed to accept you without question. Who were supposed to love you unreservedly. To know that the person that you were wasn't acceptable and that trying to be someone else was your only option.

Her father hadn't much liked the child she was, it was true, but at least he hadn't shut her out as completely as Achilles' parents had. At least he'd acknowledged her existence.

There was a lump in her throat that got worse and worse as Achilles stared at her. And what he was expecting her to do at this news, she didn't know. Perhaps show disgust that he'd married her? That he'd taken his brother's intended? Tell him that she'd rather have married his brother?

'What do you want me to say?' She fought to keep her voice level. She could feel the tension in his muscles beneath her hands; he'd relaxed as he'd told her about his parents, but now he'd tensed again.

'Aren't you appalled at my temerity?' His deep, rich voice had a sharp edge to it, a bitterness that cut like a knife. 'Disgusted by how I deceived you?'

'You didn't deceive me. Perhaps if I'd ever met your brother I might think differently, but I never met him. And I have no feelings about him whatsoever.'

'What a pity.' The words took on a serrated edge. 'You would have loved him. I hear he was a god among men.'

She took a breath, staring at the anger in his eyes, hearing the bitter note in his voice. And with a sudden lurch, she realised something: it wasn't only his parents who hadn't let go of Ulysses. Achilles hadn't either.

Because what was all of this but sibling rivalry? Wanting his dead brother's intended wife. Wanting his house. His inheritance. Wanting the love that should have been his and that had been denied him.

Her heart squeezed tight in her chest and before she could stop herself she said, 'Let him go, Achilles.'

He went very still and she felt the shift in his body, the tension becoming taut as a wound spring. His fingers had gone white around the stem of his glass, the way they'd gone white around the door handle not moments before. His blue eyes burned like a gas flame, staring at her as if he'd never seen her before in his life.

'What do you mean?' he demanded.

'I mean, your brother is gone. You don't need to compete with him.'

His expression hardened. 'I'm not—'

'You are,' she cut him off quietly. 'You're so angry with him, so bitter. You want everything that should have been his, and I get it. I understand why. He took your parents away from you and that must have been awful.'

He said nothing, his face set in forbidding lines.

'But he's dead, Achilles,' she went on gently. 'He was just a boy when he died. And it's not his fault that your parents couldn't see past their grief. It's not your fault either. You deserved better.'

He was so tense, his whole body rigid. 'I didn't get it though, did I?' he bit out.

She slid her hands wide on his thighs, pressing her fingers into the hard muscle beneath the wool of his suit trousers. 'No, and you should have. But like I said, it's not your fault you didn't get it, and it's not Ulysses' fault either. Your parents couldn't see what was staring them right in the face.' She took a soft breath, holding his gaze with hers. 'But I can see. You're an amazing man. You have the most incredible mind and I like the way you take things seriously, no matter how silly they are. You're quiet and contemplative, and you're interested in what people have to say. You're very caring too, though I think you'd prefer it if people didn't know that. But I know that. How can I not? When you've done nothing but care for me since we left for Greece?'

He said nothing, the look on his face intense, a muscle in his jaw leaping.

'I'm sorry your parents couldn't see those things,' she went on, her voice getting huskier. 'I'm sorry they couldn't appreciate what they had in you and it's not fair that they didn't. But…you're not Ulysses, Achilles. And you shouldn't try to be. You have a life and you need to live it for yourself, not to spite him or your parents.'

His expression remained taut. 'You think it's that easy? To just…let go of years of neglect?'

'No, of course not. And I'm a fine one to talk, considering my own childhood. But we both have had people in our lives who haven't moved on from the past, and we know what the consequences of that are.' Her hands closed on his thighs, gripping him hard. 'Don't you want to do things differently? Especially if we have a child?'

He stared at her for a long, endless moment and something passed between them, though she couldn't have said what it was. Then he put the wine down abruptly, leaned forward and hauled her up and into his arms.

She didn't resist him, just as she didn't resist when he shoved his fingers into her hair and pulled her mouth down on his, kissing her hard and deep, as if he had a fever and she was the only medicine that would help him.

A kiss that was desperate and demanded an answer, and so she gave it.

She leaned into him, into the hard muscularity of his body, wanting to give him what she could, because she could sense the wide, deep, unending hunger of him.

The hunger for a connection he'd been denied.

He wanted someone, she could sense that. Someone who would accept him, who wouldn't ignore him. Who wouldn't neglect him. Someone who would appreciate him not for empty charm and a handsome face, but for who he was underneath that.

She could be that person for him. She wanted to be that person.

She was his wife after all, so who better?

His mouth was hot and hungry and he was kissing her as if he was dying, and all she wanted to do was to save him. So when he bunched up her dress she helped him, shrugging out of it and her underwear too, so she was sitting astride him naked. Then he undid his belt and the zip of his trousers, and she reached for him, taking him hot and hard and smooth in her hands.

'I want you,' he growled against her mouth. 'Put me inside you. Now.'

She shifted, lifting her hips, guiding him to her, feeling him push inside at the same time as she flexed, and they both shuddered with the pleasure of it as he slid deep inside her.

Then they both were still.

His gaze was blue and dark, depthless as the sea. 'Look at me,' he ordered roughly. 'Keep looking at me, Diana.'

And she did, losing herself in his gaze as he began to move, at first slow and gradual, then becoming harder, faster. His hands settled on her hips, gripping her tight, the look on his face intense and hungry, looking at her as if she was his last chance of rescue.

She lifted her hands and cupped his face, kept looking into those depthless blue eyes, losing herself in the rising pleasure and letting him see exactly how it affected her. Letting him see how *he* affected her. And his movements become more insistent, more desperate.

But she didn't look away, and when he slipped a hand between her thighs and stroked her, and the orgasm swelled around her, she let him see her get swept away. And she called his name and felt it when the pleasure came for him too.

Willow lay against him, her head resting on his shoulder, her long, lithe thighs on either side of his, her soft breasts pressing against his chest. Her hair was a wild storm over her shoulders, the silk of it warm against his fingers. He still had one hand buried in the soft, silky skeins.

The orgasm had felt as if someone had taken a cricket bat to his head, making it ring, and he couldn't have moved if his life depended on it. But that didn't seem to matter. She'd looked down into his eyes and he'd felt more real with every thrust of his hips. With every gasp she gave and shudder that shook her lovely body. She'd done exactly what he'd said and hadn't looked away, and it felt as if she'd called him into being.

And now that strange, dissipating feeling at the edges of him had gone.

He felt real and solid and warm and lax. The agitation had gone, as if some poison had been drained out of him and the hollow that had been left in its absence had been filled up with the feel of Willow's body gripping his, her heat and her scent, the sound of his name in her smoky, sexy voice.

Let him go, Achilles...

His hand tightened in her hair. She was right, of course. She was right about all of it, he could see that now, and perhaps part of him had known all along. That in being so obsessed with having everything Ulysses should have had, he'd kept his brother alive. Just as his parents had in many ways.

But his brother wasn't alive. He was gone. And his only crimes were to have been born before Achilles and then to die before him too.

Theos, so much anger over one dead boy. A boy he might even have liked if he'd met him.

And as for his parents, well, maybe she was right. Maybe the fault lay with them and their refusal to give up their grief, rather than a failing in himself.

It was something he'd never know for certain though, since they, like his brother, were dead. All he had left of them was a name and a title, and a house that wasn't even his.

Not yet.

No, not yet. But he would have it. And maybe once he did, he could finally let go.

Achilles ran a hand down Willow's back in a long stroke, her skin damp and warm, and she shivered. Generous, warm woman. No, there would be no separate lives for either of them. She would sleep with him every night, here in this bed, because she was his now, completely and utterly. And if she wasn't pregnant now, she soon would be. He'd make sure of it.

Gathering her in his arms, he left the chair and moved over to the bed.

Then he laid her down on the mattress and stripped off his clothes and claimed her all over again.

CHAPTER TEN

WILLOW LEANED AGAINST the bathroom vanity and took a slow, deep breath. The pregnancy-test kit sat on the smooth marble, the pink lines standing out neon bright on the white strip.

Pregnant. She was pregnant.

She shouldn't feel so shocked, not given how seriously Achilles had taken the task of conception over the past month, and she definitely shouldn't feel a spiralling sense of panic either, not given how she'd known a child was required when she'd signed his contract all those weeks ago.

It just hadn't seemed real then.

It was *very* real now, though.

She and Achilles were in his penthouse apartment near Hyde Park in London—he didn't spend a lot of time at Thornhaven, telling her that he was a busy man and being close to his office in the city was preferable. But she knew it wasn't all about being busy.

He just didn't like being at Thornhaven, which, given what he'd told her about his upbringing after they'd got back from Greece, she could definitely understand. The old house had very bad memories for him, so no wonder he didn't want to be there, and letting those memories go was obviously a struggle. But it did make her question once again why he wanted to keep it so badly. Wanted to so much that he'd married her and now was going to bring a child into the world just so it was his.

But then, it wasn't really about Thornhaven, was it? It was about his brother. About his own neglected childhood. About the pain that she'd hoped to ease in him and yet it seemed as if she hadn't. Of course, that kind of wound wasn't going to magically get better with a bit of conversation and sex, she understood that. It would take time to heal. Time and care.

Time she didn't have. Because now she was pregnant, their marriage would be over. That was what she'd agreed to on the plane from Greece. They would be together until their child was conceived and no longer.

No.

Sudden tears filled her eyes, a bone-deep denial echoing throughout her entire body.

The past four weeks with him had been magical. Just being with him had been magical. During the day he went to work while she was left to her own devices, applying for places at some of her preferred universities, then exploring some of London's beautiful gardens and galleries. At night, when he came home, he would take her out to dinner to fabulous restaurants, where they had a wonderful time in each other's company, before ending up back in bed in the penthouse, their clothes torn off and on the floor more often than not.

It was perfect and she didn't want it to end.

And now all she could think about was how much more perfect it would be if it was just them, and their child. Together.

A real marriage. A real family.

Her heart pulled tight and then something expanded inside her, a ripple of light, a pure, glittering thread.

She knew what it was. It had been sitting there on the

edges of her consciousness, just waiting for her to notice, though she'd tried so hard not to.

She couldn't ignore it any more though.

The ripple of light spun harder, filling her, and for a moment Willow resisted, afraid of the intensity, afraid of the depth and strength of the emotion that tugged at her. But she wasn't the Willow so afraid of her own emotions that she tried not to feel anything at all. She wasn't that Willow any more.

She was Diana. The huntress. A warrior and a goddess, who was perfect the way she was, and so she let the light spill through her, become her, burning away her fear, filling up her hungry soul with joy and happiness and strength.

She hadn't thought she wanted love, but here it was. It had found her.

Love for Achilles and his passion. Achilles and his strength, his calm. His arms, his touch, the anchor that kept her from being battered by the storms.

Achilles, and the child she now carried. His child.

She blinked back the tears, but there was no stopping them, the stick blurring on the vanity in front of her. It was pointless to resist. There was no escape. No trying to tell herself she didn't want it, that she didn't need it.

She did want it and she did need it. She needed it with every fibre of her being.

And their child needed it too.

Would Achilles love this small life as she would? Or had this child ever only been a means to an end? Would their son or daughter grow up knowing that the only reason for their existence was a stipulation in a will? Would they find out somehow that they hadn't been wanted? That an inheritance and a university degree were more important than they were?

Willow's hand crept down to her stomach, her palm pressed there as if to protect the life growing inside her from the harshness of her thoughts.

No. *No.*

A fierce feeling of protectiveness filled her, a certainty that went down to the bedrock of her soul.

Their child would *not* grow up neglected and hurt the way its parents had been. It would *not* feel the pain of not being accepted, of being ignored. It would *not* know what it was like to be unwanted, and she would make sure of that with everything in her.

She'd always thought she wouldn't make a good mother, but the intensity of the emotion in her heart now made her realise that her doubt didn't matter. Neither did her fear.

It was love that was the important part. And it was love that would guide her.

Warm arms snaked suddenly around her waist and she was pulled back against a hard, hot male body. His lips brushed the side of her neck, his breath warm on her skin, and she shivered. 'There you are, Diana,' he murmured. 'I've been looking for you everywhere. The limo is due to arrive in about...' He stopped, his blue gaze meeting hers in the mirror, sharpening. 'You're upset. What's wrong?' There was a note of concern and tenderness in his voice that made her whole soul ache in a way it hadn't before.

Did he feel the same light inside him? He'd never spoken of love beyond that one warning he'd given her, that whatever was between them had to remain purely physical.

But that had been before their honeymoon. Before the four weeks of magic they'd created between them.

He frowned, his gaze searching her face. 'What is it, *chriso mou*? You've gone pale.'

Willow turned around and looked up at him.

He had his tux on for the gala he was taking her to, his

black bow tie undone and hanging around his neck. His white shirt was open at the neck, exposing the golden skin of his throat.

The stark black and white of his evening attire highlighted his wide shoulders and strong chest, the dramatic masculine beauty of his face. His eyes were that dark, midnight blue she'd come to love so much.

Yes. Love.

She loved him.

But your marriage will end.

Did it have to, though? Couldn't they go on with what they were doing? They were a family now, and their marriage might as well be a real one, given she and Achilles were already living together. So...why not?

Her heart was full, pushing against her breastbone, and she couldn't speak. Doubt swirled in her head, but she ignored it. This was about more than her fear and what she wanted. This was about what was best for their child.

So she picked up the stick sitting on the vanity and showed him.

Achilles went very still, his gaze zeroing in on the stick. Then he murmured something emphatic under his breath and he shifted his attention from the stick to her. His eyes glowed with something fierce and hot, a possessive kind of look that had the bright, silvery feeling inside her shining. Then he cupped her face between his hands and kissed her hard and long and deep.

Every part of her thrilled to it. To the satisfaction in that kiss and the possession, the fierce taste of his triumph.

Yes. He wants this too.

Achilles lifted his head, his eyes glowing, his beautiful mouth curving in a smile of triumph, and she knew it was true. He wanted this as badly as she did.

'My Diana,' he murmured, nudging her gently up

against the vanity. 'I can't think of a more incredible woman than you.'

She put her hands on his chest, smiling up at him, breathless with the most intense happiness. 'It wasn't all me. You had a part in it as well.'

'It's true, I did.' His hands ran down her sides lightly. She wore a golden gown in preparation for the gala that he'd handpicked himself. It was a close-fitting sheath that left her shoulders and arms bare, while the deep vee of the neckline made the most of her décolletage.

'In that case we are both amazing.' He kissed her again, hungrier this time. 'This is exactly what I wanted, *chriso mou*, exactly.'

A family with him. Happiness…

She leaned against his strong chest, loving the heat of him against her. 'I…know we agreed to be together just until the child is conceived, but…' She hesitated a moment, looking up into his eyes. 'We could stay together.'

He frowned a little. 'What do you mean?'

'I mean…perhaps we could stay being married.' She smoothed the white cotton of his shirt over the hard, muscled plane of his chest. 'We could continue living together, being together. We could even raise our child together.' She swallowed. 'We could be a family.'

There was a moment's intense silence and Willow knew instantly she'd said the wrong thing.

'Why?' The word was flat, an iron bar. 'Why would you want that?'

Her hands firmed on his chest as she tried not to respond to the cold note in his voice. 'Well, wouldn't that be best for the child? To have both parents?'

Some of the tension had gone out of him, though the smile he gave her was forced. 'Yes, I suppose that's true.'

'It is, and besides, what if this child is a girl? Would you want to stop trying for a boy?'

'No.' Something hot and fierce glowed in his eyes. 'You really want to stay being my wife, Willow?'

'Yes. Of course I want that.'

He stared at her, his expression suddenly intense and even fiercer. 'A family,' he murmured, as if half to himself. 'Yes, why not? Dad would have hated that.'

And just like that, the bright light inside her dimmed.

Because it wasn't desire for her or for their child that ran through the centre of him, she could sense it in the tension in his muscles, see it in the taut lines of his face.

It was anger. Which meant the past still had him in its grip.

That wound is deeper than you can heal.

No, it was deep, no question. But it wasn't mortal. And she already knew it was going to take time. She could help him with that, she was sure of it.

'Please don't agree just to spite your parents,' she said quietly.

The glow in his eyes focused sharply on her. 'What? What do you mean?'

'I mean, you should have a family because you want one. Because you want a wife and a child. Because you love them.' Her mouth had suddenly gone dry, but she made herself say it. 'A family isn't about gaining an inheritance or getting revenge, Achilles. A family is about love. Or do you want your children to have the same childhood you had?'

She was pushing him, she knew it. And perhaps she'd pushed too far, because the expression on his face shut down and let her go, stepping back.

Her heart shrivelled in her chest at the cold look on his face, her fingers curling around the warmth of his body still lingering on her palms. And she wanted to go to him, tell him she didn't mean to push, that if he didn't want a family then they wouldn't, that as long she could keep being with him she didn't care…

'Are you ready?' His tone was courteous, but she could hear the iron in it. He didn't want to talk about this. 'The limo will be here any moment.'

An ache crept slowly through her. Because this was familiar, the distance in his voice and the cold, hard edge to the words. He sounded exactly like her father, putting her from him as if her emotion offended him.

You shouldn't have said anything.

The ache deepened, part of her wanting to be quiet, to contain herself, do what she'd done all her life and keep herself in check. Yet there was another part, the protective, passionate part, that was urging her to fight for what she wanted, because this was important. It wasn't just about her now, but their child.

And after all, this was Achilles. Who liked her anger and her intensity. Who'd told her that she was a beautiful storm. So why not push him? Why not challenge him? So very few people did…

'Is that it, then?' she demanded, not tempering herself this time. 'Is this how it's going to be? Whenever we have a discussion about what's killing you, you walk away?'

His eyes had gone so cold, his expression a mask, but she went on, 'And what will you tell our child when they want to know how we met? That you married me and conceived them for an inheritance? That they were only ever wanted as a way to get back at your long-dead family?'

Achilles said nothing. He turned his back on her and headed straight for the door.

But that bright thread inside her was hot and it burned,

and she wasn't afraid of it, not any more. Not when she had nothing left to lose.

It was a lifeline and so she threw it to him.

'I want you, Achilles,' she said. 'I want to be your wife. I want you to be the father of my children. And I want a family and a life with you, and not because of some stupid will, but because I love you.'

Achilles stilled in the doorway, conscious of his heart giving a strange jolting leap just as it froze solid in his chest

Love. She loved him.

Shock filtered through him. He hadn't thought about love, not for one single second. Love was never supposed to be part of this and, because he hadn't thought of it, some part of him had assumed that she wouldn't either.

He was wrong though, and maybe, on reflection, he should have known this would happen. That she was too passionate a woman not to let her feelings become involved. Then again, he had no reason to think she would love him, not when no one else ever had.

You always wanted it though. You're desperate for it.

Ice swept through him, his breath catching, a deep pain unfurling inside him, but he shut it down before it could take hold.

No. He didn't need it. He didn't want it. The last time he'd been that desperate he'd been sixteen and his father had told him that he had nothing left to give him. And in that moment Achilles had felt something in his own heart flicker and go out, leaving a void inside him.

It had been a blessing, that void. Because if he didn't feel anything, then there was no pain, and he was sick of pain. Sick of hope. Sick of everything that love brought with it.

He'd been glad that it had gone, and he was in no hurry to reignite that flame.

'You shouldn't have said that.' His voice sounded cold, and he made no attempt to soften it.

'Why not?' Hers, by contrast, was hot, the fire at the core of her blazing in every word. 'Why shouldn't I love you?'

She stood by the vanity in her golden gown. She hadn't got completely ready; her hair was still loose in a wild tangle down her back, and she hadn't yet put her make-up on.

Her eyes glowed like jewels, her vivid, expressive face filled with something light and somehow defiant.

His golden goddess, blazing with strength.

Something flickered inside him, but he crushed it. Suffocated it.

She's offering you everything you always wanted.

Yes, it was true. His beautiful wife was pregnant with his child and now she was in love with him…

But he couldn't take her. He couldn't close that distance between them.

Because now he understood. Now he knew exactly what his father must have felt the night Achilles had confronted him, telling him that he had a son who was alive and who needed him. And Andrew Templeton must have felt this same void where his heart should have been. This same emptiness, right down deep at the core of him.

He had nothing to give her, which meant he couldn't take what she was giving him. If he did, he'd be no better than his father, taking love and never being touched by it. Never giving anything back. Taking it all until Achilles' heart was just as empty and barren as his father's had been.

He couldn't do that to Willow. Not to his beautiful Diana. And not to his child, either.

'You can't love me, because I have nothing to give you, Willow.' He tried to sound level. 'I don't love you.'

Another woman would perhaps have collapsed in floods of tears, or run from the room. Or turned her back on him and pretended nothing was wrong.

Women had all done that to him at various stages.

But Willow did none of those things.

She stepped away from the vanity and strode up to him, the material of her gown shimmering in the light. The look on her face blazed with something fierce, and a deep part of him gloried in how magnificent she was in this moment, even as another part killed that feeling stone dead.

'I don't think that's true.' There was a fierce note in her voice, a certainty that somehow worked its way inside him, making him ache. 'I think you're lying.'

The ache met the emptiness at the heart of him and died.

'Why would I lie?' He stared at her, let her catch a glimpse of the void. 'I told you that this was only physical. You should have believed me.'

Her gaze searched his, pain glittering in her eyes. 'It's not me you're lying to though, is it? It's yourself.'

'I don't know what you mean.'

'I think you believe you don't love me. I think you believe you don't love what we have, and this baby we conceived. I think you're telling yourself that you feel nothing, when in fact it's the opposite. You feel everything.' Her hand lifted and cupped his cheek and he almost flinched. 'I love you and I want to give you that love. And so will our child. We could—'

He'd taken her wrist in his before he could think straight, pulling her hand away, her touch burning like embers against his cold skin. 'Don't,' he ground out as an inexplicable pain flickered through him. 'Don't touch me.'

She didn't move, her gaze blazing into his. Demanding. Challenging. 'Talk to me. Tell me why you don't want this, Achilles. Tell me why you don't want me when I know you do. When I can see it every time you touch me, every time you're inside me. You look at me like you want something from me and I think I know what it is now. I think you want love.' She flung out her hands. 'Well, here it is. Take it. Or perhaps I'll just give it to you instead. I'll give it *all* to you.'

Of course she would. She would give until there was nothing left of her, until her beautiful heart gave out. She didn't know the truth about love, that you could only give so much. And if she gave it all to him, there would be nothing left for their child.

He couldn't have that. He couldn't have yet another casualty of Ulysses' death.

Achilles let her wrist go and stepped back, taking himself away from the heat of her. Because a void swallowed heat. It crushed it, suffocated it. And he couldn't do that, either.

'You've already given me everything I could possibly want,' he said carefully, wanting to keep the hurt to a minimum. 'It's not your fault, *chriso mou*. It's not your fault I can't give it back.'

She went suddenly still, tears starting in her eyes, as if she knew already what he was about to do. She was perceptive, his Diana.

'No,' she whispered. 'Please, don't.'

But he said it anyway. 'You can live at Thornhaven. When our child is born, and if it's a boy, I'll sign it over to you. If it's a girl, I'll buy another manor for you, one with lots of woods for you to ramble in.' It was the least he could do. Strange how his inheritance now seemed… unimportant, his anger at his father and his brother gone. Perhaps it meant that he'd finally managed to do what she'd tried to help him with weeks ago. Perhaps it meant that he'd finally let go.

'You will receive a generous sum of money every month for you and the child.'

'Achilles, please—'

'The divorce will be quick and painless, I promise. The woods should have always been yours.'

Tears ran down her face, fury blazing in her eyes. 'So you're leaving me? Is that what you're doing? What did I do? Was it me loving you? Was that the difference? Is it my love that you can't handle?'

He couldn't bear the cruelty of a lie, not to her, not about that. 'No. Your love is precious and you should save it for someone who needs it. And our child will need it.'

'And you don't?'

'No. Of course I don't.'

'But…that's not true.' Her face was flushed, tears staining her cheeks. 'You do need it. You want it so badly, Achilles. So why won't you take it?'

That at least had an easy answer.

'Because I can't give it back, *chriso mou*,' he said expressionlessly. 'I told you already. I don't love you. I don't love *anyone*. All the love I had I gave away, and now there's nothing left. Nothing for you or for our child, and I can't have that. I can't have you giving your heart away to another man who won't give you anything back. You deserve more than that, my Diana. So much more.'

Fury flickered in her eyes. 'Oh, that's rubbish. Love doesn't work that way. You wouldn't have spent all this time and energy on marrying me and getting Thornhaven if you really had nothing left, because you wouldn't have cared. You would have sold the house and moved on. But you didn't, did you?'

She's right.

He ignored the thought. 'You don't understand.'

But she hadn't finished. 'Oh, I understand. I understand that you love me, Achilles. You want me and you want our child, and you want us desperately. But you're afraid, and that's the real problem, isn't it? You're too afraid to take what you want and are telling yourself a whole pack of lies instead!'

That pierced the emptiness inside him, letting a hot thread of emotion in, and he'd gripped her, taken her by her upper arms before he knew what he was doing.

'You're wrong,' he said roughly. 'I gave everything I had, everything I was to my parents, and it still wasn't enough for them. They sucked me dry, Willow. And I have nothing left. *Theos*, don't you think I would love you for ever if I had a choice?'

All at once the fury in her gaze turned into something else—anguish and a terrible pity. 'But you do have a choice, don't you see that?' Her voice was hoarse. 'You can choose to stop letting your childhood dictate your own heart to you. You can choose to let that go. You might not choose me, I can understand that. But at least you can choose our baby.' Tears slipped down her cheeks. 'There's always love left, Achilles. It doesn't run out, no matter what you think.'

Dimly, somewhere inside him, there was pain, a brief, flickering agony. 'You're wrong,' he said harshly. 'Because if love didn't run out there would have been some left for me. And there wasn't, Willow. There was nothing at all left for me.'

'Oh…my Achilles…' she whispered brokenly, reaching up to him.

But he let her go and stepped away before she could touch him. Before anything about her could touch him.

Then he turned on his heel and walked out.

CHAPTER ELEVEN

AFTER ACHILLES HAD left for his gala, Willow commandeered his helicopter—because she didn't see why she shouldn't—and got his pilot to take her home, back to Yorkshire.

To get her through the agony of leaving, she gripped onto fury, letting it propel her. She took nothing with her, leaving everything behind, including the beautiful yellow diamond engagement ring he'd given her.

He'd made his choice and so she would make hers, and that was to have nothing of his ever again. The only thing she would take was his child, which was half of herself anyway. It was only fair. He didn't want it anyway, he'd made that abundantly clear.

Except of course that was a lie. Everything he'd told her was a lie. That he didn't want her, that he wasn't desperate for her. That he didn't love her. Because if he hadn't, he wouldn't have pushed her away so completely.

He was afraid, and she understood that, but he should have trusted her. He should have trusted that she had enough love for both of them and for their child too, and that was what hurt the most. That he'd held on to the lie instead of her.

Perhaps she should have stayed and spent weeks trying to change his mind. Or months. Or even years. But she couldn't face spending the rest of her life trying to get another man to change his mind about her the way she had with her father. Achilles had been right about that at least.

As the journey home stretched out before her and her fury gradually began to dissipate, the bright thread in her heart grew sharp blades, cutting her to pieces.

Love made her strong and gave her hope, but it also hurt so much.

She managed not to cry all the way back to her run-down Yorkshire cottage, but once she'd opened the door and stepped into the dark hallway, and the silence closed all around her, she leaned back against the front door and slowly slipped down to sit on the floor, tears falling silently down her cheeks.

He'd told her that it wasn't her fault, but she couldn't get out of her head the sight of his face as he'd told her that if love hadn't run out then there would have been some left for him, and there hadn't been.

He'd been so damaged by his family. So hurt. And he really was beyond her ability to heal. All she could do was push, and if she hadn't pushed, then maybe he wouldn't have pulled away from her. If she hadn't told him she loved him, then perhaps she would even now be on his arm at the gala.

But she had told him. And in the end, that love hadn't been enough for him, the way it hadn't been for her father. At least not enough to change his mind. Or maybe it just wasn't the right kind of love.

Willow lifted her hands and wiped her cheeks as her heart slowly ripped itself to pieces in her chest.

There were only two choices in front of her now: she could go back to London and beg him to take her back, tell him she didn't mean it, that he didn't have to take her love if he didn't want it. They could be together, live together, her loving him and he... Well, who knew what he would do? But that was the kind of life she'd lived with her father, where she was constantly checking herself, constantly fighting the thread of passion that lived inside her.

Or there was the other choice: staying here. And bringing up their child alone.

The thought hurt, it hurt so much. Because she knew there would never be another for her. Achilles would be the only man in her life and perhaps she'd known that the moment she'd seen him coming out of the lake.

It would be lonely, but in the end that was the choice she had to make.

He'd taught her that she was perfect just as she was, even if just as she was had been too much for him in the end. She couldn't go back to who she'd been before. She didn't want to. Not with a child to think of now. A child who needed her. And if Achilles wouldn't let her love him, then she would pour all that love into his son or daughter.

She would be strong for them.

Willow took a shuddering breath, pushed herself to her feet.

And got on with the business of living.

She was gone by the time he returned from the gala, but he'd expected that.

He sent someone to watch over her, because she was pregnant with his child and he wanted to make sure the pair of them were safe.

He did not go after her. He'd made his choice and he didn't regret it.

He felt nothing and that was a good thing.

Some time passed, he didn't know how long. He'd forgotten to keep track of such things. The member of staff he'd sent to keep track of his wife and unborn child kept him up-to-date with what was happening.

Apparently she was cleaning the cottage from top to bottom. She hadn't touched the money Achilles had sent her, so he doubled it and then got his member of staff to do a survey of the cottage and make any alterations to it that were necessary to make it a warm, safe environment for their child.

He didn't think she would argue with him on that and sure enough she didn't.

He stayed in London working. Eating when his body needed fuel, sleeping when he couldn't keep his eyes open any longer, running when his muscles needed strengthening.

He existed.

Or, at least, he thought he existed. But sometimes he'd sit in his office and the city would sparkle in the sunlight, and he felt like a shell of his former self. A shadow. Thin around the edges, mere vapour in the air that the slightest breath would scatter.

A man with a void at the heart of him.

It was a feeling he'd only ever had at Thornhaven, where he was nothing and no one. It shouldn't happen here, in his office, the sun around which the solar system of his company revolved.

More time passed and the feeling worsened. There were days where he felt as if the emptiness inside him might swallow him whole.

The only thing that helped were the daily updates from Yorkshire, keeping him informed of what his wife was doing. For whole minutes at a time he sat reading those emails over and over, feeling himself solidify and become real.

He wasn't sure why that was, and really he needed to

stop reading them, because they didn't concern him, not any more. But he couldn't help himself. Couldn't stop imagining Willow, filling up that cottage with her warm, bright presence. Couldn't stop thinking about her passion and fire, her laughter and joy.

And he couldn't stop reading those emails.

Then one day the email came with an attachment. A picture of an ultrasound examination. A picture of their baby.

He stared at it, shocked. Had so much time really passed?

You let it pass. And you did nothing. You sat here in your office pretending you felt nothing. Missing out on precious moments with the woman who loves you. The woman who is carrying your child. Your family. Lying to yourself over and over again...

Achilles shoved back his chair and got up from his desk, pain filtering through him, turning into a sudden unbelievable agony. It hurt so much he couldn't sit still, pacing to the windows and then back again.

It lit him up like a torch and he had no idea where it had come from.

He was supposed to feel nothing. He was empty inside, a hollow shell. A void. And yet...there was pain. Pain for what he was missing. Pain for what he'd done. Pain for the future he'd denied himself. Pain for the woman he'd turned away.

He tried to tune it out, tried to ignore it the way he always did, telling himself it didn't exist. Because how could it? Pain meant he cared and he didn't care. He didn't care about anything.

Yet as soon as he did that he felt himself begin to disappear, the terrible feeling of not quite existing filling him.

Because it's a lie and you know it.

Achilles stopped by the window, the thought echoing

in his head, along with the memory of Willow's voice and the anger in it.

'You love me, Achilles. You want me and you want our child, and you want us desperately. But you're afraid, and that's the real problem, isn't it? You're too afraid to take what you want and are telling yourself a whole pack of lies instead!'

He took a breath, staring outside but not seeing. Was she right? Was the emptiness inside himself, that terrible void, just a lie? A lie he held on to simply because he was afraid?

It's true and you know it.

He took a breath and then another, the knowledge sitting inside of him all this time, a truth he hadn't wanted to see.

Yes, he *was* afraid, so terribly, deathly afraid. Because if the lie was true, if love truly didn't run out, then why hadn't he been given any? Why hadn't his parents loved him? Was it really because he wasn't Ulysses? Or did it go deeper?

Was it him?

He closed his eyes, the pain running like a fault line through the centre of him. It had always been easier to tell himself that he couldn't feel. That love wasn't something he could give. That it was easier to be angry with his father and the brother he'd never met. Easier to blame them than to think it was something in himself.

Something that meant they could never love him.

He would never know the answer to that now, though. They were gone.

You have to let them go.

The pain fractured inside him, and for some reason all he could see was Willow in the bathroom the night of the gala. Willow standing tall and fierce. The light that filled her as she'd told him she loved him. The tears on her cheeks and the pain in her eyes as he'd told her he didn't want it.

Let your parents go. Hold on to her instead.

He froze, every part of him going quiet and still.

She had given him everything. She had never turned him away. Never told him that she had nothing for him. She had opened her heart, had let him give her all his anger and his pain. Had given him hers, too, without hesitation...

Nothing about her had caused him pain except her loss.

Theos, why had he sent her away? Why had he been so afraid?

There was a roaring in his ears, the lie he'd told himself all his life giving way and revealing the truth. The same truth she'd given him in the bathroom weeks ago.

It wasn't that he didn't care. He did care. About everything. And most especially about her. He loved her. He'd loved her from the moment he'd seen her watching him at the lake. And he wanted the life they could have together, the family he could create with her. And he wanted it desperately.

He stood there before the windows, his heartbeat thudding in his ears, fighting to breathe, knowing that he couldn't go on. That he couldn't keep clinging to the lie, continuing to pretend that he felt nothing, that his heart was dead inside him. Continue with this half-life, this bare existence, because that was what it was. That was *all* it was. Just existence.

If he wanted more, he had to be brave like she was. Passionate like she was. He had to step out of the shadow of his fear, let go of the lie, and believe in something else.

He had to believe in her. She'd found something in him to love and he had to trust that. Trust her. Trust the love that was in his own heart too.

He had to, otherwise what else was there?

Only existing. And existing wasn't living.

His hands were shaking as he got out his phone, but he didn't hesitate as he ordered his helicopter.

He had one last trip to make.

CHAPTER TWELVE

WILLOW HAD GONE out blackberry-picking in the woods near Thornhaven. The last of the berries were still on the bushes and she had thoughts of making a pie. The morning sickness she'd experienced over the first eight weeks was starting to ease and she had a sudden and intense craving for the tart sweetness of apples and blackberries.

It was a beautiful day, still and hot, and the woods were silent and cool.

She didn't go too near Thornhaven these days—it hurt too much, made her see things that weren't there, such as a tall man with black hair and eyes like a midnight sky. A man whose passion had taught her soul to sing.

She hated those visions. Because they were never true and they only ended up causing her pain, and so she left the area alone completely.

Just as Achilles had left her alone.

She hadn't heard from him since he'd walked out of his penthouse a month ago and she was furious about it. Not for herself, but for the baby she carried.

He might believe he had nothing to give her, but to continue to believe that when it came to his child made her furious.

Everything about him made her furious.

In fact it was better not to think about him, because she

only ended up miserable, and she wasn't going to be miserable. She absolutely refused.

She was passing by the lake when she heard the sound of splashing, and instantly she was months in the past, watching a man swimming naked. Watching him rise from the water like Neptune from the waves, a water god made flesh and just for her.

Achilles…

Her eyes filled with tears and she didn't want to look, because she would only be disappointed. And the disappointment would be so bitter.

But she couldn't stop herself from moving over to the edge and taking a glimpse through the trees…

And her heart caught hard in her chest as a man pulled himself out of the water.

A beautiful man.

Her man.

She could barely see through the tears in her eyes, a sob catching in her throat.

He was here and she didn't know why. He was here, swimming in the lake, so close and yet so far. And how dared he? How dared he come to where he must know she walked? How dared he flaunt himself like this?

And how dared she still love him when all he'd done was hurt her?

She turned away from the sight of him, walking quickly along the path, blind with tears, when a voice from behind her said, 'Diana.'

Tears were streaming down her cheeks. That voice, that beautiful voice…

'That's not my name,' she said hoarsely, not sure why she wasn't running, getting as far away from him as she could.

'I know.' Beneath the deep, lilting timbre was a note of desperation. Of pain. 'It's Willow. *My* Willow.'

She shook her head. 'I'm nobody's Willow.'

She didn't hear his footsteps, but suddenly there were hands on her hips, holding her tight, pulling her back against a hot, hard male body, still damp from the water. 'Yes, you are.' His mouth was by her ear, his breath hot on her skin. 'You're mine. I claimed you. You're *my* Willow and you were mine the moment I laid eyes on you.'

The tears wouldn't stop, pain and fury building in her heart, and she let them. Because this was who she was. A woman of deep passions. Passions he didn't want, and so what did it matter if she held them back? What did it matter if she let them out?

He hadn't wanted her back in London, so why would he want her now?

She turned in his arms, curling her hands into fists, hitting him on his damp, bare chest, wanting to hurt him for what he'd done to her and to their child.

'I hate you,' she said thickly. 'I hate you so much.'

He only caught her fists in his and gathered them together, bringing them to his mouth and kissing her knuckles. His eyes were very dark, almost black.

'I'm sorry, *chriso mou*,' he said in a low, rough voice. 'I'm so very sorry for hurting you. And you have every right to be angry. Take it out on me, my Diana. You can hurt me; I deserve it.'

His heat took all the strength from her. All she could do was look up into his beautiful, beloved face. 'Why?' Her voice was hoarse and broken. 'What are you doing here?'

'I hoped my swimming would bring you to me.' He cupped her face between his palms. 'Because I've come back to claim what is mine. You. You and our child.'

'I don't understand. You didn't want me. You told me—'

'I know.' His voice was very calm, very sure. 'But you were right about me. And I was so very wrong.'

Willow swallowed, her heart slowing, catching. 'What do you mean?'

'I told myself that I had nothing to give you, that I didn't love you. That I felt nothing at all. I'd convinced myself of it so completely that nothing could have changed my mind. And that's where you were right. I clung to that belief because I was afraid.' There was a hot glow in his eyes, a deep remembered pain. 'My father told me he had no love left to give, that he'd given it all to Ulysses. And I believed him. I had to believe him. Because if I didn't, if there was still love inside him, then why hadn't he given it to me?' His thumbs moved on her cheeks, stroking gently. 'It was easier to tell myself that it was his fault, Ulysses' fault. To tell myself I felt nothing than to believe there was something wrong with me.'

'Oh, Achilles,' she whispered brokenly, her heart aching for him. 'There's nothing wrong with you. Nothing at all. If you believe nothing else, then believe that.'

His midnight eyes stared down into hers. 'That's why I'm here, Willow. Because you sent me that ultrasound picture of our child and all I could think about was what was I missing out on and what I really wanted. And you were right, my Diana. It's you. It's our child. It's our family. That's what I want. That's what I *always* wanted.'

She swallowed, her chest tight, her voice stuck in her throat. 'Achilles…what are you saying?'

'I'm saying that I love you, Willow. I've loved you since the moment I saw you. And I can't be afraid of that pain any more, *chriso mou.* I can't.' His expression became suddenly fierce. 'I've been half-alive for so long. Existing but not living. Holding on to the ghosts of my father and brother, and I can't do it any more. I don't want to. What I want is to love you. Love you until there's no more love in me left to give.'

All her anger vanished. Just dried up and blew away, taking all the pain along with it.

'You idiot,' she said, her voice having gone scratchy and tight. 'You can't run out of love. It doesn't work that way, I told you. The more love you give, the more you have, don't you know that?'

He smiled, damn him. That beautiful, slow-dawning smile that she loved so much. 'No,' he said. 'I don't know that. But maybe you can teach me?'

She'd always been a woman of deep passions and those passions were strong and true. Her anger was a storm and storms passed, and so had hers, leaving nothing but the one passion in her life that would never change, never flicker or fade.

Her love for him.

So she gave him the only answer she had, an answer that mere words weren't enough for.

She reached up, pulled his mouth down on hers, and started teaching him right there and then.

EPILOGUE

ACHILLES INSISTED THEY renew their vows on Heiros during the university summer break, so there would be no disruption for Willow's degree, and she agreed. She wore a gown of her choosing, very Greek, a chiton of draped white silk and a golden tie at her waist. Her hair was loose and woven with wild flowers.

He had never seen anything so beautiful.

Their son, a golden-eyed terror called Alessandro, caused havoc by the water's edge during the ceremony, and Achilles had to quell him by lifting him up in his arms and making him help him say his vows.

Even Willow's father—who'd surprised everyone by deciding to attend at the last minute—agreed that it was the most beautiful renewal.

Willow somewhat mischievously had suggested they honeymoon in Thornhaven, since their first honeymoon had been on Heiros, but, since the weather was better in Greece, they stayed in Greece.

But it wasn't until deep in the night, after their passion was spent, that Achilles brought out the letter Jane had sent him, which had arrived the morning they'd left England. A letter he hadn't known what to do with and had successfully pushed to the back of his mind until now.

Willow lay wrapped in a sheet, the moonlight shining

on her bare silky skin, frowning as she read it. And then, once she was done, she put it down and looked at him, sympathy and pain and love glowing in her eyes.

The letter was written in a shaky hand:

Achilles,

I've been a dreadful father to you and I know that. I wish things had been different, but if there's one certainty in life it's that you can't change the past. I should have moved on, I should have let Ulysses go, but I couldn't. And now it's too late. But it's not too late for you. To that end, I've decided on some-thing that you may think is a punishment, but is not intended as such.

I want you to have Thornhaven, but in order to keep it you must marry and have a son. This house needs a family. It needs children and laughter and happiness. It has been a house for ghosts for too long.

You need a family too. You need to have the fam-ily that your mother and I failed to give you. And with any luck, when you do, you will make more of it than we did...

'Where did this come from?' Willow asked, a tear slip-ping down her cheek.

'Jane found it in amongst some papers in Papa's study.' He looked down at it, the same pain and love that were in his Willow's eyes in his own heart too, along with a deep regret. 'It seems I was wrong about him. He did have some-thing left for me after all.'

His beautiful wife reached out and touched his face, and just like that the pain inside him was gone, leaving behind it only a bittersweet regret. 'You see?' she said softly, her mouth curving in a smile. 'It never runs out completely.'

He smiled, the emptiness inside him, the void that had been there for so long only a memory. Because now his heart was full, with his wife and his son, with the family they would have and the future they were building together.

With love, of which he had an inexhaustible supply.

Because, as it turned out, his wife was right about that too.

Love really was infinite.

* * * * *

MILLS & BOON

Coming next month

HIS STOLEN INNOCENT'S VOW
Marcella Bell

"I can't," she repeated, her voice low and earnest. "I can't, because when I went to him as he lay dying, I looked him in his eye and swore to him that the d'Tierrza line would end with me, that there would be no d'Tierrza children to inherit the lands or title and that I would see to it that the family name was wiped from the face of the earth so that everything he had ever worked for, or cared about, was lost to history, the legacy he cared so much about nothing but dust. I swore to him that I would never marry and never have children, that not a trace of his legacy would be left on this planet."

For a moment, there was a pause, as if the room itself had sucked in a hiss of irritation. The muscles in his neck tensed, then flexed, though he remained otherwise motionless. He blinked as if in slow motion, the movement a sigh, carrying something much deeper than frustration, though no sound came out. Hel's chest squeezed as she merely observed him. She felt like she'd let him down in some monumental way though they'd only just become reacquainted. She struggled to understand why the sensation was so familiar until she recognized the experience of being in the presence of her father.

Then he opened his eyes again, and instead of the cold green disdain her heart expected, they still burned that fascinating warm brown—a heat that was a steady home fire, as comforting as the imaginary family she'd dreamed up as a child—and all of the taut disappointment in the air was gone.

Her vow was a hiccup in his plans. That he had a low tolerance for hiccups was becoming clear. How she knew any of this when he had revealed so little in his reaction, and her mind only now offered up hazy memories of him as a young man, she didn't know.

She offered a shrug and an airy laugh in consolation, mildly embarrassed about the whole thing though she was simultaneously unsure as to exactly why. "Otherwise, you know, I'd be all in. Despite the whole abduction..." Her cheeks were hot, likely bright pink, but it couldn't be helped so she made the joke, anyway, despite the risk that it might bring his eyes to her face, that it might mean their eyes locked again and he stole her breath again.

Of course, that is what happened. And then there was that smile again, the one that said he knew all about the strange mesmerizing power he had over her, and it pleased him.

Whether he was the kind of man who used his power for good or evil had yet to be determined.

Either way, beneath that infuriating smile, deep in his endless brown eyes, was the sharp attunement of a predator locked on its target. "Give me a week." His face may not have changed, but his voice gave him away, a trace of hoarseness, as if his sails had been slashed and the wind slipped through them, threaded it, a strange hint of something Hel might have described as desperation...if it had come from anyone other than him.

"What?" she asked.

"Give me a week to change your mind."

Continue reading
HIS STOLEN INNOCENT'S VOW
Marcella Bell

Available next month
www.millsandboon.co.uk

COMING SOON!

We really hope you enjoyed reading this book.
If you're looking for more romance, be sure to
head to the shops when new books are
available on

Thursday 18th March

To see which titles are coming soon, please visit

millsandboon.co.uk/nextmonth

MILLS & BOON

MILLS & BOON

THE HEART OF ROMANCE

A ROMANCE FOR EVERY KIND OF READER

MODERN
Prepare to be swept off your feet by sophisticated, sexy and seductive heroes, in some of the world's most glamourous an romantic locations, where power and passion collide.
8 stories per month.

HISTORICAL
Escape with historical heroes from time gone by. Whether y passion is for wicked Regency Rakes, muscled Vikings or rug Highlanders, awaken the romance of the past.
6 stories per month.

MEDICAL
Set your pulse racing with dedicated, delectable doctors in t high-pressure world of medicine, where emotions run high passion, comfort and love are the best medicine.
6 stories per month.

True Love
Celebrate true love with tender stories of heartfelt romance, the rush of falling in love to the joy a new baby can bring, ar focus on the emotional heart of a relationship.
8 stories per month.

Desire
Indulge in secrets and scandal, intense drama and plenty of hot action with powerful and passionate heroes who have it a wealth, status, good looks…everything but the right woman.
6 stories per month.

HEROES
Experience all the excitement of a gripping thriller, with an romance at its heart. Resourceful, true-to-life women and str fearless men face danger and desire - a killer combination!
8 stories per month.

DARE
Sensual love stories featuring smart, sassy heroines you'd war best friend, and compelling intense heroes who are worthy o
4 stories per month.

To see which titles are coming soon, please visit

millsandboon.co.uk/nextmonth

MILLS & BOON

HEROES

At Your Service

Experience all the excitement of a
gripping thriller, with an intense romance
at its heart. Resourceful, true-to-life
women and strong, fearless men face
danger and desire - a killer combination!

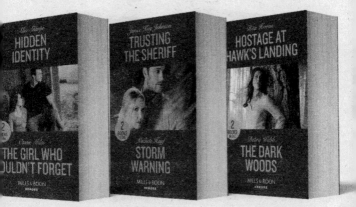